Bin Laden's Second Strike

A novel by

Charles E. Stuart

Publishing History
First Edition September, 2007

Also by Charles E. Stuart

Never Trust a Local

This book is dedicated with thanks to Joe Coons, my college chum, first business partner and very good friend. The book would not have been possible without Joe's assistance during the period of my recent personal medical travail. He edited my original manuscript and arranged for its publication when I was unable to do so.

Author's Note

This book portrays many individuals who are members or supporters of the radical organization known as al Queda, and persons and agencies trying to avoid terrorist attacks by al Queda's members, and so the book's dialogue is focused on radical, violent believers in Islam. This focus is not meant in any way to suggest that most of the followers of Islam want anything other than a peaceful, respectful relationship with those people who are not followers of this historic, ancient religion.

Charles E. Stuart

Bin Laden's Second Strike

Prologue
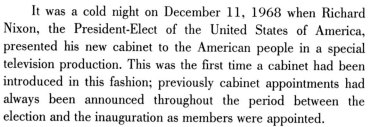

It was a cold night on December 11, 1968 when Richard Nixon, the President-Elect of the United States of America, presented his new cabinet to the American people in a special television production. This was the first time a cabinet had been introduced in this fashion; previously cabinet appointments had always been announced throughout the period between the election and the inauguration as members were appointed.

The new format proved to be a success. Simultaneously the cabinet members-elect had met each other and the American public had met them for the first time, and that time was well before the traditional post-inauguration "first Cabinet meeting".

I was an assistant to the White House Counsel John Erlichman, and I was present the next day when the newly-acquainted Cabinet-elect got together for their first actual working session in a conference room at the old Shoreham Hotel.

Here, in a kind of "retreat", they were briefed by senior members of the White House Staff: The Counselor to the President, Bryce Harlow, spoke on Congressional relations. The Director of the Bureau of the Budget, Robert P. Mayo, described the economic outlook and current financial condition of the government. The avuncular and erudite Counselor to the President, Daniel Patrick Moynihan, himself a Democrat, discussed the President-elect's agenda for domestic policy.

The concluding speaker was the National Security Advisor, Dr. Henry Kissinger, who gave an overview on foreign relations. In his thick German accent and customary intellectual and assured tone, he spoke about the current problem areas including Viet Nam, The Soviet Union, and China. Dr. Kissinger told the Cabinet that most of the current international problems were manageable, notwithstanding the current crises in several of the countries. These difficulties would all be resolved in a comparatively short time --- "several decades at the most" --- he emphatically said.

In fact, according to Kissinger, the only real problem area was the Middle East with its vast economic wealth in the hands of but a few. In a growing world of democracies, here there were still monarchies and dictatorships, even tribal structures! Here as well there was competition between Islam, Christianity and Judaism. These factors all combined to produce a powder keg in the Middle East.

"This region of the globe", Kissinger opined, "has the potential to become very dangerous to the rest of the world. Conflicts there could draw in other nations, in much the same fashion as internal dissent in the Austrian Hungarian Empire had ignited the fires that became World War I."

The sometimes pedantic but always perceptive Dr. Kissinger turned out to be very, very correct.

Charles E. Stuart
August, 2007

BOOK ONE
Fall, 1989 through September 10, 2001

Chapter 1
Someplace in Saudi Arabia, Fall, 1989
◈

After a careful study of assassination attempts against U.S. presidents, a rich, fanatical, anti-American, anti-Saudi rebel leader named Sheik Osama bin Laden had reached the conclusion that with proper planning and patience, the vulnerability of the godless leader of the free-thinking, decadent Americans could be demonstrated in a single devastating blow...and the Shiek was patiently, carefully forming just such a plan. It would take time, he knew. But he was working on it. And keeping it to himself.

Chapter 2
Washington, D.C. to Paris, Tuesday, June 19, 1990
❖

Flying along to Paris on Air France, he thought about the recent years. The marriage had gone bad! Of that there could be no doubt. He, Ipreham Belhadj, was a thoughtful man; he had worried constantly about his problems. They had even begun to affect his work.

For the first five years, his life had been idyllic. He lived in Reston, Virginia with Karen, his beautiful, blond American wife. They had a wonderful young boy who resembled his mother. Ipreham earned a good salary and had a bright future with his company. He was even spared the daily agony of commuting to Washington on Route 7, for the offices of his employer were near his home. But then problems began to develop between him and Karen.

They had met at the annual folk culture celebration on the mall sponsored by the Smithsonian Institution. At the time he was living in Bowie, MD, and working for the Prince Georges County Government in the Department of Public Works. But after graduating from the University of Maryland with a degree in civil engineering, he had unfortunately encountered the subtle racism that pervades the U.S. private sector in the development and construction industries. Because he was an excellent student, fluent in English, and respectable in appearance, he should have been highly marketable. However, when he applied for engineering positions in real estate development, or with the civil engineering firms in the area, he was always passed over.

Finally, Ipreham had realized the problem. It was his Algerian birth and Arabic name! Many of the larger private development companies were led by Jews and they, understandably, were reluctant to hire a Muslim. The smaller engineering firms were principally Christian and would rather have an American. They undoubtedly thought an American face and name would have an easier time in front of the planning commissions and regulatory boards and so their development-company clients would be better served.

Eventually he had accepted the position with the Prince Georges County Government. It was like going home! Much of the professional staff with whom he worked were from the Middle East or Africa.

As not much happened in Bowie on weekends, Ipreham found himself in Washington on most of his days off. Here, in the nation's capital, there was always something going on. Also, of course, it was an international city. His Algerian origin was sometimes even a positive factor, and that was true when he met Karen. She was a senior at American University anxious to meet people from different cultures. They met when they were waiting in line for a soft drink on one of Washington's oppressively hot July days; she was ahead of him when she turned and asked him about the heat in his own country. She was young, liberal, blond, beautiful, and eager to meet "foreigners." He was enchanted. They began dating. A year later they were married.

At first, life was wonderful. After she graduated, Karen got a job with the U.S. Department of State, in the Passport office of the Bureau of Security and Consular Affairs. This position appealed to her sense of internationalism. She was doing what she always dreamed of, participating in foreign affairs, even if it was at a minor level.

Meanwhile, after four years with the Prince Georges County government, Ipreham answered an ad in *The Washington Post* for a civil engineer with experience in aggregate production and soils. It was with the French company La Terre, a large multinational manufacturer of cement and supplier of sand and gravel to the construction industry. As his job with Prince Georges County was as a road construction engineer, he reviewed soils studies, almost on a daily basis. He had no experience in production, but he applied for the job. To his great delight, he was offered the position. It was at a significantly higher salary than his government job. Best of all, it was an opportunity to make the jump to private industry. He accepted the position, for he had seen too many of his friends spend their lives unhappily stuck in public sector jobs.

As the offices of La Terre were in Reston, Virginia, it was not practical to consider traveling from Bowie, Maryland. The beltway was just too slow at commuting times, so they moved to Reston and Karen became the one with the commute. Her offices were on 19th Street in the District.

Initially, all was well. Then Ipreham had started to notice changes in his relationship with Karen. It began when they were invited to a large picnic gathering of her co-workers. An impromptu softball game sprang up. Karen, a former member of a girl's high school softball team, was a pitcher. He was nothing. He had never played baseball and had no understanding of the game. He did not even know when to cheer. It was the first time the gulf in their cultures was embarrassing to her.

At the picnic a tall, handsome, athletic man, a player on her team, was paying close attention to his wife. When their team won, they whooped it up and embraced each other. He rushed off to get her a bottle of beer, which she readily accepted. Normally Karen, out of deference to her Muslim, non-drinking husband, tried not to drink in his presence. This time, she didn't even pretend to seek his approval by asking if he minded. It was an awkward time. The ride home was even more so.

Belhadj had considered himself a progressive Muslim. He fully understood that American women were going to be different, more independent, than Arab women. He did not expect the servility that he would have expected from an Arab wife. He did, however, feel entitled to respect. When this commodity started to decline, he was very sensitive to the change.

Karen's remoteness accelerated exponentially. She became testy and short tempered. She was no longer eager to make love, the ultimate act of defiance to an Arab male. Soon it was apparent to both of them that the marriage had been a mistake.

Now, La Terre had asked him if he wished to be considered for a management position opening up in Algeria. He had jumped at the chance! He told Karen she could have the house, both of the cars, and most of the savings. He wanted only their six year-old son, Anwar.

She thought about it for just ten minutes before accepting. Within a week he and Anwar, his beloved son, were on this plane to Paris. From Paris they would fly to Sidi bel Abbes and his new job in Algeria.

As they soared through the skies on the Air France jet (it was the boy's first flight), neither Ipriham or Anwar could possibly foresee the way their lives would soon change...and if they could, they might have welcomed the change. Or maybe not.

Chapter 3
The White House: Friday, April 19, 1996
❖

He thought about the 132 rooms in the White House, and how they were named. Four are named after colors: the red room, the blue room, the green room and the yellow oval family sitting room. One is named for a point of a compass, the East room, and one by its shape, the Oval office. Most are called by their function, i.e., the "State Dining Room", the "China Room", the "Cabinet Room", and so on. Two are named after previous Presidents: the Lincoln Bedroom and the Roosevelt Room. The purpose of the former is expressed in its title. The purpose of the Roosevelt Room is to hold meetings of small groups of perhaps a dozen people; prior to the end of the Roosevelt Administration it was simply known as the "fish room," because of a large fish which hung there. The room is furnished with a long mahogany table surrounded by fourteen mahogany armchairs. It looked like exactly what it was, a very expensive dining room suite.

The naming of the rooms was idly running through the mind of the Director of the Central Intelligence Agency as he waited in the Roosevelt Room for the President who was, as usual, late for the meeting, since he was with a group of Girl Scouts just across the corridor in the Oval office, doubtless entertaining them and himself with his bonhomie.

The Central Intelligence Agency was known around Washington and to readers of spy novels everywhere as "the Company," and to the DCI such tardiness was inexcusable and un-businesslike. He ran his own life with the precision of the Rolex Swiss chronometer he wore on his wrist.

But then, the President was a politician, doing what politicians do, wooing the public.

Across the table from the DCI, the President's National Security Advisor was engrossed in a deep conversation with the Secretary of State. Next to them were the Attorney General and the Director of the Federal Bureau of Investigation, each lost in their own thoughts. Further down the table to his left were the DCI's own deputy and a national intelligence officer (the latter was from the military intelligence branch of the Army and number three in succession at the CIA). Another person at the table, further away, was the Assistant Secretary of State for Middle Eastern Affairs, while at the far end of the room was a bookish looking young man, a Harvard professor, who had recently been appointed as the National Security Advisor's deputy. The DCI had been introduced to the professor, but could not remember his name.

Nine senior members of the United States Government were kept waiting because of a group of Girl Scouts...

The DCI took another drink from his china coffee cup, with its Presidential Seal neatly inscribed in blue. It was his fourth cup for the day and the second in the Roosevelt Room. He made a mental note that it should be his last. He did not want to leave this, of all meetings, to go to the men's room.

The door opened and the President surged into the room to a chorus of, "Good Morning, Mr. President."

"Good Morning to all of you," responded the President, with a nod to each side of the room. He sat down at the head of the table. Only in the cabinet room, with its table long enough to seat 14 people on a side was the President's seat in the middle. He gave no recognition of the fact that he was ten minutes behind schedule. Reagan, Bush or Carter would have apologized. Johnson or this President, never. Nixon, with a probable desire to escape the Girl Scouts, and his keen interest in foreign affairs, would have been early.

The President turned to his National Security Advisor. "OK. You told me you wanted to discuss something of extreme importance. From the size of this crowd, it looks as though you have intercepted word of the second coming of Christ." Everyone gave the chuckle that was mandatory when the President made an attempt at humor. The DCI had much respect for the

President's personal communicative skills, but a wisecracker he was not.

"Mr. President," began the Security Advisor, "we have a very important decision to present to you today concerning a radical, fundamentalist Muslim named Osama bin Laden. You may recall that his name has been mentioned in several briefings in the past year, as a member of the terrorist group, *al Qaeda*. In the past we have not thought him a particularly important player in this group, but just a Saudi millionaire, who was a financier of this worldwide umbrella organization of terrorists. But now the CIA has assembled additional information regarding bin Laden and his organization, which leads us to believe that our original estimates were in error: *Al Qaeda* is larger and more organized than we had originally suspected and bin Laden's role is more than that of a financier. He is the key leader. I think it will be useful at this point to ask the DCI to give us all a brief biographical sketch of bin Laden and his background."

The Advisor nodded to the DCI signaling that the ball had been passed. The DCI continued:

"Thank you. Mr. President. In the past few months we have been focusing our efforts on learning all that we can about *al Qaeda*. Using national security means, mostly satellite intelligence, including signal intercepts as well as humint...er, human intelligence from our operatives, and the security services of some of our friends, we have been able to assemble an impressive dossier on this man and his organization.

"But first, as our colleague has suggested, I believe it worthwhile to give you some historical background on the man and his group.

"Bin Laden was born in Riyadh in 1957 as the seventeenth of 52 children of the construction magnate, Muhammad bin Laden. The bin Laden family owns the largest construction company in Saudi Arabia, the bin Laden Group. They are extremely close to the Royal Family.

"Bin Laden spent his youth as a privileged young man.

After secondary school he went to Lebanon, to live in Beirut. As many of you know, this city was known as the "Paris of the Mediterranean." Bin Laden was known to have enjoyed the nightlife and women, things not available in Saudi Arabia. At this point in his life, he was not the ascetic he portrays himself to be now. He left Beirut at the outbreak of the civil war in Lebanon. He then went to Abdul Aziz University, in Saudi Arabia, and obtained a degree in civil engineering.

"In the early 1980's, alienated by the Camp David peace accords and the Soviet invasion of Afghanistan, he became a fundraiser and a trainer for the mujahedeen. In this effort, despite American support for the mujahedeen, there is no record of bin Laden ever having any contact with Americans. This is in contrast with some of the reporting in our media, which have assumed that because we backed the mujahedeen with arms and money, we backed bin Laden."

The DCI continued. "Bin Laden became anti-American and anti-Saudi during the Gulf war, for the Kingdom had permitted Americans on the birthplace of Muhammad which was considered holy soil. He was expelled by the Saudi government when they caught him smuggling in weapons from Yemen in 1991 and his passport was revoked. He then began his active career as a terrorist with his involvement in the bombing attack of a hotel in Aden on 29 December 1992. He has been increasing his terrorist activities ever since."

The Director then led the group through fifteen minutes of dates and incidents including bin Laden's presumed participation in the attack on the World Trade Center in 1993, his implication in the fatal attack on President Mubarak of Egypt, and his move to the Sudan where he attempted to develop nuclear and biological weapons. Finally, and most importantly, was bin Laden's recent letter to King Fahd of Saudi Arabia declaring a *jihad,* or holy war, until all Americans were gone from the Arabian peninsula.

The DCI read this information from a blue briefing book

with the seal of the Central Intelligence Agency on the cover. When he had finished, he ceremoniously closed the book, removed his reading glasses and placed them on the cover.

"Mr. President, Osama bin Laden is an incredibly evil man. Educated and rich, he is devoting his life to harming us. We are convinced that he is planning future operations against us that involve destruction of American property, we just don't know where or when. He may even be tempted to strike here in the United States. The Agency recommends his removal."

The group was stunned. Even those who were familiar with this bin Laden character had not known the full extent of his activities or the details of his life.

The Secretary of State was the first to speak. "Mr. President, I remind you of Executive Order 12333, which explicitly states, 'that it shall not be the policy of the Government of the United States to assassinate foreign officials'. I am reminded of this restriction virtually every time I meet with a head of government or head of state. It is a standard line for them to humor me with, 'how much safer they feel since President Reagan signed that Executive Order.'

"I certainly agree that Mr. bin Laden is a dangerous man, but there are many dangerous men in the world who are enemies of our country. We are a nation built on laws. Where would we be, if the very Government, which passes and enforces the law, broke its own laws at will?"

The Attorney General parsed in. "From a strictly legal interpretation, bin Laden is not a public official. Unless he has been secretly elected to the post of 'Secretary of Terror' of Afghanistan, he has no official standing."

The Assistant Secretary of State for Middle Eastern Affairs, a pompous man eager to demonstrate his knowledge of his specialty, chimed: "In the region which I oversee, there are 23 countries, only two of which, Turkey and Israel, have elections. The rest of the governments are monarchial, dictatorial or theocratic." This insight was ignored by the others in the room.

Then the National Security Advisor responded. "Madam Secretary, I agree with you. The United States Government should not be sending out hit men, like some banana republic or countries of the old Warsaw Pact, but this man needs to go." He turned to the Director of the CIA. "Can't we find someone to do this job for us?"

The DCI shook his head, "No, we can't. I remind you that since the Church Commission and the budget cuts of the Carter years, we have had to extensively scale back on our hiring. This means that maintaining operatives in all the trouble spots of the world is tough: We used to have more than 600 agents in the Middle East. Now we have only a handful. We don't have a single asset close to bin Laden, in his inner circle. He is surrounded by guards at all times and lives in remote areas. Getting an assassin in to that tight circle would take years."

The NSA Advisor spoke again. "How about the Israelis?"

The Director smiled. "For obvious reasons, it has proven very difficult for the Jews to penetrate Muslim organizations. Frankly, Mossad and Shin Bet can't help us on this one."

The President watched this give and take with interest. In matters of foreign policy, admittedly not his long suit, he was always slow to offer a comment. Had this been a domestic issue, he would have been leading the discussion. With foreign affairs, he preferred to wait until the group built some kind of consensus, before rendering his Solomon-like opinion.

The national intelligence officer, a major general in the United States Army, spoke up. "Mr. President, I fully agree with the Secretary of State. We cannot send an assassin to eliminate bin Laden. The law does not allow it. Further, although I am not an attorney, I have always been led to believe that what the law does not permit directly, it does not permit indirectly. We should not therefore hire a foreign national to do our dirty work. That would be wrong as well".

The President, the Attorney General, the National Security Advisor and the representatives from the Department of State were now staring at this uniformed officer with a mixture of interest and incredulity. Several of the group, including the President, had long held an opinion that "military intelligence", was an oxymoron. Where was this unknown officer going?

The general continued. "I therefore suggest that we attack not Bin Laden, but his organization, *Al Qaeda*. If, for example, we were to launch simultaneous strikes against several of his training camps, and bin Laden just happened to be in one of them, why he could almost be considered 'collateral damage.' We would accomplish our objective and remain well within the legal and moral interpretation of the Executive Order." The Army officer was looking directly at the President when he delivered this suggestion.

The President was grateful for the opportunity to jump on a clean "outside the box," solution and he did so with alacrity. "That is an excellent, excellent suggestion, General, and I thank you for it. What do the rest of you think?" He knew that the assembled group would not disagree with something he, their President, had just so enthusiastically endorsed.

Sixty-one days later, on 21 June 1995, The President of the United States signed a secret order, "Presidential Decision Directive #39", that had been laboriously prepared by his White House Counsel. It was entitled *U.S. Policy on Counter Terrorism* authorizing the Director of the Central Intelligence Agency to "use any and all means" to destroy bin Laden's network. It gave specific approval to 'render' terrorist suspects "by force...without the cooperation of the host government."

Another war had begun.

Chapter 4
Afghanistan: Monday, July 8, 1996
❖

He slept, as was the custom of desert Arabs, in his *disha-dasha.*

As was his own habit, he awoke in the fetal position, curled to the left. He was 6' 4" tall, exceptional for an Arab; too long for the sleeping bench that served as a bed.

When he sat up, having no bedclothes to turn back as it was the height of summer in Afghanistan, he was already fully dressed and ready to slip into the sandals that were placed on the floor beside his head. His Chinese *Kalishnikof* AK 47 was beside him. He was ready to fight or to flee, as the situation required.

He ran his hands over his face to smooth his full beard, and then to his head. He adjusted his turban. He thus completed his morning toilette. He had often reflected on the efficiency of this arrangement; the contrast between his current simple lifestyle and his previous one, the contrast of this life and that of most of his enemies.

His bedchamber was a single spare room about five meters by four meters. It was also his office, his dining room and his conference room. The furnishings were few, a low table on which were stacked several books and newspapers. A number of seating cushions were haphazardly placed around the walls. A single bare light bulb hung from the ceiling. There was no switch. The light was lit when the generator was running and now the generator was off. Everything was coated with the dust common to all mud buildings, and the fine desert sand that blew in when the door was opened. The gray light of the early morning filtered through a small, dirty window, set high in the wall, so that people could not see in.

He rose from his bed and, in bare feet, walked several steps to the door. He opened it, and said a few words to the guard who was posted outside. He spoke in a low voice; in the clean cultured Arabic he had grown up with and polished at Abdul Azziz University in Jiddah. Having ordered his morning tea and pita bread, he knelt on a small rug and said his morning prayers. Then he moved to a cushion and waited to break fast. Sheik Osama Bin Laden was beginning his day.

The meal was delivered as soon as he was ready for it. His men knew his habits and kept a plate of bread ready, and there was always hot tea available with the bread to be served by a young boy who entered and bowed, silently placing the plate and cup on the table and backing out of the room.

Bin Laden insisted on boys as waiters. He did not believe serving food to be a proper duty for warriors. Women, the normal servants to men, were not permitted in this training camp.

This particular boy was the son of Abdul Lazar, one of his men. After his foray to the United States, Allah had commanded him to return to his people, God be Praised. The father had gone to America to be educated and while there had fallen in love, as young men are wont to do, but with an *infidel!* After some ten years, Abdul had realized the gravity of his error and returned home to Saudi Arabia, bringing the boy with him. This move had been made without the permission of the infidel wife, Rita, who was using every means to get her son back. Fortunately, even the corrupt government provided by the Saudi royal family had not adhered to the request of the American Department of State for the return of Rita and Abdul's child.

The boy, in spite of being his Abdul's son, in spite of being dressed in a *dishadasha,* in spite of wearing a cotton *pakol,* did not look like an Arab. He had the fair skin and features of the infidel wife. Under his *pakol,* was dull blond hair. Bin Laden knew that the boy had not spoken this morning because he was ashamed of his poor command of Arabic.

As Bin Laden thoughtfully munched his Pita, an idea began to develop, just the germ of an idea. As he thought about it, turning it over in his mind, he began to become excited. It would require some investigation, beyond his limited knowledge of the subject, to determine if his idea was sound. Then it would require a major use of his pan-Arab assets. But, if he could put his idea into effect, it had the potential to be the most successful he had ever had.

He smiled to himself at the very thought of it.

Chapter 5
Afghanistan: Tuesday, July 9, 1996
◈

Muhammad Atef had been surprised when Sheik bin Laden had called him into his chamber yesterday and shared with him his idea. The conversation had lasted nearly an hour. Atef was grateful — Allah be praised — for the confidence his leader had shown in him. Atef was clearly his most trusted commander. With the help of God, Atef would do his best!

Atef left the room energized and went to his own quarters. When he was assured of his privacy, he used a satellite cell phone to place two calls. The first was to a contact in Kabul; the second was to a fellow member of their organization some six miles away. He alerted them both that he was coming. Then, accompanied by five armed guards, he set off on foot for the six mile walk to their "motor pool", two four-wheel drive Datsun pickup trucks. Although Atef did not fully understand how they did it, he knew the Americans could see things from the sky nearly all the time, it seemed. By keeping the trucks six miles from the camp, the image of the camp shown to the satellites was that of a typical Arab village, baking in the desert heat.

The six men moved slowly through the desert. The heat prevented them from moving as quickly as Atef would have wished, and it was nearly 5:00 in the afternoon when they reached the trucks, concealed in huts in a small cluster of mud buildings on instructions from Sheik Osama, who, as always, was thinking about security. Bin Laden had ordered that each of the nearly 50 training camps in Afghanistan be small, so they appeared to be no more than ordinary villages. But in fact Atef commanded several thousand men in various stages of training in those separated facilities.

Upon reaching the Datsuns, they waited until darkness before setting off across the desert, driving slowly across the rough track that served as a road. Several of the men alternated as drivers, changing every two hours, as using their Russian night-vision equipment was very fatiguing.

They arrived at Kabul early in the morning, before the city woke up, before the peddlers lined the streets.

To a man coming from the desert like Atef, Kabul was offensive. It attacked all three senses, the eyes, the nose and the ear. It was dirty. Not the clean dirt of the open desert, or the small camp in which he lived, but dirty with rubbish and sewage scattered about. It smelled with the smoke of a thousand charcoal fires, of raw sewage, with no cleansing wind to purify the air. Later in the day, the noise of street peddlers assaulted the ears. It was not a city Atef enjoyed visiting, quite unlike the Egyptian city in which he had grown up. Since his Sheik was evicted from Saudi Arabia in 1991, they had moved first to Khartoum and now to Afghanistan. The nature of their business did not permit them to choose their place of residence. But the Taliban had welcomed them when they were expelled from the Sudan — Allah be praised — and now with their training facilities spread across the country, Afghanistan was home.

The trucks went to a neighborhood of low concrete-block houses and dropped off Muhammad Atef and one man, his bodyguard. The other four drove off, two men to a truck, to purchase supplies --- there was no sense in wasting a trip to town!

Atef and his companion walked quickly down a street, turned right at the first intersection, and walked another block. Here nobody could have seen them leave the trucks. Then they joined hands, in the Arab fashion, and walked slowly, sauntering, until they came to a large two-story stucco building, surrounded by a high wall and set off by itself. Looking to any observers like two friends who had been invited for morning tea, they knocked at the gate and were promptly admitted by a servant.

They were ushered through a courtyard into an interior room with tile floors, furnished with western style chairs with gold damask upholstery. Several antique silk prayer rugs hung on the walls. A large Isfahan carpet covered the floor. The room gave a feeling of warmth, and wealth, without being opulent. The servant motioned for Atef to be seated and disappeared with the guard to fetch the tea. Atef was reluctant to sit, as his robe was covered with the dust of the desert. He remained standing. He was still standing when, several minutes later, a distinguished looking man clad in a traditional Afghan *chapan* swept into the room. The man was quite light skinned for an Arab, but had an unmistakable Arabian hawkish nose on which was affixed a pair of wire rimmed glasses with octagonal lenses, which gave him a professorial appearance. He wore a red silk *kufi* on his head, embroidered in a complex Arabic design. He was tall, though not so tall as bin Laden, and lean and tough looking. His beard was like the hair that coursed out from under his *kufi*, salt and pepper gray.

"*Ahlen wasahlan*, my friend. Welcome to my home." Mohammed al Kezir bowed ever so slightly to Atef. "Please sit down", he said, pointing to the chairs, aware of and yet ignoring Atef's discomfort. "Tea will be here shortly. If you would like to use the room to wash away the dust of our beloved desert, it is right over there." He pointed with his right hand.

Atef was reminded that Kezir's left hand was missing. It was still the practice in Afghanistan to amputate the left hand of a thief; indeed, there were almost weekly public amputations in Kabul stadium. It always made Atef feel a little surer of Mohammed al Kezir: this was a man like himself, one who lived on the edge of, if not outside, the law.

In the bathroom, Atef looked in a mirror for the first time in weeks. He did not keep one in the camp as he had no use for one for shaving. He also believed that a fighting man should have no vanity about his looks. He saw a face with red-rimmed eyes, its skin creased and burned by the sun. His once jet-black beard was showing spots of gray. The difficult life he led was beginning to show...

After he had splashed some cold water on his face and hands and dried them on his own robes rather than soil the clean towel that hung available for that use, Atef returned to the room and the awaiting host. Tea and sweet Arab pastries had been brought. The sweets were from *Semiramis,* the Middle East equivalent of *Godiva* chocolates. Indeed, their distinctive gold box was very similar to *Godiva,* as Atef had noted on previous occasions. He wondered to himself how many people in the miserable city of Kabul even knew of *Semiramis,* or *Godiva,* for that matter.

"And how can I serve the Sheik?" asked al Kezir. This was most un-Arab like, getting directly to the point. Atef was unnerved and unprepared. Bin Laden's name was seldom mentioned: he was usually referred to just as "the Sheik."

"The Sheik is seeking someone who is an expert on the subject of genetics. He wants to know more about why, over generations, people look the way they do. I was told that you could find a biologist who knows about such things, to meet with the Sheik," responded Atef, maintaining the veiled reference to bin Laden.

"Hmm. I believe one may still exist at the University, if he hasn't been removed by the Taliban. I shall have to do some investigation." Al Kezir paused, as if thinking about making a comment about the Taliban, and thought better of it. He continued, "This I will do later today. How can I reach you?"

"I'll be available by phone at 3-394-7060. It is the home of a good friend", said Atef. He frowned as al Kezir drew out a gold automatic pencil and noted the number on a small pad. "That is a very private number. I would appreciate it if you would remember the number or, if that is not possible, please destroy the paper after you have called me."

"My friend, I am becoming an old man. My memory is not as good as it once was. Fortunately, my loss remains only in my eyes," tapping his glasses, "and my memory. Other things are still working, praise be to Allah. But, rest assured, I will do as you request. Now, let us drink some of this fine tea and talk about other things. I will be very interested in hearing your views on some current happenings in the Arab world."

The two men spent 45 minutes, drinking, eating, and talking before al Kezir rose. "Forgive me, my friend, but I have a busy day and if the person you seek is not at the university, it will become busier. I will call you not later than four o'clock and inform you of my progress."

Atef rose from his chair and bowing, expressed his thanks for the hospitality. He then grew serious and grasped al Kezir by the arm. "It would be best if the person you find is not a member of your family or a friend. As you know, the desert is a dangerous place." As he said this, Atef looked directly into the eyes of his host and held the gaze for several seconds. Then he lightened and again expressed his gratitude. "*Asalam alykum* my friend."

Al Kezir responded with the customary, "*Alykum asalam.*" *Peace be with you.* It was a fine touch of irony, lost to each of them.

Atef's bodyguard magically appeared together with Al Kezir's servant, who escorted them into the courtyard and out the gate.

Chapter 6
Afghanistan: Thursday, July 11, 1996
◈

Shazeer Fahad, until recently the Professor of Biology at Afghanistan University, clung tightly to the handle on the dash in front of him. The pickup truck was bouncing severely over an imperceptible road in the Afghan desert. Fahad did not like the desert. He did not like the truck. Most of all, he did not like the men he was with.

When al Kezir had called upon him, Fahad was at home, tutoring a female student, a young woman who had shared al Kezir's fate when the Taliban took over the country. Both had been removed from the University; she because she was female, he because an unknown male student had reported an anti-Taliban comment he had unwisely made in class. Now, he was deemed to be too disloyal to the cause to be teaching the nation's youth. It didn't matter that he had taken a "first" at Oxford, that he had published widely, or that he was highly respected in continental educational circles.

"He was disloyal," some said.

"He should not be teaching," others said.

Fahad had despaired that his country was repeating the same mistake of China and the Cultural Revolution. The Taliban, like the "Gang of Four" were going to set his already backward country even further behind the West!

This "al Kezir" was not a man Fahad knew well; just that he was involved in the drug trade and, as was everyone in that business, he was rich. He had been very generous to the University and once had even made a large cash donation to enable a student of Fahad's to accept a scholarship in America, at the University of Pittsburgh. And now this morning, al Kezir had come to him with a request for a favor. There was a certain Sheik, a tribal leader living in the desert some distance from Kabul, who had some questions about genetics. "Would Fahad be so kind as to visit this man and answer his questions?"

Of course, he had said "yes". Now, as a result of his generosity, he was bouncing around in the desert with a group of heavily armed men, whose very appearance frightened him.

They arrived at their destination in the early morning hours and placed the trucks into a mud building. Then they loaded him on a small desert horse and told him to just "hold onto the saddle": The reins would be held by one of the men who would walk alongside, leading the horse.

Fahad had not ridden a horse since his childhood, but felt quite able to guide his own animal, but when he pointed this out to the leader of the group, his objection was curtly dismissed. Their rudeness contributed to Fahad's sense of unease. The men did not want to risk his getting away. He was being treated as a captive.

The sun was just coming up over the distant Hindu Kush mountains when they came to a larger cluster of huts. One of the men told him this was where he would meet with the Sheik.

Fahad dismounted from the horse with a stiffness due partially to being unaccustomed to being mounted and partially to his age. He stumbled after one of the men, and was led into a room in which there was only a bed, a table, and some cushions. There was also a man, who rose to his feet to greet him as he entered the room. He was a tall man dressed in a white *disha-dasha*.

"I am Sheik bin Laden. I thank you for making this trip on such short notice, but I have some questions that I am told you can answer. Please join me for breakfast," and waved an invitation to be seated on the floor next to the table.

As Fahad sat down, a boy appeared with tea and bread, placed them on the table, and left. Bin Laden began, and Fahad was surprised how quickly and intensely the tall man started to be serious, with none of the customary hospitable preliminaries to such talk.:

"Perhaps you noticed the boy who just left? He is the cause

of my concern. His Father is one of my tribe, a man who went to America as a student and got married to an American woman. She was, I am told, a typical American woman, fair-haired, fair-skinned with blue eyes. The child as you can see takes after his mother.

"Every other child I have seen that was the result of a union between an Arab and a foreigner is dark haired and dark skinned, but because this boy is not, the father believes the child may not be his. Is it possible for a pure-blooded Arab to have such a child?"

Fahad thought a moment before he answered. "No, Sheik, it is impossible for such an event to occur. It is not possible for a pure-blooded Arab to produce blond children. This would be a violation of Mendel's basic law of genetic dominance.

"You see, dark hair and dark skin are dominant genes, blue eyes and blond hair are the absence of color and are recessive. In any union between a dark man and a light woman, there is a small chance that the offspring will favor the mother, but blond hair or blue eyes, never. That is an impossibility."

Bin Laden's eyes narrowed and he grew pensive. "So, the father was cuckolded, the boy is not his?"

Fahad paused and chose his words carefully. "I did not say that, my Sheik. I said that 'it would be impossible for a *pure-blooded* Arab to produce blond hair and blue eyes.' But, my Sheik, it could be possible that your man is not of pure Arab bloodline..."

Bin Laden frowned. "Both his Mother and Father were good Arabs. The father was a Saudi and the mother a Palestinian. Years ago, I knew both of them, as we were childhood friends. He is of the same Arab descent as myself."

Fahad breathed an audible sigh and allowed his otherwise passive face to develop the beginnings of a smile. He was being asked to do that which he loved! He assumed the role of teacher, with Bin Laden as his student. The room became a lecture hall. "Sheik, Gregor Mendel was an Augustinian monk who lived between 1822 and 1884. As a child, in Moravia, he showed brilliance in the public schools, but his parents could not afford additional schooling. He became a monk in order to further his education.

"Mendel's research began out of a love for the natural world. He was extremely interested in subjects as diverse as meteorology and evolution. He began his experiments with plants after he had observed that some of them, in the same species, had atypical characteristics. He planted one of the atypical flowers next to the more common variety to determine what would happen to the next generation. At the time, another scientist named Lamarck, had espoused that the environment was the determining factor in a plant's characteristics. But when the second generation of the plants possessed the same traits as the first, Mendel knew that Lamarck was wrong: the environment was not a factor. It was heredity!

"Mendel began a series of experiments with pea plants, chosen because he could observe two generations a year and because they could pollinate themselves. The pea plant has both male, stamen, and female, pistil, organs. He crossed purple and white pea plants and waited to see what would happen.

"In the first generation of offspring plants, there was no change from the parents. However, beginning in the third generation of plants, and continuing thereafter, the offspring were in a three to one ratio of dominant to recessive. In the case of pea plants, this was purple to yellow. Mendel also observed factors other than color, such as size of plant, shape of seed etc. He found that in every case there was a dominant characteristic that occurred in ratios of three to one in successive generations. However, these traits were all independent of each other, even though they exhibited the same ratio patterns. Mendel had discovered the basic law of genetics."

Although Bin Laden had listened patiently to the opening lesson of the Professor's Biology course, he now grew restless. He was not used to receiving lectures. "But listen here, we are talking about men, not peas. What about men?"

"My Sheik, the basic law applies. The dominant genes of every characteristic appear in fixed ratios. However, in man, the most variable of all the species, there can be a mixture of genes. This accounts for the various shades of skin pigmentation one finds in humans."

"But this law of Mendel's still does not explain how an Arab boy could be blond," Bin Laden interjected.

"Sheik, that is what I am getting to. The boy's father was carrying a blond gene in his blood from an earlier generation. When mated with a blond woman, the chromosomes of these genes reacted to produce a blond son. A very, very unlikely event, but genetically possible."

Bin Laden looked puzzled, "But how...?"

The professor interrupted. "The British occupied Palestine during the years 1919 to 1947. There could have been a union between a British soldier and an Arab woman, a rape or even a concubine. On the father's side, westerners have been in Saudi Arabia with Aramco since before the war. Again, it was unlikely there was a marriage but, as we know, there were involvements. There are other Arab countries where Europeans and Americans have long had a presence: Look at Algeria and the French, for example. And we Arabs are a transient people." Fahad shrugged his shoulders in the universal sign of ignorance, "who knows?"

Bin Laden sat pensively for some time, while digesting the genetic lesson. Then he spoke to directly to Fahad: "Professor, you have a trained eye and are attuned to such things. Have you ever seen such an Arab before?"

"Yes my sheik, during my *hajj* to Mecca some years ago, I saw another boy, like the son of your man. I would guess there are a small number of such genetic rarities on the Arabian peninsula. It would be an interesting research project."

Bin Laden rose slowly from his seat on the floor. "Professor, you have been most helpful. It has been a long day and night for you. We will find you a place to sleep. When you are rested and when the heat of the day is past, we will return you to your home. I thank you for coming."

It was an abrupt dismissal. Fahad had wanted to ask bin Laden about his interest in the subject. Why would an obscure, uneducated tribal chief, living in a mud hut in the desert like bin Laden be so interested in the genetics of the offspring of one of his men? He had no answer, but did not want to think about it. He wanted to lie down and to sleep.

Eight hours later Fahad was awakened, given food, and returned to his horse for the trip home, accompanied by two men with the ever-present AK-47's. They set off on their journey. After two hours they stopped to rest. Fahad got down from his horse and went a few steps into the desert to urinate. It is probable that he never heard the sound of the bolt pumping a cartridge into the chamber.

The Avtomat Kalishnikova 1947 (AK-47) is the weapon of choice of communist states and third world nations. As it is simply made, primarily from stampings, it has been manufactured in a number of countries, in the tens of millions. On full automatic fire, the Kalishnikof has a cyclic rate of 600 rounds per minute. It takes just 3 seconds to empty its 30 round magazine. The professor died instantly.

As Muhammad Atef had said two days earlier, the desert was a dangerous place.

Chapter 7
Fort Meade, Maryland: Monday, July 22, 1996
❖

Danielle Lamaze-Smith was distantly related to the French obstetrician who had given his name to a concept of natural birth and the breathing exercise for pregnant women. Danielle occupied the third cubicle from the corridor in a rabbit warren of cubicles that was part of a special section of Arabic speaking interpreters and analysts on the fourth floor of the National Security Agency offices in Fort Meade, Maryland,

Her middle name "Lamaze" was a source of continuing amusement to her male colleagues, but they also noted her casual sophistication and remarkable focus when she was working on a project or talking to one of her many resources — you could see it in those intense green eyes! They could tell she was intelligent, but they liked the fact that she was never arrogant.

Compared to the cubicles of her colleagues, Danielle's was Spartan. While others had pictures of spouses and children and pets, homemade cards created by pre-school hands, "World's Best Mom" cards, jars of candy and the like, Danielle had no children. She had no pictures of her husband, Neal, nor their golden retriever, Goldie. Her sole concession to personalizing her space was the framed photo taken last Christmas in her parents' home in Sidi bel Abbes, Algeria.

Danielle's father was the Algeria CEO for La Terre, a vast multinational corporation, with its fortunes founded firmly on the cement it manufactured. Charles Lamaze and his wife were devout Catholics, and Christmas in Algeria was always a family affair, full of tradition. This past Christmas the entire Lamaze family had been together for the first time in five years: Parents Charles and Marie, daughter Danielle and her husband Neal, and Danielle's twin sister, Monique, who was a journalist in Paris.

Though they were identical twins, their parents had never tried to make Danielle and Monique carbon copies of one another.

Danielle was her "father's daughter", a serious student, committed to her work. She had been raised in Algeria, but graduated from the Sorbonne in Paris where she had taken up sociology (in which she had earned her doctorate) and languages. In addition to her native French, Danielle was proficient in English and Arabic, and competent in Pashtu. She was also conversant in Dari and several of the other minor languages spoken in the region. Danielle was, in fact, a gifted linguist. She also was a serious horseback rider while a student; she was a daring equestrienne, and had suffered more than one broken arm.

Conversely, her sister Monique was the fun-loving one, full of joie de vivre. She was gregarious, witty, flirtatious. Though they had the same striking figures with green eyes and auburn hair, and nearly-identical, strangely sexy voices, their demeanors could be entirely different. Monique joked that she and her sister were like the famous twin faces of Comedy and Tragedy. Danielle refused to accept this; she would not accept the role of tragedy for herself, although it was clear Monique was the laughing one!

So it was something of a surprise to everyone, especially Danielle, when she fell in love with the American, Neal Smith. Danielle had met Neal when his then-girlfriend had relentlessly rounded up even the most distant friends-of-friends so that Neal would have an audience for the student premiere of his Three Sonatas for Violin. At the party following his remarkably dazzling performance, Danielle congratulated the young composer, and that, as they say, was that. When they married, everyone who knew the Lamaze girls — from their Paris friends to their convent school classmates — commented that it ought to have been Monique who fell in love with a musician and even a composer, no less!

Neal had come to Paris to study at the Conservatoire and breathe the same air as his heroes, Fauré, Debussy, Ravel. When his studies finished, he held a teaching post in the music department of the American University of Paris. He was now ready to return home to the U.S., and Danielle was ready to go with him. The couple gave up their Left Bank flat, and bade a sad farewell to

Monique and the rest of their Paris friends. They moved to DC and rented a small apartment near the Catholic University of America Campus, where Neal joined the faculty of the Benjamin T. Rome School of Music.

For a few months Danielle took on various translating jobs, but when she heard that the National Security Agency was expanding its staff of Arabists because of the increased terrorist activity from that part of the world, she applied immediately, eager for the challenge.

(She told her parents she was applying to the State Department. Her father had decidedly-strong opinions about U.S. foreign policy, and was not especially pleased that she would be working for the American government. At least, with the Department of State ruse, Danielle thought that he would think that the job had, as the French say, some "cachet". Danielle would be a "diplomat", not a spy. Charles Lamaze had a low opinion of people who spent their time eavesdropping, wiretapping, reading the world's mail.)

Monique, of course, knew the truth about the position Danielle was seeking; Monique thought Danielle was being too careful of their father's sensibilities, but she would never betray her sister's secret.

The NSA interviewer was delighted with Dr. Lamaze-Smith's credentials, especially her English and her scores on the various aptitude and psychological tests to determine her skills at what might be called "puzzle-solving". But Danielle was foreign-born and a citizen of Algeria, and her "full field investigation" was more rigorous than most. It took seven months to achieve. While she waited in their small flat, Danielle translated Arabic for others, and turned her own doctoral thesis into English from the French, hoping she could offer it to an American publisher.

When word came that her NSA clearance was finally approved, Neal and Danielle broke open a bottle of fine French champagne, and considered their prospects. Neal had found that university politics (and teaching in general, for that matter) were uncongenial. They surmised that if he left the university, there was no reason to stay in high-priced DC, for Danielle would be working at Ft. Meade at the doorstep of Bowie, Maryland.

It was during a routine call to her family discussing her possible move to Bowie, that Danielle's father remarked that Ipriham Belhadj, his associate at La Terre, had once lived in Bowie where he had been an engineer for the county. So she then called Belhadj to get his thoughts, and he reinforced the idea: It was a good place, he said; a place where he had once been happy.

The following weekend Danielle and Neal drove to Bowie, scouted out a modest home where the garage had already been remodeled into a working studio, put down a deposit, and then as soon as the sale "closed", moved in. They bought furniture, and added a golden retriever to the family named, naturally, "Goldie". Their urbanite friends were horrified. When the college year ended Neal left the University, and working from home began writing music in his studio and playing violin in various ensembles, both studio and performance.

They put the empty champagne bottle on their new mantel.

In her NSA cubicle, Danielle's phone rang, and she answered automatically. "Lamaze-Smith."

"I've got to go to the Post Office", said Neal. "Do you need anything from the store?"

"Thanks, Neal, but no. And I might be a little late."

"Just come home before the janitor starts filling the office with country-western tunes." Neal was referring to the night cleaners at the NSA building who turned up their radios, too great a contrast for his classical tastes, although Danielle secretly was amused by some of the songs she heard that way, with their tales of love lost and trucks like "Phantom 409".

"Bye. Love you."

When Neal hung up, Danielle got back to work. She was pondering an unusual message that had come from a recorded satellite phone conversation. The phone number of the sending phone was one that had been previously used by members of *al*

Qaeda. The number of the receiving phone was the Saudi Ministry of Foreign Affairs.

The National Security Agency (NSA) is the major tenant on the comparatively small (5,067 acres) of Fort George Meade, in Anne Arundel County, Maryland. The headquarters building is so large that it could easily contain three U.S. Capitols, with room left over. There are more than 50 other NSA buildings scattered about the post. The size of the work force is classified, but an enterprising transportation planner on the Anne Arundel county staff took a commercially available aerial photograph from a company called Air Photographics, and planimetered the parking lots. He then divided this area by 300, the standard parking lot design square footage per car and multiplied by the 1.2 passengers per car common to Washington area commuting. From this exercise he concluded that NSA employed approximately 25,000 people at its headquarters. He also proved that anyone can do some basic spying...

Other thousands of NSA personnel are stationed at the agency's huge antenna "farms" such as Menwith Hill, England, as well as Turkey, Australia, Italy, New Zealand and Canada. From these locations the Agency operates *Project Echelon*, which was started during the cold war with the Soviet Union. This program was established to monitor radio signals and satellite transmissions from around the world and when it was begun was focused primarily on the Soviet Union and its bloc of nations, but now the capability was converted to obtain anti-terrorism and anti-drug intelligence.

The day is long past when an American Government Official would say; "Gentlemen, don't open each other's mail", as Henry Stimson had stated when he was secretary of war in the third Roosevelt Administration. Now, in a sense, "opening the mail of other countries" is the very reason for NSA's existence. It is also the world's premier code-breaking organization.

On this day in 1996 NSA was analyzing every international satellite phone transmission originating in the Middle East through its Cray Y-MP EL and IBM 6000 SP supercomputers. These computers are capable of processing one billion instructions per second and can store five trillion pages of text. They monitor two million telephone conversations an hour, and as Danielle worked in her cubicle it was the largest concentration of computer power in the world.

The computers are also set up to record all calls, local and international, from selected standard telephone numbers. When they are not fully occupied with this activity, the computers had been set up only recently to conduct random sampling of local cellular telephone calls within various countries. One of them, Afghanistan, was "covered like a blanket".

The computers are programmed with custom software for voice recognition of thousands of names and so-called "dirty words". Messages containing these names or words such as "bomb", "blow up" or "America" are recorded and transcribed. Messages from known or suspected *al Qaeda* personnel that contain a "dirty word" are automatically segregated for immediate attention and red tagged for delivery to an analyst. The transcription that Danielle had before her, was such a message:

NATIONAL SECURITY AGENCY CONTROL #96-7-146643-Q
14 JULY 96
SENDING # 50-269-4017   RECEIVING # 66-341-2917-88
ACTION WORDS: AMERICAN, AMERICA, KINGDOM
(NORMAL GREETINGS AND PERSONAL CONVERSATION)
FAREED:
    WE NEED COPIES OF THE PASSPORTS OF BOYS,
AGES 10 TO 15, BORN IN AMERICA WHO ARE PRESENTLY
IN THE KINGDOM WITHOUT THEIR MOTHERS. AS THEY
WOULD HAVE AMERICAN PASSPORTS, THESE SHOULD
BE EASILY OBTAINED.
    WE ARE PARTICULARLY INTERESTED IN THOSE
BOYS WHO HAVE AMERICAN MOTHERS, WHO MAY HAVE
FILED COMPLAINTS WITH THE SAUDI FOREIGN MINISTRY
ABOUT THEIR HUSBANDS KIDNAPPING THEIR CHILDREN

BACK TO THE KINGDOM.
WE NEED COPIES OF THE PASSPORTS AND LOCA-
TIONS OF THESE BOYS AS SOON AS POSSIBLE. BE SURE
THE PASSPORTS INCLUDE THE PHOTOGRAPHS.
MUHAMMAD

Who was "Fareed"? Danielle turned to the computer terminal on her desk and entered instructions that resulted in a list of staff of the Saudi Foreign Ministry being shown on her monitor. There were several thousand names. She entered another code to sort the list alphabetically by first name. She scrolled down. There were 11 Fareed's. Then she tapped in a code to list the positions held by the various individuals named Fareed. After removing the drivers, security people, medical staff, and other minor personnel, she had but three named Fareed who were possible. Only one was a likely prospect, since his job concerned "relations with the United States" and was not some internal embassy function. He was Fareed Khouri, a middle level manager in the section of the Ministry. Danielle next sent an E-mail to the head of the programming group requesting that all four names (the two likely ones plus the two that were unlikely just for safety) be added to the computer program for automatic attention. She had once delayed doing this and had missed a follow-up telephone call. It was not a lesson she needed to learn twice.

"Muhammad" was easier. While one could not be sure in a culture where it seemed that every tenth male was named Muhammad, Danielle was quite certain that it was Muhammad Atef, for he was a very senior member of *al Qaeda,* and after she ordered a quick computer search of cell phone numbers used previously by Al Qaeda operatives, up came the matching number.

In less than an hour, Danielle had tentatively identified both parties in the call. She was quite pleased with herself.

Knowing the probable members in the conversation was a

good start. Much of the time they could not be identified with any certainty or, not giving their names, were totally unknown. The Agency's audio technicians were skilled at matching voices to existing recordings of known individuals, but it was a time-consuming process.

A good intelligence analyst is not a linear thinker. They are similar to crossword puzzle champions. In fact, the *Sunday Washington Post* crossword puzzle was the base of a weekly betting pool in the Middle East section. Everyone contributed a dollar a week and the winner was the one who completed the puzzle. If there was no winner, the pool was added to the next week's jackpot. Danielle had won several times, but there was a man in the group who was a consistent winner. As might be suspected, he was the head of the department and her boss, Sanford (Sandy) Parcell. He even did his puzzles in ballpoint pen.

This message was mystifying. Danielle could not imagine any scenario in which *al Qaeda* could utilize the names of American-born children. She struggled with various thoughts for an hour and, reaching no plausible conclusions, wrote up a summary of her work. She "bucked this up" to her puzzle-winning department head by E-mail, with the hard copy by red tag express.

Perhaps he could figure it out.

Chapter 8
Afghanistan: Tuesday, July 23, 1996
◈

Osama bin Laden and Muhammad Atef were seated on cushions, on opposing sides of the low table in bin Laden's quarters. Atef had bought several kilos of pistachio nuts during his trip to Kabul and they were noisily involved in eating these and spitting the shells on the floor. In one of the extended periods of silence characteristic of a conversation between two men engaged in cracking and eating nuts, Atef was reminded to have the boy come in when they were done, and sweep the floor. This was not done so much out of a desire for cleanliness, but concern for bin Laden's feet. He did not wish to have his friend get up during the night and step on the hard, sharp, shells.

Atef's relationship with bin Laden was like no other he had experienced in his life. They were both approximately the same age and yet bin Laden had taken on the role of a father figure. He was a rich man, an experienced businessman, who had operated at very high levels in Saudi Arabia. Yet, he had given up all of that to organize and become the leader of *al Qaeda*. It was through his energies and brilliance that their organization had become known, and feared, throughout the world. They were called terrorists, but bin Laden maintained they were warriors for Islam. They were going to drive the Western presence out of the Arab lands. Had not George Washington won worldwide fame for driving the British out of North America? Was he not revered as a great hero?

Atef was convinced that bin Laden was going to be remembered as one of the acclaimed leaders of history, like Alexander the Great. He had often lamented to himself that it was unfortunate that Alexander had been born so long before the great Muhammad. He could only imagine what the Arab world could have been with Muhammad's religious leadership and Alexander's military skills.

Bin Laden broke the silence. "We may have to expand our search. We will probably not be able to find enough people to meet our needs in Saudi Arabia. What do you think?"

"I was thinking the same thing; it's been nearly two weeks. I have started to prepare a list of countries we could approach for assistance."

"And who do you think we should contact, Atef? Remember, the more people we approach, the more likely it will be that the Americans will sniff out what we are doing."

"Exactly. I thought of that. As there is the same degree of danger in dealing with a nation of 6 million, as 60 million, and much less likelihood of getting who we need, I eliminated many of our smaller friends. I do not think we should approach the Emirates, Qatar, Bahrain, Oman, Yemen, or Kuwait." Sensing no opposition, Atef continued. "Jordan is out, because of Hussein's love affair for the West as well as for his American wife. She is probably an agent for the CIA." (Atef knew this statement was not true, but many Arabs had it as an article of faith that Queen Noor was an American plant.)

"Also, the likelihood of success is probably lower in Sub-Saharan Africa, which eliminates Somalia, Sudan, Ethiopia and Kenya. That leaves Syria, Lebanon, Egypt, Iran, Iraq, Algeria, Pakistan, Tunisia and Morocco as the large countries, most likely to harbor individuals of the ages and characteristics we require. Do you agree?"

Bin Laden drew a deep breath, squinted his eyes and began to audibly muse. "Certainly I agree with your logic on the eliminations, the question is, which of the balance should we approach?"

"I think that Egypt is too infiltrated by the Western intelligence agencies to be considered, so we drop them. Libya, on the other hand, has the proper attitude, but is ruled by a very unpredictable man. Muammar Ghadafi might find out what we are trying to do. In his zeal to become rid of the UN sanctions against his country, he might inform the Americans. I understand that he is considering admitting to the Lockerby crash and paying reparations. No, we cannot include Libya. Certainly, the country most likely to cooperate is Iraq", continued Atef. "I think that if Saddam had thought of using boys before us, he would have started a forced breeding program." Both men laughed at the thought. Saddam Hussein could be counted on for his hatred of Americans. He had been greatly humiliated in the gulf war, the one the Americans had called Desert Storm.

They continued discussing the merits of each country, its leaders, their ability to get the information without arousing suspicion and the probability of its producing the individuals they were seeking. In the end, their list included Saudi Arabia, Iraq, Iran, Pakistan and Algeria. The last was added in spite of the fact that *al Queda* had no close contacts in the Algerian government, because the men felt that the filthy French had been breeding there for 100 years. They had to have left behind some genes!

In their first discussion of bin Laden's plan, they had agreed that the search should be limited to children with an American mother. The likelihood of their finding the characteristics they were seeking, was greater with this search criterion than in any other method they could think of. If the father had to kidnap his children and return to a Muslim country, it was probable that the mother was not an Arab. It was even more probable that the father was a dedicated Arab nationalist; with luck, even a fundamentalist regarding Islam. If this were the case, it was likely that the son(s) were already firm believers. In this regard bin Laden observed: "The largest infidel religion is Catholicism, one which has been at war with Islam since the time of the crusades. It is a false religion, but a great truth was uttered by one of their prophets, St. Ignatius. 'Give me the boy and I shall have the man for life.' We are about to put his theory into practice."

Their conversation being concluded, Atef excused himself, going to his room to make a list of contacts who could obtain the information they needed from the foreign ministries of the countries they had picked. It was convenient for him to reach the

Saudi ministry: Fareed Khouri was one of bin Laden's many brothers-in-law!

On the way out of the door, Atef had instructed the boy to go in and sweep up the shells.

Chapter 9
Sidi bel Abbes, Algeria: Wednesday, July 24, 1996
◈

The legislature of the Peoples Democratic Republic of Algeria was considering enacting a law that would ban political parties organized by a religion. In a country in which 99% of the population was Sunni Muslim, this was an indication that the public had experienced enough of the Front Islamique du Salvi (the Islamic Salvation Front) — the FIS — and their fundamentalist terrorism. For more than a decade this organization had waged a low-grade civil war, in which over 100,000 people had been killed. Now it appeared that the government would prevail and just outlaw the FIS.

Ali Idriss found this an unbelievable turn of events. After all, he thought, wasn't it the victory of the Muslim Political Party in the 1947 elections that gave birth to the FLN — Front de Liberation Nationale — a year later and led Algeria's independence from France? Ali admitted to himself that the FIS had been somewhat destructive in its methods, more than he thought necessary. But still, Algeria was a Muslim country and *should* have an Islamic government.

Idriss himself, was a low-level functionary in the Sidi bel Abbes financial records office of the very government that was promoting the elimination of the FIS, the party to which he belonged. He did not dare admit of this affiliation to any of his associates, as he probably would have been terminated. Idriss just went to his office every day and worked at his desk, pretending to like his job and the Government that employed him. In this regard he was like bureaucrats in every country of the world. He felt trapped.

Idriss tried to be obliging when the FIS asked him for help, although the organization knew he could not risk losing his job. Usually the request was to pick someone up at the airport, or provide a room or deliver a package. For that reason, he was surprised when Abassi Touati visited him with a special request.

"Ali Idriss," began Touati, "we have been contacted by our friends in Afghanistan with an unusual request, one which we do not understand. They have asked us for a list of youth born in America, to American women, but now living with their fathers here in Algeria. They must want to talk to them about something, though I cannot imagine what information a child can provide. With our position of being enemies of the government, we can hardly write the Minister of the Interior with such a request. Is there any way you can help us?"

Idriss was taken aback by the question. He had never been asked to provide information about the government and, as great as his loyalties were to the FIS, did not feel comfortable being asked to spy. Suppose he were caught?

"My friend", he began, "I am not in the department where such information is kept. Nor do I know anyone who is. What a strange request. Let us share a cup of tea and discuss this interesting matter. Perhaps with both of our heads, we will come up with something."

But, after the tea, neither Idriss nor Touati could think of any reason why the Taliban could possibly want to know about such people, nor could Idriss think of any way of getting the information. Nonetheless, he asked Touati to give him a day to think about it, before admitting defeat.

During the evening meal of rice and lamb with his wife, Idriss began telling her about the mysterious request from Afghanistan. She listened silently and then, unusual for her, made a suggestion.

"Perhaps they are talking about Anwar Belhadj. He is the young man from America I see when I have escorted the children to school. His Mother is still in the United States. I often think about her and how lonely she must be."

"Woman, I thank you for that! I would never have come up with his name."

"He is no longer such a boy, I believe he must now be 12

years old," added the wife, happy for the compliment for having added something useful to the conversation.

The next day Idriss made up a story and called the Ministry of the Interior, Office of Population Statistics. He identified himself as a journalist, thinking of writing a story about American-born children and how they made the adjustment between societies. When he was informed that the Ministry kept no files on American-born Algerians, he did not push for another response. He already had a name for the Taliban, Anwar Belhadj.

Next he telephoned the Belhadj home and asked for the son. He explained that he was with a government office reviewing the passports of those who had immigrated to Algeria within the past five years. It seems they knew that he had been one of those but could find no copy of his passport. "If you do not have access to a copying machine, you are welcome to come to this office and we will make a copy for you"

To a 12 year-old boy, such a request loomed as an order. The next afternoon the boy showed up at the office with his U.S. passport in hand. When he arrived, Idriss was quite surprised at his appearance. Belhadj did not look like an Arab. Nor did he resemble a Berber, Idress's own lineage.

Belhadj, in his jeans, with his blond hair and fair skin, looked just like an American!

Chapter 10
Fort Meade Maryland: Friday, July 26, 1996
◈

Danielle Lamaze stared at the four messages on her desk. They were virtually identical to the message she had translated a few days before to Fahreed Khouri, in Saudi Arabia. Now, she presumed, Mohammad Atef had called Iran, Iraq, Pakistan and Algeria with a similar request for passports of American born young men. Why was he interested in boys from five to fifteen years of age? What about the other countries in the region? Was there a special significance to the five countries? Was pedophilia a factor? The permutations and combinations of the unknowns were extraordinary!

Danielle researched the new messages in the same fashion that she had done with the call to Saudi Arabia. She achieved largely the same results. The calls to Iran, Iraq and Pakistan had been to Government offices. The parties to whom the calls were made were tentatively identified.

The call to Algeria was not to a government office but to a phone registered to one Abassi Touati. A computer search of Algerian government officials did not include anyone named Touati. On a hunch, Danielle accessed the terrorist data-base belonging to the CIA. This search uncovered an Abassi Touati, listed as a member of the extremist Muslim party, FIS. She decided that it was possible, indeed probable, that this was the same person.

As the telephone number was new to the system, Danielle filled out a form to add it to the watch list as well as the primary and secondary names she had uncovered. She had not devoted any attention to the FIS for several years, but the Touati name seemed to have a familiar ring to it. She just wasn't sure, but it needed to be checked out.

She picked up the telephone from the corner of her desk and dialed her department head, he of crossword puzzle fame.

"Hello, Sandy, this is Danielle. We've just intercepted four more messages from *al Qaeda*, with requests for passports. Are you available to discuss these? Now? Sure...I'll be right over."

Sandford Parcell was the archetypical NSA/CIA intelligence officer. Medium in size and weight, glasses, soft spoken and given to bow ties, he looked exactly like the college professor he was. Before joining NSA, he had been an instructor in philosophy at Skidmore College. One day, finding himself getting bored in upstate New York, idly reading the *Chronicle of Higher Education*, he was attracted to an advertisement for academics of various fields to work in Washington, DC. The rest, as he liked to say, "was history." Sandy had been in Washington for 16 years and found it much superior to Saratoga Springs in every way but one. Sandy was an avid "birder", and the birding around Maryland was more waterfowl-oriented than he cared for. Still, hope sprang eternal. A telescope sat on his window ledge and on his desk rested *A Field Guide to North American Birds.*

Danielle marched the 76 paces down the corridor from her cubicle to Sandy's office and was waved to a seat.

"Hi, Sandy. Sorry to bother you on such short notice, but we have a situation developing that I don't understand. I was hoping you might have some ideas. Yesterday, I sent you a summary of a Telcon between a man (whom I believe is Mohammad Atef) and a person thought to be Fareed Khouri, of the Saudi Foreign Ministry. It was a simple message. It requested copies of the passports of male children, born here in the U.S. of Saudi fathers and American mothers and then taken back to Saudi Arabia by their fathers. In fact, Mike Wallace and *60 minutes* did a feature on such incidents earlier this year. I know you cautioned us about 'not taking our work home,' but I found this request so unusual, almost bizarre, that I wasn't able to get it off my mind! I spent until one this morning worrying about it. Then here this morning I got four more intercepts to four more countries, with the same request."

Parcell interrupted, "What countries?"

"Iran, Iraq, Pakistan and Algeria. The telcons to the first three were to people in government offices. The call to Algeria was to a person the CIA database identifies as a member of FIS, the Front Islamique du Salvi."

Parcell interrupted again, "Who was that member?"

"Abassi Touati. The Agency base has no more information on him, just his name."

Parcell reached for a pipe and clenched it between his teeth. Since the ban on smoking in Government offices, enacted during the Carter Administration, he couldn't actually smoke, but he found it conducive to thinking to have a pipe in his mouth. He wasn't one who found it necessary to stand outside during the day and smoke the way many cigarette addicts did. But his first act, on getting to his car, was to light up.

"OK, Danielle, for starters let's get some background on this guy. Call Jurgen Heidemann at the Agency and ask him to send a NIAC [*night action required*, the second highest designation after Flash] to his station chief in Algiers. Since Touati is the only non-governmental employee contacted, it may be worthwhile to pursue that anomaly. You should also ask Heidemann to obtain the Algerian records on children who are U.S. citizens, living in the country."

Danielle scratched herself a note.

"Now, Danielle, since you have been burning the midnight oil on this, what are your thoughts?"

"Frankly sir, I don't have any. I can't come up with a single reason why *al Qaeda* would seek out children who were taken back to Arab countries. They certainly aren't being sought for intelligence reasons, so what could a child offer? The only reason that seems to make any sense at all is that they are to be used for propaganda purposes. Perhaps to embarrass us in some fashion."

Parcel pulled on his pipe, which emitted a sucking sound. "Have you contacted State to get a list of such children?"

"Yes sir, I did that an hour ago. Peterson promised to have something for me in the morning."

"Hmmm, OK." (Another fruitless inhale.) "Stay on this. We'll get together again tomorrow when you get the list from State. Maybe we'll have something on Touati by then too. I agree with you, Danielle, there is no apparent reason for what is happening but there certainly must be one! Atef just wouldn't put out these requests for his amusement. Now we have to find out why."

When she got back to her cubicle, Danielle felt strangely relieved. Her boss was as mystified as she was...

Chapter 11
Algiers: Monday, July 29, 1996
❖

CIA's Chief of Station in Algiers held the position of "Officer-in-Charge of Press Relations". It was a very transparent ruse. All of the diplomatic corps in Algiers knew what his real job was. And, if all of the diplomats knew, then everyone knew. As a class, thought Tom Dettor, diplomats were inherently unable to keep a secret.

Dettor was examining a cable that had just reached his desk from the decoding room. It had been sent NIAC, [*Night Action Required*], and was therefore considered highly important, though Dettor certainly couldn't see why. It was probably just another telex, artificially elevated in importance by some nameless bureaucrat in the DI [Directorate of Intelligence] who was working on a project and needed a piece of information. Dettor, of course, was in the DO [Directorate of Operations]. There was always friction between the two Directorates but now, with many of the new DI people being female, the DO's, mostly male, were continually disgruntled. This was particularly true of the older field men like Dettor, who had always been derisive of the DI crowd. He thought DI staff sat in their air conditioned offices and played with themselves. They were smart, but they were wusses.

26 JULY 1996
TO: TOM DETTOR, COSCIA, ALGIERS
FR: CIA DEP. ASST. DIR. HEIDEMANN
RE: BACKGROUND INFO ON ABASSI TOUATI
     WE REQUIRE BACKGROUND OF ABASSI TOUATI,
BELIEVED MEMBER OF FIS. CELL PHONE NUMBER
213-55-4679 (DO NOT USE OR DISCLOSE-FOR INFORMA-
TIONAL PURPOSES ONLY)
     ALSO, GET FROM DEPUTY MINISTER OF INTERIOR,
OFFICE OF POPULATION STATISTICS, PASSPORT

*NUMBERS OF AMERICAN BORN CHILDREN NOW
LIVING IN ALGERIA.
NEED SOONEST.
REGARDS, HEIDEMANN*

Immediately disregarding Heidemann's instructions, Dettor dialed the cell phone number. It rang three times and a voice responded, "Abassi Touati", Dettor hung up. At least the headquarters types had got the name and number right.

In every country of the world, political parties are easy to penetrate. They are always seeking new dues-paying members and additional helpers. Also, they are usually unsophisticated about performing background checks. It was the "friend of a friend" syndrome at work, as in "If you are a friend of Abdullah's, that is good enough for me." Dettor had a number of assets inside FIS, almost one in each of Algeria's 48 provinces. The FIS was his main game, easily his very *raison d' etre.*

He called his FIS contact in Algiers and was told that he thought there was such a man in Sidi bel Abbes. The good news was that Dettor had a contact, "Nadeem", in this former French Foreign Legion post. The bad news was that the man didn't have a phone and communicated by mail. As this was a "night action" request, he would have to drive the 250 miles to Sidi bel Abbes. This he would do the next morning. To hell with Washington, they could wait a day.

Dettor next called the Office of the Deputy Minister of the Interior and arranged a meeting for drinks, after work. The Minister was someone he had cultivated and was a valuable source. Every year the CIA updated their *World Fact Book* and the Minister contributed valuable, top-secret information to Tom about such subjects as the current literacy rate, the number of airports with paved runways or the percentage of people with HIV-AIDS. This made Dettor look good to the DI mullets in Washington. On the other hand, collecting this type of information just aggravated Tom. If he wanted to do this kind of housekeeping, he would have joined AID.

Of course, the Minister knew with whom he was dealing when he met with Tom, he just had the courtesy to never mention that he knew. In return, Tom had the courtesy to never ask for any information that, if the source were exposed, would embarrass the Minister. Wining and dining, at the expense of the U.S. taxpayer, was an unlisted fringe benefit of both of their positions.

They met at 6:00 PM in the current "smart" bistro in Algiers' ever-changing nightlife. The Minister, Ibu Farouk, was already seated when he arrived. He had a typical Berber face and bore an uncanny resemblance to Richard Boone, the star of the old TV show, *Have Gun, Will Travel*. Once Tom had mentioned this fact to his secretary, who had no idea what he was talking about, for she had been born long after the show was off the air. It made him feel older than his 56 years, and he never made the comparison again.

"*Bonjour, Monsieur* Dettor." The Minister greeted him in French, appropriate for the location. Dettor replied, "*Bonjour*" with an exaggerated flourish. His French was better than his Arabic, but still not as good as his English. The Minister spoke all three languages with equal facility. They continued their conversation in English.

After each had ordered a *pastis* and made the obligatory small talk, the Minister queried, "And why do I have the pleasure of your company this evening? It is not yet time for the annual report to your home office. You must be seeking something other than the dreary statistics with which I am forced to spend my days."

"As a matter of fact, Abu, I am. I have received a request for a list of American-born children currently living in Algeria." Dettor joked, "I think my government may want them returned, in order to preserve our bloodlines."

Farouk looked puzzled. "That is strange. Several days ago my assistant got a telephone call from a journalist requesting the same information. He said he was doing a story on how American children were adapting to Algerian culture."

Dettor was surprised, but did not allow his face to show any emotion. He had been a spook long enough to know this could not be a coincidence. "Ahhh, he must be the reason I have been asked to help. If you provided him with the information he requested, I will consider my mission no longer necessary."

"No, as a matter of fact, we couldn't help. We don't have the capability to segregate that data in our computer base. We never thought it important enough to set up our system programming for this purpose."

Dettor put on a smile of understanding. "Now it begins to make sense. You wouldn't help him, but the guy knows someone in my home office and figures the U.S. Government can get the information he needs. So I get a call to work on it. That's what happens when the Democrats are in office. It's probably one of the President's Hollywood friends who 'has this great idea for a movie.' I'll forget about it, ... you should too."

Farouk nodded affirmatively. Dettor was reasonably sure he had defused the issue, as far as the Minister was concerned. However, he was beginning to sense that there was a legitimate reason for the NIAC telex. One of the clowns in DI was on to some action. Something was going down.

They each had another *pastis*, chatted about a variety of things and made comments about the girls sitting at the bar. Dettor then excused himself, claiming a dinner engagement. Abu said something about "feeling like another drink." Dettor guessed that after he left, one of the ladies from the bar would be in his seat, probably before it had a chance to cool.

The importance of discretion was something they didn't teach young case officers at Camp Peary, the CIA training school, known as "the farm". It had to be learned by experience.

The next morning, Dettor left his apartment in the embassy compound before 5:00 AM in order to get an early start. Sidi bel Abbes was 250 miles from Algiers. The drive was a pleasant one, as the road ran along the coastline almost the whole way before cutting into the desert for the final 75 miles. Still, the trip would take at least five hours. Tom was thinking about how interstate highways had spoiled American drivers, until he realized he had hardly been on one since he left college. Being a field man in the "Company" didn't qualify him for many management jobs in Langley. Dettor had spent most of his adult life overseas. He didn't regret it, though it had cost him his marriage.

As he drove, he pondered the "what ifs" in his life. There were enough of them to last most the trip.

Chapter 12
Sidi bel Abbes, Algeria: Tuesday, July 30, 1996
◆

Dettor arrived in Sidi bel Abbes shortly after 10:00 AM and went to a pre-arranged contact point. His man Nadeem was fearful of being associated with the CIA and was unwilling to give any information about himself. When he wrote, it was with no return address. To contact him, Dettor had to write to a friend of Nadeem's or drive to Sidi bel Abbes. Once there, Dettor visited a certain restaurant, sat at a particular table and hoped that the waiter who served as the messenger, was working that day. Other than to give him a drink order, Dettor had never conversed with the waiter and did not know how he contacted Nadeem. Notwithstanding this torturous difficulty, the system had worked well. The government got its money's worth. The agent had provided some excellent information, and several times had even forewarned of FIS bombings or abductions. This had allowed the Federal Police, with whom Tom had shared the information, to "just happen" to be in the neighborhood and, in one case, apprehend the bombers.

"*Monsieur*, your friend says he will meet you at the Officer's Club at noon, for luncheon," the waiter mumbled to Dettor as he presented the bill for the bottle of beer that Dettor had ordered. Normally, Tom didn't drink when in the field, but the long drive had left him thirsty and feeling very deserving of a treat.

The aforementioned Officers' Club had once been the officers' mess of the old French Foreign Legion post, abandoned when the French left in '62 (a French Foreign Legion post was established in Sidi bel Abbes in 1847 upon their defeat of Abd-el-Kader to bring security to the population which was constantly being raided by desert Berbers). The people in those days, thought Dettor, were certainly a strong and hardy group...

An Algerian businessman had rented the building from the Government and had fixed it up with numerous pictures and mementos of the *Kepi Blancs*, as the Legionnaires famous hats were called; the name now applied to Legionnaires and ex-Legionnaires, as well. The sense of history in the club was palpable. Tom personally liked the place, but it was kind of a rough spot, patronized principally by retired legionnaires, those who wished they had been legionnaires and those who liked to be around legionnaires. It was hardly a place where he would be recognized. He assumed the same for Nadeem.

Tom Dettor entered the Officers' Club five minutes early and found his agent sitting in a corner booth with high sides. They exchanged greetings like old friends and Tom sat down. In a place like this, you tried to fit in with the crowd. They both ordered a cup of *gaspacho*, and chicken sandwiches.

Usually, in running agents, Tom tried to become friendly and gain the man's confidence. If the agent felt you genuinely cared about him, he would be inclined to do more for you. At least that's what the textbooks said. This man resisted all attempts at establishing any kind of personal relationship. Tom did not even know the man's real name; "Nadeem" was an alias. The agent was distant and they killed the time before the sandwiches arrived in the most mundane conversation. They waited until they had been served to begin their business, in order not to be unexpectedly interrupted by the waiter.

Tom began: "We are interested in a man named Abassi Touati and about his connections with Afghanistan. Do you know him?"

The asset wrapped his hands around his water glass and, successfully, tried to look like an old friend, carrying on a casual conversation. "Yes, I do. I know him well. We have worked together in the past. He is a dangerous, evil man, a firebrand fundamentalist who is not taking the failing of FIS lightly. Last year he went to a training camp in Afghanistan, run by the Muslim leader, Osama bin Laden. He stayed there three months and learned a great deal about bomb-making and other kinds of warfare. He returned with a renewed fervor for the Islamic cause.

He is even talking about returning there to participate in the *jihad*. If our party is banned next year by the legislature and, as you know, it looks very likely that will happen, I would not be surprised if he went back to Afghanistan."

Dettor paused, and chewed on his sandwich while digesting this information. Touati was beginning to look like a bigger fish than he had expected.

"Do you know where he lives or where he can be picked up?"

"No, I don't know where he resides, but I know that on most nights he can be found in a place, a bar called *Scheherazade*. It is not far from here."

"Do you know if the Federals know of him?"

"Yes, I am sure they do. He has a long history of crime. He doesn't hold a job, but makes his money doing a variety of things...assassination, drugs, theft, girls. As the song in your show *Irma la Douce* said: 'everything that makes life worthwhile.' He'll do anything you ask, if the price is right."

Tom was continually amazed at the extent of the man's knowledge. For Lord's sake, he had quoted *Irma la Douce!* Tom could only vaguely remember the show and none of the words or music...

Dettor, following the textbooks with another attempt to show concern, but really having some feeling for this nameless man whom he had come to respect, asked, "Would he have any reason to suspect you, if the police were to pay a call on him?"

"No, I don't think so."

"Good. You have been very helpful. In addition to your regular monthly retainer, you will be receiving a bonus. I have your normal stipend in an envelope in this newspaper, which I will leave on the table when I go. I'll leave the bonus at our regular place, on my way back to Algiers."

The asset muttered his thanks. They finished eating and drinking and continued the farce by hanging around an additional quarter hour. During this period they again discussed inconsequential events. When he believed they could safely leave without causing any attention to themselves, Tom called for the check and made a show for the waiter of buying luncheon for his old friend.

On the drive back to Algiers, Dettor put 5,000 Francs into the broken piece of culvert pipe he and Nadeem used as a drop.

Chapter 13
Afghanistan: Wednesday, August 7, 1996
◈

Thirteen days after Atef called his four contacts with the requests, three boxes of papers were delivered for pickup at a house in Kabul. In addition to the boxes from Saudi Arabia, Iran and Pakistan, there were brown envelopes from Iraq and Algeria. A day later these were delivered to Atef on the same horse that had carried Professor Fahad. As with Fahad, the horse returned back to its home without a load.

The passports from each country had been copied on British standard A4 paper, 210mm by 297mm, two pages per passport. There were 237 passports from Saudi Arabia, 179 from Iran, 133 from Pakistan, 2 from Iraq and 1 from Algeria. Apparently Iraq under Saddam Hussein was not a country to which people were eager to return, once they had left. (Atef criticized himself for not thinking of this.) He had selected Iraq on the basis of its support, not with any thought as to the probable results. Atef was reminded that Saddam had been a harsh ruler but, as the French saying observed, "you can't make an omelet without breaking eggs."

There was a note from Fareed Kouhri:

Muhammad:

Because of the 8,700 Americans in the Kingdom working in oil production and refining, there are many children with American passports. Fortunately, because we wanted to be able to identify all of the visitors related to petroleum, our computer programs were set up to do so. To obtain the list of children with American passports in the Kingdom not involved in oil, we only had to sort the list.

Call me if you want the children of oil workers merged back in.

Fareed

There was also a letter from Abassi Touati:

Muhammad:

The Ministry of the Interior, Office of Population Statistics, cannot develop a list of children with American passports presently in Algeria. They can only create a list of all American passports at large in the country. There are an estimated three thousand of these. Also, it will be very difficult to obtain the list.

Enclosed is a copy of the passport of a boy named Anwar Belhadj. He is known personally by one of my contacts in the government. As I think that most of the 3,000 Americans in the country are adults, Belhadj is probably one of the few young men.

Please let me know if you want me to try to get the list of 3,000.

Abassi Touati

Atef began by separating the passports by age. Children under five, he discarded entirely. They would possibly be considered in the future. Sorting the remaining passports took a little longer, as in many cases the photographs were blurry. In the end Atef had two boys from Saudi Arabia, one of which was the boy already in the camp, one from Iran, none from Pakistan and none from Iraq. Although the photos were a little blurred, they were as he had hoped, Allah be praised!

There was reason for his pleasure: The Saudis were 12 and 14, the Iranian 11 and the Algerian 12. Even the ages were perfect. In his hand were the passports of four young men who looked American.

He hurried off to show the passports to Sheik bin Laden.

Chapter 14
Afghanistan: Tuesday, August 20, 1996
❖

Reflecting bin Laden's corporate experience and lack of military background, he and Muhammad Atef had organized the *al Qaeda* cells and training camps along the lines of a modern corporation or university. Responsibilities and authority were meted out to a number of people, according to the skills they could contribute. There was a specific curriculum which every student was required to complete. There was considerable compartmentalization of personnel, due principally to bin Laden's vision of what he wanted to accomplish.

Generally, each cell and camp had the following management positions:

"Overall Officer-in-Charge"

"Director of Education"

"Director of Long Range Planning"

"Director of Operations"

...while the training camps themselves added "Director of Physical Training".

These positions were also in place at bin Laden's headquarters in the small village where the Sheik spent most of his time. While he filled the role of Officer-in-Charge, Muhammad Atef served as Director of Operations. No serious military training took place in the headquarters area.

Now, bin Laden and Atef were conferring in bin Laden's bedroom, together with Yousef Zubeida, the Director of Education for the whole *al Qaeda* organization. The three were discussing the kind of school they were going to establish for their "special students", for the project had expanded to the point where they needed to start bringing in other members of their group.

Bin Laden started the conversation by filling in Zubeida on his vision, their progress to date, and the need for a special educational institution for four young students. This would be unlike anything he had done to date. Instead bin Laden wanted Zubeida to create a *madrass* that would combine the traditional academic program with the bomb making and guerilla warfare skills of the regular training camp. But there would be more. Much more.

Bin Laden spoke. "Yousef, I want you to create a very special *madrass* for these four boys. It will, of course, have Islamic studies. However it will also contain what I will call "American Studies". We will teach these boys about being an American. I want the best English teachers; American English, not British English. The course work will be supplemented in English by American movies and videos of television shows. They must learn about American sports and movie stars. The magazines and newspapers they will read will be American. The politics they discuss will be American. The food in the school will be American. The clothing they wear will be American. The games they play will be American. The history they learn will be American. The products they use will be American. The boys will be given American identities, which will be used from the day they arrive. This instruction will be easier than it sounds, because the students have all lived in America and have some experience in the culture. Of course, until we meet the students themselves, we cannot know exactly how much of the culture they have absorbed."

Zubeida, eager to please bin Laden, jumped in. "I can do what you ask. We have a number of our people who have lived many years in the United States. The best of these can become the instructors."

"I want only the most trusted people involved in this assignment. No word of this project should get out. It is the most secret of efforts. In the end, the students will be involved in a major undertaking that will bring terror to the Americans in their homeland."

"A most important part of their training must be the

development of hatred for the Americans and their Jewish friends. We need to instill in these young men a love of Islam and their countries to the point that they will be willing to sacrifice their lives to participate in this *Jihad.* It is very important that this be done at an early age. As we have found, it is quite possible to send someone on a suicide mission if they have been properly taught as boys and young men. We have not had much success in recruiting people for suicide missions from the older population at large. Teaching the lessons of how terribly the Americans and Israelis have treated the Arab world is critical. Without this, we will be unable to develop these agents to their fullest value. This is a very complex educational concept, teaching them about America, and to hate Americans at the same time, but I think it possible."

"Finally, even though it is against our sacred religion and the teachings of Muhammad, the boys must be taught to drink alcohol and use tobacco products. They must also learn to eat pork and be knowledgeable about the Christian faith. They must be taught that it will be necessary to give up prayer and *Ramadan,* when they are in America. It will be dangerous for them to go to a mosque. I know you may disagree with me on this. There can be nothing," Bin Laden shook his head in emphasis, "nothing, not the slightest clue, which will give them away as being other than typical American young men. They must learn to be more American than the Americans themselves. These four agents must immerse themselves in America and be absolutely untraceable by the police. Do you understand?"

"Yes my Sheik, I do. I will start on this immediately and have a proposal ready for your review in a week! I will create an American existence, in a remote location in the mountains." Zubeida smiled, "We may even fly the American flag over our school."

"Excellent. I think you have the idea. And Yousef, I have all the money necessary to do these things. The budget is no consideration. Make a list of what you want and we'll get it. How long do you think you will need to produce these four Americans?"

"I do not know, as I have not yet met the students. Much depends upon their starting points and, of course, their intelligence is to be considered."

Bin Laden stood up, a sign that the meeting was over. "This is mid-1996. You have seven years to do your work. I want four young Americans, ready to return to their homeland, in 2003. Four blond, young Americans, each ready to die for Islam."

Chapter 15
Washington, DC: Tuesday, August 20, 1996
❖

Jerry Peterson was an assistant to the Assistant Secretary of State for Middle Eastern Affairs. A recent graduate of Georgetown University, School of Foreign Service, he had already served one tour in the embassy in Jordan, where he caught the eye of the Ambassador, now the Assistant Secretary. He was still an eager beaver, not yet worn down by the grinding inertia of government.

He received a request from Dr. Danielle Lamaze-Smith, of NSA. She wanted the passports of boys who had left the United States in the past six years for Saudi Arabia, Iran, Iraq, Pakistan and Algeria. When he tried to reach his friend Karen, at the Bureau of Passport Control, he learned that she was on vacation and would be out another 11 days. He then asked to speak to someone who could assist him with a project. After being routed around to several different people, he finally found someone who could help him. What that person told Peterson was most dissatisfying:

1) There was no way to separate children from adults, in the computer run. The program was not set up to sort by age. He could only get everyone who had traveled to those countries and then eliminate out the children himself.

2) There was no way to separate those who were in the countries for short-term visits, from those who had returned permanently.

3) The list of those holding American passports, currently in the countries specified, certainly numbered in the thousands, probably tens of thousands.

4) The computer database would produce only names and passport numbers. Copies of the passports themselves and of the photographs would have to be hand pulled from files in the central storage facility, located in West Virginia. With the

number of passports involved, this could take weeks, if not months.

5) Since there would be such an enormous effort involved in fulfilling this task, it could not be done informally. The National Security Agency needed to file a written request with the Director of the Passport Bureau.

It was enough to make a person want to take up another career.

When Peterson called Danielle with the news from the passport office, she told him to "scrub the mission." She would think of another approach.

Danielle remembered that the first intercept had mentioned that some of the American children may have been taken to the Kingdom against the wishes of the mother. There may even have been complaints filed. She called the office of the Legal Advisor at the Department of State and prepared herself for a long daisy chain of conversations before she connected with some one who was familiar with what she was talking about. She was right. It took seven conversations, with three lawyers, two administrative assistants and two secretaries before she found someone familiar with the issue. Then she got lucky! Brad Warren was actually working the problem. Although Peterson knew she was with NSA, Danielle did not want to get into a long explanation with someone in the Legal Advisor's office about what she was doing and why she needed the information she was seeking. She decided to pose as a fellow State Department employee.

"Hello, Mr. Warren, this is Danielle Lamaze-Smith, in Special Projects, Middle East. Franklin Robinson just told me that you're the attorney handling the complaints filed with the State Department by American women whose Arab husbands have kidnapped their children back to Saudi Arabia. First, is this correct; and second, can you give me any specifics on such actions?"

"Well hello, Danielle. You are in luck. I actually am the guy working with these mothers — there are about a dozen of them and they're angry — who are trying to recapture their children. Unfortunately, even with all the international laws at our disposal, we have not been able to accomplish the return of a single child. I don't think Clarence Darrow himself would be able to get anywhere with this Saudi government on this issue. With that in mind, how can I help?"

"Well, what I am really looking for are copies of the passports of the kids involved. The Deputy Assistant Secretary has asked me to look into this and see what can be done before his next trip to the region. It is not a high priority item with him, but the matter may come up in discussions with his counterparts." Since she became employed by NSA, Danielle had become quite adept at fibbing...

"Sure, I can do that. I've got copies of all the passports. Where should I send them? I'm not in favor of American kids growing up in Saudi Arabia anyway."

"You can send them to me in the interoffice mail: Danielle Lamaze-Smith, Office of Special Projects, Room 3954, Department of State."

"So, you're here in Main State too. Perhaps we could get together for lunch sometime. You sound interesting."

Danielle smiled to herself. Her voice with, its slight French accent, was still sexy and a turn-on to men. "Actually, I am in a satellite office outside of Washington, but our mail goes to Room 3354, so I'll have to decline the invitation. I thank you anyway. And I will really appreciate getting those passports this week, if you can get them off that fast. Thanks again, Brad, for the luncheon invitation. Goodbye."

If Bradford Warren should happen to try to find room 3954, he would have a difficult time. The third floor office rooms stopped at number 3950. Room 3954 was one of several addresses NSA used in various government buildings around Washington. Moreover, he would never have found Danielle at that room number; room 3954 was a men's room...

The copies of the passports arrived the next day. They were

black-and-white, Xeroxes of Xeroxes of color photographs. The pictures were unclear. Danielle did not detect that one of the boys had fair skin and blond hair.

Chapter 16
Riyadh, Saudi Arabia: Friday, August 23, 1996
◈

Yousef Zubeida was planning his work, and education was work that he knew. Zubeida had formerly been the Director of Primary Education in Saudi Arabia.

He was a Pakistani who had gone to work in the Kingdom for the same reason many others from around the Arab world went there, the lure of big money. Zubeida also was motivated by the opportunity to work in the Saudi madrasses. It was an understood reality that the Saudi royal family had ceded the operation of these schools to the imams, in return for being supported politically. Since the overthrow of the Shah of Iran by the Ayatollah Khomenei, the Saud family was nervous that the religious movement might choose them as the next target. Although Saudi Arabia was not nearly as secular a state as Iran under the Shah, permitting the Americans to be based there during the gulf war was an affront to the Wahhabis. There was much unrest in the Kingdom and Zubeida wished to be in on the ground floor of any rebellion.

Zubeida lasted six years before the Vice Minister of Education, the Saudi prince for whom he worked, determined that he was insufficiently in favor of preserving the status quo in the Kingdom. In fact, Zubeida's madrasses were really teaching and promoting fundamentalist insurrection.

So here he was operating schools for bin Laden, and it was a natural progression for Zubieda for he was a Wahabist. This branch of the Muslim religion advocated the imposition of the same strictures that the Taliban adopted as national policy in Afghanistan; the strictures the West found so unacceptable.

Now, a new task he was honored to be given, Allah be praised: Bin Laden had charged Zubeida with setting up the education for these "American" students.

First, though, Yousef had to meet with the boys and their families. He was to convince them to attend his school, rather than the public schools in which they were enrolled.

As Zubeida still had his Saudi contacts and his reputation as an educator, he decided he would start his recruiting drive in his former home country, since there were two students from Saudi Arabia. Edmund Lazar, the 14-year old boy from the camp was one and the other was a 13 year old, living in Riyadh.

Edmund had been the name of the wife's father and, like the infidel wife that Rita was, had insisted on her half of the naming process. The boy had not yet been given an Arab first name and now, given the direction of bin Laden, would never receive one. Lazar was one of the few names that co-existed in both the English and Arab cultures.

Zubeida had a sister living in Riyadh, as well as having worked there himself for many years. He was happy for the excuse to visit the city. Unlike bin Laden, Yousef Zubeida had no fascination with the primitive life style of the Afghanistan camps.

He had thought a great deal about how to approach the parents of the boys and had come to no conclusions. In the end, he decided that each case would probably be different.

He would allow each conversation to take its course.

The Saudi boy was the first to be seen; he was named Muhammad Maulana. He lived with his remarried father, stepmother and sister in a working class part of Riyadh. As Zubeida approached the home, he developed positive feelings. It was poor and run down looking. Lower income, working level people were much more likely to be militant *Wahhabis,* than the middle class and the rich.

He used a former associate in the Ministry of Education to gain some advance knowledge about the boy and his perform-ance in school, which was described as average. The associate had also contacted the father and told him that a famous educator wished to see him, regarding an educational opportunity for his son. The implication was that this was a program approved by the Saudi government. The father was receptive.

Zubeida knocked at the door, referred to his former associate and was ushered into the small, bare living room. An old, black and white TV, blaring in a corner, was turned off on his entrance. When the stepmother and daughter had been sent out of the room, leaving the father, Zubeida began.

"Sir, I am here to offer you an exceptional opportunity. In recognition of your sacrificial return to Saudi Arabia, leaving your American wife and possessions in the United States, the government would like to send your boy to a special *madrass*. This will be at no cost to you. It is entirely due to your correct, but probably painful, decision to return to your native country and your native culture.

"I personally have never been to America, but I am aware that the western world has many appealing features. You probably earned more money and lived in a better house than you do here." Yousef, as he said this, surveyed the room. It was no doubt a truthful statement. "You were married to a woman, yes, an infidel, but still someone you had once loved. You were probably enjoying what I have heard described as 'the American dream.' But you gave it all up to return to this land of Muhammad, for whom you have named your only son. This was a courageous act and should be rewarded.

"As you know, I was once the Director of Elementary education here in the Kingdom. Now I have been commissioned to establish a special school, to reward the sons of men such as you who would not otherwise be able to provide the superior education their sons deserve. It will be a unique learning experience for Muhammad; one that will be both beneficial and enjoyable. The quality of enjoyment, alas, has sometimes been missing from some of the existing *madrasses*.

"The first school is to be located in Afghanistan. It will be in the remote mountains, away from the distractions of secular life in Riyadh. The school will provide all the clothing; books, excellent food and medical care for the period Muhammad is with us. We are presently thinking this will be for a seven year period, roughly one third of that of a traditional *madrass*. This is a new educational concept. Who better to offer it to than the sons of the nation's most loyal citizens?"

During his whole presentation, Zubeida did not pause long enough to give Maulana a chance to ask a question. As he painted an ever more glowing situation, with ever increasing benefits, he could sense Maulana being captured by his word pictures. However, just to insure that was the case, he paused and assumed a thoughtful demeanor. "Finally, my friend, the government recognizes that Muhammad's opportunity would not exist, without the courage and loyalty of his father. For this reason you will also be rewarded. You will receive a stipend of 1000 *Rials* a month during the time Muhammad is in school. This is a reward for your past actions and to reimburse you for any lost income your son might have earned while he is a member of your household."

It was the clinching argument. Maulana said he considered it a great honor to have his Muhammad selected for this school and agreed to participate.

Yousef went on to explain that this was something that should not be discussed with anyone, it was a kind of experimental *Deobandi* school and needed to be kept secret. He said that someone would be by in several weeks to collect Muhammad and escort him to the school. He then gave the father the sum of 1000 *Rials* saying," take this money and spend it on your family and Muhammad during these next few weeks. Go out to restaurants. Enjoy his presence, as it will be at least seven years he will be gone." Zubeida did not say that it was likely that he would never see his son again.

Just as Yousef and Maulana were embracing in the Arab fashion, signifying a bargain being concluded, the door opened and Muhammad entered. He was even more American looking than his photographs had depicted.

He was a 13 old year, blond movie star.

Chapter 17
Isfahan, Iran: Monday, August 26, 1996
◈

Yousef Zubeida learned of the travails of Ali Sharqui's life from an al Qaeda contact in the force of the Ayatollah's religious police. Here was the story:

Ali Sharqui thought of himself as a victim. His own life was behind him, in ruins. Now, he lived only for his son, also named Ali. First, he thought he was a victim of the hated Shah, Muhammad Reza Pahlavi. As a student at the University of Iran, he had led an organization, one of many, dedicated to overthrowing the Peacock Throne. For this he had been apprehended by the SAVAK, the Shah's secret police, and thrown into prison. Here he was repeatedly beaten and tortured. The scars on his body had healed; the scars on his mind had not. When he was released from prison, he went to the American embassy and applied for a student visa to the United States. He did not really wish to live in America. He merely thought America the best place to continue his fight to unseat the Shah.

After he arrived in the United States he applied for, and eventually received, political asylum. He attended Georgetown University by day. By night, he worked with Free Iran, an organization based in Washington, DC, dedicated to ending the 300-year-old monarchy of the Pahlavi family.

In the offices of Free Iran, Ali met a beautiful blond girl named Salee Amina. Salee was a convert to Islam. She had been raised a Baptist in the American south and had never been exposed to other religions, nor to large cities or life in general. She was a "searcher" by nature and an activist by avocation. They became smitten with each other. Quite understandably, Salee was unlike any girl Ali had ever met. He told friends that, if he closed his eyes, he could still visualize their first meeting: she was dressed in a traditional flowing, white, caftan. She was tall and full breasted, things he had come to appreciate since living in the States. With her long blond hair, blue eyes and fair skin, she was easily the most beautiful girl he had ever met. She was also aggressively friendly. He was unprepared for this quality. Girls in Iran did not approach men. Within a few months she had moved into his small apartment and they were enjoying a full sexual relationship. In this lovemaking, Salee was also the aggressor. Ali could not help himself. He fell madly in love. This was something for which he was totally unprepared. Ali had expected to someday return to Iran and have his marriage arranged. In such marriages, the couples sometimes grew to love one another. Love was not a consideration in getting married.

In 1979 the Shah was dethroned and forced to flee the country. The mullahs took over Iran. Free Iran, its mission accomplished, was disbanded. However, many of its members became involved in organizations supporting Ayatollah Khomanei. Both Salee and Ali joined one of these groups and became even more religious and more nationalistic. They did this quietly at first, but with the passage of time, grew ever more strident as the Americans became more antagonistic toward Iran and Islam.

In 1984 they were overjoyed to add a son to their family. He was a beautiful baby boy who resembled his mother in form and color. They named him Ali Khomanei, in honor of the Ayatollah. One day, when the child was a little over two years old, Salee, clad in a abaya and hijab, took him out in his stroller, near their home in Fairfax, Va. They looked like a typical Arab mother and child, as the hijab, covered her blond hair.

They were attacked by a group of American school boys who started pushing them and calling them names, telling them to go home where they belonged. This was too much for Salee, who reacted with her American upbringing. To the shock and amazement of the boys, she told them to f--k off. When one boy tried to grab her, she kneed him in the groin. The other boys hit and shoved at her. When she fell, she struck her head on the curb. That was where she was when the police arrived. They found a screaming child in a stroller with an unconscious mother in the gutter. She was rushed to Fairfax Hospital, but she never revived from her coma. She died three days later from a massive cerebral hemorrhage.

The Metro Section of The Washington Post ran a story about gang violence in Fairfax. A local TV station, Channel 7, interviewed the neighbors and learned that the Sharquis seemed nice, but kept to themselves. The police were sympathetic. The Unitarian church held a candlelight vigil. The Beth El synagogue held a solidarity service. The Ahmadiyya mosque held a collection. The killers were never found.

Ali, again a victim, filled with hatred for America, took his son and returned to Iran..

By the time the end of the file was reached, Zubeida was certain that Ali's son would easily be obtained for his *madrass.* Zubeida even believed he could safely tell Sharqui a portion of the story about the *madrass,* without jeopardizing the secrecy of the overall mission.

Yousef flew from Riyadh to Teheran, where he changed planes for Isfahan. He was a man to whom flying had come late in life. As a consequence, he never felt really comfortable in aircraft. Today was no exception. The heat, reflecting from the desert floor rose in shimmering waves, causing the aircraft to go up and down in an alarming fashion. When he landed, Zubeida was dripping with perspiration from the tension. The inside of the aircraft was certainly cooler than the hut in Afghanistan in which he had lived for the past year...but still, he was drenched.

He took a cab to the Safir hotel, the best in Isfahan, and checked in. Zubeida, applying the universal logic of men on expense accounts, saw no reason to deny himself; indeed, quite the opposite. He was willing to sacrifice himself to live in the desert. He deserved to treat himself when the opportunity afforded.

He called Ali Sharqui and introduced himself as someone involved in the *Islamic Coalition Association*, a loose knit organization of many Islamic revolutionary groups. Could Ali join him for dinner the next night, the 26th? Ali, as expected said "Yes."

Later, when Zubeida retired to his bed, he felt as though it was going up and down. He had to remind himself that he was on the ground and not in the air. After an hour or two, he fell asleep.

The following day Zubeida slept late, then had a long breakfast and strolled around Isfahan. He had not visited this famed Persian city before and thoroughly enjoyed his walk. He was seemingly purposeless, but in fact, visited the city's leading carpet merchants. Like many educated men in the Middle East, he was something of a rug collector and considered himself knowledgeable, if not an expert, on the subject. He ranked Isfahan carpets only behind Kerman in their beauty. He made no purchases, but was pleased to have conversations with the merchants. They realized that he was no ordinary customer and also enjoyed discussing the fine points of particular carpets.

After his walk, Zubeida made arrangements to eat in the hotel. He did not want to go to a restaurant in which he had not eaten and didn't know the seating plan. He prearranged with the maitre d' hotel to be seated at the most private table. Then he went back to his room. He showered, a luxury, put on his Yemani-cut *Dishadasha.* Then he went down to the restaurant and waited.

When Ali Sharqui arrived, Zubeida was seated at the table, looking very much like an oil-rich sheik. He rose and introduced himself. "I am Yousef Zubeida. I am very honored to meet you. I sincerely appreciate your agreeing to meet with me on such short notice. Please join me." He motioned for Sharqui to be seated.

"Until several years ago, I was the Director of Elementary Education in Saudi Arabia. Due to a policy disagreement with Prince Abdullah, I have left my position and am now associated with an Islamic fundamentalist organization. I shall not name it at this time, but you are doubtless familiar with it. I know you approve of its goals."

"I have been asked to establish a very special *madrass* in Afghanistan. Here we will educate a number of young men in Islamic studies. They will also be trained in certain other fields and in military arts. When their education is completed, these young men will become the leaders of a new revolutionary Islamic movement. The goal of this movement will be to unify the Islamic countries in a way that they have never been unified before. It will also be a goal to drive all infidels from Islamic lands. Your son has been recommended to us as a possible candidate for this *madrass*."

As he described the ambitions of the movement, Zubeida closely observed Sharqui to determine his reaction. He could see that Sharqui was impressed and interested.

Zubeida went on. "We are well informed about your past services to Islam and to your country. We know about the circumstances that led to your going to America and to your return. I must tell you, that if you were younger, I would be talking to you about this opportunity. However, we are training the next generation of leaders. You and I are of the past. Our organization understands that you have inculcated your son with the same spirit that motivated you through the many long difficult years you endured. This will be your chance to insure that your life's work will be continued."

Sharqui interjected: "Yes, brother Yousef, I have devoted my life to our cause. I have also tried to teach my son of the true meaning of the *Qu'ran* and of the need to rid our lands of all non-believers. He seems to have inherited my fire and my beliefs. Already he has spoken about spending his life, as I do, working for Allah. However, his personality is not such to permit him to become a cleric. He is too much like his father, an activist."

Zubeida nodded appreciatively. "We have heard this. We do not need more clerics. The *mullahs* are valuable people. Islam requires them. But Islam also requires men of action. That is why we are interested in your son.

"The *madrass* I intend to create will not ignore the study of the *Qu'ran.* I will insure that our graduates are well grounded in Islamic studies. But we believe that mistakes have been made over the past centuries by Islam's failure to understand the West. This prevented the Islamic countries from defeating the invaders when they started coming to our lands. Now, to remove them, we must be their equals. This can only be accomplished by understanding them. We must know how they think. You lived in America. Can you truthfully say that there is nothing to be learned from that culture? In the past we have concentrated on the things that we believed to be impure, against the teachings of Muhammad. In so doing we have ignored what could benefit and add to our greatness. The *madrass* that your son will attend will correct the previous errors. We will also study the West."

Zubeida knew that he was touching on heresy. To some fundamentalists, it was unthinkable to even suggest that there was anything of value, not found in the *Qu'ran.* He was pleased to see nothing in Sharqui's reaction to suggest that he was one of those. Zubeida knew that had guessed right in taking the discussion in this direction.

"The *madrass* we are planning will be in a remote area of Afghanistan. There the students will be free of worldly activities competing for their attention. In compensation for this separation, they will receive the best of food, clothing and medical care. All of this will be paid for by our organization, a very rich one. They will be in a highly intensive learning environment, until we believe they are ready to leave and assume leadership positions. We estimate this to be approximately seven years. During this period you will have no contact with your son. You have my word as a brother in Islam that he will be well cared for and will emerge from the experience, a man of whom you will be proud."

At the mention of seven years separation, Yousef observed a slight grimace in Sharqui's countenance. Clearly, Ali was his fathers' life. He decided to take the disclosure another step further.

"The reason for the lack of contact is one of secrecy. There are only a handful of people in the world who know of this *madrass*. It must be kept a secret of the highest level. Our enemies, both within and without the Muslim world, must not learn of it. We assume that if it is discovered, and its purpose became known, it would be subject to destruction. This we cannot allow to happen. I regret I cannot tell you more than this, but I have taken a blood oath. My own tongue would be cut, if it were found out that I had told you more."

Zubeida correctly fathomed his man. The very thought of his son's participation in a secret organization, excited this father.

Sharqui became eager and proud. He immediately agreed that Ali would go to Afghanistan. He produced a wallet and opened it to show off a photograph of Ali. He passed this to Zubeida, who was horrified. The photograph showed a boy with coal black hair. Was there a mistake? Had he just offered the *Madrass* to a boy who looked like every other ordinary Arab boy in the country? He could feel his pulse raising and his face flushing. He scarcely heard Sharqui talking about the merits of his boy. He had to do something, but what?

"Yes, he is only 13 and 163 centimeters tall. He takes after his mother, who was also tall. Unfortunately, he takes after her in other ways too. She was blond and so is he. I have kept his hair dyed since we returned to Iran. He needs to look like an Arab. Not an American", said Sharqui.

Zubeida relaxed. Ishfahan was a rare delight after all.

Chapter 18
Fort Meade, Maryland: Monday, August 26, 1996
❖

Danielle Lamaze-Smith waited impatiently in the corridor for Sanford Parcell to finish his telephone conversation. Because of the nature of their work, it was standard procedure to leave the office when a superior received a telephone call. Even though everyone had security clearances, NSA, like all intelligence agencies, operated on a "need-to-know" system. This procedure insured that the security protocol was kept. It also saved the superior the embarrassment of having to ask his visitor to leave the room.

As she waited after her telephone had rung, Danielle read for the umpteenth time the intercepts she had been poised to discuss with Parcell:

NATIONAL SECURITY AGENCY
CONTROL # 96-8-187593-Q
23 AUGUST 96
SENDING # 66-341-1700
RECEIVING # 50-269-4017
ACTION WORDS: NONE
MOHAMMED:
    I AM PLEASED TO REPORT THAT MY MISSION
TO SAUDI ARABIA WAS SUCCESSFUL. THE BOY WILL
JOIN US. HE IS EXACTLY WHAT WE REQUIRE.
I LEAVE THIS AFTERNOON FOR IRAN.
ZUBEIDA

And another, two days later:

NATIONAL SECURITY AGENCY
CONTROL # 96-8-191476-Q
25 AUGUST 96
SENDING # 98-474-1313
RECEIVING # 50-269-4017
ACTION WORDS: NONE

MOHAMMED:
    THE YOUNG MAN HERE IS THE BEST WE COULD
HOPE FOR. HE IS SUPERIOR IN EVERY WAY. I ONLY
HOPE THE ALGERIAN WILL PROVE AS GOOD AS
THE FIRST TWO.
ZUBEIDA

    There was also a copy of a cable from Thomas Dettor,
the CIA Chief of Station in Algiers:

31 JULY 96
TO: CIA DEP. ASST. DIR. HEIDEMANN
FR: TOM DETTOR, COSCIA, ALGIERS

    MET WITH DEPUTY PRIME MINISTER FOR
POPULATION STATISTICS, ABU FAROUK. I ASKED IF
HE COULD PROVIDE A LIST OF BOYS WITH AMERI-
CAN PASSPORTS CURRENTLY IN ALGERIA. WAS
INFORMED, FOR TECHNICAL REASONS, THIS WAS
IMPOSSIBLE. FAROUK CONFIDED THAT AN UN-
KNOWN JOURNALIST REQUESTED THE SAME
INFORMATION ABOUT AMERICAN BOYS EARLIER IN
THE WEEK. I MADE UP AN EXPLANATION STORY
THAT I THINK HE BELIEVED.
    WHAT IS HAPPENING?
    MET WITH MY FIS AGENT IN SIDI BEL ABBES,
LOCATION OF ABASSI TOUATI. I WAS TOLD THAT
TOUATI IS A VERY BAD GUY. HE RECENTLY RE-

TURNED FROM AFGHANISTAN WHERE HE AT-
TENDED A BIN LADEN TRAINING CAMP FOR TER-
RORISTS. HE MAY RETURN AND JOIN JIHAD AS A
MEMBER OF AL QAEDA IF FIS IS BANNED IN ALGE-
RIA. HAVE GOT ALGERIAN FEDERAL POLICE
CONTACT GETTING ME A COPY OF TOUATI'S
DOSSIER. THIS WILL TAKE A COUPLE OF DAYS.

IS THERE A POSSIBILITY THAT LIST OF AMERI-
CAN BOYS IS RELATED TO TOUATI? ARE THE LIVES
OF THE AMERICANS IN DANGER? SHALL I PUT
TOUATI UNDER SURVEILLANCE OR HAVE HIM
PICKED UP BY THE FEDERALS?

PLEASE ADVISE SOONEST IF LIVES ARE AT
RISK. I KNOW THAT IT IS DIFFICULT TO FORM A
COMMITTEE OF DI'S AND GET A PROMPT DECISION,
BUT IT TAKES TIME TO EXECUTE ANYTHING IN
ALGERIA. IT IS SLOWER THAN WASHINGTON BY A
FACTOR OF FIVE.
DETTOR

Danielle had heard about Dettor. He was at the end of his career and sardonic as hell. He didn't care who he insulted. She was musing about this luxury when she heard Parcell call her back into his office.

"Danielle, what have we got today? Aha, two intercepts and a cable from Dettor. Good." Parcell was never more enthusiastic then when he had fresh information to digest or when he added a bird to his "positively identified" list.

She handed three pages over the desk and sat silently as he read and reread them. When he had finished, he had a worried look on his face.

"Several things bother me about this business, the principal of which is that their message style is changing. Over the past several years we have been intercepting messages of encyclope-dic length and detail. In recent months, their transmissions have been getting shorter and increasingly devoid of quantifiable information. This suggests they suspect we have the capability to monitor their telephone calls. I am sure they would never believe that we are listening to every thing they say, but clearly their conversations are becoming more circumspect. These two transmissions are the shortest ever. Do we know who Mr. Zubeida is?" As he asked the question, Parcell slid the papers back across his desk to Danielle.

"Yes sir, we think we do. When we received the first message signed Zubeida, I had no idea who he was, for the name is fairly common in the Middle East. But Zubeida made a mistake. He told us he was going to Iran in the afternoon. Our technical support people hacked into the Arabian Airlines computer and got into their passenger manifest data base. We found two Zubeidas going to Iran on that day's afternoon flights. We tracked them down through their home addresses. One was a jewelry salesman. The other was Yousef Zubeida, the former Director of Elementary Education for the Kingdom. This gentleman was fired last year for operating *madrasses*, too revolutionary for the Prince Abdullah's taste. These people are starting to upset the royal family. They see the *imams* growing too powerful. We presume it is *that* Mr. Zubeida rather than the jewelry salesman."

"I should think you're right. Certainly, bin Laden does not wear jewelry! But that brings me back to the other concern. What are these people up to? I think the Abassi Touati connection is extraordinary. I wonder what it means? And as for our man in Algiers, Dettor, his cables aren't very polite, are they?"

Parcell's mind was in gear now. He reached for the pipe and jammed it in his mouth. Danielle could just visualize the wheels turning, as he tried to assemble all the various facts and bits of information into some kind of logical order. He was interesting to watch.

Parcell continued thinking out loud, throwing out thoughts at random. "Pursuing the anomaly, as we decided to do last week with Touati, still looks like it was a good choice. We uncovered the bin Laden connection. Still, that doesn't explain the request to Touati for boys from Algeria. If they were related events, why didn't they just talk to him when he was in Afgahnistan? No, that doesn't connect. The Iran thing...Iran is the home ballpark for Hezballah...does that figure in with Zubeida's visit? And the boys, what is so special about these two boys that Zubeida remarks he hopes the Algerian is as good?"

Parcell, reminded of unfinished business, stopped abruptly and came back to earth.

"Danielle, have you heard from State?"

"Yes. I talked to Peterson and found out that what we want, the names of boys who have traveled to the ME in the past five years can't be obtained. I don't mean can't be obtained in the bureaucratic sense. I mean technically impossible." Having spent several years at the State Department, Danielle was well aware of its ponderous bureaucracy. She knew of several offices there whose people were all so risk averse that decisions were available only by a committee and then, not without consensus.

"I remembered that the intercept mentioned protests by mothers of kidnapped children and called the office of the Legal Advisor. It took awhile, but I finally got the guy who was handling the claims. He sent me copies of about a dozen passports of boys who had been kidnapped by their fathers back to the Middle East." Danielle did not relate how her sex appeal over the phone had undoubtedly helped in her efforts. "I looked at all of the passports and could find no common thread. They were just a bunch of young Saudi, Kuwaiti and Lebanese boys."

Parcell was disappointed. His facial expression broadcast his feelings. He would be a poor poker player, thought Danielle.

"Too bad. I was hoping the list of names from the passport bureau would have brought some daylight to this Stygian darkness."

Parcell was one of the few Americans Danielle encountered regularly with a classical education. She was sure that he knew the mythological origins of the word "Stygian." She enjoyed listening to him and watching his brain at work.

"Well, Danielle, we just don't seem to have enough solid information to even create a hypothesis. We will just have to keep alert and accumulate additional facts. And, of course, we must pray that our failure to comprehend what is taking place does not cause us injury."

On her way back to her cubicle Danielle reminded herself: "That's what this game is really all about, getting enough information to be able to predict injury, before it occurs."

Chapter 19
Sidi bel Abbes, Algeria: Tuesday, August 27, 1996
◈

Yousef Zubeida was enroute again, this time to Sidi bel Abbes. It was another wretched flying experience and he was pleased this was his last trip. In his briefcase was a single page summary of the person he was going to meet, prepared by a man named Abassi Touati. Zubeida did not know Touati. He did not like the sound of his report. It was not favorable.

Touati described Belhadj as a professional businessman. Some years earlier, he had returned to Algeria from the United States for a business opportunity, not for political reasons or religious reasons. Especially not for any reason connected with radical Islamic thought or action. In Zubeida's calculations, this was deducted from his standing; in fact, he did not attend any mosque or show any signs of being a good Muslim...

This was not a man who would be enticed to send his son to the *madrass* for financial gain. Nor would the free, high quality, Islamic education have any great appeal to him. There had to be a way to attract Anwar to the school. Zubeida would simply have to find it. *Inshallah*, God willing, Zubeida would find a way.

Yousef had reserved a room at the only premier hotel in town. In this case he justified staying there as being important to impress Belhadj that he was a man of substance. Zubeida had no intermediary to arrange an introduction with Belhadj. He would simply have to contact him directly. As the plane landed, an idea began to work its way into his mind.

At the registration desk he let it be known that he was visiting the La Terre company, on business. He was gratified to learn from the clerk that La Terre was a good customer; they frequently housed their clients and customers. When Zubeida casually asked about a man named Belhadj, he was informed that, as a matter of fact, Mr. Belhadj usually ate his Wednesday night dinner in the hotel dining room. Yousef remarked to the clerk that he would appreciate being introduced to Belhadj the next night, if he came in to dine. The clerk told him to be at the desk at 7:00 and it would be his pleasure to make the introduction. Zubeida nodded appreciatively. He then slipped the clerk two, 1,000 *Dinar* notes, to insure this would happen. In Algeria, as in all Arab lands, *baksheesh* was an accepted way of doing business. After his delicious dinner that evening in the hotel dining room, Yousef thanked *Allah* for his great good fortune: Belhadj came on Wednesdays, there was no need to wait long.

Zubeida spent the next day walking around town, talking to people. By the next afternoon, he had accumulated quite a bit of information about Ipreham Belhadj, the La Terre Corporation, and Ipreman's career there, including the fact that the LaTerre executive Charles Lamaze was Belhadj's mentor and friend.

At 6:45 that evening Zubeida was casually waiting in the lobby when a youngish man dressed in a white linen suit and carrying a briefcase, walked into the lobby. Zubeida, in his wanderings earlier in the day, had found out that the officers of La Terre usually wore western attire, so Zubeida wore an Armani black silk suit, rather than the robes he regularly dressed in.

The desk clerk came out from behind his enclosure as soon as he saw Belhadj enter the lobby. He started to walk to Belhadj, but Zubeida being closer, beat him to the mark. "Excuse me please, Mr. Belhadj. My name is Yousef Zubeida. I have traveled a long way to see you. Unless you are expecting someone else, I would consider it an honor if you would join me for dinner. I have an interesting proposition I would like to discuss with you."

Belhadj looked at Zubeida and observed a distinguished looking Arab gentleman man in an expensive Italian suit. He saw no reason to decline. Indeed, as would be the case with most people, his curiosity was piqued. He thrust out his hand. "How do you do, Mr. Zubeida. I would be pleased to join you."

Yousef led the way into the dining room to a previously selected table, at which he would have dined alone, had Belhadj had company.

As alcohol is not an element in an Arab dinner, the foregathering is cut short. The waiter takes the dinner order and the time between ordering and the service is the time for introductory conversation. So it was with Zubeida and Belhadj.

Yousef began: "Mr. Belhadj, I am from Saudi Arabia where I was, until recently, the Director of Elementary Education. I left that position to go to Afghanistan on a special educational mission for an organization that you are familiar with, but which shall go unnamed at the present time."

"Notwithstanding what you may be hearing and reading about the Taliban, it is far from a monolithic organization. There are some progressive members who disagree with the more conservative *mullahs*. These men are concerned for the future of Afghanistan and wish to see some western practices incorporated in the country, particularly in business and education. I have been engaged to create a new kind of experimental *madrass* that would not be so focused upon Islamic studies. Instead, it would include many of the courses, particularly in mathematics and science, which are taught in European schools. This I have agreed to do. It is my opinion that the focus on religion, to the exclusion of all else, is not a desirable thing."

Zubeida was a close observer of people. He could see that he had the full attention of Belhadj. "This same group of people is anxious to rebuild Afghanistan from all of the damages of the war with the Soviet Union all in a contemporary style. They wish to incorporate modern engineering practices and materials. It is not their wish to create a secular country, but to create a more pure Islamic nation than Saudi Arabia, but with a 20th century infrastructure. To accomplish this will require people trained in western ways, but with roots firmly planted in the Middle East. It will require people such as yourself."

"We are aware of your engineering education in America and your work experience in that country. We are also aware that, when given the opportunity, you returned to the country and culture of your birth. As you undoubtedly know, so many of our young people go abroad to study and never return. You could have done this but you did not. You are exactly the type of man we seek for a senior management position in our effort."

At this point Zubeida paused to take a sip of the lemon water from the small glass that stood in front of him. It was also a chance to collect his thoughts and to allow Belhadj an opportunity to respond. He was not disappointed.

"Mr. Zubeida" began Belhadj, "I am quite flattered, as any young man would be, with your interest, but I am afraid that you have overestimated my abilities. I am not nearly so experienced as you suggest. It is true I have a civil engineering degree from an American university, but I have none of the experience required to manage a design and rebuilding effort of the scale of which you seem to describe. I think what you need is a civil engineering consulting company with a strong Arab base. There are a number of such companies here in Algeria. I would be happy to do some research and prepare a list of them for you, if you wish. What you seek is best contracted out to a company with a record of experience and success. I would not recommend that you create your own staff."

Zubeida responded: "I agree with you. It would certainly be easier and better to simply engage a large engineering firm. But that would require entering into a contract and a vote by the governing council. This cannot be done. We can, however, hire a number of individuals in other departments of the government and assign them to the tasks we have in mind. That is what we would propose to do with you. Funding is not a problem. We should be able to double the salary you earn with LaTerre."

Belhadj was shaking his head from side to side. "I am sorry Mr. Zubeida, but I cannot accept your generous offer for a number of reasons. One, I am very happy at LaTerre. They have treated me quite well. Two, I have been told that when my superior, Mr. Lamaze retires, I will be considered for his position. If I am selected, I will be the youngest president of an operating company in the whole LaTerre organization. And lastly,

Algeria is my home. I have no desire to live in Afghanistan."

Yousef smiled at the litany of negative answers. "Mr. Belhadj, I am sorry too. We have been together just a short time, but I can see why you were recommended to us. You are exactly the kind of man we need. However, it is clear to me that you cannot be enticed to join our organization. Given your explanations, I am not sure that if I were you, I wouldn't do the same thing. Now, we will speak no more of the matter. Let us enjoy our dinners and talk of other things."

The two men sat for another hour and had a spirited conversation that proved very interesting to Belhadj. Not too many strangers came to Sidi bel Abbes. Those who did usually talked about construction and cement. The evening ended cordially with each shaking hands and then embracing the other.

When Zubeida returned to his room, he took a scrap of paper from his suitcase and dialed the telephone number written on it. He had a short conversation with the party on the other end of the line. As he hung up, he rolled his head. It would have been so much easier if Belhadj had agreed to the proposition.

The next morning an FIS random bombing occurred in a busy market place in downtown Sidi bel Abbes. Six people were killed and a dozen more injured. One of the dead was a young engineer with the La Terre company named Ipreham Belhadj.

Yousef Zubeida had found a way to deal with him.

Chapter 20
Sidi bel Abbes, Algeria: Thursday, August 29, 1996
◈

Charles Lamaze had come home from the office for luncheon on his patio with his wife. The climate in Sidi bel Abbes took some getting used to, but large old palm trees comfortably shaded them. Fortunately, a breeze was blowing from the Mediterranean Sea, some 75 miles to the North. It was thus warmed by only a short expanse of desert. When the wind came from the endless reaches of the Sahara to their south, they fled inside their air conditioned home. During such hot weather, Lamaze had found himself marveling at the Legionnaires who had lived in the city before air conditioning was invented.

They had just finished their salads when their maid came on the patio with an announcement that the police were at the door, asking for Mr. Lamaze. He excused himself from his wife, arose and followed the servant from the porch to the front door.

"*Monsieur* Lamaze"? Two officers in their tropical blue uniforms with old-fashioned high boots and black polished gun belts, greeted him with worried looks on their faces. He nodded affirmatively. "I am Captain Leon and this is my associate Sergeant, Sahwari. We are here to bring you some very bad news. One of your senior employees, Ipreham Belhadj, was killed this morning in what appears to be another bombing by the FIS. We are very sorry to bring you this news but we have learned that Belhadj worked directly for you. We also know that he has a young boy, but no wife. We thought that you might want to join us in letting the young man know that his father is dead. If you would care to come with us, we will return you here to your home. Or, if you wish, you can drive your own car and we will follow you. Again, we are sorry to bring you this most unpleasant news and to ask your assistance in informing his son."

Lamaze was shocked. The FIS random bombings were still a fact of life, but their number had greatly decreased in the past several years, as the government's security forces had made great inroads in arresting the leadership. The danger was just something you lived with. He nodded numbly, and fought back the rush of emotions that engulfed him. "I'll drive. His home is just a short distance away. Let me get my wife."

Lamaze left the officers at the door, too distraught to have remembered his manners and invite them in, and went to the patio. "Marie, something terrible has happened. Ipreham has been killed in a bombing and we must go and tell Anwar. I think we should bring him back here to be with us. The police are waiting. Let us go." He spoke in the subdued tone that one uses when speaking of death, but with the incomplete thoughts that come with jangled nerves.

The couple left the patio together, his arm around her shoulder, as they went to the front of the house and their Citroen. Marie was fighting back tears. Ipreham was a favorite of both of them. They, of course, knew Anwar less well, but he seemed like a good boy.

They found Anwar in his home, in the living room, watching an old American movie on the television accompanied by a servant. Marie said "Anwar, I must talk to you. Let's go into your bedroom so we can have privacy."

Once in the boy's room, she got down on one knee and reached out her arms to the boy. "Anwar, something terrible has happened to your father." And then with tears streaming down her face, "he was killed this morning in an accident." There was silence for a moment while a disbelieving child digested the news, followed by a scream and a rush to the outstretched arms.

Soon the both of them, Marie and Anwar, were a single sobbing mass.

In the living room, Charles had told the stunned servant about the bomb and his employer's fate. Then Charles heard the anguished screams from Anwar's room, and silently thanked God that he had brought Marie. *She knew how to deal with children far better than he.* When their Danielle and Monique were small, it was always Marie who was in charge; she meted out the praise, the punishment, or the sympathy, as the case required, with much greater skill than he would have shown. With Danielle, this changed when she became an adult, and now, Charles thought to himself, he was the one who enjoyed the closer relationship.

After a time, when the tears subsided, the police asked if they should take the child to a government agency. Both Marie and Charles answered them simultaneously. "No! We will look after Anwar." The police officers mumbled something about being in touch in the next day or two and bowed their way out. As they did so, they thanked Lamaze profusely. They too were silently thankful for Marie's intervention. Neither of them had the stomach to tell a child that his only parent had just been killed.

Marie and Anwar went to his bedroom and gathered up a suitcase full of clothing and toilet articles and then returned to the car. After sending the servant home with a promise of compensation, Lamaze found a key to the front door, which he locked upon their leaving. The drive home was silent. When they arrived at their home Charles carried the suitcase upstairs. Anwar would stay in Danielle's old room.

While Charles was coming back down the stairs to join Marie and Anwar on the patio, the telephone rang. The maid started for it. Charles waved her off. He answered it with just his name, "Charles Lamaze." He thus neatly avoided choosing the wrong language. He was prepared to converse in French, English or Arabic, as the caller willed. He did not have the language gifts of his daughter, but he spoke the three primary local languages with equal skill. The voice at the other end of the line chose Arabic, a very cultured Arabic.

"Mister Lamaze, my name is Yousef Zubeida. I am an old friend of Ipreham's. I heard on the television that he had been killed this morning in a terrorist attack. I know he was a close friend of yours too. I wanted to offer my condolences and let you know that I share your grief. I also wanted you to know that I have taken the steps to arrange his burial prayers tomorrow. As

Ipreham was technically dead before noon, he should be buried today. However, I have received permission to have him buried tomorrow. I hope you don't mind this, but I presume you are Catholic and may not be familiar with how we Muslims do such things."

"How do you do, Mr. Zubeida. I am grateful for your expression of sympathy. I know your religion requires burial within a day of death. However, even though I have lived in Algeria most of my adult life, and have had many Muslim friends, I have never been involved in arranging a funeral. I sincerely appreciate your action. Ipreham was a good friend as well as an employee. Because of the difference in our ages, we developed almost a father-son relationship. I am still in a state of shock."

"I am happy to be of service, Mr. Lamaze. I have also arranged for the washing and wrapping of his body. I will pay for everything. It is the least I can do for my dear friend of many years. I am just glad that I was able to see him before he died. We had a long and lovely dinner together last night. I will call you later today, regarding the timing tomorrow, so that you can bring Anwar to the burial site. The police told me he is staying with you. Again, Mr Lamaze, please know that I am available to do whatever I can to assist you. I can be reached at telephone number 71-439-7797. We will talk again later today."

The two men said their goodbyes.

Though Charles Lamaze had never heard Ipreham speak of Zubeida, in his grief, he did not dwell on it. He was just happy Zubeida was so helpfully involved.

Chapter 21
Sidi bel Abbes, Algeria: Saturday, August 31, 1996
◈

Tom Dettor always opened his own mail. It was a practice he had started when he was just a young field officer in India. An informant, wishing to establish a relationship, had written to him on an invoice from his dining club. This prompted much humor about having to employ a "taster" etc., by his colleagues, but it made a lasting impression. Tom never allowed his secretary to touch his mail, even the advertisements.

As he rifled through the stack on his desk, it was mostly the customary social invitations and requests for information that are the normal fare of a consular official. Toward the bottom of the stack, Dettor spotted an envelope in familiar handwriting, with no return address. He slit open the envelope and unfolded a very ordinary piece of stationary. There was no signature.

> *"The awful Sidi bel Abbes bombing was a terrible surprise, for I was alone in car driving to work, and then to the home of our mutual dear and good friend. At the last minute I decided to turn the car left, by the good grace of Allah. Afghanistan is the next country I visit. I hope to be there soon."*

At first reading it appeared to be the work of an English deficient writer, sending off a quick note to a friend. But Tom knew it was a message. He had taught Nadeem in Sidi bel Abbes to write in a rudimentary code in which every sixth word was the real message. This system would not have fooled a professional for very long, but it was a modest protection in the event an untrained person intercepted the letter.

Tom took a pencil and underlined each sixth word:

"The awful Sidi bel Abbes <u>bombing</u> was a terrible surprise, I <u>was</u> alone in car driving to <u>work</u>, and then to the home <u>of</u> our mutual dear and good <u>friend</u>. At the last minute I <u>decided</u> to turn the car left, <u>by</u> the good grace of Allah. <u>Afghanistan</u> is the next country I <u>visit</u>. I hope to be there <u>soon</u>."

"Aha, thought Tom. 'Bombing was work of friend. Decided by Afghanistan. Visit soon.'"

He ran the letter through the shredder and leaned back in his swivel chair. He would go to Sidi bel Abbes the next day. Today he had to compose a cable to Heidemann and brief the Ambassador. This Touati business was heating up.

The next morning Dettor started out for Sidi bel Abbes. It was not a happy experience. The problem was, the damned city was just too far for a pleasurable drive and just too close to warrant borrowing the Ambassador's aircraft. At 250 miles, it was on the edge. Dettor was irritated. Starting late, he arrived right at lunchtime and went directly to the established restaurant. Thankfully, the waiter was there, but gave no indication of whether or not Dettor should eat lunch. After an hour of nursing two beers to their fullest, the waiter appeared, bringing him the bill. He also brought the message to meet Nadeem in the city's main Catholic church, a new rendezvous spot. Although Dettor wasn't religious, it seemed somehow alien to conduct business in a holy place, but the meeting spot was always to be selected by the asset. The cathedral was a short walk from the restaurant and Dettor guessed that his man lived nearby and was seeking convenience as well as privacy.

Dettor walked into the high ceilinged narthex and waited for his eyes to adjust to the darkness. The church was large, quiet, cool, dim and underpopulated. Were it not for the religious aspects, it had all of the desirable characteristics for a clandestine meeting place. He saw Nadeem seated in the middle of a broad expanse of empty chairs about halfway to the transept. He genuflected towards the altar and walked slowly down the aisle.

When he reached the row of seats in front of the contact, he turned in. He stopped one seat to the left side of his man. In this way Nadeem could kneel and his face would be close to Tom's right ear. Dettor assumed that it was more important that he listen rather than ask questions.

The asset began immediately. "Thank you for coming. Last Friday night at about nine o'clock, I received a telephone call from Abassi Touati. He asked me to help him assassinate a man named Ipreham Belhadj. He wanted me to drive a stolen car he had acquired, so he could be the bomb thrower. We would wait outside of Belhadj's house and follow him. At the right time, when he was stopped for a light, or I could jam him into the curb, Touati would heave the bomb and I would race off. The intent was to make it look like a random act, instead of a targeted killing. I told Touati that I was leaving early in the morning to visit my brother in Oran and that I could not assist him. I don't know if he got anyone else, or if he did it himself. He told me he was acting on the orders of someone named Zubeida, an important member of *al Qaeda* in Afghanistan."

Nadeem had begun to tremble as he spoke, and there was a pause before he continued in a grave voice: "If you report this to the Federals, they must eliminate Touati. If they do not, he will know that I was the source of the information and order me killed. Death to those who are traitors to the FIS is not pleasant. The federals cannot just pick him up for questioning. They must eliminate him without giving him a chance to talk to anyone and tell them it was me. You are holding my life in your hands...I trust you.

"I am sorry I couldn't get to you before this happened, but there was no way. I am tired of the killings, the loss of innocent life. That is why I am helping you. Not for the money. Now go, before someone sees us together. Remember, I trust you."

Tom bowed his head in prayer for 30 seconds. Then he got up and left, without ever looking back at Nadeem. He knew what he was going to do.

Chapter 22
Algiers: Sunday, September 1, 1995
◈

Shari Massoud sat in a tea room reflecting upon his career. When he was appointed Chief of the Algerian National Police in 1991, he knew there was one thing he must do. His entire career in law enforcement would be judged on his success. More important, possibly the very future of Algeria was in his hands. He had to break up the terrorist organization, the Islamic Salvation Front, the FIS. Since the French left Algeria in 1962, the radical Muslims in this organization were attempting to destabilize the country by committing random acts of violence as well as targeted attacks against the leadership. They had to be stopped.

He knew he was the right man for the job. The son of a legionnaire, he had lived his life with and around violent men. As a youth he was a bully. He modified his behavior as an adult, but his angry, unpredictable, almost savage side was never far from the surface. He firmly believed in the principal that "the ends justify the means." This meant that he was willing to do anything to get the results he desired, including torture and killing.

Massoud had set up a secret office of seven like-minded individuals on the force and turned them into an anti-terrorism unit. This group did not operate out of police stations and did not wear uniforms. They did not drive police cars or carry police radios. They did not fill out reports or appear in court. The men were carried on the roster in various offices across the country, but they never appeared for duty at their assigned location. They operated out of a remote farmhouse in the desert outside of Algiers. They were Mossaud's private force. He was proud of their discipline.

Of course, he also knew there is an inherent danger in establishing a police force that is itself above the law. The Gestapo in Germany in the 30's and 40's demonstrated this well.

Massoud was aware of their history and was careful to not allow his force to get out of control or get distracted by other activities. He made their mandate anti-terrorism and kept them on a short leash. The results were remarkable. Almost immediately after they were formed, they began to make inroads into the FIS. Because they operated in secrecy, the FIS did not understand what was happening to them and could not conduct acts of retribution. From time to time an FIS man would simply disappear. He would never be seen or heard from again.

The anti-terrorist team's approach was simplistic. They operated with just two basic principles:(1) No terrorist acts by himself. He is always part of a group or cell; and (2) no man can endure so much pain that he will not name his associates. He might be willing to die a heroic death for them, but he will not suffer unbearable, unending pain.

Massoud had made a study of pain. He analyzed the various gruesome forms of torture practiced by such as the Marquis de Sade, Ivan the Terrible, the Gestapo, the Spanish Inquisition, the KGB and others famed for their cruelty. Shortly after he began his studies, he detected a common flaw in torture, as practiced by them all: most of their torture was performed trying to get the victim to confess to something. After enough pain, all but a very few men would confess to anything. There was also, generally, a common result. Most of those tortured died during the process.

Massoud had determined to use torture differently. His group would apply it only to those they were absolutely certain had committed terrorist acts. The prisoners would not have to confess their guilt. Both parties knew they were guilty. They would only have to name five other terrorists. Then they would be shot. They could prolong their life by naming more than five; the more named the longer they lived. Those named would then be arrested by the Algerian National Police and brought to justice through the established court system. Much of the time these terrorists gave out additional names to the National Police who were themselves not renowned for their gentility. If the tortured named innocent parties, the police investigations would soon find out they had lied. Additional pain would be the result.

Massoud had then consulted a doctor about what kinds of medicines should be administered during the torture to ensure survival and avoid passing out. He learned that in times of stress, the brain produces endorphins, a chemical that countered pain, degrading the sensitivity of the spinal receptors, in much the same fashion as morphine. There are countless stories of horribly wounded men in war, producing excessive endorphins and continuing fighting because they felt no pain. The doctor advised him that the drug "Narcan" was commonly used to counteract overdoses of morphine or to bring patients out of an anesthetic trance. Massoude introduced Narcan as an antidote to endorphins and eliminated the numbing qualities. Exquisite pain was the result. The doctor also suggested that a blood volume expander, such as Dextran, be administered intravenously to prevent the victim from going into shock.

The system had worked well. The first victim of the treatment was a Turk named Achmed Sulieman who had set off a bomb that killed 17 people. It also wounded and maimed 33 others including a five-year old girl who had both of her arms and one leg blown off. Miraculously, she survived and became a national public figure in Algeria, a symbol of heroism. Massoud ordered his men to subject Sulieman to an extremely painful death over 36 hours. He recorded Sulieman's screams and filmed his agonies. A movie was made with a detailed depiction of Sulieman's slow, terrifying death. This was shown to prospective candidates to frighten them and encourage them to believe that they had no alternative. There would be certain death. No becoming a martyr, no friends coming to their rescue; only the most terrible pain imaginable. If they cooperated, they would die a quick death and their families would receive a gift of 5,000 dinars from an unknown source. They would receive a proper Muslim burial in the desert, although their graves would not be marked.

Over four years, no terrorist had successfully resisted his organized approach for longer than ten days; most didn't go beyond two or three; only one had gone 10 before talking. One had died due to unpredictable heart failure, literally "scared to death". But the positive side was that hundreds of FIS and other Islamic extremists had been arrested as a result of only 27 terrorists being put through the process. When they were no longer needed, the men were disposed of humanely, by a "coupe de grace", a pistol shot to the head. Massoud was not a sadist nor did he employ sadists. They were merely efficient bureaucrats with a job to do...

Massoud had noted that most men were either cowardly or intelligent when faced with such a decision. Of the 47 men given the alternative, 39 decided they did not wish to test the system or themselves. They gave the unit valuable information, endured no suffering, and were shot within a few hours.

Massoud felt neither compunction nor remorse about his approach. In addition to saving his country, he was saving lives.

He was also avenging the pretty little five-year old girl with the missing arms and leg, named Lizzette. He visited with her nearly every day.

She was his only child.

Chapter 23
Algiers: Monday, September 2, 1996
◈

Abassi Touati awakened when the screaming started. It was a terrifying, animal like scream that did not sound human. But, Touati knew that it was human; someone in his death throes, in absolute, unmitigated, terrible pain.

At first Touati didn't remember anything. He had been walking out of the *Scheherazade* bar, after drinking too much of the harsh Algerian *vin rouge.* Then four men jumped him and pulled a leather hood over his head, before he even knew what was happening. He was roughly thrown into the back of a small truck where he passed out. He awoke in this place, whatever it was.

The room was pitch dark. Not a ray of light entered from anywhere. He was as naked as the day he was born, lying on a coarse concrete floor. He carefully crawled around and deduced that his cell was approximately three meters by three meters. In one corner he felt a bucket that was obviously for his waste. Across from it he felt a door made from welded sheet steel. As his watch was missing, he had no idea of the time. The screaming died down to whimpering and then stopped altogether. For the first time in his life, Abassi Touati was terrified.

Abassi lay on the cold, rough floor for what seemed like a day, when a panel opened on the bottom of the door and a tin pan and a bottle were thrust in. Touati could hear this happening, but could not see it. He crawled over to the door, moving slowly so as not to tip the bottle over, and found a pan of bread and a liter of water. He drank eagerly, knowing that he should save some of the water, but nonetheless, in his thirst, draining almost the entire bottle. He ate all of the bread. He was ravenous.

After he ate and drank, Abassi felt a little better. He felt less of the despair that had gripped him for the entire time he had been in the cell. This was based on the fear that he knew was irrational that he had been placed in the room and left to starve. He had been in many jails in his life, but this was unlike any other in his experience. Always there had been the admissions procedure, the search, the knocking around and the removal to a cell. Usually there was a cellmate or more than one person with whom to share the space and talk. Here there was nothing. Nobody.

Five times over this unknown period the feeding routine was repeated. Touati believed that he was being fed twice a day, which meant that he had been there three days. But he couldn't tell for sure. In fact, after what seemed like three days in the total darkness, feeling wretched, sore from scraping his skin on the rough floor in utter despair, he wasn't sure about anything. All he knew was that he would do anything to get out of cell, before he went mad. It was a relief when two men, dressed in black and wearing masks opened the door. Silently, they yanked him to his feet, put the leather bag over his head and dragged him down what must have been a hall to another room. Here they strapped his arms and legs to a heavy wooden armchair that was attached to the floor and removed the mask.

The room was small, windowless, dimly lit by a small overhead bulb and furnished with a desk and a chair, opposite the seat to which he was strapped. On the wall in front of him was a television set. The room had an underlying odor of sweat, urine and feces that had been soaked into the chair and the concrete floor. Touati could feel his heart beating too, too fast.

The door behind him opened. Another masked man came in and sat down at the desk in front of him. The man began to speak in French.

"*Monsieur* Touati. Take a careful look at this room. It is the last thing you will see in your miserable life. How many times you will see it, is up to you.

"This is our *petit chambre d' horror*. It is not operated by the Algerian Government, they do not know you are here. In fact, only a few people know of the existence of this place. All of them are your enemies. We are a group of loyal Algerians who are tired of the bombings and the terror. We have taken it upon ourselves to put an end it, to do what the government seems unable to do. You and your fellow terrorists are ruining our country. You are keeping tourists from visiting. You are preventing foreign investment. You are destroying our culture. Here, you will pay for what you have done.

"We have perfected the art of administering pain. You will be given special drugs to prevent you from passing out during our little sessions here. Another drug will serve to counteract the body's natural defense against pain. Additional drugs will keep you alive for the next session. Nobody has taken the full course of our treatment, without talking.

"We know that you were responsible for the bombing last week in Sidi bel Abbes. Six innocent people were killed. A person who knows you by sight observed you in the car and reported you to us. We are not going try to get you to confess that crime to us; we both know that you committed it. The only information we seek are the names of the other terrorists in your cell and sufficient information about the crimes for which they are responsible to obtain a conviction in the Federal court system. We will then turn them over to the police. That is what we seek. That is what you will give us. And you will give it to us with, or without, the pain.

"It will not be wise on your part to tell us lies and blame innocent people. We will find out and then you will no longer have the option to escape pain. The more information you give us, the longer you will live. We will verify the people you will name. After you have told us all that you wish to, you will be shot in the head. Death will be instantaneous. You will be given a proper Islamic funeral and buried in the desert. Your grave will not be marked and nobody but us will know of your death.

"If you are cooperative, after you are dead, we will make a financial contribution to your family. A sum of 5000 *dinars* to your wife and 5000 *dinars* to each minor child will be sent to them anonymously. Unlike you filthy terrorists, we are concerned with the lives of the innocent.

"And now it is my pleasure to treat you to a little cinema film we created. This will show you exactly what you can avoid, by telling us what you know. First we start with needles under the nails as a kind of an *aperitif.* Then...well, you will see *Monsieur,* you will see. And, just to make sure you watch our feature film, we are going to sew your eyelids to your scalp, so that you will be unable to close your eyes. We don't want you to miss anything. I hope you enjoy the show. I am going to leave you now as I have seen this movie before. In fact, I was a member of the cast. However, we will not leave you alone for long. My associate will be in to perform the eye surgery shortly. He fancies himself something of a doctor. *Au revoir.* "

The masked man exited the room and left Touati shaking with fear. Who were these people?

Several minutes later another man in a mask came in with a needle and thread. He grabbed Abbasi by the hair and yanked his head back. Then, as Abbasi watched at extremely close range, he pulled out an eyelid and jabbed a needle through it. Touati let out an involuntary scream. He then made a wrinkle in the forehead and stabbed the needle through the fold of skin. After he drew the thread tight, Touati could not close his left eye. The "Doctor" remarked that "I am only going to do one eye as what you are about to see was too much for both eyes," and left the room.

By the time he was five minutes into the two-hour film, Touati had seen enough. In the film, the poor bastard's screams echoed in his ears. Touati vomited over himself and lost control of his bodily functions at the sights.

He decided he would talk.

When the first man returned Touati was limp, bathed in sweat, vomit and waste. "Well, *Monsieur* Touati, have you made your decision?"

"I'll give you the names and information you need."

"You have made a wise choice. For those who cooperate with us, we try to make their last days a little better. You will be moved to another room and given clothes and better food. Perhaps, if you are good, even a little wine. Now, let's get you to a shower."

During the course of the interrogation session the next day, "the man", as Touati had come to call him, made an observation. "You were caught outside of the bar *Scheherazade*. It is ironic. The legend of *Scheherazade* is that, when condemned to death, she was able to prolong her life by telling the sultan a new and clever story each night. These became known as *The Arabian Nights*, perhaps the most famous body of short stories in the history of literature. *Scheherazade* did this for 1001 nights."

Later, Shari Massoud noted that Touati had managed only eight nights holdout before talking. The ten day record was unbroken.

Chapter 24
Langley, Virginia: Wednesday, September 4, 1996

If the people in the CIA Operations Directorate were derisive of the people in the Intelligence Directorate, both directorates were derisive of the people in the National Security Agency. They joked about NSA's having their "asses on the line" 10,000 miles from the action. The fact was, however, that since Admiral Stansfield Turner had been the DCI back in the Carter administration, their own agency was increasingly reliant on the collection of information through scientific means. To some degree the people of the CIA had brought this on themselves. They had become government bureaucrats, risk averse, virtually indecipherable from their fellow "crats" at the Department of Housing and Urban Development or Health and Human Services.

During the Second World War the Office of Strategic Services (OSS), the forerunner of the CIA, had been well known for its derring-do. Agents had parachuted behind enemy lines and into occupied territories. They had risked their lives evading the Gestapo. Sometimes they got caught. Only God knows what happened to such people.

After the war, however, there was less interest in sacrificing oneself for the country. It was far safer and easier to hire local residents to take the risks. The CIA slowly became a vast data analysis operation, with most of the data provided by foreign journals and foreign nationals. Operating out of the local US embassy, the Chief of Station controlled his agents. Thus, over a period of years, the CIA became embassy bound. If a country did not maintain diplomatic relations with the United States, there was probably no CIA presence of consequence.

Even where diplomatic relations were in place, the CIA fell into ineptitude. The invasion of Hungary in 1968, the Egyptian attack against Israel in 1973, the collapse of the Berlin wall in 1989, the coup against Mikhail Gorbachev in 1991, Saddam

Hussein's attack of Kuwait in 1990. All were major foreign policy events. All were totally unanticipated by the CIA. Their "humint" or human intelligence, had failed to predict any of these important situations. Their hired foreign spies were not spying.

While the CIA was declining in capability and importance, its competitor across the river, the National Security Agency, was increasing in stature. Its budget, a measurement of importance in government, was growing rapidly at a time when the CIA's budget was static. The nation's two "super spook" agencies began to feel adversarial about each other.

When an organization, whether a football team or a government agency, has a series of bad losses it actively begins seeking opportunities to redeem itself.

Perhaps this is one of the reasons that after the third call from the NSA's Danielle Lamaze-Smith inquiring about the dossier she had been promised on Abassi Touati, Jurgen Heidemann, the Deputy Assistant Director of the CIA found his attention piqued. Heidemann, an old Agency hand, began to sense something brewing. He telexed Tom Dettor, his Chief of Station in Algiers, instructing him to come home for consultation as soon as he got the Touati file from the Algerian National Police. Those NSA people were on to something and he wanted to know what, thought Heidemann. More than that, he wanted the CIA to be involved.

Chapter 25
Fort Mead, Maryland: Friday, September 6, 1996
◈

Danielle Lamaze-Smith made a point of writing to her parents each week. She did this by E-mail in spite of the fact that she always felt a little guilty about sending such communications; they seemed impersonal and designed for office and business use. But it was easy and the best she could manage with her hectic schedule.

It was a Friday night. Danielle and Neil had been out to a friend's for dinner and gotten home after 11:00. When Neil, pleading fatigue, had retired for the evening, Danielle said that she wanted to tarry long enough to read her mail, in case there was a message from her father. There was one:

"Dear Danielle:

"This is a very difficult letter for me to write.

"Last Saturday, a terrorist bomb killed Ipreham Belhadj, my assistant, whom I believe you met when you were home two years ago, and I think he also advised you about your move to Bowie, didn't he? Anyway, it was one of those terrible random bombings. It killed five people beside Ipreham, and wounded a number of others. The police think that the FIS were responsible.

"The police came to our house within several hours of the event and asked my help in informing his son, Anwar. Your Mother and I went to Belhadj's house not too far from where we live and found Anwar watching TV. I must say your Mother was wonderful. She broke the news to the boy and held him in her arms while they both had good, long cry. We then brought him home with us and put him up in your old room.

"Then, an unusual and very timely thing happened. I got a telephone call from an old friend of Ipreham's named

Yousef Zubeida. It seems that he had come to Sidi bel Abbes earlier in the week just to see Ipreham. Zubeida was the former Director of Elementary Education in Saudi Arabia. He is currently establishing a new school for especially bright students and had come to town to see Ipreham about placing Anwar in his school.

"Zubeida was most helpful and handled all of the funeral arrangements. He insisted on paying for everything personally, although I told him that LaTerre would certainly cover any costs involved, as Ipreham was covered by a management insurance policy. Zubeida did a fine job in an area where I would have been a little unsure how to proceed. As you will recall, Islam requires immediate burial, a remnant of the days when the desert heat required such a thing. Zubeida handled it all.

"After the prayers at gravesite, Zubeida came to our house and told us that Ipreham and he had agreed that the school was a wonderful opportunity for Anwar. He was quite distressed that he was taking the boy without Ipreham and Anwar having had a chance to discuss the school. I think under the circumstances that it is probably a good thing for the boy. He will be in a new place, with other boys his age and in a better school than those provided by the local government.

"I had not heard Ipreham ever discuss his friendship with Zubeida but apparently they go back a long time. Later in the week the Maitre d' hotel of the dining room called me to express his sympathies. He told me that Zubeida and Belhadj had dinner in the hotel dining room the night before. They had a long and animated dinner and embraced before they split up. At least Ipreham had a chance to see his old friend before he was killed.

We enjoyed having Anwar stay with us and even were considering trying to keep him. He is a lovely child with the blond hair and fair skin of his American mother.

> *I hope all is well with you and the Department of State. I*
> *also hope you will give them advice on their foreign policy.*
> *The Americans seem to continually do the wrong thing in the*
> *management of their foreign affairs. But this not new, they*
> *have had lots of practice.*
>
> *Sorry the news is so gloomy. Things are otherwise well*
> *with your mother and I.*
>
> *Love, Father*

Danielle's mind was spinning. The confluence of Zubeida, Belhadj, schools, Algeria, death, and blond hair would take her a few moments to absorb. She went to the kitchen and made herself a cup of coffee before returning to her desk.

Then slowly, it began to come to her. Suddenly, with Archimedean swiftness, she put it all together. Scribbling a note to her husband, she left the house. Even though it was 1:30 a.m., she needed to go to the office. And she needed to be there in a hurry.

She left Bowie, the community that is home to so many NSA employees, went up Route 3 and turned West on Route 32, towards Fort Meade; at this hour of the night, it was virtually devoid of traffic. Soon, in her rush to get to the office and her total preoccupation with the events in far off Algeria, she was speeding well over the 55 mile per hour limit, and her reverie was cut short by the sound of a siren. She looked in the rear view mirror and saw flashing lights. A glance at the speedometer confirmed why: she was doing 75 miles per hour. "Oh, damn", she thought, pulling into a vacant parking lot and waiting for one of Maryland's finest to get out of his car. She prepared herself.

"Officer, here is my driver's license and registration. And here is my National Security Agency identification card. There is an emergency. That is why I was speeding! I admit I was going over the limit. If you have to give me a ticket, I would appreciate your doing so quickly. I must be in my office immediately to deal with an important national security matter."

The policeman shined his flashlight in the car and saw an attractive, well-dressed woman. He looked at the NSA ID card and compared the name and photograph to the driver's license. He didn't bother with the registration. "Ma'am, I'll take you. Follow me," was all that he said, as he handed back the cards to Danielle. He didn't go over 65 miles per hour and he didn't blast through red lights, but he did keep his siren and roof lights on. Danielle had never made a faster trip. When they pulled up to the gate, the Army guard, saw the entrance sticker on the window, snapped to attention and flipped his best highball. With a police escort, it had to be somebody important.

Danielle wiggled her fingers to the police officer in thanks, and drove onto the base. In spite of all the calamitous news in the last hour, there was a slight upturn of her mouth as a smile began. Her first police escort!

She had to go through two security checkpoints to get to her floor. The guards, having less to do this time of night took longer, maybe just for something to do. Danielle was squirming with impatience by the time she got to her desk.

The first thing she did was call the Technical Support Division and inquire if it was possible to get a high quality fax transmission of a dozen passport photos from the State Department passport facility in West Virginia. She was put on hold for what seemed like an eternity. Then a different voice came on the line. "Dr. Smith, I'm Carl Noakes, the night supervisor in Tech Support. I have been following up on your request. To get the quality you seek will require the passport office to digitize the photos with a high-resolution scanner and then transmit the information over a dedicated 'D' line to a high-resolution printer. Unfortunately, NSA does not maintain a 'D' line to the West Virginia passport office. However, we do have such a line to the Department of State and they have a D line to West Virginia. And of course, we have the necessary printers. My colleague, John Wilbourn, in West Virginia will stand by to process the photos from the passports you requested, and he tells me that, although the night staff is a small force and that it may take an hour or so to pull the passport photos from the file, he will rush getting them digitized and transmitted. After we hang up, I'll contact the electronic transmission staff at State, and alert them to what is happening. Then, when we receive the photos, we'll e-mail them to you. We'll also call to alert you as to their arrival. I go off duty at 0500, but if there is anything else I can do for you, just call and let me know. Is this satisfactory?"

Danielle thanked Noakes and told him it was better than she had hoped for. She once again reminded herself how the "little people" were really the glue that held the whole place together. If Noakes were a GS-16, 17, or 18 (one of the higher ranks), she would have gotten 12 reasons why her request couldn't be handled until the middle of the following week. She made a mental note to write a salutary letter to his boss for Noakes's file.

Next, Danielle prepared a list of the 13 passports that had been provided to her by Bradford Warren, the lawyer at State. To this list she added the name Anwar Belhadj. She faxed this list directly to the passport verification office at the West Virginia facility and sat back to wait.

Danielle was sharply awakened by a ringing telephone. A young man from TSD was calling to inform her that the passport photos she had requested were available on her internal E-mail line. She glanced at the corner of her computer screen. It was nearly 6:00 AM. She had been asleep for over four hours.

Danielle had a 19" CRT. She quickly set the program for full screen display and started scrolling. In less than a minute she had found what she was looking for. Edward Lazar and Anwar Belhadj.

They were two little blond haired, fair skinned, Anglo-Saxon boys.

But they were not Anglos. They were Arabs.

Chapter 26
Fort Meade Maryland: Monday, September 9, 1996
❖

It was first thing Monday morning, and Danielle sat in front of her boss, Sanford Parcell. She was fairly bubbling with excitement as she related the story of her activities the previous Friday night and Saturday morning, giving him a copy of her Father's E-mail (with the gratuitous comments about America excised, and --- because Sanford who never drove over 50 miles per hour wouldn't approve --- she omitted the incident with the Maryland State Police; she didn't want anything to spoil her report of her discovery.) She also informed Sanford why she had never revealed to her Father that she was no longer at the State Department: Her Father had enough trouble adjusting to State as an employer, and she was sure he would never understand why she enjoyed her NSA work so much!

Sanford read through the E-mail twice, as was his custom. Then he carefully examined the two photographs of the boys. "Danielle," he said, "something tells me we are going to be seeing Anwar and Edward over here sometime soon. We had better notify INS (Immigration and Naturalization) to add their names and passport numbers to the watch list."

Danielle's first reaction was, *"My God, he doesn't see it."*

Then she realized that her boss hadn't focused on Zubeida, even though his name was in their discussion regarding the boys. "I beg your pardon, Sandy, but I don't think so. I don't believe we'll have anything to worry about for a couple of years. But then we will have *great* concerns, and by then *we won't know who we are looking for!* I think the key figure in understanding what is happening is Yousef Zubeida, the educator. He was in Sidi bel Abbes when Anwar's father was killed. I think that Zubeida is organizing, or has organized, a school for young boys where they will be trained to be terrorists. He has been trying to get students for this school who have come from the United States. That is why Atef requested the passports of young men with American mothers. Probably Zubeida is particularly interested in the Belhadj boy because he is blond and can pass for an American. If he can find the Lazar boy, he'll probably recruit him too, for the same reason. Zubeida is a teacher and administrator, why else would he be working with *al Qaeda* ?"

"That's an interesting hypothesis, Danielle", said Sandy. "Let me think about that for a minute." When he thrust his pipe in his mouth, Danielle knew that she had caught his attention. Then he went on. "OK. We have Yousef Zubeida, a former Director of Elementary Education in the Kingdom, hardly the sort of man who would enjoy living in the Afghan desert. He travels to Saudi Arabia, then Iran and then to Algeria. In the latter he meets with Abassi Touati, a known terrorist. He also visits with his old friend Ipreham Belhadj regarding his son going to his school. I think it possible that the school is to be in Algeria. That could be the reason for the Touati connection. Each of the other contacts was an official of the national government. I am also inclined to think that the Belhadj connection was incidental. As Zubeida was in Algeria working with Touati, he looked up his old friend Belhadj. They had dinner together. They get talking about the school and Zubeida offers a slot to Belhadj for his son. We started down the right road with Touati, the anomaly, and we are still on it. Has the CIA come through with Touati's file yet?"

"Sandy, the answer is 'no'; CIA has not given me anything but excuses regarding Touati. They claim to know no more than we do." Danielle shook her head for emphasis, "But I don't think they are coming completely clean with us. And I don't think that we should assume that the Touati connection is related to the school."

Then Danielle had an inspiration. Unlike many other Federal workers who used the government's telephones to call friends around the country and overseas, she never called her parents in Algeria or her twin sister in Paris. She hadn't used the lines when she was at State. She was particularly scrupulous at

NSA, where wiretapping was one of the things the Agency did best. But, what she had in mind was not a personal call. She asked Sanford to put a call through to her parent's number in Sidi bel Abbes, where it was about 8 PM.

"Hello Dad? This is Danielle. No, nothing is wrong, I'm fine."

"Dad, I am most sorry about your assistant, Mr. Belhadj, but I have a question about his friend, Mr. Zubeida. It regards something we are working on here at the State Department. Did he happen to mention to you where his school was located? He did? Ahhh, Afghanistan. He didn't say where, I guess. No? OK. You have been a big help. I have to go now but I'll write over the weekend. I love you too. Bye."

Her father's information was corroborative proof. Yousef Zubeida was working in Afghanistan for Osama bin Laden and *al Qaeda*. Now they really had to have a meeting with the CIA to tie up the relationship with Touati. Sandy said he would set one up.

Chapter 27
Afghanistan: Monday, September 9, 1996
❖

Bin Laden, Atef and Zubeida were in bin Laden's room. They were not eating pistachio nuts. They were talking about where the school should be located and how it should be set up.

Bin Laden was pleased with Zubeida's success in obtaining the four students. Now he was concerned about selecting the correct location and staffing the school. He asked some of his men who had come from the Hindu Kush mountains if they knew of a small village of no more than a few houses, in a sufficiently remote location that it attracted no visitors. Several locations were suggested. Zubeida was dispatched to check them out. Now he was back, giving his impressions.

"Sheik, I visited all the locations you told me about and only one met my criteria. It was perfect for our requirements! It's located in a valley and surrounded by mountains, the home of a wealthy opium growing tribe and consisting of several buildings, one of which can be easily converted into a classroom building. The others can be used as housing for the students and the instructors. There is ample flat ground available for athletic fields. We can drive trucks to the edge of the mountains. Then there is a good narrow trail for a horse cart ride of several hours to the village. It is the only way in or out."

"Is it available to us? What about the current residents?"

"That is the only problem. The owners do not wish to sell, at any price. They and their workers, about 15 in number, operate a profitable business in this location. They have no wish to relocate. I tried to purchase the entire village. I told them that we would build them a new village and transport them and their belongings, but they would not even consider moving. I am afraid we are going to have to take other steps. I suggest that we send some of our trusted men and forcefully remove them to a permanent location, somewhere in the desert. We must be sure, however, that we account for all of them. We cannot have anyone escape and then spread word about what we have done. Can we do this?"

"Yes. Atef, next week take ten of your best men and do what is necessary. The secrecy of this project is most important. We cannot expend all of the money and effort to build an American school and living facilities for seven years, and worry about some tribe of poppy growers." Atef nodded.

"Now, Zubieda, what else do you need?"

Zubieda was proud to show his Sheik how prepared he was.

"Sheik, I have spent a lot of time thinking about this. I have discussed this with Ziad Haznawi, one of our people who spent nearly 20 years in the United States. I asked him to create a list of everything we need to duplicate life in a small, remote ranch in the mountains of the American west. His work fills about 30 pages of your book. Zaid addresses such insignificant items as matchbooks, toothpaste and deodorant. It is a very complete list.

"The major item that must be in place first is a large Diesel generator to furnish electricity for the refrigerators and freezers for the American food. This will also power the washing machine and dryer we will need for the American clothing the boys will wear. This unit will, of course, also power the television, water pump, lights and electric stove, so it must be at least a 6,000 KVA unit and rated for continuous duty. There will have to be fuel storage in the amount of 5,000 gallons. This can be accomplished by supplying one tank of 500 gallons and then having 55 gallon drums of Diesel fuel to keep it filled. It would be very desirable to have an additional generator as a backup. By the way, the tank should have high-quality filters with lots of spare cartridges, and be equipped with fuel-polishing equipment. Dirty fuel is the principal cause of Diesel failure in the desert, as you know.

"The generator should be placed in one of the existing buildings together with the fuel storage. It would arouse great curiosity on the part of the Americans if their satellite imagery suddenly depicted 5,000 gallons of fuel drums where none existed previously. We should insulate the buildings so they don't have a bright infra-red image on their cameras from the heat of the machines.

"We should also install a satellite dish for the television the boys will watch and the video games they will play. This too must be kept invisible from the American eyes in the sky.

"As the report you hold relates, I have divided our effort into four categories and have assigned leaders:

"First is infrastructure. This includes the purchase, transportation and installation of the generators. It also includes the wiring and plumbing of the existing buildings. A septic system must be provided for the sanitary waste as the current residents use simple latrines. The buildings will have to be modified on the inside. As this effort will require construction expertise, I have placed Amed al Jarrah in charge of this effort. He is an engineer and experienced in construction. He tells me that he will need twenty men, at least half of which have some building trade experience.

"Second, the commissary chief will be in charge of setting up the kitchen, complete with such American appliances as a refrigerator, dishwasher, stove, microwave, toaster, mixer and cooking utensils. These things are available in Saudi Arabia where they are for sale to the American petroleum industry workers. Nami Omarri is in charge of this effort. He worked as a cook in New York for ten years; he will also be the cook for the school. He will buy, through our contacts in the Kingdom, American foods and products from the oil worker's central supply store.

"Third, apparel and items common to American life are the specialty of Kahlid Moqued. He grew up in Newark, New Jersey and returned to Pakistan when he was 25 years old. He knows what young men wear, talk about, play with, exercise with and think about. He did all the things that other Americans did during the time he was growing up. I have put him in charge of purchasing wardrobes, toys, sports equipment, books and the many other materials a young American would be concerned with. Moqued will also stay on as one of the instructors and will teach the students to play all of the common American sports. Because he recently returned from the United States, he is familiar with all of the slang and idioms currently popular with American youth. The language of the young, of course, is constantly changing, but the boys will keep up by reading magazines and watching television. Kahlid's experience will be extremely valuable in the Americanizing of our pupils.

"Finally and fourth, about education, my own area of expertise: I have designed a curriculum that closely follows a typical American school. We will use the latest textbooks and teaching aids. We will also utilize standard tests, as administered by The New York City Board of Education, to measure our success. Although of course I will not be at the school full time, I will be completely responsible. I intend to thoroughly monitor the test scores and to develop other tests to evaluate how we are succeeding in our effort to ingrain hatred for the American people. I have selected four instructors, all of whom, with the exception of Mullah Suqami, were totally educated in the United States. The Mullah speaks very good English, but was educated in Pakistan. He is extraordinarily capable of passing along his knowledge of the *Qu'ran.* Joining the Mullah will be three other men who spent their youth in America but returned to the Middle East to participate in our *jihad.* Abu Banshiri will teach science and math, Saad Ismael will instruct in social studies. Ferej Faqih was an English teacher in Detroit, Michigan. He will be our English teacher too.

"I believe each of these men to be superior as instructors and reliable as members of *al Qaeda.* They are loyal to our cause and I consider us fortunate to have found them within our ranks."

Bin Laden spoke. "Brother Zubeida, I am impressed and grateful for the effort and organization you have put into this job, praise Allah! I look forward to studying your report in detail. I have but two questions at present."

"One, how long do you think it will take to get all of this set up?"

"Two, when do the boys arrive and what are you planning to do with them while the school is being constructed?"

Zubeida smiled. It was really three questions, but bin Laden was being himself. Always trying to get a little extra. "Sheik, I am planning to have our three new boys join Edward Lazar here in camp. Being away from home for the first time will be strange for them. Here they will have many fathers to help relieve the stress. Their hair will be dyed and they will dress and look like other Arab youth. I will personally lead the orientation efforts. Mullah Suqami will start on the religious training and get them used to the discipline of a *madrass*. It will be time well spent."

"As for construction and how long it will take to convert the village to a school...it will take four months after Muhammad here," Zubeida turned and winked at Atef, "has turned the village over to us. I cannot tell how long it will take him and his army to conquer the place. After all, these people were *mujahedeen*. And we know what the *mujahedeen* did to the Soviets."

Chapter 28
Langley, Virginia: Monday, September 9, 1996
◈

"Your place or mine", is always a projection of strength. The stronger direct the weaker. Only in the White House is this not a consideration. The lowliest White House staffer can summon all but the very highest officers of the government, to a meeting in his office. They come willingly, even enthusiastically. Being able to say, "I was at the White House today" is a valued commodity.

When department head Parcell called CIA Deputy Assistant Director Heidemann to request a meeting, there was no doubt about where it would be held. A deputy director trumps a manager!

Sandy and Danielle took a government car and driver to the huge facility in Langley, Virginia. As they turned off Route 123, at the CIA exit Parcell remembered with derision that until the Nixon Administration the CIA managers were so jealous of their secrecy they wouldn't even allow their entrance to be marked. As an academic, Sandy thought that an example of *reductio ad absurdam...*

Their car went through the first security check and wound down the drive to the building, seven stories of uninspired concrete plunked down in the middle of the red-bricked Virginia countryside. (Sandy, with derision, told Danielle the reason the building was kept invisible to Route 123 was because the CIA was ashamed of the architecture.) Then they left their vehicle and entered the building where they were confronted by another security screening. The guard took their NSA photo identification cards and held them at his eye level while looking at each of them, as though carefully looking for a doctored face. Security was another of Parcell's pet peeves. He did not tolerate with equanimity the excessive zeal of most security people. He accepted the return of his visitor's badge with an air of defiance, a side of Parcell that Danielle had not seen before.

CIA Deputy Director Heidemann and Station Chief Dettor met them in a ground floor conference room. This made Parcell even more upset. It was as though *they* didn't trust *him* enough to let him onto the upper floors. The meeting was off to a bad start.

Heidemann started. "Welcome to the Central Intelligence Agency. If this is your first time here, I am sorry I don't have time to show you around. But this a busy day for me and the rules discourage taking visitors on a tour...."

Before Heidemann completed his sentence that was so obviously constructed to reinforce his own, and his agency's importance, Parcell shot back. "Ms. Lamaze-Smith and I are on an extremely tight schedule today. We need to be out of here in an hour, less if possible. We'll take a rain check on the tour."

"We are really interested in learning what you know about Abassi Touati.", Sandy Parcell continued. "He is figuring in a piece of business we are concerned with. We knew him only as Touati, until Danielle here, found him in your data-base as a member of FIS. Now we would like to know more about him. Ms. Lamaze-Smith tells me that she has called you several times and that each time you have told her that a dossier would be forthcoming. It has not arrived and I want to know why. What are your intentions?"

Danielle was absolutely stunned. She had never seen Sandy like this. It was as though a superman was hiding inside the "mild mannered reporter", Clark Kent. Parcell was right in the face of these functionaries. She was proud of him.

Heidemann responded. "Now Sandy, don't get upset. Our Station Chief in Algiers, Mr. Dettor," Heidemann nodded at Dettor, "has only just received Touati's file from his contact in the Algerian Federal Police. He has been trying to get it for more than a month, but somehow it was missing in their central files. Then, quite mysteriously, it showed up back in the system just three days ago. I asked Tom to hand carry it back here and meet with us. I'll have a copy for you at the end of this meeting. It is simply a long police rap sheet. Touati has a decidedly criminal past."

Dettor, in his best "don't give a damn if school keeps" style spoke next. "Now see here, Mr. Parcell," and then begrudgingly, "Ms. Smith."

"I am the Station Chief in Algiers. I have been there for seven years. I have the place wired and under control. Then you guys get involved and things start to happen. A journalist, or someone posing as a journalist, calls my friend, Abu Farouk, the deputy Minister of the Interior, and asks about American-born children in Algeria. The deputy minister doesn't know what he is talking about and can't help him. Next, I get a cable from Heidemann asking me to find out about American-born children living in Algeria and a guy named Abassi Touati. He says he has a request from some folks at NSA for this information. Then ten days later, my asset in Sidi bel Abbes writes me. I have to drive 500 miles to learn that Touati asked my man to help in an assassination and..." Danielle cut him off.

"Mr Dettor, did you just say that Touati was involved in an assassination in Sidi bel Abbes?"

"Yes, that's what my asset told me."

"Was it a bombing in which six people were killed"?

"Yes it was. Are you people reading my traffic?"

Parcell interrupted brusquely. "NSA does not intercept the communications of other agencies of the United States Government. We don't do that. Never have. Never will."

"Well then, how did she know," Dettor asked sullenly, motioning with his head to Danielle." She surely didn't get it from CNN."

Danielle sensing a developing situation, jumped in to defuse it. "I have a friend who was killed in that explosion. A mutual friend called and told me. That's how I knew and that's why I am interested in it. The friend didn't know that it was an assassination, though. Who was assassinated and why?" Danielle was now beginning to suspect the answers to both of these questions, but she wasn't going to let Dettor know she knew those answers. She wanted to have him assume that her friend was one of the other five people killed.

Dettor, feeling badly about his aggression and accusation, as well as for the death of Danielle's friend, responded in a softer, gentler manner. He did not apologize for his behavior. He merely modified it. "I'm sorry for the loss of your friend. My informant in Sidi bel Abbes informed me that the party to be killed was named Ipreham Belhadj. He didn't know the reason Belhadj was to be terminated. He did know that a man named Zubeida ordered the hit. Zubeida lives in Afghanistan and apparently has some connection with *al Qaeda*. I hope your friend wasn't Belhadj." Danielle ignored the last sentence. She chose to interpret it as a comment, not as an interrogatory.

"That is very interesting," said Danielle. "Often these bombings are random and committed by nameless, faceless people, yet here they know who did it. Have the police caught Mr. Touati yet?"

"No they haven't. Touati seems to have disappeared. He is probably laying low somewhere. But the Algerian police are pretty good. If they know who they are after, they generally get them. They are the 'Mounties of the Middle East.' "

Dettor used this last comment as a terminus; he wanted to get the conversation off Touati and on to what he wanted. The intelligence business operates on a variation of the childhood game between boys and girls: "I'll show you mine if you show me yours." He had just told Danielle something she wanted to know. Now she owed him one!

"Ms. Smith, I am curious. Just what prompted your interest in Touati in the first place? And why did you contact the Agency regarding American children living in Algeria?"

Danielle's mind raced. She didn't know the rules of the game as well as Dettor, but she knew she would have to give him some explanation. She just didn't want to tell him everything. She was developing a territorial imperative about the whole matter.

"We have been intercepting some satellite traffic from Afghanistan. It is quite open-ended, but the name Touati cropped up in a message about American boys in Algeria. It is probably unimportant, but we just wanted to try and run the message to ground before we abandoned working on it. We thought that your file on Touati might help us. Now, after our conversation today, I don't think his record will provide any useful information. He is probably just a common criminal who will do anything for a fee, including throwing a bomb."

"And now, I feel that we have taken quite enough time out of your busy day. Unless Sandy," she turned to her Department head and winked, "you have any additional questions, we shall be off and let these gentlemen deal with more important issues. Mr. Heidemann, I thank you for your time and effort. I don't think we will need Touati's dossier after all. It was nice to meet you, Mr. Dettor."

On the way back to NSA, Danielle began formulating a plan. Meanwhile, Sandy was thinking, "For a young woman, in competition with two older, experienced men, Danielle had played well. One might even say she won: game, set, and match to her!"

Chapter 29
Paris: Tuesday, October 8, 1996
❖

Danielle's sister, Monique Lamaze, lived in the 16th *arrondissment* of Paris, quite near the tennis center of *Roland Garros.* She was employed as an investigative writer by the magazine, *Paris Match.*

Monique was the one with the *joie de vivre.* She was also mischievous. Sometimes on dates when they were younger, Monique had convinced Danielle to trade places with her, but the ruse only worked with young men who did not know them very well. It was always Monique who suggested changing dates and fooling the boys. (Once, she even proposed doing this after they became sexually active, but Danielle wouldn't even consider it.) It was therefore a surprise to Monique when she received the following letter from her married sister in America:

October 3

Dear Monique:

I am sending you this by post, as I do not wish to discuss this on the telephones or E-mail. I have an unusual request. As girls, we used to trade names to fool people and have fun. Now I would like to trade names with you for a week.

I cannot tell you why, but it is important that I get into Afghanistan. I cannot do this as Danielle Smith, an NSA employee. I have my Algerian passport, and could probably enter the country as Danielle Lamaze, but I would rather be you. I need to use your name and profession as a reporter to get an interview with the person in charge of education in Afghanistan, regarding the madrasses. I will even do an article for the Match if you wish.

I also need you to get me some things for my trip. It is important that I look appropriate for this meeting. I need to dress in acceptable clothing. I don't think they expect foreigners to wear a burka, but I should be in Arab dress. Please go to a Middle East clothier and buy me three jilbabs and a couple of hijabs. Also a cotton shoulder bag. These should be ordinary cheap clothes. (Imagine, me coming to Paris and not buying the latest styles!) I need to borrow some underwear and shoes from you. I don't want to take anything into Afghanistan with an American label.

I also need you to go on a vacation somewhere. This is in case someone in Afghanistan calls to find out if I (you) work for the <u>Match.</u> I'll pay for a ticket if you want to go home and see Mother and Father. As Father may have told you, his assistant was killed in an FIS bombing. I think he is a little depressed. He could use a visit. Wherever you decide to go, don't tell your colleagues that you are going on a vacation. Let them believe that you are gone on an assignment. In fact, you might even try to get your editor to allow you to do some freelance reporting on the Taliban. That would be even better.

As an employee of the Department of State I know more than most people, that it is wrong to use another person's passport. However, even if something goes terribly wrong and the Taliban authorities report me (you) to the Algerian government, at worst they will revoke your passport. If that happens, you can apply for a French passport. You know you are eligible for one, born when Algeria was a French territory.

I know this must sound very mysterious to you, but I assure you that I am not doing anything that will embarrass you or your magazine. I just need to do this very badly. I know you will agree to help me.

I plan to arrive at de Gaulle on the Air France flight from Washington on October 22nd. I'll take a cab in from the airport.

Don't call me unless you cannot, for some reason, help me in this little masquerade.

Your loving sister,

Danielle

Chapter 30
Afghanistan: Thursday, October 10, 1996
◆

Kahlid Moqued, the teacher who had been raised in Newark, N.J., the instructor in dress, customs, sports, etc., was dispatched to Sidi bel Abbes to pick up Anwar Belhadj. Zubeida thought that Anwar, having just lost his Father, would relate best to a younger man.

Saad Ismael, the social studies teacher was sent to Saudi Arabia to collect Muhammad Maulina.

Farej Faqih, the teacher of English, escorted Ali Sharqui to Afghanistan.

As Edward Lazar was already in the camp, it was not necessary to send someone for him. However, as he would soon be separated from his own father, the cook, Nami Omari was designated as his keeper.

Each of the boys had one adult permanently assigned to them. Only the cleric, Mullah Suquami, was without a charge. Zubeida thought that the religious teacher was insufficiently flexible to suddenly become a parent to a young boy!

Each of these men had received careful instruction from Yousef Zubeida, before they left on their missions. They were told that they were to become the replacement parent of their own charges. They should start out by building a relationship of trust and understanding, of sympathy and respect, of affection and care. Zubeida saw each of these men becoming a surrogate parent during the seven-year period they would be together with their assigned student. As this was the first time any of the boys would be away from home, it was critical that the first impressions be favorable. Under no circumstances were any of the men to discipline their boys. Discipline would come later. The start of the relationship must be positive and enjoyable.

The three who were traveling with their boys were told to take a week to make the trip to Afghanistan. They were to spend at least four days in the nearest big city together. The men were to take the boys to zoos, soccer games, the cinema and other venues of interest to a pre-teen age boy. They were to stay in good hotels and eat in good restaurants. They were to develop a sense of camaraderie. Knowing how young minds worked was one of Zubeida's strengths. He was sure that if the beginnings were good, the conclusion could not help but be successful.

Lastly, the men were not to discuss what was happening with their boys. They were told to just tell the boys that they would learn more at the end of the week. Zubeida wished to preserve the orientation lecture for himself.

Now, "At last!", he thought, all of the boys and the teachers were together for the first time, in a large instruction room at the camp. They were seated on the floor, on cushions, in a semi-circle around Zubeida, who stood in the center. He began:

"We are a family. The other boys are your brothers. You have already met your fathers. The other men are your uncles. I am your grandfather." Yousef Zubeida had waited a long time to say these words. He had thought carefully about what to say. He had practiced his delivery.

"We will all become like true relatives. No, even closer than true relatives. We will be living together for the next seven years. You are now boys, but when we break up our family you will be men."

"You students have been carefully selected to play a great role in the history of the Arab world. You are destined to become perhaps only slightly less famous than the great Muhammad himself. During the next seven years you will be educated and trained to perform that role."

"There is an old saying that states: 'some men are born great, others have greatness thrust upon them.' You are both. As you look at each other, you will see that each of you is blond haired, even Ali Sharqui, who is blond under his dyed black hair. This quality has set you apart from all of the other Arab boys and men you have known. It is the mark of greatness, bestowed upon you by Allah himself. Our great God, in his infinite wisdom, has selected you for the role you are to play. It is our job, the teachers, your fathers and uncles, to educate you to fulfill your role.

"During the next seven years you will learn things that are unknown to all of the other people in the Arab world. You will be forced to study harder than you ever knew you could study, as you have much to learn. But, life will not be all study. You will have fun. We will provide you with a life that would make you the envy of every other Muslim boy in the world, if they only knew. But they cannot know. Nobody can know what you are about to enter into, as it is a secret. It is probably one of the most important secrets in the world today. You will learn these secrets on the condition, beginning right now, that you never talk to anyone, other than those in this room, about what you are learning. If you violate this vow of secrecy, Allah will be disappointed and displeased. He will exact a terrible retribution on you. He will deny you entry into his kingdom."

"Because the secrets you will learn over the next seven years are so great, we cannot risk anybody finding out about them. We will be living in the mountains alone, in a village with only ourselves and the guards who protect us. This village is now being constructed. We will move there when it is completed, probably in the next 60 days. In the meantime, you will be staying here in the camp with other men. These men do not know of our secret, even though they are our friends. If they ask you why you are here, you should just tell them you are waiting to go to a *madrass*. Because they must not see the special mark that Allah has given you, your hair must be dyed black, like Ali's. As we cannot begin teaching you the secrets until we go to the village, your time here will be spent with Mullah Suquami studying the sacred *Qu'ran*.

"This is your first time away from home. I know you will miss your parents. Your fathers know you are here and are being well cared for, but even they do not know of the secrets you will be taught. Anwar, here, has just had his Father killed by a Zionist bombing. But Anwar, before the Jews killed your father, he knew you were selected to be with us. He is watching from Allah's kingdom. You must make him very proud of you.

"That is all I have to say now. I will tell you more when we get to our home for the next seven years. Now, be good pupils of the Mullah. *Allahu Akbar!*"

Chapter 31
Paris: Tuesday, October 22, 1996
◈

As Danielle had expected, Monique agreed to participate in the impersonation ruse. It would have been uncharacteristic of her if she had not!

Monique was so eager to see Danielle that she braved the infamous de Gaulle traffic to pick her sister up. They chattered like teenagers all the way back to Monique's apartment, through luncheon, dinner and into the night. The girls, like most twins, had been extraordinarily close, particularly when they both were in Paris, before Danielle moved to the United States. Although they had seen each other at the family Christmas gathering, they had much to catch up on. Danielle wanted to find out about her sister's latest lover, the inside information on what was happening in Paris, and other gossip that only a journalist with one of the nation's leading magazines would know. So it was after 11:00 at night before Monique had a chance to ask Danielle what in the world she was doing on this mysterious trip.

"Now, tell me about Afghanistan. Why are you going there?"

"In the Department of State, there is great concern about the direction Afghanistan is headed under the Taliban. The leaders are extreme fundamentalists. They are preaching all that old stuff we grew up with. However in addition to 'there is no God but Allah' and the 'infidels must be killed', they have included some philosophy not in the *Qu'ran*. They have added instructions that teach 'the west is the cause of all our problems,' and 'there is an American/Jewish conspiracy against the Arabs.'"

"There is particular concern about these *madrasses*. We know these schools preach anti-Americanism from the time the students enter as children until the time they graduate as young men. What we want to know is: Are the *madrasses* teaching strictly Afghani students or they accepting kids from all over the

Arab world? If the latter is the case, the size of the schools and how many there are would be of great interest to the U.S. government. If Afghanistan is a center of anti-American, anti-west education, we can anticipate problems with the Middle East for years to come."

"I suppose our Central Intelligence Agency could easily find out about such things, but I needed a vacation and have not been to Afghanistan since that summer when you wanted to go to *St Tropez* and I wanted to go to Baghdad and Kabul. It was the first time we split up. Anyway, I was interviewing Afghan refugees and not learning anything. I thought to myself that I should just take my vacation in Afghanistan. I am interested in the changes in the last 9 years. At the same time I could find out about the *madrasses*. That's why I need to be you. A reporter has much more freedom to ask questions."

Monique shook her head slowly from side to side. "Danielle, where did you go wrong? Only you would want to go to Afghanistan for a vacation! But listen: I have an editor who just did a story about the situation of women in Afghanistan, and while she was there she had a female guide who was an experienced traveler there. Let me get her name. According to our editor, women traveling alone are suspect.

Danielle laughed. "Monique, you know I love you for who you are; but I am glad we are different. Two of you, or two of me, would be too much for people to bear. But I will call this woman, and perhaps use her. Now, let's go to bed. We both have a lot of traveling to do tomorrow."

Chapter 32
Paris to Afghanistan, Wednesday, October 23, 1996
❖

The next morning, Danielle dressed in her *hijab* and *jilbab*, and carrying one of Monique's old suitcases adorned with various European tourist stickers, boarded an Ariana Afghan flight for Kabul International Airport with Saraya, the guide's name and phone number, in her purse . She and Monique agreed to meet the following week at the Air France counter. Danielle's return flight from Afghanistan arrived an hour and 20 minutes ahead of Monique's flight from Algeria. Danielle promised to stay in contact with the French embassy and let them know of any of her travels outside of Kabul. They hugged each other goodbye. It was a strange sight. Even with Danielle in Arab attire and shawl, they still looked alike!

Danielle's flight path was south over Italy to the Ionian sea and then east through Greece to Turkey. Staying north of Iraq and the American "no fly" zone, the pilot turned southeast over Iran and then to Afghanistan. Danielle, like an eager child, sat in a window seat with her nose pressed against the window. She loved this part of the world with its intense variations in topography and color. She thought she could tell, even from 30,000 feet, which country they were flying over. "One benefit," thought Danielle, "of flying dressed in Middle Eastern attire is that the male passengers don't try to strike up conversations." She wasn't sure whether it was that they couldn't appreciate her body or they were reluctant to approach a Muslim woman. Whatever it was, it was the first time Danielle had flown alone in years when she hadn't been approached by some randy traveler.

The plane landed and the passengers were herded to document control. Traveling on an Algerian passport meant she avoided the need for a visa. Danielle waited in line while the lone security agent scrutinized each passport and compared the photo to the bearer. He then flipped through the pages of the book to determine if the owner had recently traveled to Israel. When she finally got to the booth and shoved her passport through the partition to the uniformed agent, Danielle could feel her heart pounding. She knew there was no way anyone could know about the switch in identities, but she was nervous anyway.

The agent looked first at the passport photo and then up at Danielle. He compared the picture of the woman in a stylish sweater and pearl necklace to the lady in front of him in a *jilbab*. Then he picked up the telephone from the counter to his side. Danielle's heart was now pounding so hard she thought she would faint. Almost immediately, a door in an office behind the passport control booth opened, and a uniformed officer stepped out. He walked into the booth where he conferred with the agent on duty. The two of them looked up at Danielle and then down at her passport. They talked another 30 seconds. Then the man on duty stamped the passport and handed it to the officer. During their conversation, Danielle was trying to be nonchalant, but was straining to control her stress. Then the officer walked out from around the booth to Danielle.

He spoke in poor Arabic. "Miss Lamaze, please come with me."

Danielle followed him down a corridor with unwashed opaque glass walls and a dirty tile floor. They came to a locked office door. The officer produced a key from his pocket, unlocked and opened the door to expose a small room with painted block walls. "Why is it that government offices around the world are lime green?" thought Danielle. A wooden table and four chairs were the sole furnishings. The officer waved her in and pulled out a chair for her to sit in. This was not done as a matter of etiquette, but to insure that she sat where the officer wished.

The officer spoke, again in poor and fractured Arabic. "Miss Lamaze, are you from Algeria?"

"Yes, I am. If it would be more comfortable for you to speak in your language, I also speak *Pashtu.*" This brought forth a smile from the officer. Danielle's fears diminished by half. She allowed herself an instant to reflect on the power of a smile. Then she returned to the business at hand.

The officer continued. "That is very kind of you. Your *Pashtu* is superior to my Arabic. Where did you learn our language?"

"I grew up in Algeria. There was a family next door to us when I was child, who had a servant who spoke *Pashtu.* I also studied it at the University in Paris, the Sorbonne. And finally, I have been to Afghanistan before, in 1987."

"That is strange, your passport doesn't show that you have ever been here before."

Danielle instantly recognized that she been "in country" for no more than 20 minutes and had already made her first identity mistake. She didn't flinch. "I am afraid that my passport was lost on that trip and I had to get a new one on my return to Paris." She smiled at the man. "I am not like some travelers, a collector of passport markings. I didn't want to fly back to Afghanistan just to get my entry stamp."

The officer smiled back. "Yes, I have seen some of those. They want additional pages added to their passports, rather than be issued new ones. Tell me, Miss Lamaze, are you a Muslim?"

"No. I am Catholic."

"Then may I ask why you are masquerading as a Muslim?"

"Sir, I am not masquerading. I don't think of a *jilbab* as being a religious garment as much as a cultural one. It is part of the national dress code. I wore this out of respect for your traditions, not as some kind of costume. I would not wear a short western skirt on the street here any more than you would wear your uniform to the mosque. It is all a matter of respect. You for the house of Allah, me for the traditions of Afghanistan."

This explanation clearly surprised the officer. He was silent for a matter of seconds while he digested this statement. "Well, seen in that light, I understand. I appreciate your desire to respect my country's traditions." The agent nodded his head to signify gratitude. "What is the purpose of your trip here?"

"Two reasons, really. I was last here some years ago and I wanted to come back and see the progress. Also, I am a journalist with *Paris Match*. My editor suggested that as long as I was on a vacation here, I should also try to pick up material for a story or stories."

"On what subject would you write about?"

"I have long had a special interest in education. I would enjoy doing some research on your *madrasses* and writing about them. Do you know how I could get a meeting with the person in charge of your educational system? I don't even know his name or title."

"That would be Seyyed Rashid. We call him the Supervisor of the Department of Education. I do not know if he will be willing to meet with a journalist from *Paris Match*, but I can contact him and ask if he will do so. Where are you staying?"

"I will be ever so appreciative if you could do that for me. I would promise to write a favorable article. All I need is an interview and perhaps even a visit to a *madrass*. You can reach me at the Hotel *Mustafa*. I don't know the number, but I am sure he will."

The officer handed the passport back to Danielle, with another smile. "I shall try to contact him for you. Welcome to Afghanistan, Miss Lamaze."

As she walked out of the office to the baggage claim area, Danielle could feel her knees shaking. She knew as soon as she gave 1987 as the date of her last visit, that she had made another mistake. She had told the truth. She did visit Afghanistan in the summer of 1987, while Monique was in *St. Tropez*. But she couldn't have lost her passport then.

Monique's passport showed an issue date of 1985.

Chapter 33
Afghanistan: Wednesday-Thursday, October 23-24, 1996
◈

At the airport currency exchange booth, Danielle changed her *francs* into *afghanis*, the official currency of Afghanistan. She didn't even want to think about the personal financial loss of trading *dollars* to *francs* to *afghanis*. It would probably be enough to purchase a silk scarf from *Hermes*. (Danielle tried to expand her wardrobe with visits to the *couturieres* whenever she visited Paris, and zealously hoarded money for this purpose.)

A cab took her to the *Mustafa* hotel, a relatively modern building in the heart of downtown Kabul. She went to her room and unpacked. Then, feeling the need for some exercise, she went outside for a walk. Danielle walked one block and found herself on Flower Street, the shopping street of Kabul. The shops were filled with rugs she liked (but couldn't buy), tourist kitsch she wouldn't own and clothes she wouldn't wear. Still, looking at the merchandise and the people on the street was interesting.

She returned to the hotel. As she passed by the desk the clerk called out to her. "Miss Lamaze, you have a telephone message," and handed her a piece of paper. "Please call Seyyed Rashid tomorrow morning at 09-138-7976."

Danielle had a congratulatory dinner for herself in the hotel roof garden restaurant. During her dinner of lamb kebabs, she refined her questions for Mr. Rashid and wrote them down. She also called Monique's contact, Saraya Ahmed, and asked her if she was available to stand by for the next two days in case she was needed to accompany her on some travels. She said she was available, and she agreed. They agreed on a fee.

The next morning she got up, dressed and went to the hotel restaurant. After a breakfast of orange juice, the local sweet pastry and tea, she returned to her room. She was anxious to place the call. As the Arab business world doesn't start as early as the American business day she was used to, or even as early as the European's, she was forced to wait impatiently for another 30 minutes before placing the call through the hotel switchboard.

"This is Seyyed Rashid", answered a voice in melodic, cultured French.

"Good morning Mr. Rashid," replied Danielle, also in French. "Thank you for taking my call. I am Monique Lamaze. A very nice official in your passport control service was kind enough to offer to call you on my behalf. I am here in Afghanistan on a holiday from my job at *Paris Match.* While I am here I hope to write a series of stories about the new Afghanistan. I am particularly interested in the educational system, the *madrasses,* and wonder if you would have enough time to tell me about them."

"I am surprised that there would be any interest in Paris, regarding what we are doing in education here in Afghanistan."

"On the contrary, Mr. Rashid. France has a large population of Muslims who are very interested in Muslim education. I do suspect they are not as concerned with where the teaching is taking place, as they are with the curriculum."

"Very well, Miss Lamaze. You know your readership and their interests certainly better than I. If you are available at 2:00 o' clock this afternoon, I can have a car pick you up at your hotel. My office is at our largest *madrass,* outside of Kabul."

"Mr. Rashid, I sincerely thank you for this opportunity. I'll be waiting in the lobby at two. Good bye."

"Good bye, Miss Lamaze."

Danielle was excited. She had briefly considered a career in journalism and had written for the *Nouvelle de Paris-Sorbonne,* the student newspaper. Now, for her first professional interview, she had hit the big time. She just hoped that she would be able to write an article that was worthy of her sister.

Danielle showered again and changed into a clean *jilbab.* Her standards of cleanliness were considerably above those of typical Afghan women, many of whom still observed the habits of desert living, for even washing was a luxury in the desert! She involuntarily shuddered at the thought. She wished to be clean and make a good impression.

The car and driver were waiting when she went down from her third floor room.

Kabul was definitely not much of a city by western definition. The hotel *Mustafa*, at three stories, was one of the tallest buildings in town. Most were mud brick buildings of just one story. As they drove out of town they quickly ran out of paved road and onto dirt roads. Dirt roads and dirty streets was Danielle's impression. Refuse seemed to be everywhere.

Finally, where the desert began, they came to a multi-building complex, surrounded by a low wall. This was the major *madrass* in Kabul.

The driver stopped at an iron gate and honked the horn. This caused a man to detach himself from a guard post, where had been sunning himself in a chair, and move quickly to open the gate. The car proceeded through onto a flat bare field, surrounded by low mud buildings. It pulled up and stopped at the corner building of the complex. She started to get out of the car, expecting to open the door herself — European manners were either not known or just not practiced throughout most of the Middle East. However, the driver, in a burst of personal speed, snatched the door open as she started to grasp the handle.

Danielle followed the driver to the building. Just before they arrived, the door opened and a craggy individual, dressed in a dark, patterned *chapan* stepped forward to meet her. He was handsome in the Middle East way, reflecting how young dark, mustachioed warriors become older, bearded graying men. She guessed his age to be some half dozen years older than herself, but he looked appreciably older. The climate and living conditions in Afghanistan caused people to age in appearance much more rapidly than in the west. Somehow, he looked strangely familiar.

"I am Seyyed Rashid. I presume you are Miss Lamaze?" His French was perfect.

"Yes, I am Monique Lamaze" as she extended her hand. He clasped it in his own which proved to be unusually large. Danielle had the brief sensation of having a cat's paw enveloped by a human hand."

"Come in, Miss Lamaze. You have arrived just in time for tea." Danielle followed Rashid into a ground floor room that ran across the width of the building.

One end of the room was an office with a desk, some chairs, a file cabinet and typewriter. The other end of the room was a sitting area furnished with four straight, but comfortably upholstered chairs and several low tables. An Afghan rug, woven in deep reds and blacks, lay on the hard floor. On one of the tables was a ceramic tea service. Rashid motioned her to sit in one of the chairs. He took the one on the opposite side of the tea service. He poured and asked her if she used sugar. She said yes. When they were each established with their tea, Sayyed started talking.

"Miss Lamaze, you may be wondering why I have agreed to meet with you. With your Algerian background, you must know that *madrasses* are only for male students. Women are not permitted, even as guests. However, I must confess, I am violating the rules due to a personal curiosity. I wanted to see if you were the same as when we last met. I do not expect you to remember that meeting. In truth, I perhaps would not recall you, were it not for your twin sister." As though to purposefully heighten the suspense, Rashid paused to sip from his teacup.

"I was finishing up my graduate work in Middle Eastern history at the Sorbonne and met your sister Danielle at a symposium. She was planning to enter the same field of studies. I was standing and talking with her after the lecture when you came along to pick her up and go back to your apartment. I come from a small village outside of Kabul and you and your sister were the first identical twins I had ever seen. I never saw either of you again, but the memory of that day is still quite vivid in my mind. You were two beautiful young women. I was most impressed."

Danielle was amazed. She had no recollection of the event at all. She and Monique were very popular. They were always being invited to parties and meeting new people. There were a number of students from Arab nations around Paris at the time. She and Monique, coming from Algeria, were often included in gatherings as hosts or hostesses tried to put together similar people. What a coincidence! Danielle was only sorry that she was now Monique. She would love to discuss some mutual friends and old professors.

"That's fascinating, Mr. Rashid. I cannot wait to send Danielle a copy of the article that I will write. I am sure she will remember you. But I must tell you, she wound up with a sociology degree! Now tell me, how did you end up back here?"

"I was a bright student in my village school. I wanted to attend Kabul University but could not afford it. Then, I was introduced to my benefactor. There is a very wealthy man named Muhammad al Kezir living here in Kabul. He is quite interested in improving the educational system of our country. Mr. al Kezir has been most generous with his wealth. He funds scholarships for students to attend both Kabul University and schools in other countries. He told me he would pay for my college and advanced studies, if I agreed to return to Afghanistan and work in the field of education. That is how I got to the Sorbonne and that is how I got here."

"That is quite a story." Danielle said as she rummaged in her cloth bag and came up with a notebook and pen, the tools of her trade. Then she pulled out a small cassette recorder and stood it on the table. "Do you mind if I record our conversation? It will assure that you get quoted correctly. It will also allow me to carry on a conversation rather than asking a question and then scribbling furiously."

Miss Lamaze, I do mind. I may tell you some things that I will ask you not to print. I think the American's have an expression: 'off the record'. I feel that I know you. We are fellow graduates of the Sorbonne. I want to trust you."

"Mr. Rashid. Of course you can trust me. A good journalist never betrays her source. If you tell me that you do not want me to use something you say in a story, then I won't. However, I must warn you. Only you will know what you wish to keep private during our conversation. You must tell me when this occurs. As you have mentioned the American phrase 'off the record', I suggest we use it. When you are expressing a private thought, say 'off the record". Danielle put on her biggest smile. "After all, we Sorbonne graduates have to stick together. Why don't we start by your giving me a general overview of Arab education and then some insight into the *Madrass* system. Shall we begin?"

"Miss Lamaze, I am an educator. I am very proud of the contributions to mankind made by the early Arabian world. The principal of these is, as you probably know, in the area of mathematics. Today the whole world uses Arabic symbols in the universal numbering system. This system began to replace the Roman system of numbering in Europe approximately 1000 years ago. Actually, it is more correct to say the Hindu-Arabic system, as the original work in this field was done by Hindu scholars around the 7th century. Their work was refined by the Arab mathematician Muhammed ibn-Musa al-Khowarizmi, who lived in Baghdad in the middle of the 9th century. He wrote an influential book that introduced the new concept of numbering. The book exists today in the Latin translation. He later wrote another book entitled *Al-jabr s'al mugabalah*. This sets forth the mathematical system known as *Algebra*, the European shortening of his Arabic title. His name was even Latinized as 'Algorismus'. This became the root of the word 'algorithm'."

Danielle was a little bored by this intellectual discourse, but she wanted Rashid to feel highly respected and at ease, so she let him continue...

"The numbers themselves have evolved over time. However, it is quite possible to relate the modern letter-forms, to a written text of an unknown author, but copied by a writer named al Sijis in Shiraz in the year 969. This is the earliest example of a work in Arabic by an Arab mathematician. Arabs surpassed the Greeks and the Babylonians in other scientific fields such as astronomy. Arabs were engaged in academic and scientific thought some 500 years before the renaissance in Europe. An example of early Middle Eastern literature is the *Rubaiyat*. This work by the 11th century Persian poet, Omar Khayyam, remains some of the most beautiful and well known poetry in the world today." And then Rashid leaned back in his chair, stared directly at Danielle, and began to recite.

> *Here with a loaf of bread beneath the bough*
> *A flask of wine, a book of verse, and thou*
> *Beside me singing in the wilderness;*
> *And wilderness is paradise enow.*

As he recited this verse, Seyyed Rashid changed from a stiff administrator into a soft poet. His voice altered and took on a kind of lilt. My God, thought Danielle. This man is still a young romantic, living in the days of his youth, in Paris.

"That was beautiful, Sayeed. I have loved Khayyam since I was a child. I have heard many people recite him, but none as eloquently and with as much feeling as you."

Sayeed blushed at the compliment. He was enjoying the intimacy of being alone with an attractive Parisian who called him by his first name. But he was also a little unsure; unsure of how to behave, unsure of what to say, unsure of where the interview was going. But he was also savoring the situation. This was the first time he had been alone with a western woman since his student days.

Danielle sensed his discomfort and turned the discussion back to Kahyyam by quoting one of her favorite verses.

> *The moving finger writes; and, having writ;*
> *Moves on: nor all thy piety nor wit*
> *Shall lure it back to cancel half a line.*
> *Nor all thy tears wash out a word of it.*

They happily spent the next few minutes impressing each

other with their memories for verses of the Rubaiyiat. By then, they had established a friendship that would have taken several meetings in Paris.

Rashid turned the conversation back to business. "Miss Lamaze, I wish to go off the record. I am concerned about the direction our education is going in Afghanistan. I came back here to teach and to introduce western ideas and thought. Since the Taliban took over, our entire educational system has been regressing. First they closed the university to women. Then they went through the curriculum and removed the courses that they thought to be in conflict with conservative Islamic thought. Now they are establishing *madrasses* across the country to teach our young men and boys to hate infidels, particularly Americans. Oh yes, these *madrasses* sound like religious schools in Islamic studies. And they do teach about the *Qu'ran*. In fact, the students are required to memorize whole sections of the writings of Muhammad. They also teach mathematics, concentrating, of course, on the contributions of Arab mathematicians. There is instruction in Arabic history and Arabic thought and Arabic philosophy. But sadly, there is no exposure for our young people to the world of modern science and contemporary western history. There is one exception to this. There is a constant beating into young heads of how the Jews and the West, particularly Americans, subjugate the Arab peoples. How they steal our oil wealth. How Israel confiscates Palestinian lands. How the infidel moral codes are creeping into Arab society. There is a curriculum of hate. That is what happens in this *madrass* and others like it across the country. This is what I wish you could write about. But, of course, you can't. If you published the truth in your magazine, I would be flung into prison and possibly even killed."

Danielle was dumbfounded. She knew of the *madrasses* from her work at NSA. Here she was getting a detailed description of their operation from the very man in charge of the system. She casually carried on their "off the record" conversation for another 45 minutes. As she took no notes, she had to concentrate on remembering the salient points and figures. She mined Rashid until the vein played out. Then, after their camaraderie was thoroughly established, she asked her final question. The real reason she had sought the interview with Rashid in the first place.

"Sayeed, I have one more question. Do you know a man named Yousef Zubeida?"

Rashid got a surprised look on his face, "Yes. He is a former official of the Saudi educational system. Why do you ask about him?"

"I understand that he is here in Afghanistan establishing special *madrasses.*"

"I am amazed at the extent of your knowledge. *Paris Match* must have a 'stringer' in Afghanistan. You probably know more about what Zubeida is doing than I do. There is beginning to be gossip in our educational community about Mr. Zubeida. He first appeared on the scene about a year ago. He lived in Kabul for a while and then disappeared. I recently heard he is now living in a desert camp with a man named Osama bin Laden. There is some talk about this camp being a training facility for a terrorist organization called *al Qaeda.* I don't know that, it is just what I hear. If it is one, I imagine Mr. Zubeida is involved in adding Islamic studies to the curriculum. He was a leader in the *madrass* movement in Saudi Arabia."

"Sayeed, you credit me with too much knowledge. I know nothing about Mr. Zubeida. My editor told me that he heard that the past Director of Elementary Education in Saudi Arabia had gone to Afghanistan. His source was probably some Saudi ex-patriot at a Paris cocktail party. If the Saudis are helping the Taliban financially or to set up a school system, it is newswor-thy." Danielle laughed. "Everyone in the civilized world is interested in the Saudis. That's what money does for you!"

And then Danielle dropped the bomb. "Sayeed, do you think I could get an interview with Zubeida?"

"I don't know. But I think I can certainly help you find out. I'll ask my friend Muhammad al Kezir. He knows everyone of consequence in Kabul, or maybe even all of Afghanistan. His range of friends and contacts is just amazing. Probably when I ask him about Zubeida, he'll answer with something like; 'I had dinner with him last week."

"It would be wonderful if you could do that for me. If I could meet with him" said Danielle with a bright smile, "I won't suggest that it be 'off the record'."

"I will work on it and call you. And now, let me get you back to the Mustafa before tongues start to wag."

On the way home in the car, Danielle thought about the two hours she had just spent with Sayeed Rashid. She knew that she would probably not be writing an article for *Paris Match*.

There was, however, a 100% certainty that she would write a long memorandum for the files of NSA and the CIA.

Upon reaching her hotel room, Danielle started writing. She lamented the lack of a computer, as she was unused to writing in longhand. She would have brought her laptop, except there was a nagging fear that it would be confiscated. She made her notes in French, as though she were writing a legitimate story for *Paris Match*. She did not include any critical comments made by Rashid or detailed information about the organization of *madrasses*.

Chapter 34
Afghanistan: Friday, October 25, 1996
❖

The next morning at breakfast in the hotel's dining room, a waiter came to her table and informed her that she had a telephone call from Mr. al Kezir; she could take it on the lobby telephone. As the waiter appeared to be impressed, Danielle recognized that Rashid wasn't joking, when he said that al Kezir knew everyone of consequence in Kabul. If he knew everyone of importance, then many times that number had to know of him. Even lowly waiters.

Danielle followed the waiter to the lobby phone and picked up the receiver that was handed to her; "Monique Lamaze." A strong male voice answered in Pashtun. "Miss Lamaze, this is Muhammad al Kezir. I understand that you speak our language so I will carry on our conversation in Pashtun. Alas, I am undereducated. It is the only one I speak with any degree of confidence." To Danielle's ear, al Kezir didn't sound undereducated at all.

"Yesterday afternoon Sayeed Rashid told me of your interview with him and of your request to have a meeting with Yousef Zubeida. Sayeed is an old and valued acquaintance. He may have told you that our friendship goes back to his student days. As a favor to him, I have contacted Mr. Zubeida and found that he will indeed consent to an interview with a reporter for *Paris Match*. He believes, as do I, that of all the Western powers, the French are the most understanding and appreciative of Arab issues."

"The interview will take place tomorrow morning at Mr. Zubeida's location. Unfortunately, this is some distance away. The trip will take at least 12 hours of continuous travel by truck and by horse. Are you willing to make such a trip?"

Danielle responded without thinking. "Yes," then added, "but I don't want to fly in the face of local customs, so I would like to bring along Saraya Ahmed, whom I have retained as a guide and travelling companion — I hope bringing her with me is acceptable, as I know about the difficulty of a woman traveling alone in the eyes of Afghanis less sophisticated than you."

"Of course. I see you've done your homework. But I must tell you that you cannot bring your companion, but you have my personal guarantee that you will be safe and treated respectfully; we are aware of the importance of good relations with the press!"

"Now let me explain what will happen. You will be picked up by two men at six o' clock at the hotel lobby. They will have a small, open truck. You will be blindfolded for the entire trip. Zubeida's location is a secret. Bring nothing with you. When the truck reaches a few kilometers from the city of Kabul, it will stop. The blindfold will be applied and you will be searched. I will instruct the men not to mistreat or embarrass you, but they must assure themselves that you are not concealing a camera, a recorder or a weapon. You will ride in the front of the truck with the driver, the other man will ride in the back. It will be a harsh and bumpy trip; the desert floor is not smooth. You need not bring food or water for the trip. The men will provide you with what you need."

"I suggest that you try to get as much rest today as you can. The trip is very fatiguing. As I have made it several times myself, I can tell you this from experience. After your meeting with Zubeida tomorrow, you will be allowed to rest for the balance of the day in a room where you can safely sleep. Then, tomorrow night, you will make the return trip back to Kabul."

"I regret that I will be unable to meet you, but I am leaving this afternoon on a business trip to Germany. As Sayeed speaks very highly of you, I feel that I am missing something. I hope you will feel free to call me if you are ever in Afghanistan again. Do you have any questions?"

Danielle thought quickly. She had the western habit of never leaving the house without identification. She wondered about being lost or killed in the desert with no ID. "Mr. al Kezir, do I need to bring my passport and press credentials to prove to Mr. Zabeida that I am Monique Lamaze of *Paris Match*?"

Al Kezir laughed. "No Miss Lamaze, you will not need to prove your identity. My word is enough. We know who you are." Danielle shuddered at the thought.

"Really, Mr. al Kezir, I can't tell you how much I appreciate your setting this meeting up. My friend Mr. Rashid told me that you are a very well known and popular man in Afghanistan. I think your kindness to a stranger demonstrates why. Good bye and thanks again."

"Miss Lamaze, I am pleased to be of service. One more thing; the men you will meet will be heavily armed. Do not be afraid. It is the custom of the desert tribes to carry guns. You both will be quite safe. Good bye."

Danielle called Saraya and advised her that her services would not be needed, and told her to stop by the hotel lobby where there would be an envelope for her in exchange for standing by unnecessarily.

After she hung up with Saraya, Danielle called the French embassy and asked to speak to the press attaché. She identified herself and told the attaché that she was going into the desert to an unknown location to interview Mr. Zubeida. If she had not checked in by Thursday afternoon, "would you contact my family in Sidi bel Abbes? My sister "Danielle" would know what to do."

Then she went to the lobby and dropped off Saraya's fee. The truth was Danielle was a little nervous, after all, about being alone on this trip into the hinterlands of Afghanistan.

Chapter 35
Afghanistan: Friday-Saturday, October 25-26, 1996
❖

Danielle tried to nap after lunch, but was unable to do so. The excitement of visiting a bin Laden camp was overpowering. She simply could not go to sleep. Finally, about four o' clock, she got up and took a long shower. She put on her dullest *jilbab*. Thinking about being on a horse, she exchanged her sandals for shoes. She went down to the lobby at 4:15 to have a light snack before her long voyage into the unknown. At precisely 6:00 PM the door to the lobby opened and a gaunt, dirty, bearded, unkempt looking man entered. He nervously cast his eyes around the lobby, looking for her. When he saw her, he didn't speak. Although Pashtun has at least half a dozen words and phrases that would have been appropriate for the time of day and circumstances, there was no salutation. With a sweep of his arm he just motioned to her to come with him. It was the kind of motion you would use if the person you were signaling was out of shouting range, not 20 feet away. Then he turned his back and went out to the street. He climbed into the driver's side of a Japanese pickup truck while Danielle was still exiting the hotel. As she got close to the truck, she saw another man, equally exotic, lying down on a mat in the bed of the truck. Danielle opened the passenger door and climbed into the cab. Had she been in America, based on the driver, she would have expected to see a floor littered with cigarette butts, beer cans and McDonald wrappers. But this was a Muslim country. There was neither smoking nor drinking nor McDonalds. The floor was dusty, but surprisingly litter-free. A gun, which she recognized as an AK 47, leaned against the dash.

Without looking to his right, or acknowledging her presence, the man put the truck in gear and pulled out into the street. Danielle noticed that he didn't look in the rear view mirror, or over his left shoulder, he just pulled out. Clearly his driving habits were attuned to the desert. (Danielle wryly observed to herself that some of the Washington taxicab drivers must be graduates of the same desert driving school and accustomed to the same level of traffic density!)

Kabul is not a large city with sprawling suburbs. In ten minutes they were out of town and entering the desert. They were heading east on the road to Jalalabad, a gravel highway. It was in pretty good shape, thought Danielle, who was quite familiar with similar roads in Algeria. In the arid, high plains country of the Middle East, erosion of roads due to rainfall is not a problem.

The truck bounced along in a quite acceptable fashion at about 30 miles an hour for another 20 minutes. Neither the driver nor Danielle had spoken to each other. He pulled off the road and, without looking at her, told Danielle that he must blindfold her for the rest of the trip and that he was also required to search her. Then he became flustered. In a state of high embarrassment he said that he had been ordered to search her but he was unable to do so. It was against the teachings of Muhammad to touch a strange woman. He said that he was going to trust her. If she said she wasn't concealing a recorder or gun, he would believe her.

Danielle was relieved. She too had been worrying about what form the search would take. In college, she had once been searched by an immaculately uniformed *gendarme* who was far less solicitous of her privacy than this poor, dirty Afghan. She quickly told him that he had nothing to worry about and thanked him for his sensitivity. Then she bent her head down so he could tie the blindfold rag about her face. Another hurdle out of the way!

The truck continued to bounce along the desert track. There was continued silence in the cab. Danielle decided to break the ice.

"Are you married?"

"Yes."

"Do you have children?"

"Yes?"

"How many?"

"Four."

"Girls and boys?"

"Two girls and two boys."

"What are their ages?"

"Two, four, five and seven."

"What are their names?"

"Their names are not important."

Apparently, her attempt to start a conversation was not going anywhere. She gave up trying.

When you are blindfolded and riding on a rough road, the bumps are intensified. You cannot see to anticipate them and brace yourself. After what must have been several hours Danielle was feeling distinctly sore. Then, there was one particularly hard encounter with a hole. Danielle was thrown forward and her head slammed into the windshield. The driver immediately stopped the vehicle. "Are you all right?"

Danielle wasn't sure how to respond. She was tired of being thrown about. Her muscles ached from hanging on to the grab bar. She was feeling very nauseous. When she didn't answer promptly, the driver said that they would stop for a rest and that he would take off the blindfold. He didn't pull off to the side of the road. There was no road. When he removed the blindfold Danielle could see nothing but desert in the headlight's beam. They were driving cross-country. The driver was navigating by the stars.

The driver got out of the truck and told her to do likewise. She pushed open the door and nearly fell to the ground. She was stiff and her legs ached. Danielle got out of the truck and walked around until she felt better. Then, feeling the need, she announced that she was going to take a walk. She added an expression common to all languages of the Middle East. She said she was going to "water the desert".

When she finished, she went back to the truck and saw that

the man in back and the driver were unwrapping a package of food. They had lowered the tailgate and offered her a place to sit and join them in a supper of bread, goat cheese and cold tea.

There is nothing like sharing a meal, even a simple one, to create a relationship. Danielle took the proffered cheese. She hadn't felt hungry till the food appeared. Now she ate with gusto. The man from the back of the truck spoke to her.

"This is a very rough way to travel, but we only have two hours more in this truck. Then we will switch to horses for the last portion of our journey."

The driver chimed in, "I will leave off the blindfold from now on. I think it is unnecessary as it is nighttime and you can't see anything anyway. I think the men at the camp are overly concerned about secrecy. I don't think you know where you are or could find your way here again."

Danielle agreed that she had no idea where she was and thanked him for keeping the blindfold off. Then they all had a short conversation about the beauty of the desert night, the quality of the cheese and the flavor of the tea. The ice was broken. The men were obviously concerned about her welfare. Danielle was beginning to like both of them.

When they climbed back into the truck, Danielle felt more relaxed than she had since they picked her up at the hotel. In spite of the fact that she knew she was a guest, with an appointment with Zubeida, there had been a slight gnawing of fear, especially since she was alone with them. Now it was gone. After eating, with no blindfold, she felt relaxed. She wedged herself into the corner of the cab and fell asleep.

Danielle awoke when the driver stopped the truck and turned off the engine. It was in the predawn and she could make out a small village of mud huts by the starlight. There were several other men outside the truck, talking in low voices. They were conversing in a dialect that she was familiar with, but could not follow. The driver turned to her and said that now they would be transferring to horseback, and that he was sorry, but the blindfold had to go back on, at least until they were clear of the village.

The driver helped her mount her horse; it was one of three small desert ponies; a squat, rugged animal capable of carrying great weight for long distances without rest or nourishment. Danielle's stirrups were only a foot from the ground. The saddle was rustic, homemade, but comfortable. It was somewhere in between an English and western saddle; a high cantle in the front and back, but no horn. The horse's step was very short, but because they were walking, it was a pleasant gait. Danielle had owned a series of purebred Arabian horses as a girl and knew how to be comfortable on horseback. She was glad the pace was a walk and not a trot. With the shortness of her horse's step, a trot would have surely been very bouncy!

They rode for about ten minutes until they were clear of the village and out of sight of the villagers and the leader took the blindfold off; then, an hour or so later, the rising sun began to outline mountains ahead of them. The leader (who had been the pickup driver) then stopped, apologized again, and said that it was necessary that the blindfold go back on. Danielle guessed that his action was only partially motivated by the need for secrecy; the balance was simply that he couldn't disobey orders and arrive with un-blindfolded visitors.

Finally after several hours of riding uphill, they stopped. Danielle could hear other voices. Someone told her to dismount, and led her up a rough path. She sensed they were entering a building.

"You may remove your blindfold now."

Danielle took off the rag that had been wrapped around her head. She found herself in a dark room poorly lit by daylight that came in through a small window, and by several oil lamps. The room was furnished with a low sleeping couch with a thick blanket; a small table approximately one-meter square, a wooden sitting bench and several cushions made from animal skins. The floor was hard packed dirt covered with a badly worn wool rug. It was certainly not commodious, but it appeared clean. Danielle was suddenly overcome with fatigue. The bed looked inviting, but first there was other business to attend to.

The unnamed driver, who Danielle was now mentally thinking of as her friend and protector, understood the women's discomfort.

"There is a building outside, to your right about 10 meters, where you can relieve yourself. I will take you there and stand guard outside the entrance so that no men come in and interrupt you. Come with me."

She followed him out into a walled courtyard that prevented her from seeing anything of the compound. The building was small and equipped with the standard sanitary facility of the Middle East desert community, a slit straddle trench. A jug of water was an uncommon accessory. When she was finished, she followed the driver back to the room.

"You should rest here until later in the morning. I will come for you in several hours, when you are refreshed and Mr. Zubeida is ready to meet with you."

She lay down upon the couch, pulled the blanket around herself, and immediately fell asleep.

Chapter 36
Afghanistan: Saturday, October 26, 1996
◈

The driver tapping at the door wakened Danielle. "Miss Lamaze, it is time to meet with Mr. Zubeida. Please come out."

She got up and made an attempt to smooth out her wrinkled *jilbab*. Fortunately her hair was entirely covered by her *hijab*. Like most desert clothing, it was made for function, not style. She began to more fully appreciate the utility of the design. She went through the door and followed her escort across the mud brick courtyard to a building flush against the other side of the wall. As there was another wall screening the rest of the area, she saw only the sky, but she began to get the idea she was in a larger than typical tribal village. The driver ushered her into a room, much bigger than hers. It was elaborately furnished with chairs, a large table, and a beautiful Afghan rug over a wooden floor. A sleeping couch was against one corner. Light streamed in through several windows.

"Mr. Zubeida will be here shortly." With that statement, the driver turned and went out the door, closing it behind him. Danielle was alone.

"Miss Lamaze, how nice to meet you at last. As I have been in the home of your family, I feel that I know you." The man who entered the room with that greeting was totally unlike the driver. He was clean, with neatly trimmed facial hair instead of a full beard. He was dressed in an expensive *galabiyya*, with the traditional black and white checked *ghutra* topped with an *agal*. He looked like an *Emir* in the flowing robes of a desert chief.

As he walked toward her, Zubeida extended his hand, an un-Arab like greeting to a woman. "I am Yousef Zubeida. I welcome you to my home." Zubeida spoke in a cultured Arabic rather than the more, coarse Pashtun. "I am sorry for the difficulty of your trip, but I hope you are now rested. I have ordered food, which should be here shortly."

Danielle took the proffered hand. "I am Monique Lamaze. My father told me you were a most impressive gentleman. Now I understand what he was talking about." She was finding it hard to believe that this obviously cultured individual could be the man who ordered the killing of Ipreham Belhadj.

"Please sit down here, Miss Lamaze," said Zubeida, as he pulled out a chair from the table for her. He then sat down opposite her.

"I must say, you look exactly like the two photographs your family has on the piano at your home." Danielle knew which ones he was talking about. As one was of her and the other of Monique, Zubeida must not have known they were twins, or else he was testing her. Danielle guessed the former and decided that it was best not to bring the subject up to this obviously intelligent individual.

"*Papa* told me he had talked with you. He didn't tell me that you visited our home. What may I ask, caused you to visit my parents, Mr. Zubeida?"

"I went to see them and poor Anwar after the terrible death of his father." Danielle noticed that Zubeida did not attribute the bombing to the FIS. "You have a very interesting father. He and I had a good conversation about the politics of the Middle East. Having lived in Algeria for most of his adult life, he has a better understanding of the Arab world than most..." Danielle thought Zubeida was about to add "infidels", but he caught himself before adding the defamatory word to the end of the sentence. He continued. "I was most interested to hear his views on the future of Saudi Arabia. He and I share similar opinions about the corruption of the royal family. We differed only about what should be done about it."

Danielle could have predicted that. Her Father was one of the staunchest supporters of democracy she had met outside of America. If he had been alive during the revolution of 1789, he would have been storming the *Bastille*. She guessed that Zubeida's cure for the Saudi problem was a theocracy.

Danielle decided she wanted to turn the conversation away from her family. "Mr. Zubeida, my Father told me that you were here in Afghanistan helping the Taliban establish a *madrass* system. He said that there was a very special *madrass* for gifted students in which Anwar would be placed. Is that correct?"

"Miss Lamaze, the Taliban are realistic about the future potential of Afghanistan. This country has very little in the way of natural resources. It can never be like a western nation. It will never be a part of NATO or participate in extensive foreign trade. Therefore, the Taliban believe that the best course for the future of the country is to steer a middle course between the past and the present. Afghanistan has existed for thousands of years without change. The Taliban want to preserve all that was good in the traditional Islamic society, and adopt only what is necessary from the culture of the west; things such as medicine. They see the way to accomplish this is to take the best students, the brightest minds, and educate them to be the future leaders of the country. They believe the *madrass* system is the best way to accomplish this. *Madrasses* stress Islamic education, traditional lifestyle and a repudiation of western culture. Because of my experience in the Kingdom, I have been asked to help accomplish this goal. As I share the convictions of the Taliban, it is an honor for me to participate in the future of this country. America is wonderful - for the Americans. France is wonderful - for the French. But not all countries should aspire to be like these two exceptional societies. We cannot allow the expectations of the common citizen to expand to the point that disappointment will occur when their individual goals are not met. This is a poor country. People cannot be allowed to dream of being rich."

"Mr. Zubeida, I accept your argument that Afghanistan is a poor country with few natural resources. However, every country has the most important resource of all, human brains. I can think of other poor countries that made commitments to pull themselves out of poverty by educating young people to the latest science of the western world. Ireland, in the past ten years, has made itself a technology center of Europe. India is developing a reputation for computer programming. Afghanistan does not have to commit to a future of poverty."

Zubeida's smile diminished. "Miss Lamaze, the difference is that we wish to remain a strictly Muslim nation. If there were too much influence from the west, the teachings of Muhammad and the *Qu'ran* would be inevitably corrupted. Now, I hear our breakfast coming. I have a surprise for you."

The door pushed open and a young boy carrying a tray, entered. He looked familiar to Danielle, very much like the photo of Anwar Belhadj. However, this boy had a full head of black hair.

"Miss Lamaze, may I introduce to you the subject of our discussion, Anwar Belhadj."

Danielle got out a "hello" to the boy and then stammered something about how sorry she was to learn about the death of his father. Still in a state of shock, she told Anwar how pleased her mother and father had been to have him as a guest in their house and how highly they had spoken of him. Anwar did not respond. He remained as silent as a mute.

Zubeida interceded. "Anwar, why don't you tell Miss Lamaze how much you are learning from *Mullah* Suquami?"

Anwar Belhadj stared up at Danielle with an unmistakable look of awe on his face. "How do-you-do, Miss Lamaze? I think your parents are the nicest people I have ever met. They took good care of me, especially your mother. I am too young to remember my own mother but, if I had one, I wish she would be like your *mama*."

While Anwar continued speaking, Danielle was fervently praying that Anwar would not mention Monique or imply that there were *two* sisters.

"This is a nice place to live. There are other boys my age to play with. The food is good and I am already learning a lot...."

Before Anwar could finish his thought, the door was opened and an unusually tall Arab man strode in. He was dressed in a white *dishadaya*, with a wrapped white turban. He was fully bearded. His eyes were set wide apart on his face and flanked a large nose. His dark pupils glistened in the center of large white corneas. Danielle was stunned. She was face to face with Osama bin Laden.

He entered the room, cast his eyes about looking for Zubeida and spoke. "I am sorry Yousef. You told me that you were going to have a visitor from *Paris Match* this morning and I forgot. I will leave the three of you alone." As quickly as he had entered, he was gone. There was no sign of recognition of the other two people in the room, only Zubeida. It was as though Danielle and Anwar didn't exist.

Zubeida spoke first. "Anwar, we have kept you away from your studies long enough. We thank you for bringing in the breakfast. Now say goodbye to Miss Lamaze and ask her to say hello to her parents in her next letter." The boy did as he was directed and slipped out as silently as a wraith. Danielle was still in a state of complete surprise. She had not expected to see Anwar, and she hadn't dreamt of seeing bin Laden.

"That was Osama bin Laden, wasn't it," asked Danielle?

Zubeida only nodded, "In France, there is some belief that he is a terrorist. Miss Lamaze, Mr. bin Laden could not be more unlike a terrorist. He is a brilliant thinker, a natural leader and a born visionary. He was asked by the Taliban to come to Afghanistan and help them form their government. It is he who proposed the development of *madrasses* including the special *madrass* for exceptional students. It was he who recruited me. He earned his initial recognition organizing the *mujehedeen* to drive the Soviets from our country. He will earn lasting fame as a result of his efforts here."

"He didn't seem to be at all interested in me, obviously your guest. Some people might even say he was rude."

"Miss Lamaze, it is the belief of the true fundamentalist Muslim that the sole purpose of women is to have children. That is why they require the *burka*. Men are not supposed to become physically aroused by women. Bin Laden did not permit himself to look upon you as you are not fully covered."

"I guess that is why the religion allows four wives," Danielle thought to herself: Zubeida would not appreciate her view of the Muslim treatment of women out loud! She needed to steer the conversation back to education before she spoke out and became declared *persona non grata...*

"Mr. Zubeida, let us return to where we were before Anwar and bin Laden came into the room. You were telling me about the desire of the Taliban to organize the country with acceptance of some things from the west. Does that mean that the mullahs will have reduced power in the future? After all, the purely religious leaders, like the Ayatollah in Iran, have little understanding of the modern world."

"Yes, I believe you could say that, although that statement is certainly subject to misinterpretation. I believe a more correct way to phrase it is that the mullahs should have some resources to call upon, people who have some education in the modern world. That is what I am seeking to do with my *madrasses*, train future leaders to operate an Islamic society in the modern world. In my opinion, there is no Islamic nation in the Middle East that has successfully achieved a proper balance. Saudi Arabia, perhaps the most rigorous Islamic state after Afghanistan, has been corrupted by their oil wealth. The leaders profess adherence to Islam but I can take you to a hotel in Greece that is a playground for the Royal family. The women arrive in *jilbabs* and *abayas* and two hours later they are in bikinis on the beach. It is disgraceful."

"The world is too small a place today for a country to exist in total isolation. News of outside events is bound to filter in. I believe we need to be equipped to, if I may coin a phrase, 'filter what filters in.' The responsibility of a ruler is to insure his people's happiness. By adhering to the traditional values, by following the traditional customs and by ignoring the siren song of the decadent western societies, I believe we can insure the well-being of the Afghani citizen."

"How are you going to recruit these exceptional students?"

"Well, Miss Lamaze, we have already started to contact the educational leaders throughout the country to get referrals of the best and the brightest candidates, young people with the self-discipline to apply themselves to learning our traditions, our history, our religion, and the reasons behind them, as well as the facts about the modern world so that sensible decisions within our cultural framework can be made about what to let in, and what to keep out."

"I'll bet," Danielle thought silently...

Zubieda continued, "And now, Miss Lamaze, you have my views on the future of Afghanistan and what we are trying to do with our *madrasses*. Let us turn our attention to our breakfast."

Danielle and Zubeida spent another half-hour together eating and talking idly. Try as she might, she could not elicit any more conversation about bin Laden or the *madrasses*. When the meal was over, he rose to signify the end of the meeting. "Miss Lamaze, you will remember, of course, that I invited you here to meet Anwar Belhadj and because I know your parents. Neither of those relationships has anything to do with *Paris Match*. You understand, I'm sure."

"Now, I suggest that you return to your room and get rested for the return trip to Kabul. It has been my distinct pleasure to meet you. I hope you have a safe and comfortable return to Paris."

During the entire trip back to Kabul, by both horse and truck, all Danielle could think about was getting back to Washington and telling her story. She fantasized about a conference with Heidemann and Dettor at the CIA. "When I met with Osama bin Laden in his camp, how did I get into the country and how did I arrange it, you ask? That information is on a 'need to know' basis. I don't believe you're cleared!"

Chapter 37
New York City: Monday, November 4, 1996
◈

In the structure of organizations, it is axiomatic that the fewer levels of management, the better. Orders from the top stand a better chance of being correctly executed if they pass through limited levels of authority.

The American Telephone and Telegraph Company, before it was broken up by the Justice Department, was one of the world's largest corporations. They were consistently praised as being one of the best-managed companies in America. From the Chairman of AT&T, the parent company, to the manager of the local office of one of the operating companies, were only ten, distinct, levels of management.

During WWII the U.S. Army, the largest army in the history of the world, had the following chain of command: National Command Authority, Theater Command, Army Group Command, Army Command, Division Command, Regimental Command, Battalion Command, and Company Command. An order from the President, the Commander in Chief, went through eight levels of command before it reached the men responsible for its execution .

The Roman Catholic Church, the oldest and largest continuing social organization in the world, with over one billion members, is organized with: the Pope, Cardinal, Archbishop, Bishop and Parish Priest. This constitutes just five levels of authority.

Al Qaeda, a transnational terrorist organization, only has three!

There is Osama himself, the senior leader in the country and the leader of the cell; then the leaders of the units; and then only men "in the trenches". That means short communications "pipes" and very few "leaks".

Further, ever the master plotter, bin Laden had agents in various countries which were unknown to anyone but himself. These

*contacts were outside of the normal chain-of-command structure.
He called upon these people for advice and to carry out particular
missions.*

Ehasan Khawalka was an Egyptian national and a senior
employee in the Information Technology Division of The City of
New York. He was a graduate of Cairo University. He was
working on his masters degree at the City College of New York in
the area of computer science. He had worked for the City six
years. He was highly respected and considered a candidate for
even higher management. He was well liked by those with whom
he worked. He was also an *al Qaeda* "sleeper agent" with a deep
and abiding hatred for the United States of America for their
support of Israel.

Bin Laden, understanding the frailty of wireless communications, contacted Khawalka only by mail and only infrequently,
when he needed serious advice. The letters were always hand
carried by a courier and posted in the United States. The address
was *Number One Vanderbilt Avenue*, a series of rental mail boxes
in the basement of New York's Grand Central Station. The
addressee was Alliance Capital Company, an inactive firm,
domiciled in Haiti with a Chechnyan Muslim as the president.
Anybody looking for records of ownership or a paper trail of the
occasional large financial transaction flowing through this
company would be totally frustrated.

Khawalka visited his mailbox irregularly, perhaps once a
week. He usually did this when he was in town, late in the
evening. The mailboxes were located two floors below the ground
level, down a long corridor from Grand Central's famous *Oyster
Bar* restaurant. At night the restaurant was closed and Khawalka
could see anyone lingering in the corridor. The mail was usually
junk, advertisements from office supply firms and printing
companies in the neighborhood. From time to time, however, he
received a business envelope with no return address. This he
would immediately put into the inside pocket of his jacket for

later reading.

One night a friend invited him to attend an important black tie dinner affair, the Second Panel of the Sheriff's Jury. This was held in the Trump Hotel, adjacent to the Grand Central Station. Khawalka seized the opportunity to visit his mailbox. He found an envelope with a familiar style. He read the letter on the train ride home, this day before the American election day.

Dear Friend:

Once again I call upon you for your help and advice. I need to acquire some American identities

I can buy the best forgeries in Europe. But I need something better than a forgery. I need the identities of four real Americans of approximately 12 years in age. These identities should allow four young men to enter the United States in seven years and apply for jobs, driver's licenses and other benefits that require documentation.

The four young men are presently American citizens, but have Arab names. I wish to give them new identities with American names. I know you understand the American system and can advise me on the best way to proceed.

It is critical that the identities be real. They must be able to withstand the highest scrutiny by police and other government officials.

The letter was unsigned, but Khawalka knew the sender could be only one man.

Khawalka knew little about the record keeping systems for American citizens. He needed to do some research. This was his value to bin Laden. His worth was based not upon what he knew, but what he could find out. He was a thorough researcher with a creative side. Ten days after he got the assignment from bin Laden he wrote to a mail drop in London, England. There his letter would be picked up and hand carried to its ultimate destination in Afghanistan.

Dear Friend:

America is a nation of over 250 million residents. From birth to death, they are accounted for by multiple and interwoven records. It is difficult to create identities. There is no national identity card, but employers, lenders and many organizations use the Social Security Administration number as a kind of national reference number. In addition, for adults, the state issued driver's license is universally used for instant identification. It generally includes a photograph. As most Americans own cars, this is a common document.

Passports are not used for identification, only for travel. Other identification documents are draft cards, credit cards, and organization membership cards. All of these, to some degree, rely upon the Social Security number which is also used for all individuals' tax returns. It is critical that any citizen who wishes to work or function in the US have a Social Security card. Only some illegal immigrants do not possess legitimate cards.

The Social Security card is applied for at age 12. The procedure is simple. The individual goes to the Social Security office with an original or certified copy, of a birth certificate and fills out a form. The birth records are kept by the state of birth; there is no federal agency that keeps citizen's original birth records. The state of birth is also responsible for the death records.

The Americans are very dependent upon computers. If a person from the state of New Jersey is killed in an automobile accident in Texas, the Texas bureau of statistics notifies the New Jersey authorities of the death of one of their citizens. This is a very efficient system. It prevents the easy assumption of a dead person's identification. It is very difficult for someone to impersonate another American without running the risk of being found out. It makes obtaining real identification documents virtually impossible. Forged and stolen documents are easily purchased, but are subject to detection.

Most of the local police forces have computer links to the Federal Bureau of Investigation. This means that someone carrying a false identification is subject to being caught, even if stopped for a minor traffic violation! However, in spite of all of the difficulty, I have determined a method to generate four original identification sets.

An example of the moral degradation of the United States is that every year three quarters of a million children disappear from home. They run away, or they are kidnapped. They are stolen by an angry spouse, or they are murdered and the bodies disposed of. These children are in a state of suspension with the authorities at the records offices. The officials do not know if the missing children are dead or alive until a body is found and identified. Most states keep records of births, deaths and marriages in their bureau of records. Records of missing children are kept by the state's police departments. The vast majority of such children are alive and ultimately return to their homes. We can take advantage of this state of suspension. The key to obtaining real identification for your boys is to have them assume the identities of missing boys.

If you are really concerned about creating unchallengeable identification for your four young men, I suggest the following:

You send a team of two men to locate four boys of the approximate age you are looking for. The boys should come from different areas of the United States, so as not to arouse suspicion. I recommend the boys be from lower income families from some of the smaller and remote cities in America. I might choose Fargo, North Dakota; Joplin, Missouri; Youngstown, Ohio; and Schenectady, New York, for example. The choice of cities should largely depend upon the ability to dispose of the bodies nearby.

These boys are kidnapped and disposed of. It will be preferable if they already possess Social Security cards. If they do not have Social Security numbers, a birth certificate will be necessary to obtain one. In either case, with a card or without, a birth certificate should be requested immediately after the abduction. This will arrive in the mail and must be notarized by the owner. As the owner is no longer available for this purpose, another boy of approximately the same age can be employed to swear to an official that he is the boy on the certificate. If desired, sons of our members could be substituted, but I do not recommend this. It would be much safer for the secrecy of the operation if another boy were hired to participate in the ruse. He could then be disposed of after this business was concluded.

This would now put you in possession of four Social Security cards and four birth certificates of boys who were real, but no longer exist. These documents can be then used to register for the draft, obtain driver's licenses, become an employee, obtain credit, etc.

Obviously, a critical part of this method is that no bodies are ever discovered. There must be no reason to change the computer designation from "missing" to "deceased". That is the real danger of such a plan. If, for some reason, an official discovers that the bearer of one of these identities is officially a "missing person" a story will suffice to correct the problem. The bearer can simply say that he ran away from home and has been living on his own until he legally became an adult. No government agency will notify the parents.

A much more modest concern, is the infinitesimal possibility that the new owner of the identity meets up with someone who knew the original owner. However, in a nation the size of the United States, this is not likely.

There are, of course, risks involved in the kidnapping and elimination of boys. In the United States, kidnapping is a major crime. It is taken so seriously that it is one of the few commonplace crimes that is assigned to the Federal Bureau of Investigation. Nevertheless, if you are absolutely concerned *with having real identities assigned to these boys, the risks are worth the result.*

Finally, it will be impossible to bring your young men into the United States under an American passport. Passports are not issued to persons under the age of 17 unless a parent or legal guardian accompanies them. Obviously, this cannot be arranged. My suggestion to you is that they fly from Paris to Quebec, Canada under French passports. Then they can travel to the United States by car or bus as tourists. High quality forgeries of French passports are very available in Europe. You have probably used them in the past.

I am, as always, pleased and gratified to be of service to our great cause.

Your friend.

Chapter 38
Washington, DC: Wednesday, November 6, 1996

The National Reconnaissance Office (NRO) was created in 1960 to end the in-fighting between the CIA and the Air Force over which was responsible for satellite reconnaissance. A battle was waged between these two giants over which group would design and operate the nation's satellite surveillance systems. As major budget and prestige values were at stake, the issue was sharply contested. President Eisenhower, demonstrating the powers of placation for which he was famous, ordered the creation of a new agency, the National Reconnaissance Office. This group would design and operate the satellites, the Air Force would launch them and the Central Intelligence Agency would interpret the information generated. It was such a secret organization that its very existence was not acknowledged until 1992.

As might be expected of a bureaucracy, the NRO did a little dabbling in image analysis itself. The Office liked to know what it was furnishing to the CIA in the "hot spots" of the world. Thus the NRO employed image interpreters to review samplings of its work product before sending it to Langley.

◈

To Harvey Saxe, the allure of secrets was overpowering. Knowing things that others could not be told was a principal source of joy in his life. He even derived gratification from reading documents marked "administratively confidential."

Harvey yearned to work for the Central Intelligence Agency. He applied for a position there, but failed to pass the psychological tests. The investigations into his motivations uncovered, quite correctly, his penchant to be involved with state secrets. As a result of being turned down by the CIA, he became an employee of another intelligence organization, the NRO. It was a lucky stroke for both of them.

Harvey became a crackerjack interpreter. It was a task at

which he excelled, his personal "highest and best use." Harvey had an unusual ability to sit at a light table for hours on end and pick out things on aerial photographs and satellite imagery that were missed by others. His only problem was that he sometimes allowed his imagination to ascribe invalid meanings to what he saw. He looked for bogeymen, and of course, since he was looking for them, he found them. That's why, in spite of his skills, he gained something of a reputation as "the boy who cried wolf."

Now the CIA was requesting an increased amount of surveillance product on Afghanistan. Harvey knew from reading *The Washington Post*, and listening to talk radio, that the Taliban were bad people. It was obvious to Harvey that Afghanistan was becoming an area of interest. He found himself looking at imagery of that country more closely. It beat watching Poland.

One afternoon Harvey noticed several horse carts on a trail in the Hindu Kush mountains. They were loaded with freight including several suspicious looking white boxes that closely resembled home appliances. As it was not an area covered by geosynchronous transmissions, he had to wait until the next day to take another look. The on the following day there was no activity, but the day after that there were clearly oil drums being moved. By the next day, Harvey began to get suspicious. What was this flurry of activity to a remote cluster of houses deep in the Hindu Kush?

Harvey was ever mindful of the alert photo analyst who spotted missile launching pads under construction in a 1962 U2 spy plane overflight of Cuba. That fellow earned a Presidential citation for his diligence. Encouraged by this example and eager to make a name for himself, Harvey asked his supervisor to take a look at the photography.

"George, I would like you to look at some interesting imagery from Afghanistan. Here is a shot from 3 October. And these from 5 October and 6 October. I don't know what to make of them, but this photo shows, what appear to be refrigerators. These other carts seem to be carrying oil drums. What do you think?

Harvey Saxe moved aside and George sat down in front of the screen. He looked at the horse carts and then he looked the half dozen mud brick houses in the village at the end of the trail.

"Harvey, I think you are right," the jaded supervisor said. "Those are refrigerators. Some tribe of rag-topped poppy-pickers is probably creating a microbiology laboratory for the production of deadly nerve agents, to use against the rest of the world. I would keep a very close watch on this. If it appears they are going to construct a nuclear bomb factory, let me know." Shaking his head in disbelief, George got up, and went back to his office. "Harvey is always looking for goblins in every closet," he thought.

Harvey turned his attention to Iran. Here there was real potential for the development of nuclear capability. And real potential for him to gain recognition.

Chapter 39
Detroit: Friday, November 8, 1996
❖

Mansukh Senna did not see any contradiction. As a Muslim, his own body could not be cremated after he died. That had nothing to do with his cremating other bodies of other faiths.

He started working for the crematorium fifteen years earlier as an ambulance driver, when he first arrived in America from Sudan. He spoke very little English, just enough to study and pass the test for his Michigan driver's license. He had hoped to become a taxicab driver, but a wonderful piece of luck had come his way. He walked by a mortuary just as the owner was placing a "driver wanted" sign in the window. He went inside and was hired. It was easier than driving a cab because, as he always said, "the passengers didn't complain, they never got mad and they didn't try to mug you."

Over time he became very close with the mortuary's elderly owner. The old gentleman paid for his tuition to mortician's school. Later, when he finally retired, he arranged for a bank loan to allow Mansukh to acquire the business. Financially, it was not a great business or even a very good business. But it paid his bills, and allowed him time to pray and to donate money to support his mosque. The clients were all black like him, but they were Baptists or Church of God, or from the storefront churches that seemed to Mansukh, to be almost as numerous as bars in the poor neighborhood in which he operated. His client's families came to him because he was cheap. It was a choice of $750 for cremation versus $4,000 for a burial. The Michigan code for cremations required him to do no more than a little paperwork, registering the death certificate, etc. prior to "cooking," as he privately referred to his work.

Occasionally, a cash rich drug dealer from the neighborhood would be involved with a killing. In such cases a body would be delivered to the rear entrance of Mansukh's business before the police found out about the death. The killer could insure the body would never be found by purchasing a quick and secretive cooking. Mansukh did this for whatever he could get, but never less than $5,000, as he was jeopardizing his license and could suffer criminal penalties. He was, of course, sure the killer would not tell the police. If, somebody else suspected an unauthorized cremation and complained to the authorities, the evidence was already destroyed. Thus it was no great surprise to him, when two men from his mosque approached him with an unusual request.

He didn't really know the two except that they were Arabs from one of the countries north of the Sahara. They told him only their first names, Dawit and Jerod. They came to him (after a prayer service, in fact) with a proposition. Over the next two weeks, they would like to rent his old ambulance for four trips to neighboring states. They would return with four bodies of young men who died of drug overdoses. As they did not want the authorities to know of these deaths, they would like the bodies disposed of immediately after they delivered them. For this they would pay $25,000. They would also return the ambulance with a full tank of gas.

Mansukh did not question how they knew there would be four young men in two weeks, or how they knew they would all OD. He did not want to know. He only wanted the $25,000. He agreed.

The two men were part of an *al Qaeda* cell in Detroit. They had recently returned from Afghanistan where they had been enrolled in the bin Laden school for terrorists. They spoke excellent English. With haircuts, polished shoes and good clothing, they could easily pass for middle class Americans. They reasoned that it would not take too much effort to fool a teen-age boy. They tried their first test in a rural area near Frankfort, Michigan, some distance from Detroit

They planned as follows: They would wait until dusk. Then they would drive their four- door Pontiac sedan until they spotted a boy who seemed to be the right age, hitchhiking or merely walking beside the road. They would pull over and offer the boy a lift home. In the countryside, in the cold winters of the northern states, people frequently offered rides to strangers. Kidnappings rarely occurred; the boys could be counted on to be unafraid. On the way to the boy's home, a conversation would be established and the boy would be asked if he had his social security card with him. They practiced several opening gambits.

"Well you're lucky we came along. A young boy your age,--- how old are you anyway--- shouldn't be out here alone on a bitter cold night like this. Suppose something happened to you, like a car sideswiping you and then not stopping. You could freeze to death. Do you have any identification on you, like a Social Security card? I always tell my boys never to go out of the house without some form of ID in their pocket."

If the response to the Social Security card question was negative, the boy would be politely driven to his home and dropped off. If, on the other hand, the answer were positive, the man in the passenger seat would hold the boy at gunpoint. The driver would activate the electric door locks. This was an automotive option that was designed for their purpose, preventing children from getting out of the car.

The Pontiac would then be driven to the ambulance that was parked in a remote location. There the boy would be killed by asphyxiation. The body would be loaded on the ambulance, wrapped in blankets and made to look, in every way, like the paying customer he was. The payment was the cash the boy was carrying, in whatever amount, and the social security card. The wallet and the balance of its contents would be destroyed with the body.

The plan was a good one. Over the course of two weeks, they acquired Robert Ziegler in Michigan, Terry McCarthy in Ohio, Peter Nichols in Illinois and Carl Kinsey in Wisconsin. In that period, in which they drove more boys home than they ever imagined they would, they had collected their four Social

Security cards as well. They only had two difficult cases.

The first tough one was Carl Kinsey. He was a scrapper. He had seen enough TV shows to get some ideas. In the darkness of the backseat, he worked a ballpoint pen from his pocket. He waited until the car went around a curve. When Dawit (holding his gun) was thrown off-balance, he jammed the pen into Dawit's hand. As Dawit screamed and cursed in Arabic, Kinsey tried to climb into the front seat by grabbing Dawit's ear and pulling himself over the seat back. In the end, Jerod had to pull the car over to the shoulder of the road and hit Kinsey with the Karate chops he had learned in Afghanistan. When they got back to Detroit, Dawit had to get a penicillin shot for his hand. He had a very sore ear for days.

The second problem was a boy in Illinois who became very suspicious immediately after he got into the car. He wouldn't talk to them. He just said "take me home or let me out of the car." They took him home. After they dropped him off, they saw him walk around to the rear of the car and read their license plate as they drove off. The boy memorized the license plate number and told his father, who called the police. The police ran a check with the Michigan police who found that the Pontiac was registered to a Jerod Jazeer, an Arab gentleman with no arrest record. Not even a traffic violation. The Illinois State police filed the incident and ascribed it to the imagination of a teenage boy. Dawit and Jerod, assuming that the boy would contact the police, decided to move on to Wisconsin for their next abduction.

The bodies were all driven to Detroit and, under the cover of darkness, unloaded and "cooked." Mansukh was paid as agreed: $25,000 and a full gas tank.

After they got back to Michigan, the two men took the Social Security cards and made Xerox copies. These they enclosed with letters to the State's records offices, with a request for a copy of the birth certificate. The return address was a postal box in a rural post office selected because it could be accessed at night and because it could be observed for suspicious activity by driving past in a car.

They visited the postbox a month after the requests were filed, but only three states had sent copies of the certificates. From the fourth state, Ohio, was a letter stating they had no record of a Terry McCarthy being born in the year specified. The men debated among themselves, whether it was better to acquire another victim or write to the United States Social Security headquarters in Washington, and request the state of birth of the owner of SS # 056-71-9918. In the end, not knowing what kind of activity they would generate as a result of such an inquiry, they determined that it was safer to simply seek a new boy.

The men returned to Detroit and offered Mansukh another $5,000 for the use of his Ambulance. Then they drove to a remote farming district near Erie, Pennsylvania where they acquired a Social Security card from George Wilkinson. They were careful to ascertain that Wilkinson was born in Pennsylvania, while he was still able to talk.

After they received a copy of Wilkinson's birth certificate from the Pennsylvania Department of Records, they bought a small piece of carry-on luggage with a lid that was constructed in layers. They slit the seam on the edge of the luggage lid and inserted the Social Security cards and the copies of the birth certificates. They had the bag re-sewn by a friend from Pakistan who owned a shoe repair shop. The man named Dawit hand delivered the bag to London, England where there were several active cells of *al Qaeda.*

The five boys were the subjects of extensive searches by the police of each state. After the customary three-day effort, the police concluded that each was just another "runaway."

The missing boys were mourned by their families. Their hopes of seeing their boys again were buoyed by the statistic that 95% of missing teen-age boys return to their homes within the first year. The fact that these boys were part of the 5% who would not return home, would not be apparent for months. Their names were maintained in the data-base of missing children.

Chapter 40
Fort Meade Maryland: Friday, November 8, 1996
◈

Danielle had a dilemma. She could not relate the full story of her ruse to get into Afghanistan without, at the most, censure; at the least, criticism. Nor did she wish to gain the reputation as someone without judgment, a "loose cannon." She had no training as a spy. That was not her job. She was simply an analyst. As such, she had no business tackling field-work without the approval of the Agency.

Additionally, she possessed secret information. Not enough or of the sort to topple a government, but enough to give the Department of State and the National Security Agency a good case of heartburn. Danielle wrestled with these problems for several hours on the Air France flight to Washington before making a decision.

She decided not to relate how she exchanged identities with her sister Monique. She would crib. She would simply say that she entered Afghanistan with a passport under her maiden name, Lamaze. She would tell the truth, just not the whole truth. This was the first time in her professional career that she had been forced to make such a decision. Initially her strong sense of ethics was repulsed by the plan. Finally, she could think of no other way. When she got back to her office she wrote the following memorandum:

Memorandum
National Security Agency
Classification: Secret
To: File 96-274-A
CC: Sanford Parcell, NSA, Jurgen Heidemann, CIA
Fr: Danielle Lamaze-Smith
Re: Trip to Afghanistan
Dt: 8 November 96

*During the last two weeks I took my annual vacation to
Paris, France to visit family. While I was there, I determined
to visit Afghanistan. I still possess a valid Algerian passport in
my maiden name, Lamaze.*

*Posing as a reporter for a French magazine was quite
simple. It is amazing how people, even in closed societies such
as Afghanistan, are willing to meet and talk with foreign
journalists. Using this ruse I was able to meet with Afghanistan's Supervisor of the Department of Education, Seyyed
Rashid. This is the individual who is in charge of the Madrass
system. I sat with him for more than two hours in his office
outside of Kabul. He was very forthcoming and I obtained a
great deal of information. At the end of the interview, I asked
him if he could set up a meeting with Yousef Zubeida (whom
we suspect of establishing special Madrasses for al Qaeda
personnel.) To my surprise and delight, he did so.*

*I met with Mr. Zubeida at his camp in the desert, some
dozen hours by truck and horse from Kabul. I found Mr.
Zubeida to be as cordial as Mr. Rashid, but not as informa-
tive.*

*During my interview with Zubeida, we were interrupted
by Osama bin Laden, who entered the room for a brief
exchange with Zubeida. Although I understood all that was
said, (they spoke in Arabic) nothing of consequence was
revealed.*

*The principal conclusion from these meetings is that our
theory of Zubeida being charged with establishing a special
Madrass is confirmed. I did not learn how many children are
involved, nor where the Madrass is located. Zubeida tried to
convince me that its purpose was to provide future leaders for
Afghanistan, but I don't find that plausible. I do not believe
Mr. bin Laden's interest is solely confined to the future of
Afghanistan. If I had to make a guess, I would predict that
the special Madrass is in the business of turning children into
terrorists. The fact that we know some of these children are*

blond and have American mothers is not reassuring. One can easily extrapolate these facts into a situation where the children are returned to America, in five or ten years, with a carefully planned mission of destruction.

We need to stay on top of this. It has the potential to be disastrous.

Attached are detailed reports on each of the meetings.

Chapter 41
Afghanistan: Thursday, February 13, 1997
◈

The completion of the school and associated living buildings was subject to the universal law of construction. It took longer and cost more than originally estimated. Amed al Jarrah had scheduled 40 men for four months to build the camp. It took 53 men five months. Admittedly, not all the delay was due to their failure to stay on schedule. Much time was wasted in waiting for materials to be delivered to Afghanistan. In the end, Zubeida's dream of building a typical American school and housing could not be accomplished. Neither the materials nor the skills were available. However, what was achieved was remarkable.

The building materials were principally Russian. After the collapse of the Soviet Union, a major segment of the industrial production segment suddenly found itself with nothing to do. All of the manufacturing organizations producing goods for the military and the government were deprived of their customer base. The cold war was over. There was no need for additional tanks or weapon systems. Almost overnight, vast manufacturing complexes laid off their workers and closed their doors.

The Government of the Unites States, specifically, the Defense Nuclear Agency (DNA) tried to help Russian industry in their crisis. Working with *Gosstroi*, the Russian Construction Ministry, they offered a grant of $20 million in a program called "Russian Defense Industry Transformation into Building Systems." This was given to the company with the most innovative approach to conversion. The winner was *Soyuzstroyenia*, the prime contractor for the SS 18 intercontinental ballistic missile. With the utter failure of the Soviet system, there was clearly no need for such giant rockets with their 6,000 nautical mile range. The directors of *Soyuzstroyenia* accepted the grant and started into civilian production. The deplorable condition of the Russian housing market led them into the manufacture of doors, window units and wall panels. With 95% of Russian citizenry living in substandard housing, there was a far greater market for such items than for rocket motors.

An engineer at *Soyuzstroyenia* was only too pleased to be working on a project to improve Afghanistan. Just a few years earlier he had been in the Soviet army and, against his will, helped to destroy the country. Now he would be able to help restore it. He designed a set of interior pre-finished birch panels scaled to be inserted in the mud houses that would become the school. He brought a high tech approach to a low tech business, woodworking. He was also figuratively fulfilling the predictions of the prophet *Isaiah*. "They shall beat their swords into plowshares and their spears into pruning knives."

As the parties to the transaction were former communists and Muslims, they saw no irony in producing wall panels where formerly rockets were manufactured. The Russians were happy for the sale, the Arabs for the product. Of *Isaiah*, they knew nothing and cared less.

All of the interiors were finished in the same light blond wood, giving the effect of being more Scandinavian modern than traditional American. The finished materials were shipped from Moscow via rail to Tashkent, then routed south to Samarkand where they were loaded onto trucks for Kabul and the Hindu Kush. Horse carts made the final leg of the trip. Even with special handling and the bribing of Russian transportation officials, it was a 60-day trip from factory to camp.

Running electricity and plumbing and finishing off the interiors of rough buildings that were never intended for such improvements was a challenge. A water line was laid to a nearby stream. Bathrooms were installed with the wastewater being piped to a large septic field. The rooms were wired with enough outlets to pass the BOCA (Building Officials Code Authority) code. When Zubeida saw the completed product he declared it a masterwork.

A new mud brick building was built to house the school

classroom. The building that was originally intended to be the classroom was converted into a kitchen and dining room. One of the houses was converted into a family room with couches, television, stereo, computers, bookcases, and even such kitsch as might be found in an average American home. This included a souvenir replica of the statue of liberty, found in an antique shop in Kabul (how or why it came to be there was anybody's guess!)

The kitchen would have pleased any American housewife. Appliances from Germany, England and Japan were the only ones available in Saudi Arabia, but they were close to what would be found in a home in the United States.

Nami Omari, the cook, was delighted. He was been given an authorization card to shop in the central commissary in Riyadh. He loaded two large trucks with his purchases. From corn flakes to Colgate toothpaste, from popcorn to parsley flakes, from hamburger buns to Hamburger Helper; frozen French fries, ice cream, spaghetti, peanut butter, bacon, chili con carne, roast beef, he bought it all. The four boys and their teachers would be treated to sit-down meals that would be the envy of most American families.

When the camp was finished, Zubeida, a student of history announced: "In 1928, when the American explorer, Admiral Richard E. Byrd, established the first permanent camp in the Antarctic he named it 'Little America.' So too, shall we call our camp in the Hindu Kush."

Kahlid Moqued, the American born and raised Pakistani, saw to it that his charges were suitably attired. For the winter there were Timberland boots, corduroy pants, heavy L.L. Bean shirts and sweaters. In summer, there would be chinos or jeans with polos or tees. These were almost uniforms in most American schools. Moqued was so in the spirit that he was anticipating the future when he would purchase button down shirts, sport jackets and neckties.

Moqued took out subscriptions to numerous magazines, from *Popular Science* to *Sports Illustrated*. They would arrive several months late, but that was not a problem. Time is not important in the Hindu Kush. He was careful to include several magazines on hot rods and motor sports. He was aware that a majority of American males were devoted followers of things mechanical. Although these things had not interested him as a youth, there was one motor driven vehicle that had always intrigued him.

Kahlid had not been the product of a wealthy family. As the rest of his friends in Newark were of the same financial circumstances, he never felt disenfranchised. Still, there were many things he would like to have had. Although there was no "dirt" open space within 25 miles of Newark, at the age of 13 he became enamored of "dirt bikes." This was prompted by a television production on dirt bike racing that showed a dozen boys his age flying through the air in a junior motocross race. Now, at the age of 25, he ordered a dirt bike. It was ostensibly for the boys; he even told Zubeida that most kids in the U.S. had one by the age of 13. It was the only example where Moqued permitted his personal desires to take precedence over what was necessary for the boys.

Game Boys, *Coca Cola* by the case, *Walkmen*, bubble gum, baseball caps, white socks, pocket knives, musical instruments, video cameras, boy scout manuals, sneakers, swim suits, camping gear, Bermuda shorts, .22 rifles, videos of *Britney Spears*, *Smash Mouth*, and the *Backstreet Boys*, *Dallas Cowboys* jackets and *Hershey* bars, were just some of over 500 items on his list as being part of the American boyhood experience. He constructed a basketball court with hard packed clay. He measured out a soccer field on the flat plain where formerly poppies had been cultivated. Here the boys and their instructors would play against the camp guards. He would do his part to insure that the boys were exposed to all things a typical American youth would have experienced during his formative years. The boys were already American-born. There must be nothing that could ever trip them up as not being American-raised!

Zubeida, in charge of the school's lesson plan, was equally thorough. He studied the curricula of various public and private schools in the United States and developed a program for the entire seven years. The boys would start their day at 7:00 a.m. with an American breakfast. At 7:30 classes would begin, with one hour of Islamic studies. At 8:30, two hours of English would be followed by an hour of American history. There would be an hour's break for lunch. In the afternoon there were mathematics, social studies, world history, special subjects and sports. His carefully-developed lesson plans contained 'disinformation' detrimental to American thought and ideals. He inserted this to instill an understanding and belief that America and Israel were the instigators of all of the problems of the Middle East, that they pillaged the poorer nations of the world.

There also had to be individualized instruction for each of the boys regarding their home state. They had to know about their state's college and professional teams, American boys loved to follow sports. Zubeida assigned this responsibility to Moqued.

After dinner there would be no homework. Instead, the boys would spend every night in front of a television watching American movies. Moqued acquired the entire inventory of a Chicago video store owned by a Pakistani (this man was willing to sell his business to another Paki who walked in one day and made him a cash offer he couldn't refuse.)

After the first six months a strict rule would be imposed. No Arabic speech would be permitted in the camp. The boys would be required to speak English at all times. In the fourth, fifth and sixth years, French studies would be introduced. If the boys were going to enter Canada with French passports, they had to have some proficiency with the language and culture.

Beginning in the second year there would be instruction in the martial arts. This would begin with rifles and move to explosives as the boys reached maturity. Personal defense would be an ongoing part of physical education.

Finally, as America was a Christian nation, in the last year

Youseff Zubeida wanted the boys to become familiar with Christianity. Of course, he knew he had to strike a delicate balance: There had to be just enough instruction so the boys would be generally knowledgeable about the subject, just not so much so that *"Love thy neighbor as thyself"* began to sound like it made sense!

Chapter 42
Afghanistan: Friday, February 14, 1997
◈

The night before they left for Little America, Zubeida assigned the American names to the boys.

Edmund Lazar, at 14 years the oldest, became *Peter Nichols*, also 14 years old. Peter was not only the elder of the group, but he also had spent the most time growing up in the America, having come to Afghanistan at the age of 12. Zubeida had anticipated trouble indoctrinating him with sufficient anti-American fervor, but was pleasantly surprised in this regard. Nichols had already spent two years in the camp as a servant. During this time he had not attended school. Instead he had been listening to his father and the other men talking about *jihads.* He was already a convert.

Ali Sharqui assumed the identity of the boy from Michigan, *Robert Ziegler*, as they were both eleven years old. Ziegler, having a firebrand for a father, was the most ideologically correct of the boys. He was ready to become a suicide bomber at any time. He was also a quick study. Mullah Suquami was very impressed with Ziegler's knowledge of the *Qu'ran*, and his fervor for Islam.

The other Saudi, Muhammud Maulana, became *Carl Kinsey* from Wisconsin. Kinsey was 14 years old and Maulana was only 12. However, Maulana was big for his age and had the most Nordic features of all the boys. He was also the slowest of the boys. Not dumb, just not from an intellectual family. Zubeida was positive that he would be believable as a big stolid farm boy from Wisconsin.

The last of the boys, Anwar Belhadj, was assigned the identity of the Pennsylvanian, *George Wilkinson*. Zubeida considered Wilkinson the best of the lot. He was smarter than Ziegler and almost as proficient in English as Nichols, thanks to the tutoring by his Father and his access to television. In spite of the calamitous loss of his sole parent, he was sprightly and upbeat. He was also convinced that the Jews were responsible for his Father's death. Mullah Suquami had been preaching against Israel and America as part of his Islamic studies during the past five months. The period of waiting for the finish of construction of Little America had been time well spent. The boys had acquired iron discipline. Eight hours a day spent studying the *Qu'ran* with Mullah Suquami will do that.

The boys were excited, as only teen-age boys can be. At last they were on their way to their new, long-promised school. They were loaded onto the back of a pickup truck in which camel skin cushions had been placed on the floor as a modest protection against the jarring. Mulla Suquami sat in the front with the driver. Zubeida and the other instructors were already at the school. The boys were all wearing *dishadashas* and *pakols*. Although they didn't know it, it would be the last time in their lives they would be clad in the garments of the Middle East. Zubeida had not told them anything about their new school, or of bin Laden's plans for them. That would come later when they had and settled in.

The trucks jounced along for almost three hours and stopped at a grassy knoll on which were constructed two modest mud houses and a barn. There were two horse carts waiting for them, horses between the shafts. The boys, now joined by Suquami, climbed into the carts. They were off.

Four hours later they arrived at Little America, their home for the next six years. The cart stopped in the middle of a cluster of seven buildings. It didn't look like a typical Afghan village. There were real windows with glass and real paneled doors. There was a uncharacteristic neatness about the place. Two of the buildings were larger than the rest. Khalid Moqued stood in front of one of them, a beaming smile on his face. He waved to them to come in.

George (Anwar) was the only one of the four who was accustomed to decent living. His house in Sidi bel Abbes was the home of an executive; small, but modern and equipped with a contemporary kitchen. To the other boys it was like walking into a fairyland. They had never been in such a place: The kitchen had gleaming appliances of stainless steel and white enamel. The dining room had two tables of four, already set for dinner. All the floors were polished.

Next, Moqued took them to their "family room" with easy chairs, electronic video games, TV and computer. They were astounded. Then they went across the street to the building where their bedrooms were located. The house, originally one large room, had been divided in half, creating two bedrooms, each with two beds. There were closets and a chest of drawers for each boy, already stocked with clothes in the right size. George (Anwar) and Robert (Ali) were roommates in one room, Carl (Mahammud) and Peter (Edmund) in the other.

Moqued told them it was necessary that they change into their western garb. He also told them to shower before changing. This brought up unanticipated problems. He had to give instructions on personal hygiene, shoe tying and bed making, and he had to set standards of cleanliness and neatness. These first organizational requirements took several hours. At the end of this, it was time for dinner.

Four very American-looking boys trooped back across the street, into the dining room, and sat down. Again, Moqued encountered unexpected issues. With the exception of George, their table manners were terrible. Moqued had to explain how they should behave in a dining room: how to eat with knives and forks so as not look like troglodytes; how they should not put their elbows on the table; why they should not interrupt when someone else was speaking; the use of the word "please," and other niceties of American family life. In respect to the teaching of manners, the dining room at Little America was no different from dining rooms in the United States where some of the occupants are teen-age boys.

The first dinner was fried chicken, mashed potatoes with gravy, string beans and chocolate ice cream sundaes for desert.

The boys loved it.

After dinner Youseff Zubeida gathered everyone in the family room and told them about their mission:

"At last we are together here in our new home. We will be here for at least the next five or six years. How long depends on how quickly you absorb the education I have planned for you.

"When we first met, nearly six months ago, I said that the four of you were chosen by Allah to carry out a secret mission. Now I can tell you what that mission is.

"The Americans have already declared war on Islam. They are bombing in our cities. They are killing our people. You will take the battle to their soil. You will be trained to speak English as well as an American. You will learn all about America, its history, its athletic teams, its government, its movie stars, etc. Then you will be sent to America where you will get jobs. You will appear to the other Americans to be one of them. You will mix with them, become friendly with them. All of this will be done in preparation for the final phase of your mission. At this time, that phase is unknown. It may be that you will be asked to send back information, to be a spy. It may be that you will be asked to blow things up, destroy bridges or power plants."

Zubeida did not think it wise, at this early stage, to talk of killing anyone. The boys would have to be brought along in their education of hate before there could be any discussion of death. Not until the end would assassination be mentioned.

"Your teachers here have been carefully selected because of their knowledge of America. Tonight you ate a typical American meal. You are all dressed as typical American school boys. This is all part of the training. It would not do if you spoke perfect English and then ate only lamb and rice. You will become accustomed to American cooking, the most varied in the world. You are wearing American clothes because we want you to learn to wear them as second nature. We want you to forget about *dishadashas*, you will not wear them until after you return home again."

Young boys are adaptable. They are also eager for adventure, always ready to try something new. Zubeida could see excitement in their faces. He tried to build on it. "You are the luckiest young men in the world of Islam. The princes of the royal family in Saudi Arabia are not so fortunate. In fact, here you will be treated better than the princes. There is one important difference between you and them, however: you will have to work for your privileged existence; they inherited theirs. You will have to study very hard to learn everything your teachers know. We are going to have the same study hours as you have had under Mullah Suquami, but there will be a much wider variety of subjects. You will work hard, but you will have a good time. I promise you that."

"And now Kahlid Moqued here, will teach us how to turn on the television and listen to Al Jazeera. In six months this will be the only Arabic language you will be allowed, the seven o' clock news from al Jazeera." Zubeida was sure that this and the Saudi network would be helpful in his indoctrination efforts. He made a mental note to limit the TV from America to sitcoms, sports and movies. He had heard the Americans complained about their network's coverage of news as being biased. However, he knew that al Jazeera was probably the most slanted news since Pravda under the communists. He counted on it remaining so.

Chapter 43
Langley, Virginia: Friday, January 31, 1997
◈

Danielle had never thought of herself as "eye candy." Attractive; yes: medium height, dark red hair, blue eyes and nicely shaped; but eye candy, no. Not in the classic sense of other French beauties such as Bridget Bardot or Yvette Mimieux. Nonetheless, Danielle always found herself the center of attraction in the company of men. She knew this was the case and always worked hard to appear her best in public even though Washington, unlike Paris and New York, did not place a great emphasis on dress. Most women, even female executives, shopped in chain stores and dressed in a nondescript manner. Being well-dressed was just not part of the Washington culture. Danielle was the only one she knew at NSA who made an effort to appear stylish. She kept up with the latest fashions. As a result, her attractiveness to men was enhanced. They were always buzzing around her. As a result of her long experience having men make a fuss about her, she was not surprised when she was invited to meet with the Director of the National Security Agency. But the Director had other things on his mind than just "hitting on her".

"Dr. Lamaze-Smith, I have read with very great interest your memorandum to the file regarding your trip to Afghanistan. I found your ingenuity impressive; your bravery exemplary; your devotion to your country and your duty noteworthy. I have the distinct honor and great pleasure to present you with this certificate of commendation. I am also pleased to announce your grade increase to a GS 13, effective immediately. You are exactly the kind of employee we need more of here at NSA if we are going to continue to fulfill our mission of protecting our nation."

A photographer was brought in to record her receiving the distinguished service award and shaking hands with the Director. Fifteen minutes later she was back at her cubicle, head whirring, wishing that she had worn her black suit instead of the knee length, dark green knock-off of the latest Yves St. Laurent design.

It was to get better.

Less than two weeks later she got a telephone call from Jurgen Heidemann at the CIA. "Could you be available to have luncheon with Mark van Rensselier, a special Assistant to the Director, in the Director's private dining room on Friday the 14th at 12:15 PM? Yes? Wonderful! I'm sure that Mark will be very pleased to hear of your availability. And one more thing, Ms. Lamaze-Smith. This is an invitation for you alone. It will not be necessary to bring Mr. Parcell with you."

Thus it was that on Saint Valentine's Day, 1996, a black Mercury bearing the seal of the Central Intelligence Agency on the front doors, picked her up at Fort Meade. The Director's personal car and driver had come to collect her.

The car whisked her up the long drive to the CIA headquarters building, went into the underground parking garage, and dropped her off at the DCI's private elevator. This time there was no producing passes or scrutiny by overzealous guards. She was an expected guest.

The elevator went up to the 7th floor and the doors opened. Danielle found herself in an executive suite with a very classy African American woman sitting at a highly polished mahogany desk "If you will please have a seat, Ms. Lamaze-Smith, I'll let Mr. van Rensselier know you are here." Danielle tried to appear nonchalant as she said "thank you" and lowered herself into a red leather chair. A previous occupant of the office, a wealthy investment banker several Presidents earlier, had decorated the DCI's reception area at his own expense. It was very tastefully done.

Ever since Richard Helms had been the Director of Central Intelligence during the Kennedy and Johnson years, an artificially high standard of style had been set. Helms wore expensively tailored suits and was always immaculately groomed. He had just looked the part of the nation's top spy-master! Subsequent DCI's tried, mostly without success, to emulate him; Helms' natural smoothness was not duplicable. The current boss didn't come close, so Danielle was surprised with what happened next.

A tall distinguished looking man appeared in the office doorway. His long hair was neatly trimmed, his blue pin stripe suit was perfectly tailored, his silk necktie formed in a perfect knot. A white handkerchief flourished in his jacket pocket. He strode up to her, his hand outstretched to both shake hers and to help her up from the chair. Danielle was immediately impressed. "Dr. Lamaze-Smith, I am Mark van Rensselier, a Special Assistant to the Director. My friends call me Mark. I hope you will too. I thank you for taking the time to come to visit us."

"In that case, Mark, I hope you will call me Danielle. I am very pleased to visit you for luncheon. I understand the DCI has the best chef in the government."

"Yes, the Secretary of State is always trying to lure him away, but we have been able to hold onto him, mostly with the aid of salary increases. Soon, I fear, he will be earning more than I do!" Van Rensselier chuckled at his own humor.

He offered her his arm and guided her down a short hall thickly carpeted in a rich gold. He opened the door to a dining room with windows looking out on a lawn trimmed to golf course perfection. There were three tables that could be joined together if desired. Two of them were pushed back to the wall. One of them, beside the window, was set with two places. She and the DCI's Special Assistant were apparently lunching alone. He helped her to a chair and took his own seat opposite. Her mind flashed back to her meal with Zubeida in Afghanistan, and then returned to the present. What a contrast!

"Danielle, I believe we're having poached salmon today. That is the one problem of having your own chef. The DCI gets a list of suggested meals at the beginning of the week, and approves the ones he wants. Then he frequently spends the rest of the week complaining about the consequences. There is no changing of minds and substituting, say, Chinese food, at the last minute. However, it is a cross I would gladly bear."

"Now, as you probably know, there is an old Federal regulation that prohibits the consumption of alcohol in government buildings. Fortunately, it is a regulation that is universally observed in the breech. In recognition of your French ancestry, I have ordered a *Pouilly-Fuisse*. May I pour you a glass?"

He started to reach for a bottle from a silver ice bucket, where it had been cooling, just as a white-jacketed waiter entered the room. "Ahhhh, George caught me doing his job and is afraid I am going to want to split the tip. Danielle, this is George Wilkins, who has been here serving every DCI since the Kennedy administration. He should be retired, but he is too good. Besides, he knows too many secrets." As he said this, van Rensselier smiled warmly at George, a handsome man the color of *café au lait*. Danielle found herself liking the man even more, a man who could banter with service employees with obvious regard. She had observed too many men in public life at much lower levels who took themselves too seriously and others too much for granted.

Over the meal, beginning with an excellent *vichyssoise*, Mark casually pumped Danielle about her background. He did this in a conversational manner so that Danielle found herself recounting a great deal of information about herself without realizing that she was doing so. He was a master inquisitor. He also asked about her husband. Danielle had noticed over the years that men were always more interested in her spouse than she was in their wives. A psychologist once told her this was just part of the dominant male syndrome; that men were interested in finding out about the mates of women they were attracted to.

"What does your husband do?"

"He is a composer and musician."

"Tell me about him."

"Well, he's an American. We met at a Paris recital where

he was performing his student composition, *Three Sonatas for Violin.* Of course, he was playing, too. I was in the audience. We fell in love, got married, and soon he got the itch to come home to America and I was interested in some new, challenging experiences, so we moved to D.C. He taught at American University, but he got bored with the same curriculum planned for each year and the political maneuvering among the faculty at the university, so we moved to Bowie where he has a studio in our home, he teaches a few favored students, he performs and he conducts occasionally. It's perfect for us. And because we aren't functioning in the same environments, we can still be interesting to each other without overlapping. It's perfect.

"How does he feel about your job, and your working?"

"Well, he is very supportive of me. I am glad I had the good sense to marry an American. A European man would not be so understanding."

"Do you have children?"

"No, we don't. I am afraid I am caught in that classic trap of choosing between a career and family. Obviously, I chose the career. My job has been so exciting and satisfying to me that at this point I couldn't even think of doing anything else."

Van Rensselier paused. His body language suggested that he wanted to make a comment, but he remained silent. After a moment he turned the conversation back to less personal matters. When they got to desert, a delicious hazel nut *torte* and coffee, he finally began to speak what was on his mind.

"Danielle, I cannot tell you how impressed the DCI and I are with your actions these past few months regarding the *madrasses* and Osama bin Laden. We have read your memo on your trip to Afghanistan as well as your previous memos internal to NSA." At mention of the National Security Agency, Danielle raised her eyebrows. "It's OK, we have the appropriate legal access to all of your written work. I have found your insight and intuition nothing short of brilliant." He paused to sip his coffee. "Finally, your trip to Afghanistan and your posture as a French journalist were inspired. You collected data and developed a hypothesis. You then proceeded to validate your theory with a process of discovery in the field. You took your own vacation time and spent your own money. You did it all. I wish our own people were half so good."

"Thank you, sir. I just did what I thought was necessary to solve a problem that nagged at me, nothing more. But I do greatly appreciate your kind comments."

"Danielle, I know better. There are not twenty people in this Agency who would have behaved as you did. They would have formed committees, held meetings, written memos, gotten the opinions of others. They would have stretched the process out over four months before recommending a course of action. Then they would have found six reasons why their conclusions might not be correct. They would do this to cover their derriere in the event they were wrong. Watching you work was like watching Michelangelo execute a work for the Medici. You knew what you were going to do and you did it, knowing that the outcome would be its own justification."

Danielle appreciated men who invoked the classics in their conversation. She knew that Mark's comparison of her with Michelangelo was hyperbolae to the extreme, but she found it gratifying nonetheless. She was about to utter a protest when the he finished his thought.

"Danielle, the Director has charged me to completely rejuvenate the CIA. In recent years it has not, as you probably know, been performing up to the requirements of its mission. To make the necessary improvements, we are going to need good people, people like you. I would like you to transfer from NSA to the CIA. You have already made one change in your career with the government, from State to NSA. Make another. Come join us."

Danielle was taken aback. She had not expected such a development and had no immediate response. She needed to collect her thoughts.

Just as nature abhors a vacuum, prospective employers cannot tolerate a lull in conversation when they are soliciting a superstar they really want. Van Rensselier jumped back into the void. "You are qualified for a position in either the Directorate of Operations or the Directorate of Intelligence, I would be pleased to have you in either. We'll send you to Camp Peary, which we call 'the farm', our training school in Southern Virginia, for a year of education. And one more thing, I believe we could jump you up a couple of grades by giving you some management authority."

Danielle put on her most serious face. "Sir, I mean Mark, I am very flattered. I would like nothing better than to work for the CIA, but at sometime in the future. I'm not yet ready to leave NSA for two reasons: First and most important, I am still learning. I have been there less than two years and am not finished with my technical and systems education. Second, I am in the middle of an exercise that is important to me. I want to run the bin Laden matter to ground. I want to find out more about the *madrasses,* and if I went to your school for a year, I might miss out on something important, a situation where I could add something of value. For these two reasons I must decline your flattering offer. I say again that someday in the future, if the offer is still open, I would like very much to work for the CIA. And, of course, at that time I will be of greater value because I will have more experience. I am only 31 years old, and perhaps not ready for a management position."

Mark van Rensselier put a scowl of disappointment on his face. "Danielle, I reluctantly accept your reasoning. But, and I am going to hold you to this, at some point in the future, I am going to come looking for you and then, I won't take no for an answer."

On the way back to Fort Meade, riding in the soft leather backseat of the Director's car, Danielle found herself wondering if she had done the right thing. There had been no intercepts that mentioned anything about boys or *madrasses* for several months.

Muhammad Atef had not talked on his satellite phone. To add to the mystery, nothing had been heard from or about Abassi Touati. He seemed to have vanished from the face of the earth.

Nothing was happening.

Chapter 44
Fort Meade Maryland: Monday, February 18, 1997
◈

Four days following her luncheon with van Rensselier (President's Day on the 17th had delayed her), Danielle went to Sanford Parcell with a request.

"Sandy, I want to take the next week or ten days to work on a special project. I believe that we are in for a very difficult future with al *Qaeda* and other terrorist organizations. I don't believe our government is taking their threat seriously enough. I want to take some time to do research and write a paper with my conclusions. Jack Carson can easily pick up any of my urgent work and, if necessary, I'll be available. I just need some uninterrupted time to concentrate. I will have a report with my findings in ten days, maybe less."

As she knew he would, Parcell agreed to her request. Nine days later, Danielle completed her work. It was her *magnum opus* to date...

Memorandum
National Security Agency
Classification: None
To: Bradley Fisher, Director, National Security Agency
CC: File 97-1-T
Fr: Danielle Lamaze-Smith
Re: The Gathering Danger of Islamic Terrorist Organizations
Dt: 27 February 97
Executive Summary:
        The attached report explores the clear and growing
danger of Islamic extremism.
        As one who grew up in Algeria, a country wracked by
terrorism, I am acutely aware of the growth of Islamic
fundamentalism. It is an insidious cancer spreading through-
out the Middle East. I do not believe our government is paying

sufficient attention to this new and extremely dangerous threat.

The Department of State publishes an annual listing of significant terrorist incidents. This is well known. However, their work is a global log of all terrorist activities. It includes acts perpetrated by other terrorist organizations such as the Irish Republican Army. The following report is compiled from several data-bases. It focuses only upon terrorist acts committed by extremist Muslims, or acts that are in some way connected to Islamic ambitions. The results are startling.

Following is a compendium of Islamic terror for 1996. I have included it in the executive summary as an illustration. It shows the geographic extent and the organizational diversity of the terrorist's work:

Chronology of Terrorist Incidents with Direct Relationship to Islam during the year1996

1 January, Iraq
Three individuals attempted to leave a vehicle containing explosives near UN offices in Irbil.

8 January, Indonesia
Two hundred Free Papua Movement (OPM) guerrillas abducted 26 individuals in the Lorenta nature preserve, Irian Jaya Province.

16 January, Turkey
Seven Turkish nationals of Chechen origin hijacked a Russia-bound Panamanian ferry in Trabzon.

18 January, Ethiopia
A bomb exploded at the Ghion Hotel in Addis Ababa, killing at least four persons and injuring 20 others. The injured included citizens from the United Kingdom, Mali, India, and France. In March, al-Ittihaad al-Islami (The Islamic Union), an ethnic Somali group, claimed responsibility for the bombing.

26 January, Yemen

Al-Aslam tribesmen kidnapped 17 elderly French tourists in the Ma'rib Governate to pressure authorities into releasing one of their tribesmen.

11 February, Bahrain

A bomb exploded at the Diplomat Hotel in Manama, injuring a British guest and two employees and causing significant damage to the hotel. The London-based Islamic Front for the Liberation of Bahrain claimed the bombing, but later denied responsibility.

20 February, Turkey

Two members of Mujahedin-e Khalq (MEK), an Iranian dissident group, were found dead in their Istanbul apartment. In April 1996 authorities apprehended three Islamic militants and several Iranian and Turkish nationals in connection with the killing. The militants later claimed they had received their orders from Iranian diplomats stationed in Turkey.

25 February, Jerusalem

A suicide bomber blew up a bus, killing 26 persons, including three US citizens, and injuring some 80 persons, including three other U.S. citizens. HAMAS's Izz al-Din al-Qassem Brigade claimed responsibility for the bombing in retaliation for the Hebron massacre two years before, but later denied involvement. HAMAS also issued a leaflet assuming responsibility for the bombing signed by the Squads of the New Disciples of Martyr Yahya Ayyash, the Engineer, claiming the bombing was in retaliation for Ayyash's death on 5 January 1996.

3 March, Jerusalem

A suicide bomber detonated an explosive device on a bus, killing 19 persons, including six Romanians, and injuring six others. The Students of Yahya Ayyash, a splinter group of HAMAS, claimed responsibility for the attack.

4 March, Israel

A suicide bomber detonated an explosive device outside the Dizengoff Center, Tel Aviv's largest shopping mall, killing 20 persons and injuring 75 others, including two U.S. citizens. HAMAS and the Palestine Islamic Jihad (PIJ) both claimed responsibility for the bombing.

14 March, Bahrain

Assailants poured gasoline at the entrance to a restaurant in Sitrah and threw Molotov cocktails inside, killing seven Bangladeshi employees and destroying the restaurant.

27 March, Algeria

Armed Islamic Group (GIA) extremists kidnapped seven French monks from their monastery in the Medea region. On 26 April the GIA offered to free the monks in exchange for the release of GIA members held in France. On 21 May the group stated that they killed the monks in response to the French Government's refusal to negotiate with them.

1 April, Egypt

Four al-Gama'at al-Islamiyya (IG) militants opened fire on a group of Greek tourists in front of the Europa Hotel in Cairo, killing 18 Greeks and injuring 12 Greeks and two Egyptians. The IG claimed they intended to attack a group of Israeli tourists they believed were staying at the hotel, as revenge for Israeli actions in Lebanon.

5 May, India

Islamic separatists killed eight Hindu Nepalese migrant workers near Srinagar.

13 May, West Bank

Arab gunmen opened fire on a bus and a group of Yeshiva students near the Bet El settlement, killing a dual U.S./Israeli citizen and wounding three Israelis. No one claimed responsibility for the attack, but HAMAS is suspected.

28 May, France

Unidentified gunmen shot and killed a former Iranian deputy education minister under the Shah at his home in Paris. No one claimed responsibility for the killing.

Greece, A bomb exploded at a building housing the main offices of IBM in Athens, causing extensive structural damage but no injuries. The group Fraxia Midheniston (Nihilist Faction) claimed responsibility.

4 June, Tajikistan

Gunmen shot and killed two Russian servicemen's wives while the victims were visiting a cemetery in Dushanbe. No one claimed responsibility. The Tajikistan Internal Affairs Ministry believes the gunmen were members of "Muzlokandov's Gang," an Islamic extremist group.

9 June, Israel

Unidentified gunmen opened fire on a car near Zekharya, killing a dual U.S./Israeli citizen and an Israeli. The Popular Front for the Liberation of Palestine (PFLP) is suspected.

25 June, Saudi Arabia

A fuel truck carrying a bomb exploded outside the U.S. military's Khubar Towers housing facility in Dhahran, killing 19 US military personnel and wounding 515 persons, including 240 US personnel.

8 July, Ethiopia

Two Somali gunmen opened fire on the Minister of Transport and Communications as he arrived at his office in Addis Ababa, wounding him and killing two guards and two passersby. Al-Ittihaad al-Islami claimed responsibility for the attack.

1 August, Algeria

A bomb exploded at the home of the French Archbishop of Oran, killing him and his chauffeur. The attack occurred after the Archbishop's meeting with the French Foreign Minister. The Armed Islamic Group (GIA) is suspected.

11 August, Somalia
Suspected Al-Ittihaad al-Islami gunmen killed two Ethiopian businessmen in Beledweyne to avenge Ethiopia's two-day military incursion into Somalia earlier that month.

25 August, Bahrain
Three Bahrainis shot and wounded a Pakistani policeman guarding the Russian Consulate.

16 October, Ethiopia
In two separate incidents, unknown assailants shot and killed a French national and a Yemeni national near the Taiwan Market in Dire Dawa.

20 October, Yemen
Assailants abducted a French diplomat while he was driving in Sanaa. On 26 October the diplomat was turned over to local tribe members who then detained him until 1 November, when the government agreed to their conditions for his release.

24 October, Uganda
Several gunmen attacked a Sudanese refugee camp in Palorinya, western Moyo, killing 16 Sudanese refugees and wounding five others.

12 November, Bahrain
Two propane gas cylinders exploded behind a strip mall near the Shia village of Wattyan, damaging the Gulf Motors Agency Hyundai dealership and injuring a security guard.

15 November, Algeria
Unidentified assailants beheaded a Bulgarian businessman who was the former Bulgarian defense attache to Algeria. The victim was found at the entrance to Bainem Forest, west of Algiers.

17 November, Turkey
A fire broke out at the Tozbey Hotel in Istanbul, killing 17 Ukrainians and injuring more than 40 persons. On 22 November the group Turkish Islamic Jihad (TIJ) claimed responsibility for starting the fire.

3 December, France

A bomb exploded aboard a Paris subway train as it arrived at the Port Royal station, killing two French nationals, a Moroccan, and a Canadian, and injuring 86 persons. Among those injured were one U.S. citizen and a Canadian. No one claimed responsibility for the attack, but Algerian extremists are suspected.

31 December, Bahrain

Eight assailants surrounded a building in a Shia village, set several tires on fire, and threw Molotov cocktails inside, killing an Asian man and injuring two others.

There were a total of 31 terrorist attacks in Islamic countries, or that can be attributed to organized Islamic movements. Of the 83 incidents of terror committed worldwide in 1996, 40 % are related to Islam.

The largest and most deadly incident was the attack on the Khubar Towers in Saudi Arabia on June 25th. This action, possibly the work of al Qaeda, killed 19 U.S. military personnel and wounded 515, of which 240 were American. However, it is clear from reading this list that al Qaeda is just one of a number of terrorist organizations operating in the Middle East.

In this regard, I believe that we do ourselves a disservice by referring to these many organizations by their initials. Sometimes the terrorist's works are even termed "civil wars" or "separatist movements." We need to remind ourselves the GIA, FIS, GFLP, TIJ etc., the war in Algeria or the Moros in the Philippines, are all motivated by radical Islamists. While we professionals know these are all radical Islamic organizations, there is a tendency to forget this and only remember, for example, that the FIS killed 100,000 people. We should always identify such organizations as "Radical Islamic." The public needs to understand this.

A major failure of our current policy is that we treat terrorism as a criminal problem. That is how we reacted to the 1993 attack on the World Trade Center. Six people were killed and over 1000 injured. A worldwide manhunt was mounted to apprehend the perpetrators and bring them to justice. This is the American way. Find and punish, not identify and destroy. We are in the midst of a world-wide war with Muslim extremists. It is not too far-reaching to consider it WWIII. Our reaction to terror should be military, not law enforcement.

It is going to get worse. The demographic projections are frightening. Europe had a total population of 728 million in 2000. It is projected to be 600 million in 2050. Only one of Europe's principal 23 countries has a positive birth rate, Muslim Albania. All of the rest, including the great powers of France, Germany, Russia and England do not even produce enough children to sustain a level population, much less growth. They are all shrinking, even Italy. The seat of Roman Catholicism projects a decline of its present population of 57 million to 41 million by 2050.

In contrast, the populations of Islamic nations are expanding rapidly. By 2050 there will be 700 million people in the South Asian countries. Another 500 million Muslims will live in the area between Morocco and the Persian Gulf. Europe will have 600 million people with 1.2 billion Muslims as neighbors. If the <u>percentage</u> that is radical stays the same, it is clear <u>the number</u> will grow rapidly.

In the attached report is an analysis of terrorist incidents for each year of this decade. It is an alarming picture. This issue needs to be addressed by the highest levels of the Government.

(The detailed exhibit was attached hereto.)

Chapter 45
Fort Meade, Maryland, Friday, February 28, 1997
◈

On 28 February 1997, Danielle received a response to her memorandum from NSA Director Fisher:

Memorandum
National Security Agency

Classification: None
To: Danielle Lamaze-Smith   *CC:*
File 97-3-T
Fr: Bradley Fisher, Director, National Security Agency
Re: The Gathering Danger of Islamic Terrorist Organizations
Dt: 28 February 97

> *Your report was both interesting and insightful.*

> *I agree with much of what you state. Islamic radicalism does present "a clear and growing danger" to this country.*

> *I need us all to be aware, however, that the National Security Agency is not a policy-creating organization. Our mission is to help the policy makers make decisions by providing timely intelligence, obtained through scientific means.*

> *I continue to commend your enthusiasm for this subject. It is a worthwhile follow-up on your report on Afghanistan. Keep up the excellent work.*

"But", Danielle thought in exasperation as she put the memo down, "are we going to do anything about the threat besides study it?"

Then, on the way back home to Bowie that afternoon, Danielle heard on the radio that a gunman had conducted a sniper attack on tourists at the Empire State building in New York City. One person was killed and almost a dozen injured.

The gunman finally shot himself, leaving a suicide note that claimed the killings were a punishment against "the enemies of Palestine."

Danielle pulled into a parking lot and removed her bulky cell phone from her briefcase. She called the NSA switchboard and asked to be patched through to a Mr. Mark van Rensselier at the Central Intelligence Agency. Apparently, the NSA switchboard had his direct line, but he was not in. She got his voice mail.

"Hello Mark. This is Danielle Lamaze-Smith. I would like to come visit with you when you are free. I'd like to discuss the position you offered me at the CIA, if it is still open? I'm available next Tuesday at 10.00 AM if that will work for you. Please let me know." Leaving her call-back number, she disconnected.

As she swung back on the road and resumed her trip home Danielle was excited. She was already planning her presentation, what she would say. And what she would wear.

Chapter 46
Langley, Virginia: Tuesday, March 4, 1997
❖

This time there was no Director's car to transport her in style. Danielle drove her own POV (privately owned vehicle, in Government parlance) to the CIA headquarters in Langley, Virginia. Van Rensselier had notified the gate security post that he was expecting her. She drove into the complex and parked in the visitor's lot. The front security desk was also alerted and assigned an escort to conduct her to the seventh floor. Van Rensselier was waiting at the elevator to relieve the escort. As before, he was impressed with her appearance, for she was dressed in well-tailored clothing that emphasized her professional bearing but still looked attractive, and she was carrying a briefcase that obviously was of high quality. "This lady has class beyond her years", he thought. Then he spoke aloud:

"Well Danielle, I didn't expect to see you again for another year and here it is just two weeks after we met." He approached her with his arm outstretched and a smile on his face; actually, Danielle thought it was more of a grin. "So you've decided to join the first team."

"Hello, Mark, it's nice to see you again. Yes, a woman always reserves the right to change her mind. I didn't think that I would have to explain that to *you*", was Danielle's *riposte*. She delivered this with a Cheshire cat smile of her own.

"Let's use the Director's conference room. He is at a NATO meeting, so he won't be needing it today." Mark led the way to a room that had its door in a corridor about 20 feet from yet another door which had the word "Director" in bronze letters.

When she entered the room, Danielle saw a round mahogany table with eight chairs around it and another door that led directly to the Director's office. Built into the wall were three 27" CRT's. Two telephones were on the table, one of them red. Danielle wanted to ask if it was a hot line to the White House or the SecDef or the Kremlin, but she refrained, for what she was about to present would require all the stagecraft she could muster. It would not benefit her if she acted like a tourist.

"Would you like coffee or something else?" asked Mark.

"Not at this time, thanks." Danielle was about to perform and she didn't want any props to distract her.

"So, what made you change your mind so quickly? You don't strike me as the sort of person who does that. What happened?"

"Mark, when I left here two weeks ago, I was convinced I was at the right agency and doing the right thing for this stage of my life. I did want to come to the CIA at some point in the future, but not until I had another year at NSA. To be honest with you, however, the first doubt began to creep in on the way home. When I got back to NSA, I asked my boss if I could be relieved of most of my responsibilities for a week or two, that I needed some time to do research and write a report. He agreed."

"My work on the *Madrasses* in Afghanistan got me interested in the whole subject of terrorism in the Middle East. I have been educating myself in the subject for the past six months. The more I learned, the more concerned I got. I don't think this Administration is taking *al Qaeda* and other terror sponsoring organizations as seriously as they should. I did an analysis of all the terrorist's incidents in the Middle East since 1990, who did them, where they occurred, the targets, etc. I prepared an extensive report and submitted it to Fisher. He returned it to me a few days later with a short covering memo admonishing me that making policy was not the purview of NSA. I got that report on the same day of the Empire State incident. I heard of it on my way home and called you. That was the action-forcing event."

"I want to be part of an organization that helps create policy, not a technical organization whose task is to supply information. I want to be part of the Central Intelligence Agency. Incidentally, in my briefcase, I have a copy of the report for you." With that statement Danielle flipped the locks on it and pulled out a bound report with a red cover.

Van Rensselier reached for the report. As Danielle sat quietly, he flipped through it for some five minutes. "I am struck by the quality of this work. I look forward to reading it carefully. In the executive summary, you predict a grim future for this trend. What would you advise the National Security Council and the President to do?

"Well, ...that is a good question. I think I shall begin by saying what we should not do."

"First, we should not be treating Islamic terrorism lightly. Except for the World Trade Center bombing in 1993 and now, of course, the Empire State building, they have only hit targets overseas. I am convinced that, sooner or later, they will strike us here in the homeland again. The World Trade Center bombing was only a foretaste of things to come."

"Second, we must understand the nature of the Islamic *jihad.* There is a tendency to relate all of this to our support of Israel. To that end successive Presidents, from Nixon forward, have focused on getting Arafat and the current Israeli Prime Minister, Meir, Rabin, Begin, Natenyahu, whomever, to declare a truce. We have sponsored meetings from Camp David to Oslo, to no avail. The simplistic belief has been that if we can get the Israelis and the Palestinians to kiss and make up, our troubles will be over. Nothing is further from the truth. The Palestinians and the Israelis are not the root cause of terror in the Middle East. They have nothing to do with the Taliban in Afghanistan. They have nothing to do with the FIS or the GIA in Algeria, they have nothing to do with Saddam Hussein in Iraq, They have nothing to with Ghadafi's blowing up Pan Am 107. We must remember also that terrorism is a tactic used by others such as the IRA or the Basques separatists. It is an absolute mistake to relate all of the terrorist activities in the region to Israel. The real problem is that *Islam is a ninth century religion run amuck!* It has simply not made the adjustment into the modern age."

"In Islamic countries, the status and treatment of women is

archaic. Human rights abuses are rampant. In a world in which democracy spread through the West in the 18th century, it is, no pun intended, a foreign concept to the Middle East. Instead, malevolent and cruel dictators reign supreme. It is an area of grinding poverty. The oil and mineral wealth is in the hands of a few who squander the riches of their countries. The birthrates are high, which just exacerbates the poverty. Unemployment is rampant. For an area called the 'cradle of civilization', the lack of emphasis on higher education is appalling. These conditions create a giant petri dish for the incubation of terrorist movements."

"So Danielle, I ask again. What would you advise the President"?

"I would say; 'Mr. President, the only solution to the problem of terrorism is to be aggressive. Act with strength. If a country supports terrorism or harbors terrorists, make it painful for them to do so. Impose sanctions. Rain cruise missiles down upon them. Pursue their political leaders with the military. Make the average citizen recognize that supporting terrorism is unrewarding. *That* is what must be done."

"But Danielle, isn't that approach what we abhor in despotic dictators? Are we not visiting the sins of the Father on the children? As a great country, we should not adopt a policy that embraces such a concept."

"No, Mark. Terrorism is different from officially adopted policy. It is unlike the other wars we have fought in the 20th century. Terrorists are not conscripted. They are volunteers. Terrorism is the result of individual action within a society. It is more indigenous than even guerilla activity. Certainly there are national leaders who encourage terrorism. Saddam Hussein is such a man, as is Muammar Ghadafi. But most terrorists are inspired by other leaders like Osama bin Laden; men who have no official political status. They will continue to attract support from the masses until the masses understand that there is no benefit to be derived from participation in their leaders' ambitions. Terrorism is unique. I don't believe our national leadership understands that."

"Danielle, you have just enunciated a most interesting analysis, and you have done it succinctly. It is certainly something I would like to think about. Now more than ever, I would like to have you with the Company. Yours is just the kind of analytic ability we need more of. Originally, based upon your success in Afghanistan, I imagined a career for you in the Operations Directorate. Now, after observing your ability as an analyst, I think you are more suited for the Intelligence Directorate. Which would you prefer?

Danielle took a deep breath. Then, looking directly into the eyes of Mark van Rensselier, she gave her answer. "Neither."

"But I thought you wanted to join the CIA?"

"I do. But I don't want to work in either of the directorates. You are an Assistant to the Director. I want to be your assistant. You have a charge to rejuvenate the Agency. I believe that a major part of the Agency's future is going to be concerned with Islamic terrorism. I want to help you reorganize the CIA to deal with the future. Charge me to handle the issues that loom on the horizon in the Middle East. When we met, two weeks ago, you told me that most of the people in the Agency form committees and hold meetings. I intend to be different. I promise you I am not trying to build a bureaucracy around myself. All I need is an office, a good secretary, and a clear thinking superior. That's why I want to be your assistant and not report to someone else. We both know how easily good ideas can get buried in this town, if they are at all controversial. Well, *I intend to produce some controversy.*"

As she finished her preplanned speech, Danielle looked closely for signs of rejection from Mark. She detected none, only a poker face, void of any expression, positive or negative. Then a broad van Rensselier smile appeared.

"Danielle Lamaze-Smith, you've got a deal. Welcome aboard." And Mark stuck out his hand to seal the bargain.

Chapter 47
Afghanistan: Thursday, August 7, 1997
◆

Osama bin Laden and Muhammed Atef were sitting on a low bench, their backs against the mud brick wall that shaded them. As is the custom of in-laws the world over, they were talking about the marriage of their children. Atef's son was married to bin Laden's daughter.

The Sheik spoke: "My daughter tells me that her husband complains that he cannot be a part of our efforts here in this camp. The fact is, I believe they would both like to be closer to us, rather than in the more remote area where we have them stationed. However, it is for their own good. You should remind your son of that whenever you speak."

"I do," said Atef. "Whenever we are together, he harasses me about not being part of the action. I remind him that being around you and me is dangerous for his health and for that of his bride. Ever since that attempt on our lives in the Sudan, I am concerned about such things. It is one thing for us to be killed and quite another for our children. They are both so young. Their lives are just starting."

"Yes, Muhammad, I quite agree with you. When I was your son's age, I was enjoying life in Beirut, not climbing around in the mountains with an AK 47. There is time enough for that later. Once one starts this life of ours, there is no going back. But let me change the conversation. I am concerned about this friend of yours, Kahlid Sheik Muhammad. I have been thinking about our meeting."

"Sheik, I tell you again, I do not call him a friend. I met him through his nephew, Ramzi Yousef. As you will recall, it was Yousef who came up with the scheme to blow up the American building, the World Trade Center in 1993. It was because of this relationship that I suggested we meet with Kahlid to hear what he had to propose. Yousef and Kahlid had also developed a plan to blow up American aircraft leaving the Philippines. I am inclined to believe this was mostly the thinking of Yousef. However, since the Pakistanis arrested Yousef in 1995, he is not available to give his side of the story. Kahlid can exaggerate a little without fear of being contradicted. I must tell you, however, that I was impressed with the idea Kahlid presented to you."

"Yes Muhammad, I was also impressed. I must admit, the idea of using aircraft as weapons was one that had not occurred to me. His other schemes regarding the destruction of US aircraft over the Pacific do not have any real appeal but, using an airplane as a fully-equipped, fully-armed, steerable bomb is a fine tactic in our struggle."

"Sheik, I agree. Killing Americans in quantity by destroying buildings full of them with aircraft is a step beyond which we have gone. It is much better than a car bombing, for instance. How can they defend against it? You have invited Kahlid Sheik Muhammad to join *al Qaeda*, now I'll be curious as to what he does. I understand that he is close to Massaud and the Northern Alliance, sworn enemies of our friends in the Taliban. It will be very interesting to see his decision."

The two men continued their conversation about Kahlid Sheik Muhammad and his revolutionary ideas for another quarter hour before bin Laden again changed the subject.

"What are you hearing from Zubeida and our special students?"

"I met with him briefly last week, when you were away on your tour of the nearby camps. He told me that things are going very nicely. The boys are well established. They are learning English, and the American customs faster than he had thought they would. Zubeida is quite pleased with the progress."

"That is good news. I have already begun to think about their first assignment. How many of these do you think we still have?" With that question, bin Laden reached under the bench and produced a brown cardboard tube three and one quarter inches in diameter and 15 inches long.

Atef reached across and took the tube from bin Laden. He hefted it and thought a minute before responding. "As you know, we used the majority against the Soviets, with great effect. Others have been expended in training exercises. Still, I think we must have several thousand scattered around the country. Why do you ask?"

"I want you to gather one hundred of them and find a means to smuggle them into the United States. I should think that going through the Philippines might be a good way. Contact our friends who ship opium through Manila. They should know how to do it. Now that I am thinking about it, paint over these tubes and tell our friends that they are filled with drugs. I want as few people as possible to know what we are doing. There should be no rush to do this, we have plenty of time." Then bin Laden's face lit with a curious smile; "the Americans gave us these to fight the Soviets. Now, as Allah commands, we will begin returning the ones we didn't use."

Chapter 48
Langley, Virginia: Thursday, November 18, 1997
◈

There was a difference in culture between the CIA and NSA. Danielle felt it immediately.

Because she had continuing loyalties to her old organization, she initially had some difficulties adjusting. It wasn't that the CIA people just thought they were superior, they *knew* they were superior. After all, the CIA was the stuff of public imagination. It was the organization upon which dozens of books and movies were based. Nobody ever made a movie about the National Security Agency!

Further, most of the employees at NSA were, in some way, technical. They programmed computers, or they designed antennas, or they broke codes or they translated messages. They did their jobs with quiet efficiency. They were relatively unconcerned with the private nature of their work. They were not all caught up in the importance of working for America's spy agency, as were the people at the CIA. Here people seemed engulfed in the cult of secrecy. They all delighted in their knowledge that they knew things that others didn't know. Even the vast numbers of employees who were engaged in reading foreign newspapers and magazines, trying to glean nuggets of information, were guilty of this attitude. Everyone, it seemed to Danielle, operated under an aura of conspiratorial secrecy.

When Danielle arrived for her new job as Van Rensselier's assistant, there was no authority in the Table of Organization for such a position. He could, however, appoint a deputy. Thus Danielle's official title became "Deputy Assistant to the Director". Even though the job was the same, it was much different than being as assistant to an Assistant to the Director. As Danielle would have said in French, one had '*cachet*'. The other did not. She was surprised to learn that the term was also part of the English language.

The CIA was in the process of creating a special bin Laden unit. This was a task force whose job it was to gather and maintain all the intelligence available on one individual. It was the first time in anyone's memory that a group of analysts had been put together with the responsibility for just one person. Danielle was made a member of the task force, although her mandate was the much larger subject of Middle Eastern Terrorist Activities. While bin Laden was currently inactive with regard to new acts of terrorism, other groups and events kept her busy:

4 September 97: Three suicide bombers from HAMAS detonated a bomb in a crowded shopping center in Jerusalem, killing eight and wounding 200.

30 October 97: Al-sha'if tribesmen kidnapped a U.S. businessman in Yemen.

12 November 97: Two gunmen from the Islami Inqilabi Council (Islamic Revolutionary Council) shot and killed four U.S. businessmen from Union Petroleum in Pakistan

And then just yesterday, *17 November 97:* Al-Gama'at al-Islamiyya gunmen shot and killed 62 tourists and wounded 26 in the Valley of the Kings in Egypt.

With the possible exception of the Valley of the Kings incident, it is likely that none of the above activities were reported on the evening news in most American cities. Danielle was concerned that the terrorists would grow bolder, sensing that America was unconcerned with the random deaths of its citizens. She was convinced that the terrorists would continue to probe, pushing, pushing until they got a reaction. She was almost alone in this opinion at the CIA. Only a few others on the bin Laden task force saw revolutionary Islamic terrorism as she did: the global threat of the future.

In the next year, Danielle's hypothesis would be proven correct.

Chapter 49
Washington DC: Friday, August 7, 1998
◈

The Department of State of the United States of America carries the following entry in its official Chronology of Significant Terrorists Incidents:

> ***U.S. Embassy Bombings in East Africa, August 7, 1998:*** *A bomb exploded at the rear entrance of the U.S. Embassy in Nairobi, Kenya, killing 12 U.S. citizens, 32 Foreign Service Nationals (FSNs) and 247 Kenyan citizens. Approximately 5,000 Kenyans, 6 U.S. citizens and 13 FSNs were injured. The U.S. Embassy building sustained extensive structural damage. Almost simultaneously, a bomb exploded outside the U.S. Embassy in Dar es Salaam, Tanzania, killing 7 FSNs and 3 Tanzanian citizens, and injuring 1 U.S. citizen and 76 Tanzanians. The explosion caused major structural damage to the U.S. Embassy facility. The U.S. Government held Osama bin Laden responsible.*

It was not the means by which Danielle wished to be proven right. She had been working in her office when the news of the embassy attacks came through as a "flash" on her computer screen. Special software allowed such a message to take precedence over whatever else is being displayed or worked on. As most people in the CIA have computer displays on their desks, always lit, the "flash" is an effective way to disseminate announcements about important events affecting national security.

The initial news was simply that two U.S. embassies had been struck by what were assumed to be terrorist's bombs. Minutes later, when the countries of the embassies were listed, Danielle knew instantly that Osama bin Laden and *al Qaeda* were responsible. No other organization had the capability to simultaneously attack in two such geographically separate locations. No other terrorist leader had the diabolical hatred of America to sacrifice hundreds of innocent Muslims in order to kill just a handful of U.S. citizens.

Danielle reviewed the message on the screen several times in disbelief for a minute or two and collected herself. Like most employees in some way connected to the State Department's Foreign Service, her second reaction was to wonder if she knew any of the injured. A moment of mentally reviewing the postings of friends, relieved her of this anxiety. As van Rensselier was out of the office, she began to write a position paper setting forth her thoughts on appropriate responses.

Danielle worked nonstop, fueled only by coffee and some peanuts from the snack machine. After nearly twelve hours of uninterrupted activity, her paper was concluded. She knew that most other analysts were constrained by organizational structure. They would have to wait for committee meetings with their colleagues. As van Rensselier's Deputy, she had no such protocol to follow.

When van Rensselier stopped at his office on Saturday morning as was his custom, hers was the only paper on his desk. He read it and made a copy for the Director. This he hand delivered to the Director's secretary with a covering memo with instructions that it be transmitted to the home of the DCI so it could be read over the weekend . In his memorandum, he stressed the following points:

1: *The paper was written by a single person.* It was not the product of a committee.

2: *The author was a bona fide expert on Middle East terrorism.* She was from Algeria and understood the problems of the region.

3: *It was a good starting point for discussion at the NSC.* The other players including Defense, State, WSAG, and the rest would probably not be able to pull anything together for at least another day. This paper would stimulate other thinking.

4: *The paper was good.* It was logical and well written. It reflected a point of view that would, when the dust settled, probably be the consensus opinion.

5: *The author actually had met bin Laden in 1996.* This was a bit of panache that should be exploited.

The DCI came home after a round of golf on Saturday to find the memo from van Rennselier and its attached analysis by Danielle. He read them, read it a second time and called van Rensselier on their direct line.

"Van, I have just read the paper you left for me. I found it an extremely impressive work to be produced on such short notice. I am attending a meeting of the National Security Council at the White House at 1500 on Monday (the DCI liked to use 24 hour 'military' time). I am going to try to get us 10 minutes on the agenda. I would like you and Ms. Lamaze-Smith to accompany me. She can present her paper in the lion's den. It will do her good to see how the CIA and the NSC interact at the White House. I'll meet you at my car, in front, at 1430. See you then."

Chapter 50
The White House: Monday, August 10, 1998
◈

Danielle had, of course, met the DCI. She had even been in meetings with him. But, except for the time when Van (as her boss had asked her to call him) took her into the DCI's office to be introduced on her first day on the job, she had never been alone with him. Now, she was riding in the front seat of his car on her way to the White House. She was highly excited. She was also, as usual at such important times, lamenting the fact that she wasn't wearing something different.

As the car sped down Route 123 and onto the George Washington Memorial Parkway, the two men in the back seat ignored her and talked about other matters. It was only after they turned onto the E street bridge that the DCI asked her a question.

"Danielle, have you ever been in the White House?"

"No sir, I haven't. I hope the excitement I am feeling isn't too apparent."

"Don't worry. I think the first time in the White House is exciting for everyone. I know it was for me...and I was a lot older than you on my first visit. It's just that there is so damn much hype about the place. From the time we were children it has been presented as almost mystical. A sort of OZ-like place with the President being the Wizard! Do French children have the same feelings about the *Elysee Palace?*"

"I don't think so. I didn't. Of course my formative years were spent in Algeria after we became independent. But I don't think French children view the Palace with the same awe that Americans seem to have for the White House."

"We are strange people. I think we take after the English. They disagree on everything except respect for their Royals. Then they unify. We are the same way regarding the White House. We may hate its occupants, but we love their residence."

"I understand. The White House seems to have an aura of its own. It is famous just *as a place*. It is like Buckingham Palace or the Kremlin. To Europeans, the White House simply stands for America." Then Danielle asked the question. "Do you think the President will attend the meeting?"

"No, he is not scheduled to. He usually stays out of national security discussions until after the staff has bloodied themselves over the issues. It is amazing how much disagreement there is between departments...State and Defense for example. Still, having all sides represented with healthy discussion is best in the long run. We generally come up with the right answer. Also, of course, the President currently has other problems on his mind."

While Danielle was pondering this statement the car pulled into West Executive Drive and stopped at the entrance to the West Wing of the White House. Danielle was amused. They were going in through the basement door, the entrance used by the White House staff. At the front entrance, she knew from watching the TV news, there were always members of the press "hanging out."

The meeting was in the Situation Room, a conference room in the area occupied by the NSC staff. It really *was* in the basement! Danielle was expecting something special, she didn't really know what, but she was disappointed. The Situation Room was just an ordinary conference room.

Danielle knew several of the attendees by sight, the National Security Advisor, the Chairman of the Joint Chiefs and the Under Secretary of State. The eight or ten others were simply staff, like her. The NSC director started the meeting by asking those with unfamiliar faces, nodding to Danielle and a Lt. Colonel, to please introduce themselves. When it came Danielle's turn, the DCI jumped in and cut her off.

"Dr. Lamaze-Smith is a new addition to my staff. She recently transferred to us from NSA. Before that she was at State. She grew up in Algeria, speaks fluent Arabic and has an amazing clarity of understanding of the Middle East. In October of 1996 she actually met Osama bin Laden. She has prepared a paper that succinctly sets forth her views on the background of the embassy bombings and what our response might be." Looking directly at the National Security Director, the DCI continued. " I suggest that we start the meeting by asking Danielle to present her case." The leader of the NSC nodded in assent.

All of the heads in the room were suddenly looking at this attractive, smartly dressed, young woman who was so enthusiastically endorsed by the Director of the Central Intelligence Agency. Danielle was on.

"Good afternoon. My title of Dr. Lamaze-Smith is only used for introductions. I hope you will all call me Danielle." The Chairman of the Joint Chiefs and the other two uniformed officers smiled.

"Having been raised in Algeria, where my Father is the president of a La Terre subsidiary, I grew up with terrorism. As an adult here in Washington I have made a specialty of studying radical Islamic terrorism. I know what they believe. I know what they think. I know what they hope to achieve. What I am about to present to you are not random thoughts, but the result of years of analysis and study."

"The first question is why. Why are there terrorists? Why do they go around blowing people up? Why do they hate Americans? Why is the Middle East such a hot bed of animosity directed at the United States?"

"It is a mistake, albeit a common one, to assume that the genesis of the problem is Israel. It isn't. It is a facet, an important issue that must be resolved, but it is a sidebar. And incidentally, the issue is not Israel, but Jerusalem. I'll get into that later. But neither Israel nor Jerusalem is the root cause of terrorism in the Middle East."

"I hear the discussion that we are fighting a 'war on terror.' That is incorrect. Terror is simply a tactic used by the enemy. We are fighting a war on radical Islam. Yes, I know there are some seven million peaceful U.S. citizens who are Muslims. As a matter of fact, those very people have prevented our government from focusing on the facts. In a desire to avoid offending such a large group of people, people who are likely to vote as a bloc, our politicians tiptoe around the issue." The chairman of the joint-chiefs perked up. This woman was not just some liberal professor proposing Pollyanna ideas. He leaned forward in his seat.

Suddenly Danielle was interrupted. The door behind her opened and she totally lost her audience. Several in the room started to rise from their chairs. There was a chorus of "Good afternoon, Mr. President." The President entered the room and motioned for people to keep their seats. He moved to take a chair across from her.

Danielle, now somewhat flustered, introduced herself. "Mr. President, I am Danielle Lamaze-Smith with the Central Intelligence Agency. I was just making some observations about the nature of Islam. With your permission, I'll continue." A nod of his head was all she got.

"The radical Islamic movement has existed for 1,000 years, since the time of the crusades. Their goal is not the pluralistic world to which we Christians aspire, where there would be three great monotheistic religions, Christianity, Judaism and Islam, all living in harmony. Their absolute ambition, their holy cause, is the domination of the world. This is the true meaning of *jihad*. Their struggle will continue until Islam rules supreme, until there are remaining no infidels, no non-believers, period. Demographically, there is ample reason to believe they will be successful in achieving this ambition."

"Islam is the world's fastest growing religion. It has expanded by 500%, *five times*, since the middle of the 20th century. In contrast, those who profess Christianity have grown by only 50%. Already, in Europe, what we have always thought of as a Christian culture, Islam is the second religion. It will predominate by 2025." Several in the audience shifted in their seats as though discomforted by the thought.

"It is true that currently most members of the Islamic faith are not driven by these ambitions. However, much of their leadership subscribes to the dictum of the supremacy of Islam. They absolutely believe in the goal of Allah, to rule the earth through armed conquest. That is what we are currently facing in the Middle East, where over 90% of the population is Muslim. In these countries, with their systemic poverty, lack of education, mass unemployment, brutalization of women, huge birthrates and total lack of appreciation of western values, we are seeing increasing unrest. The embassy bombings are just the latest manifestation of their determination to expel infidels from their lands." Danielle paused to gauge her audience. She had their rapt attention. Even the President seemed alert to what she was saying.

"It is important that we understand this. Negotiation, by its very definition, implies that the parties are trying to reach a common goal. That is not the case with the leaders of radical Islam. They view negotiation as a sign of weakness. They cannot comprehend our desire for peaceful co-existence. They understand only *Al Harb,* the religion of the sword. It is therefore particularly important that we react to the Embassy bombings with a sign of strength. We must take military action. I cannot emphasize this too strongly."

The President interrupted. "Before we hear from our folks from the Pentagon, what would you suggest as an appropriate military response?"

Danielle's brain raced. It was one thing for her to propose a strong reaction, quite another to suggest to the President a specific response. She was out of her area of expertise. Still, she didn't want to be seen by the President as someone with only information and no answers.

"Mr. President, my field is the Middle East, not military tactics. I don't have an exact answer for you. However, as a student of history and an observer of current events, it would seem that we have three choices:"

"One is to do nothing. If this is our course, we should be

prepared to do as De Gaulle did when faced with the same problem in my native Algeria. He didn't think he could win over the Muslim separatists. He just ceded them the country, over the strong objection of the one million *pieds noirs,* French residents of Algeria, and pulled out. I don't believe that should even be a consideration for us."

"The second option, it seems to me, would be a limited response of some sort, bombing of the *al Qaeda* camps or hitting them with cruise missiles."

"The third choice would be a military invasion of Afghanistan, the home base of *al Qaeda.* I think that would be a real wake-up call for the entire radical Islamic movement. It would show them that we are not the paper tiger they think we are. We must remember that Saddam Hussein invaded Kuwait because he didn't think the United States would do anything. I will not presume to suggest policy decisions of this level, but those are the choices."

The President didn't show any facial reaction. "Thank you." He turned to the Chairman of the Joint Chiefs, "General, what's your view, what should we do with the terrorists?"

"Mr. President, I agree with the options outlined by Ms. Lamaze-Smith. As we have so often discussed, even in this very room, the choices are limited. One of the problems is, as you know, there are no worthwhile targets. Bin Laden's camps are nothing but jungle gyms and a few mud huts, nothing worth wasting a cruise missile on. We previously agreed, several years ago, that if we ever got a solid fix on bin Laden's location, we would launch some strikes. To date the intel people have never been able to give us more than a best guess, insufficient in everyone's opinion to raise the balloon. However, with this latest atrocity, I think we should hit several locations with Tomahawks, with or without bin Laden; the sooner the better."

Next, to speak was the DCI. "Mr. President, we have identified a number of priority targets in both Sudan and Afghanistan. In Khartoum there is a tannery owned personally by bin Laden. Destroying that would cause him some financial hardship. In *al Shifa* is a pharmaceutical plant that we believe may be making VX, a sarin-like nerve gas. We believe this because a ground team exfiltrated some earth samples from around the plant. When we analyzed them, they tested positive for EMPTA, a precursor chemical. In Afghanistan, of course, are a number of small training camps. It is true, as the general observed, that these are not really worthwhile targets. On the other hand, we might get lucky and catch bin Laden or Atef visiting one of them."

Danielle watched in fascination, for the next half-hour, as various parties discussed various pros and cons of hitting various targets. In the end it was determined that the tannery was out, due to the potential for collateral civilian damage. The pharmaceutical plant and several camps would be attacked and destroyed.

Finally there was a discussion about notifying the Pakistanis. The missile cruisers were in the Arabian Sea. Their rockets would have to overfly Pakistan to reach Afghanistan. It was determined that a member of the Joint Chiefs should personally go to Pakistan to assure their president, that the missiles were not an attack by India. Nobody wanted to risk an inadvertent nuclear war.

Danielle disagreed with this decision! She was sure that the Pakistanis would alert bin Laden. *"If it were up to me, I would have the US President call the Pakistan president the instant the strikes were launched, not before,"* she thought.

On the ride back to the CIA, the DCI complimented her on a fine presentation. When she protested that she didn't get to make even a third of the points she had hoped to present, the DCI commented, with a little more sarcasm than Danielle thought necessary: "You never do with that crowd. Welcome to Washington."

On 20 August 98, ships of the U.S. Navy, operating in the Arabian Sea, fired off their cruise missiles at a number of *al*

Qaeda training camps. The majority of these were on target. There was much physical destruction and the loss of some 20 lives of terrorists. Unfortunately, neither bin Laden, nor any of his senior leaders, were part of the damage. They had been forewarned and left the camps.

Danielle was right.

Chapter 51
The Philippine Islands: Thursday, November 26, 1998
◈

On the West Coast of the island of Luzon, some 100 kilometers northwest of the Philippine capital of Manila, lies one of the world's great natural anchorages, Subic Bay. It was established by the colonial power of Spain as a coaling station and arsenal in 1885. When Spain lost its war with America in 1898-99, "Subic" was taken over by the U.S. Navy. For nearly 100 years it was almost continuously expanded and improved as a principal Navy Ship Repair Facility. Subic Bay, and the town around it, Olongapo City, was famous to generations of American sailors as the best port-of-call in the Pacific. All of this ended in the first two years of the ninth decennial of the 20th century. In 1991 the Philippine Senate declined to renew the navy's lease for the Bay. In 1992 Mount Pinitubo erupted. The latter event buried the entire navy base under several feet of volcanic ash. The Navy pulled out.

As the U.S. Navy had some forewarning of the termination of their lease, they had been able before the volcano erupted to empty their vast storage warehouses and specialized workshops such as electronics, meteorological instruments, and submarine periscope repair. They then struck a deal with the Philippine government to leave behind the largest of the repair facilities, the machine shop. This complex with its huge boring mills, lathes capable of machining 30-foot-long parts, and giant milling machines was capable of undertaking repair and rebuilding work on all but the largest marine engines in the naval service. The Philippine government anticipated establishing the Subic Bay Free Port Zone, and wished to preserve the employment of hundreds of skilled machinists and technicians. The government wisely chose not to operate the new enterprise, but to put the entire machine shop up for lease. The winning bid was from two brothers.

Epifanio and Pepito Panillo were deemed to be the ideal operators. Epifanio was a trained accountant and businessman.

Pepito was a highly skilled machinist and shop manager. Unfortunately, both were also experienced and resourceful smugglers of contraband, especially drugs. The latter skill was unknown to the government, but it inured to the benefit of both parties. Epifanio ingeniously laundered the drug proceeds through the machine shop. This facility, having some of its overhead costs paid for by smuggling, was able to undercut its competitors. Thanks to Pepito's shop management skills and the experienced workforce, the shop gained a reputation for quality workmanship. Customers from around the world sent large marine engines to The Cabanataun Machine Works for rebuilding. (The company name was taken from the Japanese prison camp, in memory of their father who died there in WWII.)

Initially, the brother's drug-smuggling customers were the Moro tribesmen of Mindanao, suppliers of opium and heroin to the American market. Under normal circumstances the Moros, who were Muslims, were loath to transact business with non-Muslims. However, an early small commercial dealing had evolved into a friendship with the Catholic Panillos. Both sides grew to trust the other. Religion was put aside in favor of profit. It was a classic symbiotic relationship.

Under the Taliban, Afghanistan became a major supplier of the world's opium production. Shipments to Europe went overland, through Russia. Shipments to North America went by ship, through the Panillos.

On November 26 Epifanio received a telephone call in his office from a man who identified himself only as Muhammad, requesting a meeting. It was set for 4:00 o'clock that same afternoon at the Manila Hotel, downtown, where Epifanio had a private suite.

In the small but luxurious rooms they met as planned. This old establishment, once the home of General Douglas McArthur, was still ranked as one of the world's finest hotels. Even Atef, who had stayed in some of the best hostelries in the Middle East, was impressed. He had announced himself at the desk and was escorted to the third floor by a solicitous bellman. The bellman knew Epifanio, and had benefited greatly from his ongoing generosity.

"Good Afternoon. I am Muhammad Atef. I appreciate your taking the time to meet with me. I was given your name by a mutual friend, a Mr. al Kezir, of Kabul in Afghanistan. He tells me that he has a longstanding and pleasant business relationship with you."

"Good morning to you. I am Epifanio Panillo. Yes, Muhammad and I are old friends; he stays with me whenever he is in Manila. I am pleased to be of whatever service I can to one of his associates." Atef followed his host into a sitting room furnished with highly carved oriental teak chairs. Chinese watercolors hung on the walls, a blue Chinese rug covered the floor. On a low table between two chairs was an antique porcelain tea set. Panillo poured two cups of tea. He began the meeting with a discussion of their mutual friend. He did this partly in order to probe the *bona fides* of Atef and partly because he wanted to know of the health of al Kezir, who had not been to Manila for more than a year. When he was satisfied that Atef was genuine, he began the business conversation.

"As you are here at the suggestion of Muhammad al Kezir, I presume you are in need of my services as an exporter. What specifically can I do for you?"

"I am going to need to ship 100 cardboard tubes, each three and one quarter inches by fifteen inches. They will each weigh about 6 pounds. The tubes contain very, very valuable items and should not, must not be found by the American customs authorities."

"What is in the tubes, the usual commodity, or will these require something different?"

Atef paused to think. Bin Laden had told him not to discuss the contents of the tubes with anyone, to let everyone believe they contained drugs. But Atef knew that drugs would not show up on an X-ray, whereas the contents of the tubes would be plainly disclosed. He decided he had to bring Panillo into the secret just enough to help him determine how best to provide the shipping. "The content of the tubes is a very great secret. We are letting all of our people assume it is drugs. I would hope that you would do the same. However, between us, the tubes are filled with a metal object that will be apparent to an X-ray. As the metal is iron, I presume it can also be detected by a magnetometer. This shipment must go inside another metal container, a steel box that is not subject to opening. What you use is your business. That is your field of expertise and that is what we are paying you for; in fact, paying you very well if the tubes are safely delivered."

"And when do you need these tubes to be shipped?"

"There is no hurry; not this year or even the year following. I took advantage of a trip to the Philippines on other business to meet with you. If I am to be successful in my business, I must do long range planning. I am sure it is the same with you. Take whatever time you need. I tell you again that the tubes contain items of extreme importance. Their safe arrival at their ultimate destination is worth a great deal of money to my organization. Is this a project you would like to undertake?"

"Yes. Yes, I always appreciate a challenge. I will find a way to get your tubes into North America. But, I forgot to ask: Is the location important? We have a facility in Vancouver, Canada from which we service the northwest fishing fleet. That is the normal port-of-entry for our goods. We are constantly shipping crates of engine parts to this location. Also the Canadian customs inspections are less rigorous than the U.S. Customs Service. Of course, if we ship to Vancouver it will require that you arrange to get the tubes across the Canadian/American border. Will that be a problem?"

"No. The port is not critical. We expect to have to move the tubes once they are on land. I am not even sure of their final destination at this time. That is yet to be determined. You get them to North America. We'll do the rest." Atef, though he knew nothing about the border security between Canada and the United States, was certain that they could find a way to get the tubes across.

"Finally," said Epifanio, "I must ask this, even though I suspect the answer. Must the contents be shipped in the tubes? Sometimes it is easier if the dimensions are not rigid. We normally pack our merchandise in plastic bags."

Atef smiled. "You probably suspect correctly. I have 100 tubes, three and one quarter inches by fifteen inches. They must be shipped in the tubes."

Panillo, having gotten all the information he needed about the merchandise to be shipped, asked, "and how do I get in touch with you?"

Atef shook his head from side to side. "You don't. I will be back in the Philippines in the next year. I will call upon you then."

The two men rose and shook hands. Each always felt more comfortable if the other man with whom he was dealing had black hair. Neither of them trusted or liked associating with fair skinned westerners.

When they parted company, each was thinking the same thing. "Just how *would* the tubes be shipped?" And Epifanio recalled a radio report he had heard in Manilla: Today was the Americans' Thanksgiving Day. He wondered: "Would they be thankful?"

Chapter 52
Afghanistan: Monday, December 14, 1998
◈

Osama bin Laden and Muhammad Atef were interviewing an interesting man. He had come to them at the suggestion of one of the camp directors, Abu Zubaydah. The camps attracted many resourceful and dedicated people, but this man was exceptional for someone so young. He was smart, talented and technically oriented. Most importantly, he has already proven himself. As Ahmed Ressam recounted his life's adventures, both men listened attentively.

"I was born in Algeria, in Sidi bel Abbes, in 1971 and grew up in that city. If you have ever been there, you know there is not much for a young man to do. I was ambitious. I wanted more out of life than most of my friends, who were content to sit in coffee shops and pass their time in meaningless conversation. In 1994, I bought a fake French passport. Then I took all of my money, most of which was stolen from the many Christians who live in Sidi bel Abbes and went to Montreal, Canada. There I was able to convince the authorities that I was escaping government persecution. This was the truth. The government would have put me in jail for my life of crime. Of course, I didn't explain this to the Canadians. They granted me political asylum. I spent the next several years living off the infidels, cheating them, robbing them and even killing several. It was easy. In Montreal the people were so trusting. They had no suspicions and were happy to befriend a young man with a hard-luck story.

"After a year of knocking around, I met Raed Hijazi, a man who had recently been in the training camp run by Abu Zubaydah in Kahldan. He convinced me that I was wasting my life with my aimless ways, that I could better serve our cause if I had some formal training. So last year I determined to come to Afghanistan to attend the camp in Khaldan.

"I bought a blank baptismal certificate, stolen from a

Catholic church, and filled it out in the name of Benni Antoine Noris. With this document I was able to obtain a Canadian passport, so that I could fly to Pakistan, go onto Afghanistan, and return. Of course, I planned on removing the pages with the Afghan stamp, before I went back to Canada.

"I found the camp experience exciting. There I learned about making bombs. I was also taught how to place cyanide in the intakes of the air conditioning of buildings, to kill the occupants. I think this is a superior approach to killing infidels. You can kill large numbers of people with minimum risk of being caught. I am eager to put in practice the things I have learned. At night, I dream of blowing up American embassies. When can I start?"

Bin Laden had learned, in his years of experience with young men, that sometimes the tough talk is not matched with the courage and capability necessary to back up the braggadocio. But Ressam seemed different. On his own, without any training or direction, he had done things that most young Arab men his age, only dream about. Bin Laden was ready to take a chance.

"You have had an interesting life for someone so young. You have proven your ability to make your way in the western world and elude, even fool, the authorities. I am looking for someone to lead a mission to the American homeland to destroy a major American airport. I think you are my man!"

"I have several other Algerians with whom you can work. I want you to go to London. There one of our London cells will take care of you. They will give you precursor chemicals that you can smuggle back into Montreal. Once in Canada you will set up a cell with the other Algerians. You will have to use your talents to arrange travel documents for these people, but that should be easy, given your skills. You will rent space and set up a bomb-making facility, as you have been taught. You will acquire weapons and other explosive chemicals. When your associates join you, you will make your way to Vancouver on the west coast of Canada. In the West, we have some other men, Abdelghani

Meskina and Abdel Hakim Tizgah, who will be available to help you."

"I am not going to direct you to a particular airport, you will have to select that on the basis of research. I will insist that you go into the United States from Vancouver. I will be very interested in your recommendations on the best route into the United States from that city. It is very important that you investigate several routes and border crossings as we have another operation planned that will require going through Vancouver. Do you think you can do all of this?"

Ressam put on a resolute and determined look. He sat straight up and squared away his shoulders. "Yes, my sheik. You have made me a very proud man to be trusted with such a difficult and dangerous task. I will do as you direct or I will die trying."

Chapter 53
Afghanistan: Thursday, March 11, 1999
◈

When the British Prime Minister Neville Chamberlain met with the German Chancellor Adolf Hitler in Munich in 1938, the civilized world breathed a sigh of relief. A general European war was averted. There would be "peace in our time", as Chamberlain put it.

Had the same world known of the secret meeting in the spring of 1999 between Osama bin Laden, Muhammed Atef and Khalid Sheik Muhammad in al Matar, near Kandahar, Afghanistan, it would have shuddered. The meeting was the final planning of an act that would lead to war in the Middle East.

Bin Laden now endorsed Kahlid's final plan of using loaded commercial aircraft as weapons. Bin Laden wanted to hit the White House and the Pentagon. Kahlid wanted to strike the World Trade Center. All three of them wished to destroy the U.S. Capital.

Detailed planning including the selection of the participants, who would take pilot training, the financing, the obtaining of passports and visas, and the selection of flight schools, started in earnest. It would culminate two and a half years later on September 11, 2001.

Bin Laden correctly foresaw the reaction of the US Government. He remarked to Atef; "Muhammed, this will cause the Americans to tighten up their borders. It will be very difficult, if not impossible, to infiltrate any more of our people into the United States after this attack. We should increase the size of our cells in America immediately, before they close the borders. It makes the American boys in our training camp, our second strike, all the more important. I just hope Zubeida is doing the job we are paying him for."

Chapter 54
Langley, Virginia: Monday, December 15, 1999
◈

Danielle thought the report from the Federal Bureau of Investigation was almost unbelievable. On Sunday, December 14, an alert agent of the Bureau of Customs had apprehended a man trying to smuggle explosives into the country at the Port Angeles, Washington border station. He was going to use them to blow up a target at LAX, the airport serving Los Angeles.

As she read the entire report she grew pensive. This was her worst fear, her personal nightmare, come true. *Al Qaeda* was striking at the American homeland.

The report detailed how a man named Ahmed Ressam, attempted to smuggle powerful explosives in the spare tire well of his rented Chrysler sedan. He seemed nervous to the customs officials. When they detained him for questioning, he tried to flee. The car was then searched and the explosives found. At the end of the report she read even more chilling news. Ahmed Ressam was from Algeria.

Danielle remembered a much younger brother of a friend of hers in Sidi bel Abbes named Ahmed. It could be the same person. Her first instinct was to immediately fly to the Seattle FBI office where Ahmed was being held prisoner. Then she thought better of it. She was not in any sense of the word a clandestine operative of the CIA. However, there was a remote chance that other *al Qaeda* members would be watching the building, observing who entered and left. If she were photographed, it certainly wouldn't do to have her picture possibly make its way back to Afghanistan. She decided that she would request the FBI to ask some questions of Ressam that would be helpful to her research. She wanted to know if he was the same Ahmed Ressam she remembered, if he was being directed by bin Laden, when and where Ressam had last met with bin Laden, who else had been in the meetings, and other inquiries relating to Ressam's training. She prepared a list of 37 questions and e-mailed it to Francis Reilly, the FBI's Special Agent in Charge.

Osama bin Laden was raising the stakes.

Danielle was worried.

Chapter 55
Afghanistan: January, 2000
❖

Osama bin Laden and Muhammad Atef had been very disappointed to learn of the failure of the Ressam mission. They had high hopes of its success. However, the plans for the "Kahlid plan" as they had taken to calling the aircraft plot, were still firmly on track. In addition they had another action underway.

For nearly two years, several of their personnel, al Rahim al Nashiri and an associate named Kahallad, had been working on a scheme to attack a ship off the coast of Yeman in the port of Aden. Originally they had conceived of a plan to ram an oil tanker with a small boat filled with explosives. Bin Laden convinced them that they would gain greater reaction if they targeted a U.S. warship. Blowing up an oil cargo carrier, even a "super tanker" would be a one-day's news story. Sinking a US Navy vessel would be a major blow to the Americans. The effect would reverberate around the world.

The ship plan was a source of pride to bin Laden. He did not conceive of it nor did he direct the actual operation or planning. He merely approved it and suggested improvements to an already good concept. It was an example to him of how *al Qaeda* was maturing as an organization. Cells around the world were coming up with concepts for terror and destruction and submitting them to him for approval and funding. His dream for a worldwide terror organization, with him as the senior leader, was being realized. He didn't get involved in details except on very, very special projects. The "American boys" was the principal of these. He and Atef were talking about this project this January day while resting around a fire in an over-warm hut.

Atef spoke. "Ah, my friend, I talked to Youssef Zubeida the day before yesterday. He told me that the boy's schooling and their rate of progress is exceeding all of his expectations, praise Allah! He said that all of the boys are significantly ahead of young Americans their age in terms of education and knowledge. He told me the boys tested higher in math, science and history than boys two years older in the United States. He is very proud of his achievements. I think it would be a good idea for you and me to invite him for a special dinner when he is next in the area. I am not being critical, but I don't think he gets the same kind of psychic reward that we get when one of our people is successful with a car bombing or blows up a building. Those things are not his mission in life."

"That is a very good suggestion, Muhammad. I sometimes forget that everybody is not motivated by the same things that we are."

Atef continued. "To change the subject, I believe I mentioned to you, that the Philippine smuggler, Panillo, told me he would probably deliver the tubes to Vancouver, in Canada. I agreed. I said that as long as he got them to North America, we would do the rest. Now I am not so sure. If a quick-witted operator like Ahmed Ressam failed to get a small amount of explosive across the border, how are we going to import a hundred tubes? The customs search must be much more rigorous than I imagined. I have great confidence in Panillo, he has been doing this for a long time and seemed quite confident he could deliver our goods to Canada. But I have real concerns about our capability. We had better put our best people to work on it."

Bin Laden turned to Atef and flashed that little smile he got whenever he was pleased with himself. "Muhammad, I have already determined how it will be done." Then bin Laden got up and went to a table where he picked up a book entitled *Soils Mechanics for Civil Engineers*. He walked back to where Atef was sitting and opened the book to a marked page with a photograph. "We are going to get the tubes across the border in one of these. The custom's officials will be afraid to open it."

Then bin Laden smiled again. "Our best people have already been at work."

Chapter 56
Carlisle Barracks, Carlisle, PA: Tuesday, October 10, 2000
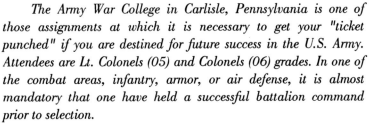

The Army War College in Carlisle, Pennsylvania is one of those assignments at which it is necessary to get your "ticket punched" if you are destined for future success in the U.S. Army. Attendees are Lt. Colonels (05) and Colonels (06) grades. In one of the combat areas, infantry, armor, or air defense, it is almost mandatory that one have held a successful battalion command prior to selection.

The War College is on the grounds of The Carlisle Barracks, one of the oldest posts in the Army dating from 1783, and it prepares its students for duty in the Pentagon for service on army, Joint Chiefs or Department of Defense staffs. It deals with strategy, logistics, war gaming and joint operations. The motto of the War College is, "Not to promote war, but to preserve peace", taken from the original mission statement by Elihu Root, Secretary of State under President Theodore Roosevelt.

In addition to military subjects, the curriculum includes history and geopolitics. This prepares the future leaders of the Army with an appreciation of world affairs. Each of the services operates a similar institution: The Navy War College is in Newport, Rhode Island, and The Air Force War College is at Maxwell AFB in Huntsville, Alabama.

High-level civilian employees of the government attend the National War College or the Industrial War College of the Armed Forces. In order to promote a greater understanding of the nation's defense team and to reduce parochialism, each of the services selects a number of students to attend colleges of the other forces.

Colonel Don "Red" Prather, so nicknamed because of the flaming red color of his closely cropped hair, stood in the front of his Army War College classroom. Here he taught his students about the history of the causes of the wars of the 20ᵗʰ century. The creators of the College's curriculum were firm subscribers to that expression finely chiseled in the marble frieze of the U.S. Archives building, in Washington, D.C.: "What is past is prologue."

It was almost the end of the class period, and Colonel Red Prather was concluding his lecture on the Philippine Insurrection. "It is a little remembered fact that this war was the direct cause of the development of the Army's Colt M1911 .45 caliber pistol, until recently our regular weapon for officers, tankers and others who would be encumbered by a rifle. In 1893 the Army's ordinance board adopted a Colt .38 caliber revolver as the Army's standard sidearm. In the Spanish war, this small caliber performed well in Cuba. However, in the Philippine Islands, it proved incapable of stopping the Moro tribesman. These people, charging with their razor sharp *krises*, kept right on coming at our troops, even after being shot a number of times. They were fanatics. As the *Kris* is a slashing weapon, rather than one designed for puncture, like a bayonet, we lost a lot of men to beheadings and dismemberment. The Army was forced to immediately develop a more powerful weapon, the .45 ACP (Automatic Colt Pistol). A shot from this pistol, firing a 350 grain bullet at 1900 feet per second, will, as you know, knock a man off his feet."

"Does anyone in the class know what inspired the Moros to their high level of ferocity?

"No? Well, let me tell you something about them."

"The Moros had been fighting the Spanish for 300 years. They also fought those Filipinos whom the Spanish had converted to Catholicism. When the Spanish withdrew from the Philippines, the Moros turned against us. Their descendents are still fighting. They now conduct operations in two organizations, *Abu Sayyaf* and *Jemaah Islamiyah*. The Moros are Islamic Jihadists. They believe that all people are either Islamic or Infidels with no right whatsoever to be on this earth.

The United States had its first exposure to Islamic terrorism over 90 years ago. That's something to think about this day after we celebrate Christopher Columbus and his coming to this land that now, under our constitution, practices freedom of religion; today is also the day after the Jewish holiday of Yom Kippur!"

"The class is dismissed."

Colonel Prather was a knowledgeable and proficient lecturer. He practiced the art of finishing every talk with a "zinger" closing line as the class ended and his students left the room. Now, class done, Prather stuffed his lecture notes into a brown Army issue attaché case. When he snapped the lid closed, a thought jumped into his mind. "If only we could solve today's terrorist problem as simply as we did in the past. The invention of a better weapon."

Prather mused about the thought. He liked the line. He resolved to use it on a future class.

Chapter 57
Zamboanga, The Philippines: Monday, Dec. 4, 2000

Bong-Bong Makaisa rolled down the steel shutters of his little shop as he had done, nearly every night for 23 years. He would perform this ritual just 16 more times. Then he would be on his way to the United States.

In the early years of their marriage, Makaisa ignored the importuning of his wife to move to be with her sister in Washington, D.C. Finally, he relented and applied for a visa. Now, a dozen years later, the confluence of several events caused him to be happy when the visa was finally granted. The first and most important of these was economic. A western-style shopping center opened up less than a mile away and reduced his business by one-half. His customers now bought their *barong tagalogs* from a large company that imported them from China. These were marketed at less than the price that Makaisa had paid local women to sew the merchandise he sold.

The second reason was Khadaffy Janjalani. Janjalani's older brother, Abdurajik, and Makaisa had been friends for many years. When Abdurajik was killed by the armed forces of the Philippines, Khadaffy had taken over their Islamic organization, *Abu Sayyaf*. He vowed revenge against the government.

Makaisa was a Moro. He was an affirmed Muslim separatist, as was his Father before him, as was his Grandfather. From the time he was a child, Bong-Bong had heard about the heroic deeds of his male relatives. Killing infidels was part of the family history. He himself had participated in numerous armed raids against government installations. They would sneak into Army posts at night and kill the government soldiers as they slept. Now, with the killing of Abdurajik, there was additional incentive.

When he met with Khadaffy Janjalani several months earlier to announce his impending departure for the United States, his leader expressed pleasure. "It is a good thing. My brother

Abdurajik long wanted to organize some loyal fellow Muslims in the United States. He wished to work against the Philippine government's interests in America. Now you can help me to set up such an enterprise."

Then Khadaffy did something most impressive to Makaisa. He told him that they would communicate in a secret code over the Internet. Bong-bong did not have a computer, but he knew about the Internet. Some of his friends possessed these wondrous machines. He had long aspired to own one. The shopping center had put an end to that dream.

Khadaffy took Makaisa into the hill country to visit an old man he knew in order to learn about the secret code. The man was a Japanese, a soldier in WWII, who had gone into the mountains at the war's end, rather than surrender. There he had met a *Filipina* and started a family. During the war the soldier had been a code clerk, and when he fled, he took his codebooks with him. They were still in his possession, in their original waterproof cases with the rising-sun seal of the Japanese army. As he and Khadaffy had been friends for many years, he was only too happy to make a gift of the codebooks. He was also pleased to offer instruction on their use to Khadaffy and Makaisa. As the books were for the coding of Japanese words, it was necessary to acquire Japanese/Tagalog dictionaries for both the sender and receiver of messages.

Makaisa arrived in the United States and settled in a large Filipino community in the Oxen Hill area of Prince Georges County, Maryland. Five weeks later, he purchased a computer. Using the code machine and dictionary, he sent the following message to Khadaffy:

> *Have safely arrived in Washington and rented an apartment. My e-mail address is MindanaoBongo@AOL.com. I have found a management job with a contractor cleaning government and office buildings. I have already met several friends who will be helpful to our cause.*
>
> *Bong-Bong.*

Chapter 58
Fort Meade, Maryland: Wednesday, April 25, 2001
◈

Charles Myers inserted the floppy disc into the "A:" drive of the computer terminal on his desk. The disc was dated February, 2001. Meyers was 60 days behind in his work. The disc was a copy of an encoded Internet message. It was directed to Myers because he was a cryptographer.

The entire National Security Agency crypto section was always running behind. They attacked the high priority messages first and barely managed to keep up with those. The priority mail included all transmissions from several select Middle East countries, North Korea and the Peoples Republic of China. The latter was treated as high priority, thought Myers, only through force of habit. He hadn't gotten any really worthwhile intelligence in months. The commies were now almost exclusively concerned with commercial interests. Their overseas traffic was principally directions to their agents in the U.S. about what technical designs the engineers at home needed to have lifted from IBM, Microsoft and other developers of civilian technology in the computer fields. It was interesting reading, but hardly of consequence to national security. When he was caught up on the priority transmissions, Myers turned to the other mail.

Myer's monitor lit up with the introductory information display:

> *Encrypted message taken from an Internet transmission, 18 February 2001. Sender located in Zamboanga, Republic of the Philippines. Screen name Mecca5. Possible terrorist communication. Break and send results to Sanford Parcell, Chief, Islamic Terrorist Section.*

The screen next showed the garble of numbers and letters of a coded message. It was strange, unlike any code that Myers was familiar with. He directed the message to the Cray supercomputer on which was stored all of the codes currently in use around the world. Because a simple thing like the transposition of letters in a word before encoding would create something the computer couldn't recognize, the program had to contain all of the variations that man could envision. The program was enormous. The computer went to work. Monitoring lights flashed as it began to run through all of the permutations in its logic base. 17 minutes later, his CRT flashed the message, "No known structure."

This was going to be interesting. Myers enjoyed a challenge.

The next step was to load up a computer with a program of older codes, not current within the past 10 years. This program was larger than the one containing the current codes. It was huge, too large to keep permanently stored. Myers had to e-mail the computer control room and request a special loading, as the supercomputers were always booked up. He filled out a computer time-requisition form and waited for a response. Nine minutes later he received notice that the program he requested could be available at 0315. As Myers fully expected to be home in bed at such an ungodly hour, he e-mailed the disc to the geeks in the computer room with the request that they run it for him. As it was close to quitting time, he closed up shop and went home. By the time he pulled in his driveway in Bowie, some 40 minutes later, he had forgotten all about the message from Zamboanga.

Myers, in fact, didn't really remember the Zamboanga message until he pulled into the NSA parking lot at 7:40 the following morning. At that point he became mildly curious about what the geeks had come up with. He skipped his customary coffee stop in the cafeteria and went directly to his desk. He would get his coffee later. Unfortunately, later was not to come.

When he arrived at his cubicle, Myers immediately noticed a blinking light notifying him of a priority e-mail. He entered his personal code, *10reddog56* (his birthday and dog's name) and opened his mail.

This is what he saw:

> *To: Charles Myers, Crypto section #3*
> *Fr: William Warren. Chief, Computer Control*
> *Re: Message for analysis by the "Old Codes" program*
> > *Where did you come up with this?*
> > *This is the code that Herbert Yardley broke in 1942.*
> > *It is one of the oldest codes we have in the program. It is a Japanese military code from WW II. This is a variation of the same code that was used to fake the water evaporator report on Wake Island. The Japanese bit on our fake report and moved their fleet. We won the battle of Midway as a result.*
> > *The message follows in clear Japanese. I didn't send it up to the translation section. You will have to do that, unless of course, you are a Japanese speaker.*
> > *You guys in crypto continue to amaze me.*

Myers was stunned. Everyone in NSA knew about Yardley. He was the nation's preeminent code breaker in the 1940s. He had successfully rendered Code Purple, the Japanese naval code. Now the 60-year old code was being utilized again. Why?

This couldn't wait for e-mail. Myers picked up the telephone and called Peter Hutchins, Director of Translation-Oriental Languages.

"Peter, this is Chuck Myers in Crypto. Do you have a minute? I would like to come up and meet with you regarding a message we just decoded. It is in Japanese so we are going to need a Japanese translator. No, I don't know how important it is. That's what your translator is going to find out. I'll be right up."

Myers walked down the hallway, past the elevators he normally used, to another bank of them at the far end of the building. On the way he passed two sets of fire stairs. In the past, he would have taken the stairs up the two flights to the translation section. However, a year earlier, in yet another effort to improve physical security, the stairwells were wired. If any of the stairway doors was opened, a very loud bell went off and guards came running. The theory was that in the event of a fire, the alarm wouldn't matter. It seemed to Myers that the place was going security crazy.

Myers shared the elevator with an attractive girl whom he had not seen before. He smiled. She smiled back. Just as he was fumbling to develop a snappy comment, he arrived at his floor. He would have to ride this bank of elevators more often.

Hutchins's office was at the end of the hallway, on the outside wall as befitted his position. Most of the employees at NSA were stuffed into small, windowless cubicles constructed of chest-high "space management" systems. Hutchin's office was not on a corner. Those were reserved for the Assistant and Deputy Assistant level. But it was a large office with three windows. Myers blinked at the brightness as he walked in. Although they were not close in their personal or business relationship, Myers was on a first-name basis with Hutchins. Myers spoke as he moved to Hutchins, his arm outstretched to shake hands.

"Good morning, Peter. I appreciate your seeing me on such short notice! I think I have a hot potato that needs immediate attention. I have been advised by the boys in computer control that a message I am working on is in Japanese, in their WWII code Purple. As this is a code that hasn't been used in 60 years, we are all a bit curious to see what the message is about. There is always a chance that it could be from army headquarters, directing General Homma to place additional troops on Guadalcanal, but I don't think so."

"Morning, Charles. I got your request for translator. Mr. Furakawa should be joining us in a minute. Before he gets here let me tell you a little about him. He is a child of *nisei* Americans. He was born in an internment camp in California at the end of the war. Apparently, he never held anything against our government, because he joined the Department of State as a

translator when he graduated from UCLA. He is ahaa.....
.....Good morning, Saburo. I would like to introduce Charles
Myers from cryptology. Mr. Myers has an unusual problem. He
has been working on a message which turns out to have been
encrypted in a code I think you are probably familiar with. Pull
up that chair and have a look."

Furakawa pulled up a seat to the edge of Hutchin's desk
and took the single page that was handed to him. He read the
first several lines and stopped. "This was written by someone
who is not a Japanese speaker. The word order and the grammar
are extremely crude. No Japanese of even the slightest literacy
would express himself in this manner." I will have to paraphrase
the message I think is being sent. A direct translation of this work
would be almost unintelligible." Furakawa took a yellow pad and
began writing, as Hutchins and Myers looked on intently. He
wrote, crossed out and wrote again, for almost five minutes. Then
he laid down his pen and began:

"My dear friend: I was very pleased to learn of your safe
arrival in Washington, also to learn of your new contacts. Now
that you have a home, I will send weapons and explosives packed
in the luggage of travelers. They will arrive as tourists. Send me a
telephone number where they can call you. K"

Hutchins was the first to speak. "Who sent this to you,
Charles?"

"Sanford Parcell."

"When was it lifted?"

"Damn, it's over 60 days old!"

"Then I think you had better get this to Parcell before our
'dear friend' gets his explosives and blows something up. I hope
he understands what is going on with this old Japanese code,
cause I sure as hell don't."

Chapter 59
Justice Dept., Washington, DC: Monday, April 30, 2000
◈

When principals from agencies outside of downtown Washington meet with principals of agencies located in the District of Columbia, there is a tendency to hold the meetings in town and start around 10:00 AM. In this method the commuters avoid the congestion of the normal inbound traffic. Unless the meetings are unusually short, and meetings of principals rarely are, the attendees can also enjoy luncheon together. This is of special interest for those coming in from the suburbs where the nearby restaurants are generally of the chain variety. Accordingly, at 10:00 AM on April 30, 2000, the following people assembled in a conference room in the Department of Justice building on Pennsylvania Avenue: Hugh Morrison, Deputy Assistant Attorney General, Department of Justice; Carl Walker, Assistant to the Director, Federal Bureau of Investigation; Mary Henderson, Assistant to the Director, Bureau of Immigration and Naturalization; Sanford Parcell, Chief, Islamic Terrorist Section, National Security Agency; Dr. Danielle Lamaze-Smith, Deputy Assistant Director, Central Intelligence Agency. These people were gathered to discuss the resolution of the mysterious coded message intercepted by NSA the previous week

As the matter of terrorists operating within the continental United States was within the jurisdiction of the Federal Bureau of Investigation, the meeting would normally have been held in the J. Edgar Hoover building. However, Mark van Rensellier of the CIA, having been told of the developing situation by Danielle, called a friend at the Justice Department and managed to get the venue moved to more neutral turf. As it was in his conference room, Hugh Morrison chaired the meeting. After the normal pleasantries and introductions, Morrison began.

"As we all know, last week NSA intercepted and broke the coding of a message that suggests explosives and weapons are going to be coming into the United States. As I see it, this meeting has been convened to make the following determinations that I have listed on the agenda." As he spoke, Morrison passed around a printed page.

AGENDA
INTER-AGENCY TASKFORCE
DOJ, FBI, INS, NSA, CIA
27 APRIL 2000
1: Assign responsibility to determine the origin of the message and whether it is an individual or a group.
2: Assign responsibility to identify the recipient of the message and whether it is an individual or a group.
3: Attempt to determine the nature of the threat.
4: Evaluate the significance, if any, of the use of an old Japanese code.
5: Discuss possible courses of action, when the participants have been identified.
6: Discuss long-range threat assessment

"I think this covers everything. Shall we get started? As item number one involves an offshore situation, let us hear from the CIA first. Dr. Lamaze-Smith." Morrison nodded at Danielle.

"Thank you. As it is clear under federal statute that all intelligence operations on foreign soil are the within the mandate of the Agency, I don't think there is any disagreement on who the responsible party is." Danielle delivered this salvo right in the beginning, in order to prevent the FBI from even thinking about getting their liaison agents in the Manila embassy involved. She continued. "Item one, identifying the sender has already been accomplished. Our people in the Philippines worked over the weekend. They contacted the local Internet Service Provider (ISP) and obtained the identity of the screen name Mecca5. K turns out to be (as I suspected) Khadaffiy Janjalani, the leader of the Islamic terrorist group *Abu Sayyaf*. He operates out of

Zamboanga and has been getting more aggressive since his brother was killed. This is a threat we should take very seriously."

"Thank you, Ms. Lamaze-Smith." Morrison was taken aback. He had not anticipated that the CIA would be so aggressive. They were lucky, working in areas where there was no government concern about privacy. They could move more quickly in foreign countries. Now he was going to be embarrassed by a Justice Department agency, the FBI. He sought to ameliorate their lack of progress.

"Mr. Walker, I know that you have to work within the legislation that protects the privacy rights of individual citizens. As it was over a weekend, you have not yet gotten a court order to enter and gain access to the files of AOL. When do you think you will have the identification and other information on Mindanaobongo?"

"Well, the fact is, we already know his identity. I was 'surfing the net' last night when I got an inspiration. I sent Mindanaobongo a phony questionnaire from a fictitious government agency. I just checked my e-mail before I came to this meeting. He fell for it. We are dealing with a man calling himself Bong-Bong Makaisa. He lives in an apartment on Fort Foote Road in Oxen Hill. I just sent a couple of agents to the landlord's office. By the time this meeting is over we should have his real name and other particulars."

He assumed a large smile and became almost jovial. The FBI was not being out-performed by the CIA!

"That was very resourceful of you Carl. Between you and the CIA in the Philippines, we are much farther along in this case than I thought we were an hour ago, when I dictated this agenda."

"I've asked Ms. Henderson to join us this morning to fill us in on the size of the Filipino community in the Washington area."

"Thank you Mr. Morrison. Before I give you the statistics, I do want to correct the misapprehension of Mr. Walker. Bong-

Bong is not a codename or a *non-de plume*. It is a real name in the Philippine Islands. I know it sounds like the nickname of a drummer in a rock group, but it isn't."

"As we all know from personal observation, the Washington metropolitan area is becoming a destination for immigration from all over the world. The estimated total population of the Standard Metropolitan Statistical Area is about 6,800,000. This should be confirmed when this year's census data becomes available. Approximately 832,000 of this population, or 12%, are foreign born. The Philippine immigration count was 11,800 nationally over the last decade. Of these, more than half, 6,800 settled in Washington.

There is a large population of people from the Philippines in lower Prince George's County as well as in Fairfax County in Virginia.

"I don't have our documentation on Mr. Makaisa as yet, but I will certainly send it to any of you who wish it when I get back to my office. Just leave me your cards with your e- mail address.

"Finally, as you all know, the procedures for admittance to this country leave a lot to be desired. Obviously, we deny entry to known terrorists or criminals. However, the ability to get information on individuals in other countries is frequently difficult. Sometimes it is impossible. It is not too hard for an enterprising individual to slip through our net. My agency has been concerned about this for years. To add to the difficulty, the Congress has refused to budget the enormous investment in computer hardware in will take to insure that entry points have access to all the information they need. Without this, we cannot always refuse admission to people we don't want in our country. I have the feeling, which I'm sure is shared by many of you, that we are going to have a major incident sometime in the future. Something will happen and then all of us, the INS, the law enforcement and the intelligence agencies, are going to take the blame. I don't mean to blow off steam, but this is how I feel. Thank you."

"Thank you Ms. Henderson. I for one certainly agree with you. Our country is going to take a hit someday and then all of us will be the fall guys. As I am nearing the end of my career, I hope I finish my watch before the stuff hits the fan."

"Next for discussion is our joint best-interpretation of the nature of the threat. Who has an idea?"

There followed some 20 minutes of discussion, at the end of which nothing conclusive had been established. Since only Danielle had any knowledge of *abu sayyaf*, the others didn't doubt her characterization of them as serious, they just had no independent knowledge. The group concluded that the CIA should undertake a thorough analysis of *abu sayyaf's* recent activities in the Philippines to determine if there were any clues as to what they might try in the US. Concurrently, the FBI would survey all of its field offices for information on Filipino arrests and gang-related activity. It wasn't much, but it was a start.

With regard to what should be done with Bong Bong Makaisa, screen name MindanaoBongo, initially there were divergent views. Walker wanted to pick him up for questioning. Danielle and Morrison wanted to monitor his communications and try to learn more about what *abu Sayyaf* was planning. After weighing the possible benefit of any information obtained versus the risk of Bongo, as they all now referred to him, committing a destructive act, they determined to wait and watch. Morrison told Walker to place him under surveillance for the next three weeks.

Henderson asked the question, "Why only three weeks? Suppose he blows something up or kills somebody in the fourth week? Morrison then proceeded to educate the group on the "random walk theory" of personal movements:

"Some year ago the Germans did a great deal of research on the subject of continuing surveillance. I know it sounds simple, you just put a tail on your suspect and follow him around. However, watching a man for 24 hours, without letting him know you are watching, is an enormously expensive and difficult process. It is very consumptive of manpower and technical assets.

The Meinhardt studies demonstrated that placing a person under surveillance for a period of three weeks would provide approximately 80% of the significant information you need to know about that person. You know where he gets his hair cut, what restaurants he likes, who his friends are, where he goes to church, where his girlfriends live, etc. The 20% of the information you miss takes virtually the rest of a year to obtain. That is why we only follow a person for three weeks, unless of course there is the risk of flight. We will obtain a court order to place a tap on Bongo's phone and perhaps put a bug in his apartment. I promise you, we will know all about Mr. Makaisa in the next three weeks, except what he does for Christmas. Dr. Meinhardt called his studies the 'random walk' series because what may seem like random movements are generally repeated over a three-week period."

In response to Morrison's inquiry if anyone had any explanation for the use of the old Japanese code, there were no ideas. NSA hadn't seen the code since the end of hostilities in WWII. If the nation's code experts had no thoughts, how could the rest of the group come up with anything?

On the final agenda item, the long-range threat, there were no ideas either. There was, however, unanimity of opinion. The Islamic terrorists were on the march. Their activities were on the upswing around the world. Everyone in the conference room believed that inevitably, the Jihadists would strike in America.

Chapter 60
The Philippine Islands: Saturday, May 19, 2001
◈

Captain Sadeki Nakabayashi knew his ship was in trouble. The *Shinbun Maru*, heavily laden, was in danger of foundering. They had sailed from the port city of Davao, on Mindanao Island just eight hours earlier, on the way to Luzon. A sudden squall of the type the natives call a *chibasco* had sprung up. It blew off an improperly secured hatch cover allowing the ship to take on water. The *Shinbun* now lay very low in the enormous troughs of the storm, not that there was any danger of running into an underwater obstacle, for they were in the middle of the Mindanao trench, at 35,000 feet the second deepest trench in all the oceans. Only the Marianna's Trench was deeper, and it by a mere 300 feet. Nakabayasha couldn't think of a worst place to be. He had reversed course and was now headed back to Mindanao, the second largest of the more than 7,000 islands that make the Philippine Archipelago. It was a race that he had to win. The ship's pumps were fighting a losing battle trying to keep up with the inflows.

Captain Nakabayashi had spent 35 years running coastal steamers around the islands of the western Pacific. Never had he been more uncertain of survival than the present. He ordered the seven Maylays who served as his crew to stay in his cabin just aft of the bridge, instead of going below to their berths. Not that being topside would make much difference if they foundered, for they would never get their lifeboat launched in such a raging sea. Now he was alone in the wheelhouse with his mate, a Filipino from Manila; the mate was audibly praying to the Virgin Mary even as Nakabayasha silently prayed in Shinto. If only he could get to the island, he would run the *Shinbun Maru* up on the shore and beach it. Re-floating his ship was a problem that he hoped he would have.

The ship's radar, with its revolving antenna located at the

top of a relatively low mast, was useless. It was fouled by the return of the spray and by the tops of the waves when the ship was in a trough. What was working, splendidly, was the big Fairbanks Morse diesel engine. It had been rebuilt just the previous year by the *Cabanataun Machine Works* in Subic Bay and was running perfectly. The Captain silently thanked the god who looked after engines.

Finally, after some additional three hours, during which time his ship continued to sink ever deeper in the water, the storm began to lighten up. At almost the same time, Captain Nakabayashi spotted a shoreline. He didn't know exactly where he was, but undoubtedly what he was looking at was the northwest shore of Mindanao. He was unsure about whether to run hard up on the beach, which could rip his bottom out. An alternative was to cut his power and allow his ship to be carried ashore by the waves. This course ran the risk of causing him to lose steerage and being turned broadside. This could result in the destruction of his ship by the waves dashing it on the volcanic rock that typically lay a little offshore. He chose to cut his power to the point where he could just maintain headway and steer straight in.

There was a grinding crunch as welded plates were stretched and ripped. Then, so abruptly that Nakabayashi was thrown to the deck, even though he was bracing himself, the *Shinbun Maru* stopped. The captain told the mate to cut off the main engine but to keep the auxiliary running, to provide electric power. He, the crew and the ship were saved.

Approximately 35 minutes after the *Shinbun Maru* was beached, a dozen men armed with AK 47 automatic weapons appeared out of the darkness. They boarded the ship at the bow by throwing up a line and snagging a rail. They hardly got their feet wet. They went forward to the bridge and shot the Captain and mate. When the crew came up from below decks where they had been since landing, they were also dispatched. The killers were members of *Ajemaah Islamiyah*, an Islamic terrorist organization.

A short, swarthy man with blazing dark eyes, gave orders.

"Tanzi, get the bodies off the ship and to the truck. Galib, you and Abu get some water and wash away any bloodstains. We want to make it look as though the crew were all swept overboard and drowned in the storm."

Riduan Hambali surveyed his newly acquired property. He knew they had a day, two at the most, to strip the ship of everything valuable, before they were detected. Someone, a fisherman, a low flying inter-island aircraft or a beachcomber would spot them. Then it would take another six hours for the authorities to arrive. It would be tight, but they could remove everything of value in 24 hours.

Hambali went below deck to inspect the engine room. Gleaming like a new jewel in an old setting was a beautiful diesel engine. A brass plaque announced that it had been rebuilt by the *Cabanatuan Machine Works* in 1998. They would have to use an acetylene torch to cut the drive shaft and the engine mountings. That would be easily done. The hard part was going to be getting an engine that weighed over ten tons out of the engine room, on deck and into a barge, but it could be accomplished. They could use the ship's own boom and electric winch. Hambali knew where he could find a barge and a small tug. The Panillos would pay handsomely for an engine they had rebuilt just last year.

He climbed the ladder back to the deck where he could use his cell phone. He had to get additional men and an acetylene torch. Allah had performed a miracle and dropped a small fortune in their laps.

Chapter 61
The Philippine Islands: Saturday, July 7, 2001
◈

On the morning of July 7, 2001, Khadaffy Janjalani was having a cup of coffee and reading *The Star*, a Philippine newspaper. The story in which he was so engrossed was an account of how his organization, *Abu Sayyaf,* had received financing and training from Osama bin Laden for an assassination attempt on the life of the Philippine President, Gloria Macapagal Arroyo.

The paper referred to an intelligence report that had been released on July 5, that described how the Islamic terror group *al Qaeda* had provided funds to "deploy highly trained bomb experts and suicide bombers to assassinate Arroyo."

The story further reported that "security measures around the president had been tightened, that "vehicles were being searched in the vicinity of Malacanang compound and the elite Presidential Security Group (PSG) was placed under heightened alert due to possible bomb threats.

"Security was also tightened around members of the president's family, after a separate report of an *Abu Sayyaf* assassination plot against Arroyo's eldest son, who serves as the vice governor of Pampanga.

"The day after the intelligence was issued, Sen. Rodolfo Blazon revealed that *Abu Sayyaf* are again training in the Taliban-run camps in Afghanistan. According to Blazon, some 50 members of *Abu Sayyaf* are currently training with the Taliban under bin Laden's auspices, a claim confirmed by Vice President and Foreign Affairs Secretary Teofisto Guingona Jr.

"Senator Blazon recently moved to convene the National Security Council (NSC) to assess the security situation before the 12th Congress convenes on July 23. Blazon made the appeal a few days after the *Abu Sayyaf* declared that the kidnappings of American nationals would continue if the government refuses to grant them a separate homeland.

"The demand was not new, however the group has now demanded an end to American support for Israel as well. While the *Abu Sayyaf* has always made vague political demands, it was the first time the group issued such a grandiose condition. Philippine intelligence sources claimed that the demand was one of the conditions specified by bin Laden for financial support.

"Sources at the Department of Foreign Affairs (DFA) confirmed that the Taliban is providing training for the Moro Islamic Liberation Front (MILF) as well. DFA sources claimed that while the Taliban actively supported the MILF's plan to create a separate Islamist state in Mindanao, most of the foreign assistance to the MILF is routed through non-governmental organizations (NGO's) from foreign countries, making it difficult to trace funding to its source.

"'What is established is that there is a flow of foreign assistance to the MILF", the DFA source said. 'Most of them are coursed through the NGO's. We can't really say whether government is involved except for the Taliban.' The Philippine government suspects that Pakistan and Libya also have NGO's that support the MILF with various forms of assistance."

The Star's story did not please Janjalani. As a proud and vain man he resented the emphasis on Osama bin Laden and foreign help. His own name was not even mentioned once. He would show the world that he was as capable as bin Laden, even if he were not rich. He would make the name of *Abu Sayyaf* as famous and as feared as *al Qaeda*.

He would find a way to assassinate president Arroyo and make international newspaper headlines doing it.

Chapter 62
Seattle, Washington: Wednesday, July 25, 2001
◈

Muhammad Shariff was well satisfied with his position in life. He had money. Not as much as he would like to have, but enough. He owned a chain of fourteen dry cleaning shops and was negotiating to acquire two more. He was a half-owner of two jewelry stores. He also owned a Middle East restaurant, *the Ahlambra*, in partnership with two other Saudis.

He had a fine family, Three children, two boys and a girl. His wife was probably pregnant again with a fourth. They expected to hear a confirmation from the doctor next week.

He had respect. He was one of the financial advisors to his mosque. The Imamm regarded him as one of the strongest supporters of Islam in the membership. He was on the committee that visited new believers in the Seattle area. He was frequently able to offer new émigrés employment in his shops.

Most importantly, he had satisfaction. He was a contributor to the *cause*. As one of *al Qaeda's* most active members in the United States, he was responsible for the development of cells on the West Coast of America. Muhammad and Osama bin Laden had been friends since their days in Abdul Aziz College together.

Muhammad maintained a separate office from which to conduct his *al Qaeda* activities. Only a few very close associates, not even his wife (especially not even his wife!) knew of its existence. It was near the SeaTac airport and was disguised as an import/export operation. From here he carried on a regular correspondence with bin Laden, who used a courier to mail and collect his letters from Djakarta, Indonesia. Muhammad visited the office several times a week to make telephone calls and collect his mail.

It was on a bright sunny day in July that Shariff visited his office and found a letter from his friend, Osama. He remembered the day particularly, because the weather had turned to rain virtually while he was contemplating his friend's request. He did not think it a good omen.

Dear Friend:

I am writing you to request some help now, as I believe I may be unable to do so in a few months. This could be as a result of something we have been planning for several years and expect, God willing, to accomplish in the next few months. I may not be alive to write you or I could be in hiding.

I need you to provide an apartment for two young men and to be of whatever other help you can be as they are unfamiliar with the area. The apartment should be close to the Canadian border.

I expect they will be calling you sometime in the last quarter of the year. They will identify themselves by ringing you and using the word "Wusool". They will have only the special telephone number we created, years ago, that cannot be traced to you.

It is important that you not meet these young men. Do not take them to your mosque, introduce them to your friends, arrange a dinner for them or put them in an apartment house with any of our brothers. You should only deal with them on the phone. They will have money to live on, you don't have to worry about that.

I want you to investigate a soils engineering school where they can get good instruction on being field technicians, running compaction tests, etc. They both want to pursue this career. I don't want them to get involved in a one or two year program or anything longer than eight weeks. Just enough to learn about field-testing. Again, do not get involved in enrolling them. Just be able recommend a school.

The young men are on an important mission. If they are caught, they should not be able to identify you in any way. This is very important to me and to our struggle. I know you will not fail to be of service.

I am being guided by Allah to punish the Americans.
Keep me in your prayers,
Your Friend

Chapter 63
Afghanistan: Tuesday, August 28, 2001
◈

Because of the increased danger from random missile attacks, bin Laden determined that no more than two senior members of *al Qaeda* should ever be together at one time. Today he was meeting with Aman-al-Zawahari who along with Muhammad Atef formed the ruling triumvirate of the *al Qaeda* organization. Bin Laden was clearly number one, of that there was never any doubt in anyone's mind. However, he purposefully left the number two position undefined. Sometimes it seemed to observers, if not to the individual, that Atef was the favored son. On other occasions bin Laden behaved as though al Zawahiri was the leading contender for the deputy position. Each had their attributes and made their own contribution, but neither had been named as senior assistant.

Zawahiri was a Pakistani, four years older than bin Laden and a medical doctor. He had been active in the *jihad* terror movement for years. There were some that thought him more devious and ruthless than bin Laden. He certainly knew the *Q'uran* better than bin Laden, almost as well as most mullahs, in fact. However, in spite of his experience in the movement and his knowledge of religious dogma, Zawahari lacked the charisma of bin Laden and the imposing command authority of Atef. The three of them liked to joke about the Americans' rewards of $5,000,000 for bin Laden and Atef, but nothing for Zawahiri.

Bin Laden spoke. "Kahlid Sheik Muhammad was here yesterday. He told me that at present the planned date of attack is September the 11th, the week after next. He is convinced that we are going to be successful and that tens of thousands of Americans will be killed. We are still planning to hit the World Trade Center, where most of the deaths should occur. But we are also trying to hit the U.S. Capitol and the White House. This will psychologically injure many more. I have been waiting for this day for years."

Zawahiri responded. "Yes, even if only several of our heroic martyrs hit their targets, it will be a powerful lesson to America and the rest of the world. It makes it all the more important that we have a television program prepared and ready to be recorded." Zawahiri had been working on a TV program to be broadcast from *al Jazeera* after the attacks. The substance of this program had led to the first serious disagreement between him and bin Laden.

Zawahiri had traveled extensively in the United States. He thought he had a better feel for the American people than bin Laden, who had never been to the U.S. Zawahiri wanted the post-attack broadcast to be unmistakably directed to all Americans, an absolute depiction of cause and effect. "You support Israel, this is what you get in return." Even though he had the most limited ability with the English language, Zawahiri was convinced that a plain direct message was what was needed. He and an English-speaking associate had collaborated on a text and submitted it to bin Laden earlier in the week. Although their draft was in Arabic, the English speaker assured him that the translation would be very strong.

Bin Laden rejected their work out of hand. Instead, bin Laden had prepared his own text. It seemed to Zawahiri to be vague and unclear and was directed to the normal Arab audience. Only in the last paragraph did he speak directly to the Americans, and then to impart just two thoughts. There will be no security for their country until the Arabs are back in Palestine and until the infidel armies are out of the lands of Muhammad.

As Zawahari read through bin Laden's work his unhappiness increased. The message completely missed the mark, he thought. It failed to take advantage of the opportunity to drive a wedge between the United States and Israel. Zawahari had observed in his travels around the U.S. that the Jewish population of the country was primarily concentrated in the big cities, and he had also learned that the average middle American didn't understand the reasons for their country's support for Israel. Here was an Allah-given chance to take advantage of a situation, and start to destroy public support for Israel. However, Bin Laden was still writing for an Arab audience.

Here was bin Laudin's text:

"What America is tasting now is something insignificant to what we have tasted for scores of years. Our nation, the Islamic world, has been tasting humiliation and this degradation for more than 80 years. Its sons are killed, its blood is shed, its sanctuaries are attacked, and no one hears and no one heeds. When God blessed one of the groups of Islam, vanguards of Islam, they destroyed America. I pray to God to elevate their status and bless them. Millions of innocent children are being killed as I speak. They are being killed in Iraq without committing any sins, and we don't hear condemnation or a fatwa [religious decree] from the rulers in these days, Israeli tanks infest Palestine – in Jeni, Ramallah, Rafah, Beit, Jalla and other places in the land of Islam, and we don't hear anyone raising his voice or moving a limb. When the sword comes down (on America) after 80 years, hypocrisy rears its ugly head. They deplore and lament for these killers who have abused the blood, honor and sanctuaries of Muslims. The least that can be said about these people is that they are debauched. They have followed injustice. They supported the butcher over the victim, the oppressor over the innocent child. May God show them his wrath and give them what they deserve."

"I say the situation is clear and obvious. After this event, the senior officials have spoken in America, starting with the head of infidels worldwide, Bush and those with him. They have come out in force with their men and have turned even countries that belong to Islam to this treachery, and they want to wag their tail at God, to fight Islam, to suppress people in the name of terrorism. When people at the ends of the earth,

Japan, were killed by the hundreds of thousands, it was not considered a war crime, it has something that has justification. But when they lose dozens of people in Nairobi and Dar es Salaam, Iraq was struck and Afghanistan was struck. Hypocrisy stood in force behind the infidels worldwide, behind the cowards of this age, America and those who are with it. These events have divided the whole world into two sides. The side of believers and the side of infidels, may God keep you from them. Every Muslim has to rush to make his religion victorious. The winds of faith have come. The winds of change have come to eradicate oppression from the island of Muhammad, peace upon him."

"To America, I say only a few words to it and its people. I swear by God who has elevated the skies without pillars, neither America nor the people who live in it will dream of security before we live in Palestine, and not before the infidel armies leave the land of Muhammad, peace be upon him.

God is great, may pride be with Islam. May peace and God's mercy be among you.

Zawahari was very unhappy with the speech as it was written. Here is what Zawahari thought should be the essence of the speech, to be broadcast right after the attack:

"I bear witness that there is no God but Allah and that Muhammad is his messenger. There is America, hit by God in one of its softest spots. Its greatest buildings were destroyed, thank God for that. There is America, full of fear from its north to its south, from its east to its west. Thank God for that."

But now he dared not raise the issue again. Instead, he chose to console himself that bin Laden was willing to make a video at all. The Taliban were against an attack on the United States, they would certainly be against a speech directed to the

American public. As they were guests of the Taliban, there was some question in Zawahiri's mind just how far they should push the Taliban's hospitality. The Taliban were much more concerned with the Northern Alliance and were requesting help from *al Qaeda.*

Still, bin Laden's was a dreadful speech, even allowing for the fact that Osama's degree was in engineering.

"My sheik, I think the text you have written is fine. It addresses both our people and the Americans. I think we should wait and broadcast it several weeks after the attack. This will insure that everyone in the world will pay attention to it. The enormity of our power should sink in before we make any statements."

"I agree with you, Zawahari. If the attacks go off on the 11th of September as planned, this program should be aired by *al Jazeera* in the first week of October. Let us say on the 7th of October for ease of memory."

"My sheik, your mention of the 11th of September made me think of something. In America they write the dates differently than we do. Here the 11th day of the 9th month is abbreviated 11/9. In America it is written 9/11. When I was in the United States, I remember being highly impressed with their national emergency telephone number system. Over the entire country the number is the same, 911. On 11/9 we will create an emergency so great that the President himself should answer the 911 calls."

Both men laughed. Bin Laden clasped Zawahiri by the shoulder. "The President may not be able to answer the phone. With luck both he and his phone will be out of order." And both of them laughed again.

BOOK TWO
September 11, 2001 - May 24, 2003

Chapter 64
New York City: Tuesday, September 18, 2001

Ehasan Khawalka had only received nine letters from Osama bin Laden since he had advised him on how to obtain real identities for young boys five years earlier. One of the letters had been a note of appreciation for such an excellent job of research. Seven letters had been regarding the disposition of large amounts of money that were being directed to Alliance Capital Company, the firm whose place of business was only a mailbox in New York's Grand Central Station. The last letter had been a warning to Khawalka to stay away from lower Manhattan on the morning of September 11. Khawalka worked at The New York City Department of Records on Chambers Street. He did not understand the message but trusted bin Laden. He found reason to be late for work last week on the 11th!

It was becoming increasingly difficult to move significant sums of money around the world. The U.S. government instituted various reporting requirements on banks and investment houses regarding large financial transactions not in the ordinary course of business. This was done in an effort to complicate the lives of the Colombian drug lords. It also served to make life more difficult for al Qaeda. Developing plausible stories for the generation of this money and producing the paperwork to support the stories turned out to be another of Khawalka's many skills. He was very creative. He invented receipts from sales of imaginary property, inheritances from the deaths of imaginary relatives, imaginary gambling winnings and other more complex reasons to justify large amounts of cash moving through Alliance.

The tenth letter to Khawalka from bin Laden was different from any previous requests. It requested his advice and assistance in a specific murder. The fact that this letter ironically arrived on the Jewish holiday, Rosh Hashanah, escaped both their attention.

Dear Friend:

What I am about to tell you will be, Inshallah, God willing, another great triumph over the infidels and their debauched country, the United States, that evil supporter of the filthy, cheating Jews and their stolen land called Israel they insultingly took from us. You saw the effect of Allah's power on the 11th of September. The aircraft that was piloted by Hani Hanjour, American Airlines flight 77, was planned to hit the White House. For some reason known but to Allah he diverted and crashed into the Pentagon. Now we must complete the unfinished business. We will prove that no one in America is safe from the wrath of God and al Qaeda. Not even the President.

Five years ago your help was extremely valuable. You gave the directions for obtaining the identifications of four boys. We followed your advice and now have four young men who are undetectable, as they possess real identities. These young men have been in training for five years to learn how to become American citizens. They have learned well. If you were to meet them, which you will not, I think you would be completely fooled. They have also learned about explosives and how to use them in assassinations. The explosives we have in mind will not require that we be close to the President, although the effect will certainly be better if we are a kilometer or less in distance.

I would like you to study the movements of recent presidents and determine an event that can be predicted. An event where the President is going to be outside the White House for a known period of time. An event where it will be possible to drive a truck to within one kilometer of the President's location.

Presuming you will be able to identify such an event, we will also need you to acquire a piece of property within 60-75

*kilometers of Washington. The property should be large
enough to afford privacy while the truck bomb is being
constructed. I believe a farm of about 20 or 30 hectares would
be ideal. Do not be concerned about the price. We will pay
whatever it costs.*

*I know that this assignment will be a burden on you, as
you live in New York and the research is in Washington. It
will probably take a number of your weekends.*

*Ehasan, this is a very important undertaking with a
great deal of risk. The Americans have already identified all
of the people in the plane operation. They know where they are
from, what countries they passed through, where they stayed.
They have enormous resources. It is absolutely important to me
and to our cause that you not be connected with this in any
way. Your role will only be to transmit messages and to lay
some groundwork. Your great value to me is that Muhammad
Atef and I are the only people who know about you. I am
confident that you have never discussed our relationship with
anyone.*

God be with you.

Bin Laden knew about men. He knew they could be divided
into three categories: killers, fighters and lovers. He was a killer,
as were most of the men around him. The only exception that he
could think of was Yousef Zubeida, who was a fighter. Fighters
had no compunction about being involved in the deaths of others;
they were just not willing to kill with their own hands. Bin Laden
had only met Khawalka once but had pegged him, quite
correctly, for a fighter.

To bin Laden, lovers were quite useless.

Chapter 65
Washington DC: Thursday, September 20, 2001
❖

In the aftermath of the attacks of September 11, the nation's intelligence agencies were all beehives of activity. Danielle found herself in meetings virtually all day, every day. There were internal meetings within the CIA to search for and analyze any missed signals that might have alerted them to the attack. There were meetings with the National Security Council and the Department of Defense to discuss an appropriate level of response and what other attacks might be imminent. And finally, there were meetings with the Congress of the United States to investigate the CIA's failure to predict the event and to make sure there would be no more surprises. It was the latter meetings that Danielle found so troubling.

In both the internal meetings and gatherings with other agencies, the participants were largely professional, and were experts in their fields. There was a collegial atmosphere. They were all involved in trying to assemble data. They dealt with facts. There was no attempt to assign blame. It was quite the opposite with the Congress.

Danielle's first experience with the United States Congress was both educational and depressing. She had accompanied the DCI and van Rensselier to a subcommittee hearing in which the Chairman seemed to be more interested in appearing dynamic to the audience than he was in getting information. Other members of the committee read questions from lists prepared by their staffs. Sometimes the question had already been asked and answered. At best the members had not been paying attention, otherwise they would not have asked the same question; at worst, the member may have recognized that their question was redundant, but wasn't smart enough to come up with an alternative on their own. Danielle knew that in a representational democracy it is not necessarily the smartest people who get elected. Indeed, she had formed an opinion from watching television news that the smartest people didn't run for public office. She had worked with many people at the National Security Agency who were absolutely brilliant. They were scientists and engineers who had no interest in becoming public officials.

◈

One afternoon, after spending the morning on the "hill" trying to explain to a group of Congressmen why the movements of Osama bin Laden were unpredictable, the three of them were riding back to Langley. Danielle, following the custom they had established when the three of them went places together, was in the front seat with the driver. The DCI and van Rensselier were talking in the back seat. The new administration had elected to keep the DCI in place. As both Van and Danielle were part of his personal staff, they had not been asked to leave the CIA either. In any event, Danielle wasn't concerned about her employment. Although she had technically left the career civil service to take a Schedule C position as Van's deputy, she was sure she that she could easily make the move back.

Suddenly and without warning, the DCI reached out and put his hand on her shoulder. "Danielle, forget the party line we have been giving to the politicians. What do you really think is going to happen next? What should we be doing?"

Danielle was taken aback. Although she was always careful not to contradict her superiors and believed that she was a truthful witness, no one had ever asked her personal opinion about what *she* thought should be done. Now the DCI was seeking her advice.

Danielle waited thirty seconds before responding. "Sir, sometimes I find the process of eliminating what won't happen to be a helpful exercise in predicting what might happen."

"The Congress, the FAA and the airlines are all focusing on preventing future airplane take-overs. They are strengthening cockpit doors, adding more sky marshals and installing more security apparatus for the passengers to contend with. I don't think any of these steps is really necessary. Osama bin Laden will not use airplanes in his next attack. I don't know what he will use, but it won't be airplanes."

"Bin Laden is a shrewd and wily character. He believes he is smarter than we are, he is enjoying the game of trying to outwit us. It would be offensive to him to use the same technique he did the last time. That would make us think that he had run out of ideas and he wouldn't want that to happen."

"Let's review his actions in the past. He carefully planted a truck bomb in front of the Khobar Towers in Saudi Arabia. When our security people started paying close attention to trucks, he switched to cars for the embassy bombings in Nairobi and Dar es Salaam. Then he blew up the "Cole" with a small motor boat. Finally, he introduced mass suicide bombers and plane loads of explosives. Each time he changes his *modus operandi*. The next time it will be something else."

"There are some things that I just don't worry about, such as poisoning water supplies. There are only a few known toxins strong enough that wouldn't require thousands of gallons or pounds of the substance to contaminate a typical reservoir system, with millions of gallons of water. Also, the toxins are hard to acquire. We can take water supplies off the list."

"Also non-risky now are large sporting events. I read that that the Redskins are not permitting people to bring hampers and back packs to Fed Ex Field. As we beef up security at these large events, I think that will have an effect upon Mr. Bin Laden's interest in using them as venues for terror. He has shown no inclination to push in areas where there are protective systems in place. This would also eliminate large chemical plants and nuclear facilities. In spite of the fact that we read stories about security penetrations in such places performed as tests, these kinds of facilities are really only susceptible to suicide bombers. And I believe *they* are in short supply in this country."

"All of the nineteen participants in 9/11 were from the Middle East. Most were from the Kingdom. al *Qaeda* went to great effort to infiltrate these people into the United States. If bin Laden had sleeper cells of people willing to commit suicide for Islam, he would have used them in the largest terrorist incident in history. He wouldn't be holding them in reserve for some future activity. The fact that *al Qaeda* had to import people tells me that he has no really radical folks in this country. He probably has a lot of people who are "sneaky Pete's", people who would be willing to plant bombs and kill, as long as they are not killed themselves. I think we can eliminate car bombers of the type who pull into a busy intersection and blow themselves up. It is not going to happen."

"Wait a minute, I spoke too fast. Let me back up. Five years ago, when I was with the National Security Agency, we got a lead on a special *madrass* school in Afghanistan. I thought then, and still do, that it is a special school for boys who will be taught to be terrorists and then inserted into the United States to wreck havoc. We haven't heard anything about the school for some years. However, now the boys ought to be about the right age to operate on their own. I would guess they now are sufficiently brainwashed to believe in the 67 virgins that await their dying for Allah. I presume these could become suicide bombers. Men!" she said, shaking her head.

"And what do I worry about? I personally worry about bombs being placed along the AMTRAK lines in the Northeast corridor. It would cause mass casualties if detonated when a train was passing. Better yet, pick a spot where two trains pass and blow up the track when they are both in the area. Railroad wrecks are spectacular and make great disaster photographs. We are putting airline travelers through the most thorough screening system that money can buy, because it is simple and something we can do. We are impounding nail files and small sewing scissors. We are not working on the security of 1000 miles of rail, because we have no ability to do so."

"Another worry of mine are shopping centers. They are impossible to control. People are coming and going all the time, most carrying packages. There are cars and vans always pulling up to the building to drop people off or pick them up. If bin Laden chose to start hitting random shopping centers around the country, people would be afraid to go shopping. The economic consequences would be very serious."

"Bin Laden doesn't do things that are expected. He does the unexpected. Do you remember the James Bond movie *Goldfinger?* The villain seeks to rob the U.S. Treasury of its gold stored in Fort Knox. This is located in the middle of the Army's Armor training facility of the same name. Goldfinger enters the post with a convoy of US Army trucks. That's the kind of stunt that I think would appeal to bin Laden; using army trucks to get into a restricted area. There will be a second strike, of that I am convinced"

"I'm afraid I've sounded off, but you asked me."

The DCI was thoughtful before he responded "Your analogy to Goldfinger seems very much on target. Two men, each extremely devious and entirely amoral. One motivated by money, the other by Muhammad."

As the car was at the junction of Route 123 and the George Washington Parkway, just minutes from the office, there was no more conversation. Each became lost in their own thoughts.

Chapter 66
Afghanistan: Saturday, October 6, 2001
◆

Osama bin Laden was a master of manipulation. He played people off against one another with a skill that had been learned and practiced since childhood. (If one has 51 brothers and sisters, such skills are necessary for survival!) Bin Laden also kept information compartmentalized. He did not tell the whole story to anyone. Only Atef had enjoyed his full and absolute confidence.

Although he had no reason to distrust Yousef Zubeida who was, of course, deeply involved in the secret of the boys, he did not inform Zubeida of his plans for them. This was not because he had no confidence in Zubeida; it was because Zubeida could no longer add value to the mission. His task was the education of the boys. He performed it well.

On the other hand, Kahlid Moqued, the young Pakistani who had grown up in America, was vital to the success of the undertaking to kill the American President. He would be responsible to get the boys accustomed to American life, help them rent apartments, acquire driver's licenses, get jobs, etc. He must be the one to do this because he had to remain the only one in America who knew about the boys and the secret of their hair color.

In late September, anticipating the American invasion of Afghanistan, Osama bin Laden had sent for Moqued. It took Kahlid five days to make the trip to the Tora Bora.

"So you are Kahlid Moqued. I have heard very good things about you from Yousef Zubeida."

"Thank you, my sheik. I have tried to the best of my abilities to contribute to the education of the Americans. I think your idea is brilliant. I am very honored to be a part of the program."

"Kahlid, do you have any idea of what the boys you have

been training are going to do in America?"

"No, my sheik. I only know that it will be a very important secret mission, perhaps blowing up U.S. government buildings or the United Nations."

"It is none of those, though you have just given me a very good idea. I had not thought of destroying the UN. It is something I shall now have to think about. It will show our contempt for their organization ruled by a so-called "Security Council" that includes not one Islamic nation as a permanent member! Yes, it is an excellent suggestion."

Kahlid beamed at the praise. "Thank you, my sheik."

"Kahlid, the task I have set for the young men is even more important than blowing up buildings. Six years ago when I conceived of this idea, I did not know what the boys' ultimate use would be. But now it is apparent. They will complete the undone work of September 11th. One of those airplanes that day was supposed to crash into the White House and kill the President of the United States. As we now know, not only did that pilot not hit the White House, but our intelligence was also faulty. The President was not even at home!"

"We are sending these boys over there to finish the job that was left undone in September, 2001."

"Now here is my reason for asking you to come here to see me: You grew up in the United States. Do you think you can be involved in this effort? Is there any reason why you would not want to do this?"

"My Sheik, I am a Pakistani Muslim, not an American. Although I was born and grew up in America, in my heart I have always belonged to the country of my Father's birth. I hate America for its anti-Arab, pro-Jewish policies. At my first opportunity, when I was old enough, I came home to Pakistan. Then I crossed the border to this country to join your forces. I am glad that my growing up in America was of use to our cause. I would like to continue to be involved in such an important objective."

"That was the answer I expected to hear. Good. I had heard what a great soldier for our cause you are!" Bin Laden nodded his head in affirmation of his pleasure.

"Khalid, I do not think it is possible to have you involved in the final action, that is the sole purpose of the American-looking boys. But, you can be very important to the success of the plan by insuring that the young men are properly set up. Even though they have been educated to be Americans, for a few months they will be like desert Bedouins coming into Riyadh for the first time. The Bedouins speak the language, they dress the dress, but they are uncomfortable in the city. I think it will be the same for our boys. I need you to help them get settled in and feel at home there. When you feel the boys are ready to be on their own, you should come back."

"I understand, my sheik, I think I will be able to know when is the correct time. I have lived with these boys for five years. They are like younger brothers to me. What do you want me to do?"

"You should help get them acclimated to America. I think it is a complicated country with many rules and regulations, We do not want our efforts of the past five years to be exposed because of the failure to observe a simple law. Each of the boys should get an American driver's license and own a car or truck. If what I read is correct, most young Americans own their own car. They should not have bank accounts or credit cards, as those financial connections will leave too much paper behind that can only help the American police. All transactions should be in cash. You will have to rent mailboxes in your name and arrange for monthly cash replenishment.

"There are two that will be staying in the countryside, close to the city of Washington where the government is. A house there has already been purchased for them to live in. These two should go to a welding school and get jobs as welders. The other two are going to the northwest coast of America, near the city called Seattle. I have made arrangements for them also to go to school, not as welders but as what the Americans call 'soils technicians', to learn to test the dirt on construction projects. Just as we have a house for the first two boys, an apartment has been located for these two in the Northwest. On both coasts you will rent yet another apartment as an address for their driver's licenses."

"We have to face the reality that since our attack on September 11th, the Americans have greatly increased their airport security. That is why you should travel by bus from Canada to New York City. You should then drive to Washington and Seattle. It is important to leave as few trails as possible.

"In New York City, your contact will be Sayyid Qutb. You will only be able to reach him at a mailbox number that I shall give you. Then, when you get to Seattle, you will contact another friend of our cause, Muhammad Shariff, at a private telephone number — I'll give you the number but you must memorize it before you go to America. Shariff will be helpful to you. He is a member of our organization, but you should be cautious not to tell him anything about what you are doing, particularly about the boys. It is very important that nobody but you know about them. Your identification sign for Shariff will be the single word *'Wusool.'*"

Bin Laden and Moqued spent the next day and a half going over additional thoughts that bin Laden had regarding the boys and their mission. During these conversations bin Laden asked many questions of Moqued about America. The shiek had obviously spent a great deal of time in planning, and Moqued was highly impressed with the leader's attention to details. Even the smallest elements had been carefully thought out! His sheik had an uncanny understanding of "how things worked" in a country in which he had never visited. He was so impressed, Kahlid thought it sounded like another American citizen was coaching bin Laden. But he didn't ask.

Kahlid Moqued was convinced the mission, with so much advanced planning, must be successful! *Praise Allah!*

Chapter 67
New York: Tuesday, October 9, 2001
❖

Ehasan Khawalka possessed several sets of business and credit cards as well as two driver's licenses. One was his real name and business affiliation: Ehasan Khawalka, Senior Operator, Information Technology Division, City of New York. The other was Sayyid Qutb, Principal, Alliance Capital Company.

Qutb was a member of the Muslim Brotherhood who had been executed in 1966 for trying to overthrow the Egyptian Government. Khawalka greatly admired Qutb and chose the name to honor him. In normal circumstances, Khawalka used his own name and address. On *al Qaeda* missions where he wished to remain anonymous, he became Qutb. Today at the Hertz rental car counter, he was Qutb.

His other wallet with his real ID was at home on his bureau. He used to be concerned that if he were killed in an auto accident or street mugging, there would be no way to identify him. He got over this by reminding himself that if such a thing happened, he would be dead and wouldn't care.

He wore a suit and tie, overcoat, a fedora hat pulled low, and dark glasses. There was no chance anyone would ever be able to recognize him on any videotape from some unseen camera. He made a point of telling the clerk that he was going to drive to Pennsylvania and asked about maps for that state. Even though he was only going to Washington on a three-day tourist mission, Khawalka conducted himself as though he were planning to rob the mint. His meticulous nature was helpful in such planning. He tried to think of everything, knowing that even the smallest detail could become important.

Khawalka had spent eight evenings reviewing microfiche files at the New York Public Library on 42nd street. He was looking at newspaper photographs from the *Washington Post*. He specifically wanted to see photos of Presidential travel and of the

President outdoors. He learned from this research that there were a number of activities that took place outside if the weather was decent. These were conducted in the Rose Garden, right in front of the oval office.

One was due to the President's association with diseases: the photo with the March of Dimes poster child, the muscular dystrophy child, etc.

A second activity was the various bill-signing ceremonies. These were set up when there were more guests than could be accommodated in the oval office.

Then there was the annual Thanksgiving presentation of a big tom turkey by the turkey growers. This had to be done outside. Nobody wanted to risk a forty-pound bird in the oval office.

Lighting the Christmas tree was obviously an outdoor event, as was the Easter egg roll on the White House lawn. This was traditionally conducted for underprivileged children from the District of Columbia.

Then he found it. A large gathering on the White House lawn with the President and other important dignitaries. It clearly stood out above all others as being ideal for his purpose. He knew that he had found the perfect venue for bin Laden's plot.

Khawalka drove to Washington. In the past, he would have flown. But after 9/11 the security procedures included a photo ID check. Although he had his Qutb driver's license, and used it to rent the car, somehow having security people at the airport examine his credentials made him uneasy. He didn't know what security checks AMTRAK required, but he guessed it would be similar to the airports.

Khawalka checked into the twin bridges Marriott in Virginia. After he unpacked, he returned to his car and drove south on Route #1. He got on the Washington beltway and drove over the Woodrow Wilson Bridge to Maryland. He took the first exit South and got on the Indian Head highway. He had checked some land and realtor listings on the Internet and found a couple of small farms for sale in an area called Southern Maryland.

The first farm he looked at was in Accokeek. It was 15 acres of open field and was surrounded by houses. He told the real estate agent that he was looking for something larger and more private. They continued driving south and entered Charles County, Maryland. There, in an area called Nanjemoy, he found exactly what he wanted. It was an old tobacco farm with a run down house and a large barn on 39 acres of land. The land was principally woods that the real estate agent called wetlands. "Mr. Qtub, these woods are considered to be 'upland wetlands'. Even though there is no standing water, they are protected by federal statute. I have to be honest with you. You will never be able to develop this property. All you will ever have is one house and that barn."

"It is perfect, just what we are looking for. I am certain my wife will like it as much as I do, after I get the house fixed up. I don't think women have the same ability we men have to visualize how things can be. They only see what is. It is just as well that she is not with me today."

Khawalka and the real estate agent went back to the man's office in LaPlata and wrote out a contract. The agent said the asking price was $250,000. When Khawalka asked about a deposit, the agent said, "one or two thousand dollars would be enough." Khawalka counted out twenty $100 bills and gave them to the agent. Khawalka said he would send a check for the balance when he got back to New York. The real estate agent said the settlement could be done by mail two weeks later, when the title search was completed.

Khawalka did not drive back to the hotel in Virginia. Instead, he went directly to the White House. The trip took exactly one hour and ten minutes, less time than Khawalka expected. This site was just perfect, he thought. *Allah be praised!*

Chapter 68
Afghanistan: Monday, October 29, 2001
◈

On October 29th, 2001, one month and 18 days after the greatest tragedy ever staged in the American homeland and a few days after the farm transfer was complete, Ehasan Khawalka wrote to Osama bin Laden with suggestions for an encore performance.

Dear Friend:

I have done as you requested.

I have studied the movements of recent past presidents. As you know, they travel a great deal of the time out of Washington and around the country. While it may be easier to get close to a president when he is in another city, as did Lee Harvey Oswald in Dallas, he used a rifle. As you tell me we will be using a truck, there is little ability to pre-position it in a city other than Washington. For this reason I agree with your conclusion. The assassination must take place in the city where the President lives.

Most of the time when the President is at home, his movements out of the White House are not announced. When there are public appearances in Washington away from the White House, the Secret Service use different routes to drive to the destination. Sometimes they clear the streets of other vehicles. It would be impossible to leave a truck parked on a street that the President's motorcade was certain to use.

After much analysis, I have concluded that our action must take place at an outdoor event at the White House. Such events are held in one of two locations, either in an area directly in front of the Oval Office, called the Rose Garden, or alternatively on the South Lawn of the White House itself.

The outdoor events are many and varied. There is one

however, that seems ideal for our purpose. It occurs on the south lawn of the White House. Because it is a major event, the President will be outside at least one half-hour. Exact timing for the placement of the truck will not be necessary. There will be several thousand spectators and participants, so the numbers killed may approach those of September the eleventh. There will also be another Head of State or Head of Government present.

It is called an arrival ceremony.

The White House has the Treasury building on one side and a strange looking building called the EOB on the other. However, 17th street (the street with the EOB) remains open to traffic. It will be possible to drive a truck within the kilometer you specified. This will put the truck at an oblique angle to the ceremony, but I presume this can be accommodated. It would be better if we could get the truck directly to the south of the lawn, on the ellipse (see map), but this is where the army parks four cannons for the 21 gun salute. I am sure the ellipse is secured and we could not get a truck into the area.

I have enclosed a map that shows the ellipse, the White House and 17th street. Also enclosed are some photographs and news stories of previous arrival ceremonies.

Meanwhile, I have bought a small farm of 13 hectares. It is located a little more than an hour's drive south of Washington. The farm is at the end of a long dirt road and quite private. It has an old house which needs some repair, but can be fixed up for the young men. There is also a barn in which the explosive truck can be parked.

The price was $250,000. I had that amount of money in our account, but now have only $47,000 after buying the farm. As that is much less than you usually keep in Alliance, you may want to replenish the bank account.

I am very pleased. I think both of these locations meet our needs.

Your friend.

Bin Laden continued to correspond with Khawalka. He wrote long lists of questions and alternative scenarios. Also there were additional items to purchase. Khawalka reinforced his amazement at bin Laden's ability to visualize a country he had never visited.

Chapter 69
The Philippine Islands: Thursday, November 22, 2001
◈

It was a ritual. Every Thursday night the owners of the *Cabanataun Machine Works*, brothers Epifanio and Pepito Panilio, had dinner together. Sometimes Epifanio went to Olangapo, sometimes Pepito made the trip to Manila. Sometimes they met at a small restaurant in between.

They did not meet for social reasons, although certainly the social interaction was important to each. They did not meet on the business of the *Cabanataun Machine Works*. That was discussed during the normal workday. And they certainly didn't meet to celebrate the American "Thanksgiving", which happened to fall on this day. They had never heard of it. No, they met on Thursdays to discuss their secret business of smuggling.

Tonight Pepito was especially jubilant! He had just acquired the means of getting the mysterious Afghan tubes to Vancouver. He could hardly wait for the waiter to leave the table before telling Epifanio about it.

"I have some very good news. On Tuesday I was visited by one of our friends from Mindanao. He had something he wanted to sell me. It seems that an old inter-island freighter lost its crew in a storm earlier this year. I think I remember reading about it. At any rate, the ship was washed up on the beach with no crew. The international maritime law of salvage was in effect. Our friend and his people stripped the hulk of everything of value, including the engine, a fine Fairbanks Morse that had just been in our shop for rebuilding a year ago. They cut it out of the wreck and brought into the yard as deck cargo on another ship. I got it for the bargain price of $15,000."

Ever the accountant, Epifanio asked, "And what do you think we can sell it for?"

We're not going to resell it, my brother. We have just found a way to ship those mysterious tubes the Afghanis want us to move to Vancouver. The engine is a Morse Model 251. It has eight, nine-inch cylinders. If I remove the crankshaft, the cylinders and the sleeves, the valve train, cam and cam gearbox, I think I can easily get a hundred three-inch tubes inside. The crankcase alone will hold almost three quarters of that amount. If I really need more room I'll take the rotors and fields out of the starter and generator. And I haven't even considered the turbocharger. When I get the tubes inside I'll bolt the engine back together. We'll even use the correct torque on the cylinder heads! Then I will add our usual paint job and brass plate with the date of rebuild. No customs inspector will even think twice. They'll just see another marine engine rebuilt by *Cabanataun*. We will have a custom-made steel shipping container, one that is X-ray-proof and not subject to being opened for inspection. I don't know why I didn't think of it before.

Epifanio could only look on with admiration. "Brilliant brother" he said, as he raised his glass of scotch in salute. Their dinner continued in good style.

Chapter 70
Afghanistan: Sunday, December 9, 2001
❖

Osama bin Laden mourned the loss of his friend, Muhammad Atef. Even though he had been a *jihadist* for many years, bin Laden had served but little time as a combat soldier. He was unused to having his close friends killed.

Atef and seven other *al Qaeda* fighters had been killed in an air attack outside of Kabul on November 16. The men were caught in the open by the accursed Americans. Bin Laden could not go to the body of his friend, but he was told that it was badly torn up. Even today, almost a month after the death, he still regretted his inability to be present at the burial. He knew in his heart that the loss of Atef was a small price to pay for the deaths of 3,000 Americans! He remembered what the German, Adolf Eichmann, had said when he learned of his own death sentence from the infernal Israeli court: "I will gladly leap into my grave knowing that I have killed six million Jews." Bin Laden agreed with Eichmann. Eichmann may have been an infidel, but he had the right idea about Jews!

As he shivered in the dank and wretched cave in the Tora Bora mountains, bin Laden admitted to himself that the Taliban had been right and predicted the American reaction. They did not want him to attack the Americans. They told him that he was "playing with fire." *Of course, they were only concerned with saving their positions. He was concerned with saving Islam!*

Now he knew he had to be on the run. He and several dozen of his most loyal men left their camp near Kandahar and had taken to the hills. It nourished him to know that all of the more than 300 men in the camp begged to be allowed to accompany him. Of course, that was impossible. It was hard enough to hide 30 from the Americans, much less 300

The Americans were everywhere. They had started bombing and missile attacks on the seventh of October. By the ninth of

November they had driven *al Qaeda* and Taliban forces from *Mazar-e-Sharif* in the north. Four days later the Taliban evacuated Kabul. Bin Laden was amazed at the speed of the Americans. He was also surprised at how little resistance the Taliban troops had offered. Not at all like the *mujehadeen* and the Soviets.

As he lay shivering in his robe, for the first time in his life he felt mortal. But now this new mission that he had conceived and nurtured with the boys was inspiring him to take chances and use all his management skills, all his charisma: this plan *must be* executed to its conclusion! He must get the boys out of the Hindu Kush and into the United States. Even if Yousef Zubeida did not think them ready, they could not be caught by the Americans. He decided that, in the morning, he would send the code word for the operation. It was a single word but it would cause them to evacuate "Little America" and start on their journey. With their French passports they would work their way to Paris. From there they would fly to Canada and go on to the United States.

The word was *"wusool,"* Arabic for "arrival."

It would be his second strike. The world would remember him for it!

Chapter 71
Afghanistan: Tuesday, January 15, 2002
◈

Youseff Zubeida had been anticipating the order from bin Laden to abandon the school, and yesterday the word had come. *"Wusool."*

Bin Laden originally had originally given Zubeida seven years to educate the boys. The American invasion of Afghanistan unexpectedly reduced that to only five years. Nonetheless, Zubeida believed they now were ready. They had mastered the English language and American history. They were at the level of a senior in high school in math and the sciences. While most others in the Arab world had only *al Jazeera* and state newspapers as sources of information, he and the boys had access to US television. They even had watched Fox news and CNN's coverage of the invasion of Afghanistan. Zubeida felt comfortable allowing the boys to see this. He used the event to raise their hate level for America. The boys were equipped with enough colloquial information to be contestants on Jeopardy, a game show they watched each week. The only thing Zubeida was at all concerned about was the age of Ali Sharqui, the Iranian boy, (now *Robert Ziegler from Michigan*). He was just 16 years old and wouldn't be 17 for five more months. Zubeida was unsure about how old you had to be in America to live on your own. But that really was not his problem. He had done his part. He had produced four Americans.

The plotters had prepared, and now were following, a plan of evacuation. The boys were each taking two suitcases with clothing, nothing else. As they owned no personal items, photos, etc., there was none of that to pack. There was a considerable amount of clothing, sports equipment and "toys" that they could not take. Bin Laden originally had wanted all of this destroyed so as to provide no clues that young men had been in the camp. Zubeida had talked him out of this decision and was distributing the clothing, bicycles, game boys etc. to the children of the guards. The appliances, generators, etc. were to be hauled to Kabul and sold. In the end there would be nothing left but the mud huts with their birch paneling. The American army, if it ever got to the Hindu Kush, would be amazed, but there would be no clues as to what had happened for the past five years. Let the Americans try to figure it out.

The boys all had their French passports, purchased from the finest forgery shop in Europe; although *al Qaeda* operated its own document "factory", bin Laden was unwilling to use it for security reasons. He didn't want anybody in the organization to know about the boys, except for the dozen or so who had been associated with the project over the past five years. The project had successfully been kept a secret until now. He didn't want to take any chances.

So, on Tuesday evening, January 15, the boys, once again with blackened hair, left the camp in the same horse cart in which they had arrived, five years earlier. There were tearful partings with their guards and teachers, even mullah Suquami. Kahlid Moqued, the instructor in American sports and customs who had become their close friend would be going with them to Paris and Canada and would stay a few months to help them get settled in the United States. Then he would return to Afghanistan (he was deemed a liability, due to his dark Middle Eastern appearance — even with his American passport he was obviously foreign.)

Bin Laden had been very specific in his instructions to Zubeida. No associating with anyone who looks dark or appears to be from another country. When they got to the United States the boys were to befriend Americans. Even though they were trained to behave as native citizens, they were young and still lacked the discipline of an adult. They might slip and forget their training in the company of other Arabs.

There had been much discussion between bin Laden and Zubeida about how they should leave Afghanistan. Zubeida wanted them to fly out of Kabul airport if it was functioning: he was sure the boys' French was good enough to pass whatever official questioning they would be subject to in the Afghan capital. But bin Laden was leery. He could visualize a French member of the multi-national force meeting the boys in the Kabul airport and firing off a stream of questions in French, faster than they were equipped for with their schoolboy language training. Bin Laden just felt Kabul was too unstable a departure point.

So it was in response to bin Laden's concerns that Zubeida had mapped out a travel plan that had them going back to Kabul by truck, then by rented van through Jalalabad to Peshawar and on to Rawalpindi in Pakistan. If they couldn't get an international flight out of Rawalpindi they could drive on to Lahore, where there certainly would be flights. Or, they could simply catch a plane to Delhi and then fly to Paris. It was difficult getting information in Kabul because the city's central telephone exchange had been damaged and was out of service, and obviously, they did not want to risk making international flight reservations on a cell phone...

As they left the camp this evening, the boys were delighted with the situation. After being cooped up in "Little America" for five years, they would have been willing to drive south and across India to Madras, 2500 kilometers distant, if necessary.

Chapter 72
Paris, France: Thursday, January 17, 2002
◈

With the start of hostilities, all regularly-scheduled airline flights into or out of Kabul had been suspended — the airlines were wary because standard airline insurance policies do not cover entry into a war zone. But by the time Zubeida, Moqued and the boys got to Kabul, the airport had reopened, and international flights were arriving with personnel from Red Cross, AID, UN and various other non-governmental organizations (NGO's). The passport control was loose. With the flights running again and security sloppy, Zubeida was relieved. He dropped the plan to travel across hundreds of miles of bumpy roads into India, cramped in a car with the four boys and Moqued. He made that decision without consulting Bin Laden, justifying to himself that conditions had changed and bin Laden was unreachable.

With outgoing flights filled to capacity, there was little scrutiny given to a Saudi businessman, an American and four young men with French passports exiting the country: they were just part of a flood of people who had been waiting to leave Afghanistan since the start of the war. Today's flight to Paris was smooth and uneventful, so Zubeida could relax. In fact, he enjoyed the flight more than any that he could remember. He, like the boys, was looking forward to visiting the great city.

When they arrived at De Gaulle, the boys were in awe. They were transfixed. They had been living in isolation for five years and suddenly, within three hours, they found themselves in one of the world's great metropolises. They were seeing things that they had read about but never experienced. But above all else it was the women that held their attention.

Yousef Zubeida had originally intended that they stay only a day in Paris before flying on to Canada. Now, before they even picked up their luggage, he could see that his plan needed to be revised. It was necessary that they spend several days, perhaps even a week in France. Strange, he thought; people normally went to Paris on a vacation to "decompress" from the rigors of their working life. The boys needed Paris to "compress" from the isolation of their home in the Hindu Kush!

Staying in Paris was not without risk. Although the boys were passable in French, they were clearly not as proficient as if it were their primary language. In the hotel their passports would identify them as French citizens. Away from the hotel they could adopt the role of American tourists, on a winter break from their school.

They needed this "compression" — but they needed some experience in the mysteries of sex.

Zubeida knew that sex in Islamic society is on a totally different plane than in Paris or the US. Young Arab men are usually virgins when they get married, particularly in countries like Saudi Arabia and Afghanistan where the teachings of Muhammad are the basis of civil law. Marriages are arranged. Women do not flaunt themselves, but remain chastely covered in *burkas* or *jilbabs*. The redeeming side, from the male point of view, is that a man is allowed four wives. He can also simply terminate a marriage by declaring it dead and marry someone else. This system assures that a man can enjoy the pleasures of the flesh throughout life to a far greater degree than in the western societies. Also, women are subservient to men, as Zubeida thought they should be. He preferred it the Arab way and had, himself, several wives...

However, he also knew the boys were going to be thrust into a society that seemed to be ruled by sex. Zubeida had never been in the United States and had, in fact, spent very little time in Western Europe. He was amazed at the amount of sex in advertising in the magazines and on the television. The boys, on the other hand, had all reached puberty while in "Little America." They had little recollection of life in the Arab culture. They saw nothing wrong in bikini clad pretty girls advertising automobile oil filters.

In the van, all the way into Paris from De Gaulle airport the boys were in a high state of excitement. They had never seen so many cars, so many tall buildings, and so many well-dressed people. Zubeida was glad they were talking in English. Let the driver be disgusted with the young American tourists!

Once they reached their hotel, Zubeida contacted an *al Qaeda* cell member in Paris. "Sherriz, this is Yousef al Wabi. Your name and telephone number were given to me by a mutual friend, a sheik now living in Tora Bora. I am sure you know whom I mean. I don't know why exactly he has an interest in this. I think it is for an old college friend of his now living in America. There are four boys around 17 years old. We need four young *poules*, about in their 20's, for a week, to show them the sights of Paris. I mean *all* the sights. The boys are from a private school in the 'States and are in Paris for the first time."

"Yes, I know it will be expensive, the cost is of no concern. The boys are from rich families. Sherriz, these girls should be very high class, clean *poules,* not cheap street girls." It would be well if they spoke some English. The boys have all studied a little French, but I don't think they learned in their French classes some of the words they are going to need." Zubeida paused in the conversation for a moment while he pondered what he was about to say next. "And one more thing Sherriz, I need a couple of older girls for the next several nights. We are at the Montfaucoln hotel. Can you call me back here with the arrangements by four o'clock this afternoon? Good, I'll wait to hear from you."

Zubeida pondered the next move. He was unsure just how much the boys knew about sex. What he was sure of was that the boys would rather be informed by Moqued than himself. It was always best to learn about this subject from an older brother, a role Moqued had played for the past five years, rather than from your Father.

At the meeting with Kahlid Moqued on what he wished to discuss, Zubeida had two points that were absolute. One, condoms should be worn at all times during intercourse. He did not want anybody coming down with a venereal disease or, Allah forbid, the new disease of AIDS, which he had heard about. Number two, there were to be no photographs taken. No tourist shots in front of the Eiffel tower or Versailles. None. The boys were going to be in their American identities. They could have no photos floating around for the Americans to discover. Zubeida didn't know how they did it, but he had great respect for the sleuthing powers of the U.S. government. Hadn't they, unbelievably, tracked down mir Aimal Kasi, the man who positioned himself at the entrance of the CIA in Langley, Virginia and killed several employees? It had taken four years, but the CIA finally bagged him in Pakistan.

Zubeida could take no chances.

Chapter 73
Montreal, Canada and Paris, France:
Thursday, January 24, 2002

In traditionally Catholic France, Islam is the second largest religion: there are more than 5 million Muslims in a total population of 60 million, over eight per cent. In Canada the ratio is less, some 600,000 Muslims in a total population of 32,000,000; that works out to slightly less than two percent. However, as most of this population is in several major cities, it is safe to project that of Montreal's 3.4 million inhabitants, about at least 75,000 or two-and-one-half percent are of the Islamic faith. This is a large enough group to support several organizations of Islamic extremists in Montreal. The intensity of feelings in the community can be seen at the "Montreal Muslim News Network" website which is substantially devoted to complaints about treatment of Muslims in Montreal and environs, especially in the courts, newspapers, broadcast media, and in public opinion. The website is headed "In the Name of Allah, the Beneficent, the Merciful"...

One of these extremist groups was Fayteh al Islam. While not a formal cell of al Qaeda, it enjoyed a close working relationship with bin Laden's organization.

Pirouz Matasar, the leader of *Fateh al Islam* received an internet message advising him that five fellow believers were coming from Paris and would stay Friday night in Montreal before catching a bus to New York on Saturday the 29th. He was requested to make bus and hotel reservations for Kahlid Moqued and four companions. Matasar was advised that he would be contacted by Moqued when the group arrived in Montreal, and that nothing else need be done by him for the visitors.

Meanwhile, tonight, on their last night in Paris, Zubeida took the boys out to a wonderful dinner at a pricey restaurant,

Chez Flambeau. He ordered wine for them, thinking it was a "first time" (unbeknownst to him, the boys and their *poules* had been drinking *vin* all week!) When they got back to their hotel he gathered everyone in his room for his final lesson.

"Tomorrow, Friday, after five years of being together, we will part company. You started those five years as boys, but today you are men! Like men all over the Muslim world, you have a sacred duty to perform. Your brothers in Islam are fighting and dying to protect our world and our traditions from the infidel incursion. Now you will have an opportunity to contribute."

"Five years ago I said that you four were especially marked by Allah with blond hair to blend in with the American invaders of our lands. Osama bin Laden himself has determined that you should take the battle to America, to carry on the work of the brave heroes of September 11. Tomorrow you will be in Canada, an infidel land. It is not the Great Satan that is the United States. But as soon as the next day, Saturday, you will be in the den of the enemy!"

"In America, you will all go to a house we own outside of Washington, DC. You will all stay there for several weeks until Kahlid feels you are properly settled in. Then he will leave Peter and George and take Carl and Robert to the West Coast of America, to the city of Seattle. After he has seen to it that all is well with Carl and Robert, Kahlid will return to Afghanistan. You will be on your own.",

"I do not know what our great leader has planned for you. I only know that you will be required to blend into American society, to live and work among them, to become trusted friends. When a mission is assigned to you in the future, it will be easy for you to carry out. You have been well trained. Most importantly, you are now *Americans,* not from the Middle East. The authorities will not suspect you. They will be looking for dark haired men with Arab names, not blond American teen-agers."

"One final reminder. You have all been extensively trained

in explosives. You have learned how to make suicide belts. If you are on any mission in which capture may occur, you must remember to wear your killing belts. The Americans absolutely must not take any of you alive. They will torture you and use drugs on you. You will not be able to resist. As you are the only ones in America who know about each other, you cannot risk the missions of the others. Of course, if you have to use your explosive belts, try to be close to some Americans so they will die with you. As the Mullah taught you, Islam does not condone suicide. But dying in the cause of Islam, particularly if an infidel dies with you, will assure your entry into Allah's kingdom."

"Now, I want to wish you all great success. I am very proud to have been a part of your lives for the past five years. May God be with you."

Zubeida could not go on any further. He was starting to choke up. He was not like the people at home who sent others on suicide missions, when those "others" weren't family or friends. Those people sending off the doomed followers were trained persuaders and inspiring speakers who could convince poor, uneducated, young Arabs that dying for Allah was a noble death.

This was different. Zubeida had grown to love these wonderful boys...

As they were preparing to leave the hotel for the airport at the end of a glorious week of excitement, sightseeing and sexual experimentation, Kahlid Moqued asked the boys, "Who has got their girl's address and has promised to write? Three sheepishly admitted to doing so. Moqued asked the three to produce the paper on which the address had been written. When these were collected, Moqued tore the paper into bits and flushed them down the toilet. "Men, remember to leave no traces of who you are or where you live. You must always be alert to this. Think!"

Moqued didn't know before that moment that the boys had their girl's addresses. But he was still young enough to remember that boys have a tendency to fall in love with their first sexual partner.

Chapter 74
New York City: Saturday, January 26, 2002
◈

The border crossing on the bus from Quebec province to New York State was uneventful. If the INS agent saw anything unusual in four young Frenchmen touring together in the United States, he didn't say anything about it. Kahlid Moqued, with his American passport, did not warrant so much as a second glance.

It was a long monotonous trip. The countryside from Montreal to the edge of the Ramapo Mountains just north of New York City was covered with snow, typical for the date and the result of a snowstorm that had passed through a few days before. As the distance was over 400 miles, the Greyhound bus ride took nearly nine hours in spite of the route being nearly all on the New York State Northway and then the Thruway. When they finally pulled into the Port Authority Bus Terminal, the boys were all asleep. They were unprepared for what they saw when they stepped outside of the terminal. To someone living in the Hindu Kush, Kabul was big and busy. This was surpassed by Paris and Montreal. But to them, New York was unbelievable. Even though they had seen many American movies and TV shows set in Manhattan, they were unprepared for the hustle and the crowds, even at this late hour. The terminal itself was a shock. It was a giant multistory facility serving more than 7,000 buses a day. The boys were in awe.

Khalid had booked three rooms at the New Yorker Hotel, across Eighth Avenue from Pennsylvania Station. Because Khalid needed to take the train to Newark and get his New Jersey driver's license renewed, and since he also planned to spend a few days with his parents, he knew that soon the boys would have their first test on their own. Khalid reasoned that even if they made some mistakes in representing their identity and origin, New York was big enough that it wouldn't matter. As it happened, their first test was in the taxicab from the Port Authority to the New Yorker.

Khalid had booked two cabs, talking to one of the drivers in Arabic. When two black-haired young men got in the cab, the driver asked, also in Arabic, "Where are you from?" Carl was just about to respond when Edmund, sitting beside him in the back seat, gave him an elbow and jumped into the conversation with, "what did you say?" When the driver repeated himself, Carl responded in perfect English, "I'm sorry, I don't understand you." The driver apologized, saying that he thought they were also from the Middle East. When they told him they were from Illinois and Wisconsin, the driver accepted the answer without question. They had passed their first test as Americans!

When they got to the hotel, the boys stayed in the background while Kahlid dealt with the registration. This was because they intended to rinse out the black dye in their hair when they got to their rooms. It would not be good if the desk personnel saw them first as dark-haired young men and later as blonds. Even in New York, that might cause some questioning on the part of the desk clerks.

They went to their rooms, washed out their hair, and watched TV until one in the morning, then they went to bed. The next day, Kahlid was going to take the train to New Jersey to visit his parents and renew his license, and to rent a car for the drive to the house in Nanjemoy. The boy's were going to go sightseeing around New York, a perfect Sunday adventure! Everyone was eager to get an early start. Kahlid was anxious to see his parents, the boys were anxious to be in New York on their own.

Kahlid thought of himself as a sibling. To the boys he was a major parental authority.

Chapter 75
The Philippine Islands: Monday, January 28, 2002
◈

Epifanio Panillo was working at his desk when he received a telephone call from a man who did not introduce himself by name. Instead, he identified himself by saying only that he was following through for Muhammad on the matter that the two of them had discussed three years earlier. He wanted to meet Epanifio the next day, at the machine works.

When Epifanio arrived at the *Cabanataun Machine Works* the next morning, he found a man who would give only his first name, Aman. He explained that Muhammad was unable to make the journey as he had been involved in a serious accident.

Aman asked if Epifanio had developed a secure way of transporting the short tubes. Epifanio took him to a corner of the machine shop where the Fairbanks Morse #251 was standing, already assembled. Pepito showed him how they could store 116 tubes in the crankcase, the cylinders and under the overhead valve cover and then the engine could be reassembled. Aman became ebullient in his praise. Like Epifanio, he told Pepito that the concept was "brilliant."

Then Aman issued another request. "In addition to these tubes, I need one hundred pieces of steel pipe, each two and one half feet long and 61 millimeter inside diameter. The pipe should be approximately one eighth of an inch thick First, can you provide such pipe and second, can we get them into Canada along with the engine?

"Of course," said Pepito, "we stock boiler tube pipe in various sizes. It may not have quite the wall thickness you have requested, but it is stronger than common cold rolled steel pipe because it has to withstand high-pressure steam. As I think your planned use involves pressure, I am sure it will be adequate for your needs. I don't believe we have any pipe with a 61 millimeter inside diameter, but that is not a problem. We will turn a 61-

millimeter mandrel on a lathe. Then, on a pipe machine we force it through a smaller pipe with hydraulic pressure. When we finish, you will have 100 pieces of pipe, two and one half feet long and stretched to 61 millimeters in diameter. With regard to shipping them to Vancouver, it won't even be necessary to conceal them. I will bind them in bundles of twenty-five and label them "repair sleeves for water tube boilers-61mm ID...... Wait a minute, I have an even better idea. I'll make two bundles of fifty, seven and one half-foot tubes and just label them "Replacement Tubes for Water Tube Boiler." You can cut them into thirds with a simple power metal hacksaw, a couple of hundred dollars new. Then no one could possibly have any questions."

Aman immediately saw the value in the last suggestion and said "excellent."

Pepito then looked straight at Aman. "You know of course, you are going to have to weld caps with firing pins on the end of each piece of pipe after they are cut?" Aman just gazed back. He gave no hint of understanding the comment.

The three of them went back to Pepito's office and quickly came to an agreement on price. Aman would give them $250,000 before the engine and pipes left the country and $350,000 more when the engine cleared customs in Vancouver. Surprisingly, there was no negotiation. Aman agreed to their request without objection.

After Aman left, Epifanio made a few telephone calls. He learned that Aman was Aman-al-Zawahari, a senior official in *al Qaeda*. He also learned that the "accident" in which Muhammad Atef had been involved, was a bombing raid in Afghanistan by the United States Air Force. Muhammad Atef was dead. When he heard this last piece of information, Epifanio slowly hung up the phone and turned to Pepito.

"Brother, we should have asked for even more money! I think we are getting into some very deep water with this transaction. When we ship out that engine and those pipes, let's not put our brass plaque with the date of rebuild. In fact, let's create a fictitious company as the shipper. It would even be worth the cost to rent a small warehouse in Vancouver and use it as the shipping destination. We don't want to do anything that could cause this business to be traced back to us."

Pepito agreed.

Chapter 76
Nanjemoy, Maryland: Wednesday, March 27, 2002

Kahlid Moqued thought it was time to head west. He had done everything necessary to insure that George Wilkinson and Peter Nichols were established and settled in. The power service had been ordered from the Southern Maryland Electric Cooperative, the phone service from Verizon, the oil for the furnace from Southern Maryland Oil. These were all done in the name of the property owner. He had enrolled them in driver's school, gotten them Maryland driver's licenses, secured car insurance and bought them each pickup trucks.

The driver's licenses were obtained in a slightly fraudulent manner. A day after arriving in Maryland, Kahlid rented an apartment in the nearby town of Indian Head. He did this not because he needed an additional place to live, but because he wanted to maintain the Nanjemoy farm as an untraceable address.

Kahlid told the landlord that he had no credit rating, as he had just returned from Pakistan where had been in college. Now he had a job at the nearby Naval Station working as a chemist. As his job required him to travel a great deal, he would probably have some friends stay in the apartment from time to time. If the landlord would give him a 10% discount, he would pay cash for a year in advance. Of course the landlord jumped at the offer. Kahlid put the telephone in Peter's name and the electricity in George's. Armed with a utility bill and a copy of the lease (in their Uncle Kahlid's name) each boy could go to the Maryland State Motor Vehicle Agency and prove he lived in Indian Head. This would be the address that appeared on the driver's license.

Then Kahlid did something else that had been suggested to bin Laden by Khawalka. He had the boys trade birth certificates and file applications for stolen/lost licenses. This necessitated going to several different MVA centers to be re-photographed but, at the end of the day, each boy had two Maryland Driver's Licenses, his own and one in his roommate's name. They could change identities at will. Khalid would also do this in Seattle for Robert and Carl.

Moqued found them a welding school that promised to secure employment for its graduates. In the event this didn't occur, Kahlid called a series of contractors and made a list of those looking for laborers. He taught them such cooking as he learned from his Mother and bought several cookbooks. This was something they had overlooked in "Little America," where Nami Omari kept them all so well fed. Kahlid bought paint and brushes and together they painted the inside of their house. They went shopping in the thrift stores in nearby Waldorf and furnished their home, having only to buy new rugs, bedding, linens and drapes at Wal-Mart. The house ended up looking like a typical home lived in by two young, working class bachelors. It was time to go.

The night before he left, Moqued took George and Peter to the barn for a private conversation. He went over their mission for the last time, carefully reiterating all of the details he had received from bin Laden. The boys were silent as they listened. The enormity of the proposed deed made them thoughtful. However, like Moqued, they were impressed with bin Laden's planning. All they had to do was follow his highly detailed directions. They couldn't fail.

It was just like one of their newly acquired cooking skills, baking a cake. All they had to do was follow the recipe!

Chapter 77
Vancouver, BC: Thursday, March 28, 2002
◈

Jimmy Byrnes and Alexander Harrison were customs inspectors of incoming freight at the Port of Vancouver dockyards. They were reviewing cargo that had just arrived on a ship from the Philippines.

"Hey Jimmy, look at this," said Harrison, who was fascinated by the big machinery which came through the port. "It looks as though *Cabanataun* has some competition, eh? Here's an engine for one of the factory trawlers from an outfit I haven't heard of before: *The Manila Engine Company.* What a knock-off! It looks just like the ones that we get from *Cabanataun,* even down to their trademark of chrome-plating the fuel injector diesel lines. And look here, the same paper tag labels that *Cabanataun* uses wired to several points on the engine."

WARNING! Crankcase oil has been removed for shipping. Do not attempt to start engine before adding oil to the proper level.

It always struck Harrison that the unnecessary warnings were a sign of quality and concern on the part of *Cabanataun.* Of course the oil was removed for shipping. Who would ship an engine with oil in the crankcase?

"And here. In the same place where *Cabanataun* always screws their brass plate; *Manila Engine Company-rebuilt 6/02.*"

Jimmy, who was not an machine enthusiast like his partner, mumbled a response. "Hell, Alex, it's probably some ex-employees of *Cabanataun* who saw there was a buck to be made in servicing the Canadian fishing fleet. Well, the competition probably means our lads got a better price!"

They stamped the bill of lading and other import paperwork without further comment. It never even occurred to them to run the engine through one of the new Magnaflux X-ray machines recently installed by the Vancouver Port Authority.

Chapter 78
Seattle, Washington: April 5, 2002
◈

For the trip across the country to Seattle, Kahlid had bought a used crew-cab pickup truck. He planned to sell this to one of the boys when he left to return to Pakistan. It offended bin Laden's sensitivity for secrecy that Robert Ziegler and Carl Kinsey, the two boys who were going to Seattle, knew where the other two boys lived. He would have preferred that the west coast contingent not know the whereabouts of their east coast brothers. However, it was simply not possible to arrange such secrecy without bringing other cell members in the United States into some portion of the plan. After a great deal of thinking about alternatives, bin Laden determined that the approach he was using posed the least risk. At least, George and Peter would not know how to contact Robert and Carl.

Moqued and his two charges took ten days on U.S. Interstate 40 to drive across the country, avoiding the northern route on I-80 or I-90 which could be snowy even in April. They took time on the trip for a two-day detour to visit the Grand Canyon. Even if one did hate the United States, the Canyon existed long before there was a country. It was something Moqued had always wanted to see.

Several hundred miles before they got to Seattle, Moqued called Muhammad Shariff. Moqued got no answer, not even a recording. This worried Kahlid, who had a tendency to be concerned about even the slightest deviation in plans. Finally, just before they started across the Cascades range in Yakima, he tried again and this time he reached Muhammad. He was told that the instructions from "the sheik" were a bit in conflict. He was required to find a soils engineering class and an apartment close to the Canadian border. That had proven impossible. There was a soils technician course of one semester at a community college in Seattle, but it was 100 miles from the border. He had therefore exercised his judgment and rented a furnished apartment in Seattle for 12 weeks. When the course was over, they could move to Bellingham if they wished to be closer to the border. This concerned Kahlid as he did not wish to remain in America for more than another three weeks. He was uncertain about Robert and Carl's ability to conduct a move without his assistance.

Kahlid need not have worried. Robert, having watched Kahlid go through the process in Maryland, took charge. He got a telephone, got the power turned on, registered himself and Carl in school, all without coaching. The only thing he required direction on was the acquisition of a vehicle for Carl. Left to his own devices, he would have bought a bright red Le Baron convertible. Kahlid thought if they were to pass as soils technicians, he should have a pickup truck and so he bought a four-wheel drive Toyota Tacoma, popular both with contractors and younger men. He did bow to the boy's wishes somewhat. The pickup was red.

Kahlid Moqued hung around Seattle for three and a half weeks. He busied himself by renting a furnished apartment in Bellingham, Washington. He used a fictitious name with the landlord. Paying cash in advance for a year insured that no questions were asked. At the end of that time he got a small brown envelope from a man whose name and phone number had been given to him by bin Laden. The man was a member of an *al Qaeda* cell in Seattle. The envelope was mailed from the Philippines and contained a letter and a key.

"Enclosed is a key to a small warehouse in Vancouver. In the warehouse you will find a large marine engine mounted on a skid, so that the oil pan can be unbolted and removed. You will also find the necessary wrenches for doing this. The street address for the warehouse can be obtained by calling Abdul at 444-9764 in Vancouver. Memorize this telephone number. You have been instructed what to do. May Allah guide you to success."

Kahlid Moqued left Carl and Robert in class and drove north to the border and into Vancouver. He called Abdul and got the address of the warehouse. He drove to the address and found a solid masonry building with both a steel entry door and a heavy steel roll-up door through which a large truck could easily fit. He put the key in the lock of the entry door and opened it up. An enormous Fairbanks Morse Diesel engine was in the center of the floor, and beside it were two bundles of steel pipe, seven and one half feet long.

Kahlid went nearby and used a pay telephone to contact a motor freight company in Abbotsford that advertised shipping to freight terminals in all of the major cities on the east coast. He arranged to have a truck meet him at the warehouse the next morning to pick up the pipe for delivery to Baltimore. He decided that he would only ship one bundle at a time. After it was safely delivered, the other bundle would follow. Bin Laden had warned him about risking the whole operation on a simple thing, like a lost shipment.

Kahlid next went to an after-market automotive store and bought two lockable tool chests, one for the Toyota and one for the crew cab Ford. He also purchased a 2,000 pound floor jack, and four padlocks that he snapped on the empty tool boxes. Then he returned to the warehouse and unloaded one tool chest and the jack. When he finished, he carefully locked the door and returned to Seattle, where he sent the shipping paperwork to the Maryland address by the U.S. Postal Service only, avoiding the cross-border delays that he had been told applied when sending mail by Canada Post to the U.S.

The next morning Khalid retraced his steps northward, but stopped in Bellingham, Washington. He looked in the Yellow Pages for mini-warehouses near Meridian Street and rented one large enough to drive the truck inside and close the door. In this room he left the other toolbox.

Kahlid spent the 90-minute drive to and from Bellingham concentrating on the instructions from bin Laden, making sure he hadn't missed anything. Later that night Moqued carefully went over their mission with Carl and Robert for the last time. He reminded Carl to call Peter in a week to check on the pipe's delivery. He should go to a pay phone, call and ask the simple yes or no question "Has the shipment arrived?" He should get his answer and hang up. He should not carry on a conversation with Peter. They should get in the habit of treating every phone call as though it were being monitored.

The next day Kahlid Moqued left for Pakistan. The boys were on their own.

Now, it was in Allah's hands.

Chapter 79
Washington, DC: Tuesday, July 18, 2002
◈

Herr Meinhardt's "random walk" surveillance theory had been utilized on Bong Bong Maikisa over two years earlier. The monitoring uncovered nothing out of the ordinary. Bongo went to work each night for a contractor who cleaned an office building on K Street. Several times a week he visited *The Islamic Society of Southern Maryland* in Upper Marlboro, MD, to pray and socialize. The Bureau planted an agent in that organization that duly reported back that Makaisa was just exercising his religion. Moreover, the *Society* was not planning any violent acts against the country. Indeed, quite the opposite. Many government employees worshiped there. The Imam was patriotic and regularly condemned those Muslims who were committing terrorist acts and causing problems for the rest of the believers.

The tap on Makaisa's telephone divulged that his wife liked to gossip and complain about the people in the neighboring unit. The bug in Makaisas apartment discovered nothing except that Makaisa, like millions of other men around the country, Islamic or not, took his wife out to dinner on Saturday nights, after which they came home and made love.

Nor was there any e-mail traffic between "MindanaoBongo" and "Mecca5." It was as though they had discovered their communications were compromised. Then on 18 July 2002, Michael McNulty, the special agent Carl Walker had placed in charge of the case, received an e-mail from Sanford Parcell at the National Security Agency.

James:
Attached is an e-mail to Bongo from Khadaffy Janjalani in the Philippines sent four days ago. It was decoded yesterday and translated this morning. It looks like this group is coming to life again.

> *Sometimes I wish I were a G-man. You guys have all the*
> *fun.*
> *Sandy*
> *CC: Danielle Lamaze-Smith, CIA*

McNulty rarely read attachments to e-mail on his screen. To do so, he had to lean over his desk till his head was 15 inches from the tube and squint. This position was injurious to his image. He clicked the download/print icon.

> *National Security Agency Control #02-7-185347-q*
> *18 July 02*
> *Sender: Mecca5*
> *Recipient: MindanaoBongo*
> *Malacanang has just announced that next spring Arroyo has been invited to visit the President of the United States. This gives us a great opportunity to act. If we could eliminate Arroyo while she is in America, it would be a big embarrass-ment for the Americans. It would show that they couldn't protect their guests. It would also demonstrate the power of Abu Sayyaf and the worldwide Muslim jihadist movement.*
> *I want you to start to investigate the opportunities to remove Arroyo. This will probably be when she is not in the company of the American President. I understand that he is very closely guarded by the Secret Service, an organization that, so I have heard, is one of the world's best security forces.*
> *You have a long time to study this. Make a list of what and who you need to carry out your plan. This is a God-given opportunity to help our cause.*
> *K*

Special Agent James McNulty read through the message twice. Then he got up from his desk and walked about 50 feet to a similar cubicle occupied by an agent who, early in his career, had served as a liaison agent to the Philippine embassy.

"Arnold, who are Malacanang and Arroyo?"

As he was engrossed in reading a brief, Arnold responded without looking up from his work. "*Arroyo* is Gloria Macapagal Arroyo, the president of the Philippine Republic. *Malacanang* is the name of the president's house, kinda like our White House. Why do you ask?"

Chapter 80
Washington, DC: July 19, 2005
◈

The latest e-mail from Mecca5 aroused a number of sleeping government departments and agencies. The Director of the Federal Bureau of Investigation personally called the White House and the Department of State to warn them of the threat to Arroyo's life. This precipitated much internal discussion about whether or not to warn president Arroyo. In the end, the Secretary of State determined against it, unless and until a specific danger emerged. The presidents of most of the countries on the globe were always receiving threats. It was just part of politics in the modern world.

The Secret Service was also informed and consulted. Their feeling was the only time of any real risk to Arroyo was during her trip from Blair House to the White House and during the arrival ceremony. She could be subject to a suicide car bomber on Pennsylvania Avenue and 17th street. It was an extremely unlikely event, but could be dealt with by closing traffic on both streets for five minutes before the motorcade left Blair House. This was a decision that could be made at any time.

The FBI was responsible for counter-terrorism. They instituted another three-week surveillance of Makaisa in accordance with the "random walk" theory. The FBI's electronic expert replaced the bug that had been removed from Makaisa's apartment. The old bug was dismantled, as such illegal invasions of privacy are never left in place longer than necessary. This is not done out of respect for individual privacy rights, but out of respect for the slight chance of discovery. Although the court order for the wiretap had long since expired, it was not necessary to get a new one. The phone tap had never been disconnected.

Prior to September 11, 2001, residents of the Philippine Islands were afforded relatively easy entry for visiting their families in the Continental United States. But after 9/11 immigration into the U.S. had become more difficult. But now, after the message intercepts, the Immigration and Naturalization Service had paid even greater attention to applications for visas. They scrutinized every document and caused long delays in the list of people just coming to visit family members. One of the agents that Mecca5 hoped to send to assist Mindanaobongo, was caught in such a delay.

The Department of State had advised that Philippine president Gloria Arroyo was scheduled to visit the American President sometime in the spring. Danielle Lamaze-Smith had never attended an arrival ceremony, but after the memo to Bong Bong was intercepted, she determined to be there.

Osama bin Laden had never attended an arrival ceremony either, nor did he intend to be at the celebration for Gloria Arroyo. He would, however, send a surrogate. He made arrangements to send word to Esam Khawalka that this was the time, and that the word was "*wusool.*"

Chapter 81
Nanjemoy, Maryland: Tuesday, July 30, 2002
◈

Three weeks after Kahlid had left the United States, both George and Peter were taking a three-month welding course, and both had found jobs at the same steel fabrication shop. They were surprisingly skilled with their hands, and they found the whole concept of work for compensation quite exciting, and they never had monetary concerns. They were excellent employees, and "getting paid" fascinated them. Of course before this they had spent five years where they worked only for Allah.

On July 30, they received a letter from Kahlid informing them that the pipes were being shipped by truck, prepaid to a freight terminal in Baltimore. They would arrive within a week. The letter included a receipt so they would not have to identify themselves by name when they went to collect the load.

On the following Saturday, August 10, when they had no welding classes, they took their pick-up truck to Baltimore and returned with the pipes. Then they purchased a metal-cutting band saw. As the saw had an automatic cut off switch, they loaded it with two pipes each morning before they left for welding class. Most of the evenings when they got home, they did the same thing, so they were cutting four pipes each day. In several weeks, just as they were finishing cutting the 50 pipes of the first load, Peter got a telephone call from Carl asking if the shipment had arrived. No sooner did he say yes, than the phone clicked dead. The next week a letter arrived with another receipt for shipping. The second load of pipes went as the first.

In the steel fabrication shop where the boys worked, Ben Russell, their foreman, shook his head in amazement as he talked to the owner of the company. "I don't know how I got so lucky. I look for help for months and all I get is lazy, longhaired pot-heads. Then in the same day, two guys from different parts of the country who just met in welding class, show up. They turn out to be the most enthusiastic, hardest working guys I've got on the payroll. And they are just like brothers. They are closer in a few months than I was with either of my brothers, and we grew up together."

"These guys' parents certainly did a great job. There is nothing like being raised in the Midwest to instill good old fashioned American values."

Chapter 82
Raleigh, North Carolina: Monday, August 5, 2002

Gamma rays have the smallest wavelength and the highest energy of any waves in the electromagnetic spectrum. They are generated by nuclear explosions and by radioactive atoms in a series of man made and natural isotopes.

Science progresses not nearly so much by revolution, than by evolution. Thus, in the middle of the twentieth century, scientists around the world were experimenting with beneficial uses of radioactivity, particularly gamma rays. In Sweden a Rumanian neurosurgeon with a PhD in nuclear physics named Ladislau Steiner, conceived of the idea of focusing a stream of gamma rays from Cobalt 60 to a single point in the brain. This would be done to treat tumors without invasive surgery. Today Steiner's "Gamma Knife" is an internationally recognized protocol for the treatment for brain tumors. Gamma rays kill a number of types of cancerous cells in the human body.

Almost contemporaneously, in Raleigh, North Carolina, a man named William. F. Troxler was working in his basement laboratory to develop a device that would measure the density of soils using the radioisotope Cesium 137 to generate gamma rays. He would then measure the deterioration of photon strength as the rays passed through soils of various densities. Troxler was highly successful in his experimentation. Now the Troxler Company is the world leader in construction test equipment. Their Model 3340 Surface Moisture Density Gauge, the industry standard, consists of a high-impact plastic box 16 inches long, 10 inches wide and 4 inches thick. There is a probe, ¾ of an inch in diameter and two feet long, at the end of which is a small piece of radioactive material. The probe is placed in a prepared hole in the ground. The photon flow and moisture are measured by a meter on the face of the box. The meter is directly calibrated to read moisture and compaction, both expressed as percentages.

As the instrument depends upon the use of radioactive material, Federal regulations require the display of the triangular nuclear warning symbol. On the large blaze orange carrying case are several labels stating WARNING-CONTAINS RADIOACTIVE MATERIAL. This is required, even though the actual amount of the isotope is quite small and poses no harm to the operator. A label also appears on the instrument itself.

Margaret Inverness, a large, breezy and jocular woman with oversized breasts, manages the mail order department at Troxler. On July 21, 2002, she was surprised to receive an order for two Models 3340s without the isotope or the electronic circuitry. The order did specify that the dial was to be in place and that the units should look, in every way, like fully operating units. The letter was from AQ Enterprises, a new soils engineering company that was being organized in Bellingham, Washington. The units were to be used for classroom instruction. As Margaret had never before received such an order, she went to see Wayne Irish, the Vice President of Sales.

"Wayne" she said, as she marched into his office, "I have gotten an order for two 3340s without the guts. We have no such animal in our catalog. What shall I do?"

"What do they want them for?"

"The order says they want them for classroom instruction."

"Aaha, they are trying to save some money and not spend $8,500 for the machine with the isotopes and electronics. It is probably a good idea. As a matter of fact, we might consider adding such a unit to our line. I think the plastic box with probe and fiberglass carrying case probably cost us around $1,500. Tell them you will be pleased to fill their order for $2,500 apiece. We should get a higher markup on a special order, don't you think?

"Sure we should. But how do I fill the order? Do you want to notify production to make up two bare bones units?

"Yeah, I am going to meet with Larry Owens of production

later this morning anyway. I'll ask him to make up two 3340's for you and send them to shipping to hold till you get a check. Sound OK?"

"Works for me. You get me those units and I'll tell the customer that I had them made up especially for him."

As Inverness left Irish's office, she found herself wondering what the AQ in AQ Enterprises stood for. Knowing the lack of literary creativity of most engineers, she guessed it was probably something off the wall like "always quick", "authenticate & quantify", "assured quality", or some similar goofy acronym.

She could never understand how engineers could be so anal about so many things.

Chapter 83
Bellingham, Washington: Thursday, August 22, 2002
◈

Carl and Robert decided that on the first day they would ride together in the crew cab pickup. Thereafter, they would each take a truck and a Troxler tester which they had received from the manufacturer only two days prior. They were just a little bit nervous and needed the reinforcement of the other's company. The Troxlers were in their orange carrying cases in the back of the truck, in plain sight for the customs agent to see. They also determined that on their first trip they wouldn't try to bring any tubes back with them. They took this precaution in the unlikely event some curious customs agent was unfamiliar with nuclear test equipment and asked to see a demonstration. Obviously, they couldn't do this. Their Troxlers contained no isotopes.

Going into Canada was easy. They crossed from Blaine, Washington, to Surrey, British Columbia, at the famous "Peace Arch." On both sides of the border they were simply asked to show their birth certificates and driver's licenses. When the guards asked the purpose of their visit, business or pleasure, they both said "business." They were even a little disappointed at the simplicity of getting into Canada, as they had carefully rehearsed stories about their role as soils engineers.

Once in British Columbia, they went to the warehouse and spent the first day taking the engine apart. They removed the oil pan, thankful that Kahlid had briefed them on how to do it. The oil pan, formed of heavy steel, was heavy enough on its own. When loaded with the tubes it weighed over a quarter of a ton, far more than the two of them could lift. However, with the aid of the floor jack and the wood braces provided by Mohquid, it was fairly easily handled. The valve cover was easier. It was in two pieces.

After they removed the 116 cardboard tubes, they carefully locked them in the toolbox and reassembled the engine. This exercise took all day. When they were finished, the engine, except for some paint they scraped off the oil pan, looked like it did when they arrived. It was rebuilt and ready to be dropped in a boat — if only it had enough of its components to run!

Going back across the border was easy on the Canadian side. The American customs agents asked them to open the fiberglass carrying cases for the Troxlers. This was an opportunity to start telling the story they had so carefully rehearsed. "We are soils Tec's on a large earthmoving site in Canada. Any day the weather permits filling and compacting of earth, you are likely to see us on the job."

The agent waved them through.

Chapter 84
Justice Dept., Washington, D.C.: Tuesday, Sept. 17, 2002
❖

The original "Inter-Agency Task Force", less Ms. Henderson from Immigration and Naturalization, but enlarged by Special Agent McNulty, was meeting to discuss an interesting message NSA had intercepted from Bongo to Mecca5. Bongo was getting cold feet. Sanford Parcell read the decoded e-mail aloud to the group.

National Security Agency Control #02-9-196754-q
16 September 02
Sender: MindanaoBongo
Recipient: Mecca5
K:

 I have spent a great deal of time on your request. As I work at night, I have had much time to do investigation.

 I have determined there are only two ways to do what you wish. They involve using shooters or car bombs. These would be utilized when Arroyo is entering her car at Blair House on Pennsylvania Avenue for the one-block drive to the White House. If a large amount of explosive was available, a truck bomb might be detonated in 17th Street during the ceremony on the south lawn of the White House

 I am not certain either of these methods will succeed. In fact, I don't believe either of these methods has more than a 10% chance of success.

 The most important thing is, I am not willing to undertake either of these attempts. I am enjoying my new life. I am too old to commit suicide or spend the rest of my life in prison. I no longer feel the violence I once did. Unbelievably to me, the United States is a good place to live. I am happy here.

 You have known me for more than 30 years. You know

that I am not a coward. Many times I have risked my life for Islam. Now it is someone else's turn. Someone who is younger and has nothing to lose. I want to spend the rest of my days with my wife and her family. I think it is an old man's right.

I hope you won't be too disappointed with this decision of mine. In all honesty, Arroyo will be much more easily killed in the Philippines. There the security will not be as difficult. There you have many younger men eager to prove themselves

Please don't send me more messages. I don't want to get involved with assassinations in any way.

I am sorry for this disappointing news.
May Islam rule supreme!
Bongo

When Parcel finished reading, he laid the piece of paper on the table, stared out at the group and stated: "*Casus fortuitus non est sperandus et nemo tenetur devinare.*"

There was a table full of blank faces. Even Danielle didn't remember much Latin. She had not studied it since secondary school. Latin was of a wholly different linguistic family from Arabic and the other Middle Eastern languages with which she was familiar.

Parcell queried, "Are there no lawyers in the room?" Morrison, Reilly and McNulty all nodded weakly.

"I am always amazed that one can graduate from law school without knowing the basic legal terms much beyond *habeas corpus, et al* and *de minimus non curia lex. Casus fortuitus non est sperandus et nemo tenetur devinare* is a Latin expression meaning, "a fortuitous event not to be expected." Danielle thought she could detect an ever so slight look of smugness, as Parcell nodded at Morrison to begin the meeting.

The fact is, Parcell did have such a look. A mild and unassuming man in a bow tie, a former academician, Parcell needed to assert himself in the world of the Justice Department and FBI, where toughness was of preeminent importance. He started out the meeting on just the right note. He reminded the group that there were other qualities besides masculinity. He had them in abundance.

In his position in the hierarchy at the FBI, "Assistant to the Director", Reilly had access to all of the personnel records of those on whom the FBI had done any kind of field investigations. It was almost certainly an abuse of power, but he had the files pulled on everyone with whom he was going to meet. He had read Parcell's file two years earlier.

Reilly managed to get out, "So the professor is going to give us our daily Latin ...", before Danielle cut him off.

"As the only female present, I hereby assert my right, no, my obligation, to bring order to warring factions. I don't work in this building or within walking distance. I have a half-hour ride to get back to my office. Shall we get started?"

Morrison spoke. "Well, unless that message was strictly for our benefit, and I don't think that is the case, I think we can remove Bongo from our target list. He sounds like he really means what he is saying. I guess the question is, are there any others?"

Danielle answered his rhetorical question. "No, I don't believe so. In the last months I have done a lot of research into *abu Sayyaf*. They are a very potent force in the Philippines. There they are capable of a great deal of mischief. However, there is no indication that they have developed any international organization. In fact, Bongo seems to be their only foreign agent. They are quite unlike *al Qaeda* in that they have never been able put together financing to support transnational operations. They seem to be almost exclusively the creation of Khadaffy Janjalani, a man not to be compared with Osama bin Laden. Janjalani is a serious danger in the Philippines. He should not be considered a threat in the rest of the world."

Special Agent McNulty asked a question. "Dr. Smith, I am new to this terrorism business. I was only brought in to monitor our Bongo character. But I have always gotten the impression that these different Islamic groups, even with different leaders, tended to cooperate with each other. Shouldn't we be concerned about *al Qaeda* sort of jumping in and "picking up the pieces" so to speak?

"Mr. McNulty, it is true that there is a great deal of cooperation between certain groups, particularly when they have a common goal. That is not the case in this instance. *Abu Sayyaf* is a Moro separatist organization. Their goal is a Muslim republic in Mindanao. They have been trying to achieve this for hundreds of years. Of course bin Laden would be delighted if they were successful. He is pleased with Muslim achievements everywhere. But he cannot take his eye off the ball. *al Qaeda* is concerned with the United States, other targets are sideshows. No, in this one we don't have to worry about some sleeper cell of bin Laden's coming with in the big guns. Also, we have managed to penetrate *abu Sayyaf*. Our asset tells us that Janjalani is extremely jealous of bin Laden. He wouldn't think of asking him for help."

The group continued the discussion for another forty-five minutes. They resolved to do three things:

1) The FBI would pick up Makaisa a couple of days before president Arroyo got to the United States and put the fear of God in him. The FBI would threaten him with the death sentence, life imprisonment and deportation. What he got would be up to him, how cooperative he was. Privately, the lawyers didn't think they had much of a case. But that wouldn't stop them from making his life a living hell for a couple of weeks. They certainly wouldn't have to worry about Bongo hiring Alan Dershowitz as defense counsel.

2) They would recommend that the District of Columbia police close Pennsylvania Avenue and 17th street to all vehicles from five minutes before the movement of president Arroyo's motorcade until the arrival ceremony had begun. It would screw up traffic in the District for a half-hour, but it couldn't be helped.

3) They would see to it that the District Police and the

Secret Service "heavied up" on uniformed and plainclothes law enforcement personnel on both streets and around the ellipse from two hours before the arrival ceremony, until it was over.

As she took the Government Chrysler back to the CIA headquarters, Danielle was not her usually worried self. She was confident they had done everything necessary.

Chapter 85
Nanjemoy, Maryland: October 8, 2002
❖

With the necessary and invaluable help of Khawalka in the United States, bin Laden's directions to Moqued had been extraordinarily specific. Moqued in turn had passed along absolute instructions to the boys, telling them they came from bin Laden. All, particularly Moqued, were impressed at the amount of detail the leader of *al Qaeda* had developed and how carefully he had planned.

The instructions said that not sooner than six months after they received their driver's licenses, George and Peter should acquire their Maryland Commercial Driving License (CDL). These would be required to operate the truck that bin Laden specified they use for the operation, as it had ten wheels and was nominally rated for 10,000 pounds of cargo. Khawalka had determined the exact type of truck and even provided a list of places where such a truck could be purchased. Accordingly, since the six months' period had elapsed, the boys each took CDL driving courses at the College of Southern Maryland. Then it came time to purchase the truck.

The first dealer on the list, Brandywine Trucks, in nearby Brandywine, Maryland, did not have exactly the model they were looking for. They had to buy a special advertising magazine to locate the vehicle bin Laden specified. They found a perfect one that had been thoroughly restored by a collector in Chambersburg, Pennsylvania. They bought the truck and told the man that they would be back the following week to pick it up, after they made arrangements for insurance and picked up temporary tags from the MVA. When their insurance agent in La Plata asked them what in the world they intended to do with such a truck, they told him they were going to convert it into a welding truck.

The explanation satisfied the agent.

Chapter 86
Nanjemoy, Maryland: Tuesday, January 7, 2003
◈

People who enter into engineering or science as a career generally have advanced capability to visualize designs in three dimensions. They have a highly refined sense of spatial relationships. So it was with Osama bin Laden. From the instant he conceived of the idea, he had a clear vision of how the racks should be constructed in the back of the truck. He could see in his mind's eye exactly how the entire framework would be welded together. He could place the pipes in this framework by a sixth sense. Given the materials and tools, bin Laden could have manufactured what he required without a set of plans. This is not a gift enjoyed by everyone.

Khalid Moqued had an excellent memory. Perhaps even a superior memory. He absorbed all of the detailed operating directions bin Laden imposed on him over two days and could repeat them back, almost word for word. He remembered telephone numbers of various cell members in America whom he could call upon if he needed assistance. He had an almost endless capacity for minutia. But he couldn't quite grasp what bin Laden wanted welded in the back of the truck. And bin Laden knew that if Moqued could not picture it himself, he would be woefully unable to explain it to the actual fabricators. With this realization, bin Laden violated his cardinal rule with regard to operation "wusool". He committed something to paper.

Bin Laden sent for graph paper and a straight edge and provided both a plan view and isometric view of exactly what he wanted constructed. These two sheets were carefully folded and stored in the false bottom of a piece of ordinary carry-on luggage that was given to Moqued. Bin Laden did this reluctantly, but consoled himself with the thought that, if discovered, it would seem innocuous to an ordinary custom's agent. To someone whose mind worked like bin Laden's, the purpose was clearly apparent.

When Kahlid had left Peter and George eight months earlier, he gave them the drawings saying, "This is why you must study welding and become welders. This is what you must build in the back of the truck."

By this day in 2003, Peter thought they were ready to begin construction of the device. They had already cut the pipe into 100 pieces 30 inches long. Using their metal band saw they also cut 100 pieces of one-quarter inch thick metal into three-inch squares. In the very center of each of the squares they drilled a hole in which they welded a one-half inch long pin, three-sixteenths of an inch in diameter. They had a wood shop turn a 61 millimeter shaft, three feet long. Then, in the exact center of one end of the shaft, they drilled a hole to receive the pin. This was their jig to assure that the plate was welded on the tube with the pin at the very center.

They slid the wooden shaft down the pipe and placed the plate on the end of the pipe with the plate's pin inserted in the shaft's hole. This assured them the pin was centered. Then they tack-welded the plate to the tube so as not to burn the wooden jig. After removing the jig, they finished the weld soundly. (If they were constructing a device that was to be used many times, this pin would have been made of hardened steel. But this weapon was to be used only once.)

From the fabricating company where they worked, they purchased 12-foot lengths of three-inch wide, one-quarter inch thick angle iron to construct the main frame. The inner dividing frames would be fabricated out of one and a half-inch angle iron three-sixteenths of an inch in thickness. The bed of the truck was eight feet wide by twelve feet long, so if the frame openings were one foot square, there would be openings for 96 tubes. They deemed this sufficient, even for Sheik bin Laden!

Eight inches from the other end of each of the tubes they mounted an electric solenoid. This device, essentially an electromagnet, had a pin that projected into the tube to prevent an object inserted in the tube from sliding down. It was arranged so that when a current was applied to the electromagnetic coil of the solenoid, the pin withdrew from the tube, and the tube's contents would slide down the other 22 inches. A switch in the cab would control the current. To get these solenoids, Ehsahn Khawalka found The Detroit Coil Company on the Internet. They manufactured just the right solenoid for the purpose! Using a money order, purchased with cash, he had placed an order for 100 solenoids to be delivered to a temporary postal address in New York. When the solenoids were delivered, he collected and re-shipped them to the address of the farm he owned, in the name of Sayyid Qutb, in Nanjemoy, Maryland.

He knew there was no sense in giving any secrets away. Once the FBI got started, they were famous for their ability to piece things together...

Chapter 87
Fort Lesley J. McNair: February, 2003

The "Military District of Washington" is the name of the Army Command responsible for the military security of the nation's capital. However, as Washington was last invaded during the war of 1812 when the British landed nearby in Maryland and burned the White House, invasion by a foreign military power is no longer an issue. Now the primary purpose of the Command is ceremonial. The principal unit performing this function is the 3rd U.S. Infantry (The Old Guard). This splendid troop is the oldest active infantry unit in the Army, serving continuously since 1784. They furnish the sentinels at the Tomb of the Unknowns, provide military escorts for interments at Arlington National Cemetery and participate in a variety of other official ceremonies, many involving the Commander in Chief, the President of the United States. They also maintain their proficiency as field solders by constant training at Forts Pickett and A.P. Hill in nearby Virginia. Together with the U.S. Army Band (Pershing's Own), the 3rd Infantry performs at over 6,000 functions a year. Of these ceremonies, the two largest are well known to television audiences, the inauguration of a new President and the funeral for a dead President.

There is also a third major task. It is less well known than the other two, as it does not receive significant television coverage. Indeed, it takes place exclusively on the privacy of the White House lawn. It is the "arrival ceremony" for a visiting Head of Government or Head of State.

The phone rang on a desk in the "ceremonies" office of the MDW at Fort McNair.

"Ceremonies, Sergeant Stryker. Captain Peterson? Yes sir, he's in. Who's calling? Office of Protocol, hold on sir, I'll transfer you."

"Captain Peterson. Good afternoon sir,......yes sir, the

president of the Philippines, Gloria Macapagal Arroyo, on 19 May. Yes sir, we can do that. Can I expect the usual confirmation in writing? Thank you sir."

"Sergeant Stryker, put out a memo to all concerned parties. Standard arrival ceremony at the "House" on 19 May 2003 at 0900 for president Arroyo. And start a personal count-down-time-line tickler file for me."

Because he took his job very seriously, Captain Peterson immediately began to worry. Indeed, there was much to worry about in a drill with so many moving parts. As always at these events, the major concern was security. But there were many others with that responsibility.

Captain Peterson's primary anxiety was *rain*.

Chapter 88
Bellingham, Washington: Tuesday, May 6, 2003
❖

By May 2003, Robert Ziegler and Carl Kinsey had each taken 51 trips across the Canadian border. On each trip they carried back one tube apiece in their Troxlers. They were careful not to make crossings when the ground was not at the proper moisture content for "controlled fill", which would require the use of a Troxler measuring instrument. This was done, as it was quite possible that one of the customs officials had at one time worked on a construction job. Anyone who had ever spent the slightest time around a construction site would know that soils couldn't be moved and compacted unless they were at the right moisture. Coming from a desert country, the boys were appalled at the number of rainy days in Vancouver. The ground never seemed to dry up. Since they began going across the border at the end of September, they had gotten in only 51 trips. However, in talking to construction people in their soils class, they learned that in the winter in the northwest, not much got accomplished in the earthmoving business.

On this Tuesday, Carl and Robert, each in separate trucks, approached the Peace Arch border crossing. They made it a practice to maintain about a five-minute separation between vehicles in case there was some problem. They had purchased CB radios and always turned them on to the same channel, so that one could alert the other to any difficulty. On this day Robert, arriving first in the crew cab truck, got through both borders without difficulty, as usual. During the time it took for Carl to arrive at the border the shift changed on the U.S. side. A new man named Arthur Mathews waited to inspect Carl's truck. Mathews was not someone Carl had encountered previously.

Carl pulled up and automatically handed over his birth certificate, driver's license and auto registration. Mathews took them. Then he walked around to the rear of the truck and looked at the large orange carrying case for the Troxler. He walked back to the driver's window.

"Mr. Kinsey, will you step out of the truck, please?"

"Yes sir. Is anything wrong?"

"Will you open this case for me please?"

Yes sir, but I cannot open the instrument inside. It is a sealed nuclear testing gauge. I am a soils technician working on a big earth job in Canada."

"OK, explain to me just how this device works."

"Actually, it is very simple. There is no real radiation to worry about. There is a little piece of Cesium 137 at the end of this tube. When the tube is inserted in a hole I make for it in the ground, it measures the flow of radiation between the Cesium and the sensor unit. The smaller the flow of photons, the greater the density of the soil. The reduction is expressed as a percentage of compaction on this dial. Except for making the hole in the ground, it is a very easy process."

"Mr. Kinsey, the U.S. Government has installed equipment at this Port of Entry that detects radiation and sounds an alarm if any is encountered. Can you explain why that equipment is not detecting radiation from your machine? Is it some kind of special radiation which doesn't set off Geiger counters?"

"Sir, I am not an expert in radiation. I only know that the amount of nuclear material, its Cesium, is very small. Perhaps your equipment isn't that sensitive." At this point Carl began to get a little nervous. He knew the monitor wasn't picking up radioactivity because there wasn't any isotope in the Troxler.

"Mr. Kinsey, please bring your test device into our office building. I wish to try subjecting it to one of our portable testers. You may pull your truck over to the parking area."

Of the four boys, Carl Kinsey was the least well equipped to deal with intellectual pressure. He grew noticeably agitated. This caused Mathews to become suspicious. He started with just a technical curiosity about why the radiation wasn't setting off alarms. Now, as he walked into the building with a badly shaken youth, he began to sense something else was wrong. He sat Carl down at a table, went into the next office and asked his superior to join them.

Customs inspectors, while technically law enforcement officers, are not well trained in basic police procedures. Dealing with dangerous criminals is not second-nature to them. If they wanted to be cops, they would have joined the BATF or the FBI! To a police officer, conducting a body search is a prerequisite to conducting an interrogation. Had the customs officers even done a basic "pat down", they would have discovered the toggle switch in Kinsey's left front pants pocket. They would also have discovered the wire connecting the switch to the battery pack and to the blasting caps as well as the five pounds of urea based homemade explosive in two plastic bags in Kinsey's jacket pockets. Discovery of these items would have saved their lives.

The explosion of the homemade bomb caused a sympathetic detonation of the three pounds of Composition B that Kinsey was carrying concealed in the Troxler device. The result was an explosion that blew off the wooden roof of the concrete block building in which the customs offices were located. Parked in his truck on the side of Interstate 5 a quarter-mile away, Robert Ziegler heard the explosion and saw the tell-tale plume of black smoke rising through the clear spring sky. He knew instantly what had happened.

Even as Ziegler mourned the loss of his friend, he was thinking about the changes he would have to make in the plan. Fortunately, their great leader, Osama bin Laden, had thought through the consequences of such an event. He had carefully specified an alternative procedure.

Robert Ziegler launched into "plan B" as easily as he slipped back into traffic on I-5. Or more graphically, as easily as Carl Kinsey made the decision to click the toggle switch in his pants pocket.

Both boys were perfectly trained to deal with the unex-pected.

Chapter 89
Bowie, Maryland: Wednesday, May 6, 2003
◈

Danielle first learned of the explosion at the Peace Arch border crossing, as did most Americans, on the television news. The explosion occurred at 4:33 PM, Pacific Daylight Savings Time, which was already 7:33 PM, Eastern Daylight Savings Time. She was watching an 11:00 PM network news show when the item was aired. There were no details, as no one really had any idea what had happened. There had been an explosion. That was all. Danielle called her office to see if there were any facts that hadn't been released to the public. The CIA emergency operations center didn't have anything to add to what she already knew. Danielle went to her computer and composed an e-mail to Carl Walker at the FBI.

Carl:

It is 11:25 PM. I have just learned of the explosion at the Peace Arch border crossing. I contacted our ops-center and learned no more than was on the news.

Perhaps it is only because the Peace Arch was the crossing where Amed Ressam was apprehended in 1999, on his way to blow up LAX, but I have the very strong feeling that this incident is terrorist related.

I have no training in law enforcement and would not suggest that I have any knowledge in that field. However, I have spent the recent years of my life focusing on Islamic terrorism. I think I might be helpful to your efforts.

If you were planning on using Special Agent Francis Reilly to supervise the case, I would be delighted to work with him again. As you may recall, we worked collaboratively on the Ressam matter. As I did then, I might provide insight on possible Middle East connections.

While I will not contact Reilly without your approval, it

seems to me that this is an opportunity for the FBI and the CIA to demonstrate that our two agencies can work collegially, when it is for the benefit of the country.

I look forward to discussing this matter with you in the morning. I'll call you at 9:30 AM.
Danielle

As she did not have Walker's e-mail address at home, Danielle sent the message to her own office. She would forward it to Walker when she got to her desk in the morning, at 7:30 AM.

After she sent the e-mail, Danielle spent two hours thinking and writing down thoughts on how she would develop the case. She was certain that with her pointed reference to cooperation, that Walker would feel obligated to let her get involved.

Chapter 90
Bellingham, Washington: Wednesday, May 6, 2003
◈

Normally Robert Ziegler drove directly to the rental storage unit to unload his Troxler, after crossing the border. After the explosion, he instead went to the rented apartment. He knew that even though his driver's license and vehicle registration showed the address of their apartment in Seattle, and even though their apartment in Bellingham had been rented by Khalid Moqued, it was probable that the authorities would ultimately trace him to the new location. He needed to collect the $11,000 cash they kept hidden in several locations in the apartment. He also needed to pick up the clothes and toiletries that were his, before leaving the apartment for the last time. He was pleased that dusk was falling as he left. Like most people evading the law, he felt safer in the dark.

Ziegler drove to a store that sold truck tool boxes and bought a heavy steel box with locks. Then he drove to the rental unit, pulled the truck inside and unloaded the Troxler. Next he unlocked and unloaded the toolbox that they used for storage. There were 103 tubes including the one he had just carried in. He loaded the empty toolbox onto the truck and divided the cardboard tubes between the two boxes. He carefully counted out the tubes into two piles, 51 in one pile and 52 in the other, including the tube he had just brought with him. He loaded one pile of tubes into one of the toolboxes, the other pile into the remaining box. Although the toolboxes were now too heavy for him to lift alone, he believed he could easily slide them from one truck bed to another. When he finished this task, it was past dinnertime. He locked up the truck and the tubes in the storage unit and walked down the street to a fast food restaurant. After dinner he checked into a nearby motel using a fictitious name. Tired from the strain of the previous day, he slept through until morning.

After he arose and showered, Ziegler called a taxicab and asked to be taken to a rental car company that would rent a van "cheap" for a couple of weeks. The driver took him to a local company called Rainwater Rentals where he picked out an older van that had been used by a local delivery company that had failed. It was dinged and dented, but had relatively low mileage. As he had no credit card, he was required to leave a cash deposit of 110% of the van's value. Many of the rental agency's customers had their credit cards cut off. Cash deposits were not uncommon. He told the clerk he needed to drive to Florida to pick up the rest of his belongings from his apartment and not to expect him back for two weeks.

After renting the van Ziegler drove to the storage unit and, with some effort, managed to push both tool chests from the pick-up into the van. He took the license plates off the pick-up truck and again locked it in the storage unit. He then went to the office of the storage unit and prepaid for an additional six months. He was thus assured that the pick-up truck would not be found for at least that length of time. This was in keeping with Moqued's constant reminding them that they had to build "cut-outs" into their trail. The rental van was an example that Moqued had given them. Locking up the pickup truck was his own idea. He was sure that Moqued would be proud of him.

Ziegler drove the van to the Seattle branch of the trucking company that had shipped the steel pipes to Baltimore. He unloaded the tool chest containing 52 tubes and prepaid the shipping charges. He was about to set off on a drive back to Nanjemoy. If anything happened to him, at least Peter and George would have 52 tubes with which to work. He would stop at a mailbox along the way and send off the shipping receipts, just as they had done for the pipes.

Ziegler hadn't really fully appreciated the genius of bin Laden's planning until he was asked to provide a driver's license at the rental agency. Instead of producing his own license, he gave the clerk the one with his picture and Carl Kinsey's name.

If, as was likely to occur, the authorities began looking for him, he would not be found. Nobody would look for Carl Kinsey.

Carl Kinsey was already dead.

Chapter 91
Indian Head, Maryland: Thursday, May 8, 2003

In 1890, the United States Navy purchased 880 acres of land on Mattawoman Neck in Charles County, Maryland, to establish a proving ground. Here would be tested the guns manufactured at the Naval Gun Factory in nearby Washington, DC.

In 1898, the Navy established a gunpowder factory at the site. The facility was expanded by the acquisition of an additional 10,050 acres in 1900, when it became a primary manufacturing source of the Navy's explosive propellants, later used in WWI and WWII. In true government fashion, the name changed frequently. From Naval Proving Ground, to Naval Powder Factory, to Naval Propellant Plant to Naval Ordinance Station-Indian Head. Currently, the plant is formally known as The Indian Head Naval Surface Warfare Center, part of the Naval Sea Systems Command. The latter title is in recognition of the little town of Indian Head, Maryland, that grew up along one edge of the property. Future names cannot be predicted.

Located at the "installation of the evolving name" are two important units. These are the Naval Explosive Ordinance Disposal Technology Division and a detachment of the Naval Explosive Ordinance School, a joint services Explosive Ordinance Disposal (EOD) training facility. These entities contain the government's foremost experts in bombs and explosives. They are called upon to investigate unidentified explosions on Federal property across the country.

Immediately after the explosion at the United States Customs Service office at the Peace Arch, in Blaine, Washington, the FBI requested that an EOD team of forensic specialists be dispatched to the scene.

The EOD team carefully measured the extent of the damage. They calculated the distance from the center of the blast point, to points where various building structural members were destroyed. They painstakingly collected metal fragments from the scene. They chemically analyzed the residue from the powder burns. Within 36 hours the EOD team produced a report for the FBI:

DT: 8 May 2003
FR: Naval Explosive Ordinance Disposal Technology Division (NAVEODTECHDIV)
TO: Federal Bureau of Investigation (FBI)
RE: Explosion at US Customs Service Office, Blaine, Washington (USCSBLW)
   SUMMARY: The initial explosion was an Improvised Explosive Device (IED) constructed of approximately five pounds of standard commercial nitrogen fertilizer, UREA, combined with diesel fuel. This was fired off with several blasting caps, believed to be manufactured by the Atlas Division of the American Cyanamid Company. The explosion of the IED caused a sympathetic detonation of 3 pounds US military explosive, Composition B. This was contained in what is positively identified as an M720 60 mm, high explosive (HE) mortar round.
   A detailed report of the methods, findings and conclusions is attached.

Chapter 92
Seattle, Washington: Friday, May 9, 2003
◈

Special Agent of the Federal Bureau of Investigation Francis Reilly was from a large Catholic family in New York City. Although his parents kept trying for additional male progeny, Francis was their only boy. It may have been growing up in a family with six girls, or it may have been the toughness of the Sisters at St. Michaels where he went to parochial school, or it may have been his wife, whom he freely admitted was smarter than he was (Phi Beta Kappa in aeronautical engineering, currently working for Boeing), but Francis was very comfortable working with females. This made him unusual in the FBI. With its exclusively masculine background and macho image, women were generally not appreciated. However, when Francis learned that Dr. Danielle Lamaze-Smith from the CIA was coming to Seattle to work with him on the Peace Arch explosion case, he was pleased. He had enjoyed the association by e-mail when she helped him with interrogation issues for Ahmed Ressam. Now he was looking forward to meeting her.

Reilly picked up Danielle at the SeaTac airport two days after the explosion. He was prepared for the intellectual power. He was unprepared for her strikingly attractive appearance!

"Hello, I'm Dr. Danielle Lamaze-Smith. I hope you will just call me Danielle."

"Well, my full name is Francis James Reilly, but everyone calls me 'Fran.' I never liked it. I've always thought it sounded feminine, but it's stuck since grade school. You might as well call me 'Fran' too."

Danielle put on her biggest smile. "I'll never feel comfortable calling a clearly fit FBI agent like you 'Fran.' I'll give you a choice. You can be James, as in 'My name is Bond, James Bond', or you can be 'Jim.' I recommend 'James.'"

Reilly grinned. "If James is what you recommend, 'James' it

is."

The two of them bantered back and forth while they waited for Danielle's luggage to come down the carousel. James's car, with U.S. Government plates and a windshield card stating FBI-ON OFFICIAL BUSINESS, was in a "no parking" zone, right by the exit. They didn't talk about the case until James had them safely out of the airport.

"Bring me up to date. Have you ID'd the perpetrator?"

"Well, yes and no. It was a young man, a boy really, named Carl Kinsey from Wisconsin. At least that was the name on the birth certificate and driver's license he had been using for identification. We located his parents yesterday afternoon and learned that their son has been missing since 1997. When the agents from our Racine office showed them the Motor Vehicle Administration photograph of the perp, they said it didn't look anything like their son. So I don't know what to think. I guess somebody stole Kinsey's identity back in '97."

"Let me ask you something. Was Kinsey blond haired?"

"As a matter of fact, yes. Why do you ask?"

"Well, it's just a hunch, but I have been expecting something like this for over five years." Then Danielle explained to James her theory of the *madrass* for young terrorists. By the time she finished her narrative, they had pulled up in the garage in the basement of the FBI office in Seattle.

When they got to Reilly's office, his unit secretary Cindy Ericson was walking out. "Mr. Reilly, I just delivered a fax from Washington with the EOD report on the explosion at the Customs office. And while you were out, I typed a message from the Washington MVA regarding Mr. Kinsey's truck. It's also on your desk. Let me know if I can do anything else. Would your guest like a cup of coffee?" Cindy was angling for an introduction to Danielle.

"Thank you, Cindy. This is Dr. Smith from Washington, she is going to be helping us on the Customs case for a few days. Dr. Smith, this is Cindy Ericson. She has been with us for nine years and is more valuable than any three agents in the place." Danielle and Cindy shook hands. Just as with Mark van Rensselier of the CIA, Danielle liked this man who valued his staff. (Cindy also liked Reilly, he was easily the handsomest man in the office and very pleasant to work for.) Danielle turned down the coffee and asked Cindy where the ladies room was.

When she returned, James had already read the EOD summary and the MVA message. He gave them to Danielle who quickly scanned them.

"James, I think we have a serious problem. This is not an isolated explosion. The car's chain of title shows that it was owned by a Kahlid Moqued, clearly an Arab. And the EOD report confirmed the presence of a 60mm mortar round. That scares me. My understanding is that mortars are the most effective indirect fire weapon available to terrorists. Only artillery and rockets are more deadly, and they are very difficult for the average terrorist to get hold of. Here's what I think: I think Mr. Kinsey was involved in smuggling mortar shells into the country! Can we find out from Customs if he had crossed the border previously?"

"Well, sure. If you don't mind, I've got us scheduled to drive up to Blaine after lunch to talk to the Customs agents. If we get our timing right, we can talk to both shifts. My plan was to speak to them in a group, rather than spend the time to meet with them individually. We can always do that later."

Reilly and Danielle spent the following half-hour discussing the next steps in the investigation. They agreed to immediately do the following:

1) Apprehend Khalid Moqued and bring him in for questioning. The truck was previously titled in Maryland. The search for Moqued should start with that state's motor vehicle agency. James would task the FBI office in Baltimore to follow up with that responsibility.

2) Contact Customs Headquarters and get their thoughts as to where 60mm mortar shells might be coming from.

3) Contact Canadian Customs and see if they had any ideas as to where 60mm mortar shells might originate.

4) Contact the Department of State and determine if individuals named Carl Kinsey and Kahlid Moqued had recently entered the country. Such a request should include passport country of origin and numbers, points of entry or exit (POE), dates, etc.

Reilly called in Cindy and explained what he wished her to do while he and Dr. Smith were out. Then he and Danielle left for a quick luncheon. They had a two-hour drive to the Peace Arch customs office in Blaine, Washington.

Chapter 93
Blaine, Washington: Friday, May 9, 2003
◈

When James and Danielle arrived at the Blaine Customs office, workmen were just about finished with the repair of the damaged offices. Reconstruction had started the morning after the blast; now, about 70 hours later, all of the windows had been replaced, the roof was rebuilt, and the damaged masonry walls were re-laid. Only the doors, ceilings, electrical and mechanical, drywall and painting remained to be finished. These items were scheduled to be completed over the next five days. This all occurred only because the U.S. Government was not required to obtain building permits from the local government, although Blaine's reputation for permit service was far better than Bellingham's, 20 miles south. The General Services Administration (GSA) had men on the job as soon as the EOD team was finished with their research.

Reilly and Danielle went inside and introduced themselves to the site manager. They asked for permission to speak to the incoming shift, about 15 agents. These were assembled in the lunchroom, the only large area that was undamaged by the blast.

"Good afternoon. My name is James Reilly. I am a special agent of the Federal Bureau of Investigation. I am working on the deliberate explosion that you suffered here this week. With me is an associate from Washington, Dr. Danielle Lamaze-Smith. Before I go any further, let me express our sincere condolences over the loss of two of your fellow employees in this terrible event. Even if you are Customs Service and I am FBI, we work for the same employer. We view your loss as our loss. We work hard on any crime, we work just a little bit harder when one of our own has been killed. We *will* find the responsible parties."

"Dr. Smith and I have several questions we would like to ask you. We are speaking to you as a group in order to save time. If any of you would like to meet with us privately, we will make ourselves available at your convenience."

"First, do any of you know the suspected bomber, Carl Kinsey?" Suddenly nearly every hand in the room shot up. The incoming shift leader spoke up.

"Mr. Reilly, nearly everyone of us has dealt with Mr. Kinsey or his co-worker, Mr. Ziegler. They have been coming through here since last August. They were two of the nicest young men you ever wanted to meet. That's why we just can't believe that either of them would do this."

"Can you provide us with the records of how many times they came through your inspection?"

The shift leader spoke again. "Sure. I was a Bellingham city police officer before I was accepted for a job with the Customs Service. I got some training as a detective. I've already put together a schedule of the dates and times, of the exit and return, of both Mr. Kinsey's vehicle and Mr. Ziegler's."

"That's wonderful. I am sure you will be very helpful. Do you by chance have copies of Ziegler's paperwork, birth certificate, driver's license and auto registration as well?"

"It's all in the file folder I've prepared for you."

"That is excellent. Now, tell us about Kinsey and Ziegler. Why were they traveling back and forth to Canada? What did they tell you?"

"Well, they claimed they were soils inspectors, working on a big earthmoving job. They had these nuclear test gauges..."

Reilly stopped him. "Nuclear test gauges, what are they?"

Danielle interrupted. "My father is the president of a company that produces aggregates for the construction industry. His company uses nuclear testing to determine the optimum moisture for the compaction of various batches of aggregates. Basically, it's a piece of radioactive isotope mounted in a testing probe. The better the compaction, the more dense the material. The denser the material, the lower the flow of radiation, gamma rays, if I remember correctly; I was never very good at physics. I don't know the difference between gamma rays and x- rays."

The shift leader spoke again. "She's right. That's just the way Ziegler explained it to me. He had this small suitcase-sized piece of equipment with dials on it. It couldn't be opened because it was radioactive and....."

Suddenly the enormity of the fraud dawned on him. "None of us opened the case because we believed the warning labels, we believed there was radioactivity. What a perfect device for smuggling. I can't believe how gullible I was." He shook his head in disgust. "What a fool I was. If I was thinking properly, Wechsler and Mathews would still be alive."

Reilly jumped in to deflect the self-incrimination. "You can't blame yourself. Any customs official in the country would have believed there was danger from radiation. And, besides, the boys were wired. They were taught to blow themselves up if anybody began to ask questions. That is obviously what happened. For some reason, who was it, ...Arthur Mathews, asked Kinsey to step into the office. Kinsey waited until he was in a building before pulling the pin. He wanted to maximize the effect of the blast. He knew he was about to be found out."

Danielle addressed the audience. "Does anyone happen to remember seeing a manufacturers name on the testing unit?"

A lady in the middle of the group spoke up. "Yes, I do. I remember it because it was an unusual name. Working at a busy border crossing like this one, you would think that you would encounter every name known to man. But this was a new one. I have never seen the name Troxler before. And after this incident, if I ever see it again, it will be too soon."

On the trip back to Seattle, Reilly reminisced about the cases he had worked on; about the different kinds of people you encountered on investigations. Some were belligerent or resentful. Others were frightened and unwilling to talk. But sometimes you got lucky. You found people like the shift leader. A former law enforcement officer who anticipated all your questions and had the answers ready in a file folder.

Because of the time difference, it was Saturday morning the

8th before they reached Troxler. Through the Raleigh, North Carolina police they had contacted someone who could give them information about recent sales and got connected to Margaret Inverness.

"Sure I shipped two model 3440's to some company in Seattle. I distinctly remember their cockamamie name. A. Q. Enterprises."

Danielle gasped. "My god, *al Qaeda* enterprises!" She could visualize bin Laden in his mud hut in Afghanistan, laughing at them.

Chapter 94
Seattle, Washington: Friday-Monday, May 9-12, 2003
◈

Danielle stayed in Seattle four days. During that time not only did they have positive accomplishments, Danielle got an inside view of how to conduct a criminal investigation.

The first thing James did was to run the names Carl Kinsey and Robert Ziegler through the State of Washington Department of Licensing in Olympia. He did this to obtain their photographs and listed residential address. This turned out to be an apartment in Seattle. The rent was paid for a year in advance, but the apartment was not being lived in. In fact, the electricity and phone service had both been disconnected for non-payment of the monthly maintenance fee. A call to the power company confirmed that the lights and stove had last been used in September of 2002. The DOL also confirmed the ownership of a 1999 red Toyota pick-up truck, registered to Robert Ziegler.

James told Danielle that the DOL was usually a good place to start an investigation. It was difficult to exist in the U.S. without a car. The Motor Vehicle Agencies made it difficult to obtain licenses. There were plenty of fake Social Security cards floating around in the hands of undocumented aliens. But fake driver's licenses, that was something else again. You had to have a permanent address and prove it with utility bills, a lease, or some other validation.

James concluded that the suspects had rented another apartment closer to the border. He levied three agents from the Portland FBI office and had them start calling apartments, working from the border south. On the second day they found a building in Bellingham that had rented a two-bedroom unit to Kahlid Moqued. A squad of agents was sent to the apartment prepared to make an arrest, but found clothing and shaving gear for only one man. Robert Ziegler had already left. He was one step ahead of them.

A group "brainstorming" session came up with the idea that the "suspects," as Danielle was learning to refer to them, may have rented a warehouse space. This would be a safer place than the apartment to store the 103 mortar shells they calculated had been smuggled in on the 51 trips over the border each suspect had made. The agents from Portland were put to work canvassing the area's self-storage units.

The sixth phone call produced a mini-warehouse that had rented a unit to Khalid Moqued in May of 2002. Then, just several days ago, a young man had come in and paid the next six months in advance. When the owner agreed to unlock the unit without a court order, the agents arranged to meet him at the site. When they unrolled the overhead door, they found a plateless 1999 Toyota Tacoma pickup, red in color. Nothing else.

It was now clear to all of the FBI agents that Robert Ziegler, whatever his age, was highly trained. He had anticipated being tracked down through his truck and driver's license and abandoned the truck by locking it up for six months. Clearly he had rented another vehicle.

Hertz, Avis, National and several smaller local car rental agencies were contacted. They conducted computer searches of their transactions for the last two weeks in both the Vancouver and Seattle markets. Nobody named Ziegler had rented a car or truck. The agents called a small company called "Rainwater Rentals" and asked if a Robert Ziegler had rented a vehicle. The owner responded that the only thing he had rented all week was a van to some kid named Cantsey, or something like that, who needed it for two weeks to drive to Florida to pick up the furniture from his apartment. "Would the agent like him to dig out the file and check the exact name?"

The brain is a peculiar organ. Unless directed to do otherwise, it submits completely to the power of suggestion. The agent should have picked up on the name Cantsey, but he didn't. The only person in the case with a similar name was already dead. The touch about needing a truck for a couple of weeks to go to Florida to pick up a load of stuff was the final straw. The agent said, "No, it wasn't necessary." They were looking for a trained foreign agent named Ziegler. Not some kid with furniture in Florida.

The Department of State did provide information about Kahlid Moqued. According to the Canadian Foreign Ministry, Moqued arrived in Montreal on 13 January 2002, from Paris, France. He apparently stayed overnight in Montreal, since he crossed the border the next day at Bernard-du-Lacolle on a Greyhound bus to New York. He left the country from Los Angeles; (LAX) on 26 May 2002 ticketed for Pakistan. There was no record of either Carl Kinsey or Robert Ziegler entering the country. In fact, there was no record of a passport having ever been issued to either of them.

With Kahlid out of the country and the trail of Robert Ziegler dead as suddenly as it had started, there was nothing more to do in Seattle. Danielle returned home. On the flight back to Baltimore/Washington International (BWI) she had six hours to concentrate. She couldn't wait to get to the office the next morning.

Chapter 95
Langley, Virginia: Tuesday, May 13, 2003
◈

When Danielle got to her office, she placed a call to the headquarters of the Greyhound Bus Company. Because there are statutes forbidding the CIA to undertake any investigations in the Continental United States, (CONUS) she was treading on very thin ice. She knew she should have contacted the FBI and asked them to follow up on her idea, but she couldn't do it. She was developing a real sense of ownership about the whole matter.

"This is Danielle Smith at the US Immigration and Naturalization Service. I am looking for the passenger manifest of one of your busses that left Montreal on the 14th of January, last year and crossed the border at Bernard-du-Lacolle into Champlain, New York. No, there is no problem with any of your personnel; we are trying to determine the passenger list. Yes, I'll wait."

"Hello, Ms Snider. This is Danielle Smith at the INS. I understand you can help me with the passenger list of a bus that left Montreal at 9:00 AM on the 14th of January last year, bound for New York City. ...Yes, of course I'll hold while you get it up on your screen. Got it? First, was a U.S. Citizen named Kahlid Moqued on the bus? He was, excellent. Now at least, we have the right bus. Who were the other passengers?"

"Ms. Smith, we have a couple of trips a day we call our "drug runner" specials. These are filled with elderly passengers going to Canada to get their prescriptions filled. I think its probable that everyone on the bus was of that category. But wait, hold on a minute, on this bus, there were four young French tourists, in addition to the geezer brigade."

"May I have their names please? OK, Peter Bouchet, Charl Moussou, Thomas Bragunier and Pierre Lamale. Thank you very much Ms. Snider, you have been quite helpful. I hope you are still running those specials in a few years, when I retire. I may someday be a customer. Good bye."

Next Danielle called the French embassy and asked for the passport office.

"Bonjour, Le m' appele Danielle Lamaze-Smith, Le travaille pour le services Amercains d' immegration et de naturalization. Pourriez-vous faire pour moi la ve'rification de quatre passpeports? Peter Bouchet, Charl Moussou, Thomas Bragunier, Pierre Lamale."

The passport clerk was impressed with the quality of Danielle's French. It was both excellent and authoritative. Clearly this was a person to be reckoned with. Without insisting on the normal procedure, that the names be faxed on an INS letterhead, she complied with Danielle's request.

Merde'. According to her database, only two of the four names had ever been issued a French passport. Was *Madame* sure of the other names? When Danielle asked for the birthdates of the two persons with valid passports, the clerk told her 1937 and 1959. Danielle thanked her for her time.

Danielle now knew that the four boys had entered the country with false passports. Somewhere along the line at least two of them, Carl Kinsey and Robert Ziegler adopted their American identities in order to obtain driver's licenses. Wasn't it probable that the other two boys would do likewise?

When she really had serious analytic thinking to do, Danielle needed to be alone. She had to be free from the distractions of her phone, desk and office. She left her room and went to the ground floor of the CIA building to the auditorium. She was in luck. The big double entry doors were still open from a briefing on retirement issues by the Agency's Human Resources Department. She slipped in, closed the door behind her. She then sat down in the back row of seats and closed her eyes to concentrate.

She thought about the bus trip from the border. It was a long tiring trip, almost nine hours. The New Jersey Motor Vehicle Agency had given the renewal date of Kahlid Moqued's license as January 16, 2002. They arrived in New York on the 14th. Wasn't it logical that they stayed in New York for several days? If they did, perhaps it would be a hotel near the Port Authority building. She needed to check out the hotels in the area.

Then, why would Moqued rent an apartment in Seattle for just two boys? Only if the other two were going to be dropped off somewhere along the way. Wouldn't it make sense to have two operatives on the east coast and two on the west coast? If all four of the young men were going to be used in the west, wouldn't they have flown there? Why put everyone on a bus for the long drive to New York City?

The more she thought about the circumstances, the more she became convinced. Khalid Moqued and the boys stayed in New York before he got his driver's license renewed in New Jersey. And why did he get his license? Only if he needed to rent a vehicle and use it to drive somewhere. If he were going to borrow a car, he wouldn't have bothered to get a new license. And, if he rented a car, where was it turned in? She knew that he bought a truck in Maryland, it was in the title chain of Kinsey's truck. Were the other two boys in Maryland?

Danielle's mind was a symphony. Organizing a criminal investigation was not much different from being an NSA or CIA analyst. You just established a logical sequence of events and pursued it. In a sense, it was like her father's business. You started mining a rich vein of gravel. You worked it till it played out, or led to another vein. She had a lot of leads to follow.

Danielle went back to her office. It was clear to her that she was not going to be able to do this alone. She needed the resources of the FBI. She thought about calling James in Seattle, but rejected the thought. If she gave her ideas to him, he would take them and run with the case. It wasn't that she wanted to preserve credit for herself. Credit was not a concern. Control was. Danielle was exhibiting the characteristics that caused her to go to Afghanistan. Once she got involved in something, she wanted to carry it through to the end.

Danielle decided to call Special Agent Michael McNulty. He was younger than she and looked at her as a superior. That was the relationship she wanted.

"Hello, Michael. This Danielle Lamaze-Smith. I wonder if I could buy you lunch tomorrow. I am going to be in town and I have a matter I wish to discuss with you. Yes? Wonderful. I'll see you at the Old Ebbits Grill at noon. Goodbye."

Then she wrote an informal memo so that he would have a written record of the information she needed. There would be no official interagency request.

> *I am working on a related element of the Min-danaoBongo matter. I need your help.*
>
> *Can you find out if the individuals, Khalid Moqued, Robert Ziegler and Carl Kinsey registered in a hotel in New York City, probably near the Port Authority Terminal, on the night of 14 January 2002? Were two other young men with them? If so, what were their names?*
>
> *Can you find out if Kahlid Moqued rented a car in NYC on the 17th of January, 2002, or a day or two later and, if he did, where it was returned?*
>
> *If you can find out the names of the other two boys, can you find out what state MVA has them registered as owners/ drivers. You might start with Maryland as Moqued purchased a truck there that later was sold to a suspect on the West Coast.*

Danielle printed this out and erased the original. She folded up the hard copy and put in her purse.

Back at home that night, she had difficulty sleeping. While Neal lay beside her dreaming of great music, she tossed and turned, anticipating the meeting the next day.

Chapter 96
Washington, DC: Wednesday, May 14, 2003
❖

The Old Ebbits Grill was a favorite of Danielle's. She loved the leather seats, the gracious large tables and the ambience. Although she never recognized any of the people at the nearby tables, they always *looked* important.

When she arrived ten minutes early, McNulty was already there. Since the days of J. Edgar Hoover, the FBI had a reputation for conservative dress, white shirts, sincere ties and blue or gray suits. Still, it was possible to sense when an extra sartorial effort was being made on the part of a man. Danielle noted that was the case with McNulty. He was no rumpled cop!

"Now before we start, Agent McNulty, I am going to lay down some ground rules. I asked you to this luncheon, I am going to pay the bill." When he started to protest and mentioned "going Dutch", Danielle would hear none of it. She wanted him to feel ingratiated; going Dutch would not contribute to her desired effect.

Neither had a drink. Danielle had a glass of wine with her meal. McNulty did not. When the food arrived, Danielle got down to business.

"As we both know, counter-terrorism in the US is within the purview of the FBI. The Company is banned by statute to conduct investigations on American citizens. However, what I have is sort of a cross-boundary jurisdictional issue. I read recently that the Prince George's County police force had worked out an agreement with the Washington police to pursue suspects across the District line, if they believed a felony had been committed. I think I may have a similar situation. I have been pursuing suspects from other countries who are now in the United States. I want to continue to pursue them until I know if they are guilty of a terrorism-related crime. If they are, I'll gladly turn the matter over to a law enforcement agency. However, at this point I still don't have anything on them. In fact, I need your assistance just to find them. I could go, perhaps should go, to Walker or somebody at his level, but I am afraid he will cut me out entirely."

McNulty knew the feeling of having a case taken away by a superior. Everyone in law enforcement has had it happen to them. He also knew the feeling of pride that comes with developing a case from scratch. You get a severe case of territorial imperative.

"How can I help?"

Danielle took the memo from her purse and laid it on the table. "You'll notice this is not a formal request in any way. There are no copies of this anywhere. You have the only one."

"McNulty scanned the memo and put it back down on the table. "This stuff is easy. I used to be in the New York field office. We worked a lot with the NYPD, excuse me, the New York Police Department. I've still got a lot of friends in the PD. They have a whole hotel division. Some law enforcement agency in the country is always looking for someone staying in a New York hotel. You were smart to suggest that your suspects might be staying close to the Port Authority terminal. The PD boys have the city divided into zones, they'll send an e-mail or a fax to all the hotels in a ten-block radius. If they don't get any success, they'll expand the search by another ten blocks. By tomorrow, I'll have an answer."

"The next request, finding out about the rental car is also easy. Some 85% of the vehicles rented in this country are with the major companies, Avis, Hertz, National and a couple of other large regionals. The Bureau has a link to all of them. If Moqued rented a car, we'll learn all about it. Perhaps not by the close of business today, but by first thing tomorrow morning."

"Finally, IF we get lucky with the hotel registration, and get the names of the other boys, the MVA information is the easiest of all to get. We have direct computer access to every state motor vehicle agency in the nation. You give me a name and in minutes

I can give you the individual's age, weight, address, insurer, drivers' license number and, in most cases a head shot. There are still some states that don't require photographs. I can get you this information without any undue effort. I'm happy to do it for anyone involved in counter-terrorism. I'll do this with the understanding, of course, that if there turns out to be a law enforcement matter, the FBI will get the job. Rather than looking at this as a case of me helping you, I can justify the assistance as a case of you helping me. OK?"

Danielle felt quite relieved. She was more than a little nervous about violating a federal law by going "off the reservation" and exceeding her authority.

Danielle:

Following is the information you requested:

1) Kahlid Moqued rented three rooms in the New Yorker Hotel from 14 January to 19 January 2002. Occupants were Kahlid Moqued, Carl Kinsey, Robert Ziegler, Peter Nichols and George Wilkinson.

2) Kahlid Moqued rented a four-door Pontiac from Avis at their 42nd street office on 19 January. He used a valid New Jersey driver's license to complete the transaction. As he did not have a credit card in his name, he used the card of Kampfi Moqued, his father. The car was turned in at the Avis office at Reagan National Airport on 9 February. There were 487 accumulated miles.

3) Peter Nichols and George Wilkinson are both licensed drivers in the state of Maryland. They obtained their passenger car licenses on 18 April 2002. Six months later they each received their Commercial Driver's License (CDL) on 9 October. Peter Nichols also has a motorcycle license.

The following vehicles are registered to George Wilkinson:

- *1999 Ford 150 truck, VIN (vehicle identification number) SMZ1999-72423986, color white, LIC.*

> *PT37987*
> - *1987 AM General 10 ton truck, VIN 87-9007. Note: This truck had temporary (30 day) tags issued, but permanent tags have never been applied for.*
>
> *The following vehicles are registered to Peter Nichols:*
> - *1998 Ford 150 truck, VIN STR 1998-57850612, Color green, LIC, CL68071*
> - *1996 Kawasaki 500cc motorcycle, VIN Ka798652, LIC 47613*
>
> *The vehicles are insured through Southern Maryland Insurance in La Plata, MD. Tel: (301) 934-4007.*
>
> *The registered address for both the licenses and the titles is: 4081 Indian Head Highway, Indian Head, Maryland.*
>
> *Remember our deal on law enforcement.*
>
> *Glad I could be of help.*

Michael

Danielle sat and stared at the paper. A week ago she didn't have any names. Now she had all five. She felt like screaming for joy, but didn't.

Such an act would be widely misunderstood in the Central Intelligence Agency.

Chapter 97
Indian Head Maryland: Thursday, May 15, 2003
◈

According to *MapQuest*, it was 39 miles and 53 minutes from Langley, Virginia to Indian Head, Maryland. Danielle printed out the directions and left her office at noon. She told her secretary that she had some meetings to attend and would be "out-of-pocket" for the rest of the day. Of course, she would be reachable on her cell phone.

In reality, it was 41 miles and 67 minutes to the apartment building listed as the address for George Wilkinson and Peter Nichols. As Danielle drove up to the rather old and dilapidated building on Indian Head Highway, the main street of Indian Head, she noticed the entrance to a military facility a block away. She remembered that the report on the Peace Arch bombing was written by an EOD team located at the Indian Head Naval Surface Warfare Center. It had to be the same place. She figured she would do a little networking while she was in the area. She would stop in to congratulate the team on their good work, after she finished scoping out the apartment. This far out in the boondocks, the EOD people probably didn't get many visitors. Such acts never hurt. Sometime in the future she might require their cooperation.

She pulled her car up past the apartment building, got out and walked back. An elderly black man was mowing a very small patch of grass in the rear of the building. When Danielle got close to the man, he turned off the mower and asked if he could help her. It was obvious from her dress that she wasn't interested in renting an apartment, she must be looking for something.

"Yes, thank you. I am looking for a Mr. Wilkinson and Mr. Nichols. Do they live here?"

The lawn mower man looked perplexed. "Well, the answer is 'yes and no'. They rent the apartment next to mine, but I've never seen them. They're never here, so they must be living somewhere else. I've got their new phone book and there are some bills in the mailbox from the power company. I asked the building owners about them because I have a friend who is looking for a place. The owner told me they paid a full year's rent in advance, in cash. Since the year's end, he has gotten a money order each month. That's all I know about them."

Danielle thanked the man. It was Seattle all over again. The apartment was only rented in order to provide an address to the Motor Vehicle Administration, so they could obtain driver's licenses. As the black man correctly observed, they were living some place else.

Danielle returned to her car and drove the block to the gatehouse of the Navy facility. When the guard asked her the purpose of her visit, she pulled out her CIA identification and explained that she wished to visit with the EODTECH team. The guard suggested that she needed to see the base commander and directed her to his office. It was turning out to be a bigger deal than Danielle had anticipated. As she pulled into the parking area reserved for visitors, she was sorry she had started the whole process.

Captain James Peterson, USN, was in the 24th year of his 25-year hitch. He was an EDO (engineering duty only), not a line officer, and had spent most of his career at sea being concerned with "pipes and pumps." The Navy, in recognition of his career of meritorious service, had rewarded him the command of the Indian Head Naval Surface Warfare Center. The base Technical Director was essentially in charge of most of the 3,600 employees. However, the Base Commander enjoyed quarters in a lovely old home on the bank of the Potomac river, as well as a good deal of local prestige in Charles County. It was a pleasant way to end a career.

Captain Peterson's secretary came to the door of his office. "Sir, a Dr. Danielle Lamaze-Smith from the CIA is here to see you."

Captain Peterson rose to his feet. He had no idea what the

lady wanted, his visitors were normally Navy or industry. He was curious. "Show her in."

"Dr. Smith, welcome to Indian Head. I am Captain Peterson, the Base Commander. Please have a seat."

"How do you do, Captain Peterson. I am Dr. Danielle Lamaze-Smith. I am afraid I am disturbing you for a very insignificant reason. I found myself in Indian Head on other business and thought I would stop in and meet the EOD tech team who did such a fine job on analyzing the explosion at the Peace Arch border crossing earlier this month. I presume they are part of your command."

"Actually, Dr. Smith, that group is only quartered here. They are not part of my command. I make explosives, they investigate explosions."

Danielle's brain went into overdrive. Was there a connection between the Indian Head apartment of the terrorists and the Navy base? "You manufacture explosives...what kind."

"Well, one of our products is called Energetics, the explosive that propels the ejection seats in military aircraft. We developed the explosive for the "bunker buster" bomb used in Afghanistan. The world's largest producer of nitroglycerine, the Biazzi Company of Switzerland, is a contract operator of the only government-owned nitration facility in the country, here at Indian Head. We were originally a gunpowder plant, but in the early 1960s, we began the manufacture of nitroglycerine for the third stage of the Polaris missile and for Otto Fuel II used in torpedoes. We make a variety of specialty explosives. You look surprised. Is something wrong?"

Danielle thought quickly and decided she needed to fully explain.

"Captain Peterson, I am tracking some Middle Eastern terrorists. Two of them have rented an apartment here in Indian Head. As they are not living in it, I believed they rented it in order to have a lease address to get their driver's licenses. Now I fear that they may have needed a location from which to attack your facility. Just how vulnerable are you to terrorist attack? What kind of explosion could they create by blowing up your base?

"Ms. Smith, one of our base's problems is that we are surrounded by development. This makes us vulnerable in the BRAC (Base Realignment and Closure) process to a site in the California desert called China Lake. The people at China Lake have tried for years to get the work we do. One of their arguments has been the question you just asked. What if there was an explosion? Our response to that question has been to limit the amount of explosives we keep on site. When we finish manufacturing a batch of something, it gets shipped out. What is stored here is in hardened magazines with blast directional features. Even if the security to one of these magazines is breached, and that would be difficult, if the explosives it contains were detonated, the blast would be dissipated upwards. It may not even break any windows in downtown Indian Head. I don't see what your terrorists think they could accomplish by targeting us. And as far as stealing anything, forget it. We are surrounded by water. They would never get off the base. Your terrorists would be much better advised to make a bomb out of nitrogen fertilizer, like Mr. McVeigh in Oklahoma. The directions for making bombs are on the Internet."

"Captain, I am much relieved to hear all that you have told me. I had a few worried moments. Now I am inclined to believe that the whole thing is just a coincidence. There is no sign that the terrorists are living in their apartment. Moreover, it is hard to imagine what they could accomplish if they were living there."

"I dropped by to thank an EOD team for their good work. Instead I got an education. I thank you very much for your time. When you see the team, kindly give them my thanks and my regards."

As it was late in the day, Danielle drove directly home. Two thoughts nagged at her. Where *were* the boys living? And, what *if* Indian Head was not a coincidence?

Chapter 98
4:14 a.m., Nanjemoy, Maryland, Monday, May 19, 2002
❖

Robert Ziegler had left Bellingham and Seattle thirteen days ago, driving slowly, off the Interstates, at night. Several times he had slept in the car when he was able to find a deserted road where he felt it would be safe to rest; sometimes he stayed in old "tourist cabins" that were on the now-bypassed old roads. Because in the Northwest especially, the nights were getting short, and he had averaged only about 230 miles per day.

He pulled into the driveway next to the Nanjemoy house and honked the horn to wake the residents up. He got out of the van when he saw lights go on in the house. As he had not telephoned, he was not expected.

"It's Robert!", George shouted to Peter who was still in his bedroom. "My God, we have been concerned about you. We've read about Carl. Of course, we had no idea of what happened to you. As the TV didn't say anything about you, we thought you might be all right"

Peter came out of his bedroom, rubbing the sleep from his eyes. He and then George embraced Robert. George suggested they all go in the kitchen. He would make a pot of coffee, but he didn't want to miss any of Robert's stories.

It took an hour and a half for Robert to take the other two through what he and Carl had been doing for the past 14 months. Then George asked a question. "Did you bring the rest of the mortar rounds with you in the van? We have already gone to Baltimore and picked up the tubes you shipped. They arrived in the nick of time. Today is the very day we have been directed to put into effect operation *Wusool.*" When Robert said that he had the shells in the back of the van, George became excited. He insisted that they all go out to the van and unload the rounds. Then they would take the mortar shells from their shipping containers, remove the safety wires, and place them in the steel mortar tubes. Both boys wanted to show Robert what their skill with welding had produced.

They came back in the house a little after 7 o' clock. George and Peter had both told Ben Russell, their foreman, that they would be unable to come to work on the 19th as they had a funeral to attend. (They did not realize that they were a little premature in describing the event as a funeral.) Nor did they tell Mr. Russell that they were not going to come back to work. They had received directions from Sayyid Qutb to immediately drive to Detroit after operation *Wusool* and contact Dawit al Zaret. He would arrange a place for them to stay while awaiting directions for their next assignment. Now, of course, they realized would also have Robert with them.

The original plan was for Peter to be waiting on his Kawasaki motorcycle in a spot where he would be protected by the Washington monument. After George set off the mass mortar attack, Peter would then speed across the ellipse and pick him up. With the confusion that would be generated by the explosions, they did not think this would be difficult. Together they would then ride into southeast Washington where one of their trucks would be parked. They would leave the motorcycle behind with the key in the ignition. This would insure that it would be stolen before the authorities picked it up. With luck, the police would never find the motorcycle. Certainly, they were not going to file a stolen vehicle complaint.

Now, with the addition of Robert, there was a change in plans. They decided to use his rented van to drive to Detroit. He would wait for the motorcycle at the corner of New York Avenue and 13th street. The van would be more comfortable than a pickup truck. It was also less subject to being stopped. Each of them had drilled into their heads the efficiency of the FBI at following the skimpiest of leads. The people at Rainwater Rentals wouldn't even consider the van missing for at least another week.

They packed up the van with their clothing and personal gear. They had a big day ahead of them.

Chapter 99
Fort Myers, Virginia: Monday, May 19, 2003
◈

Of the many varied events that occur at the White House, none is more impressive than the arrival ceremony for a visiting foreign head of state or head of government.

The foreign dignitary lands at Andrews Air Force Base where greetings are conferred by the Chief of Protocol from the Department of State. The visitor then boards the President's own helicopter, Marine One, and is whisked to downtown D.C. A few minutes later it lands in the "ellipse", as the park adjacent to the Washington monument is called, where cannons have been placed for a later ceremonial 21-gun salute. At the ellipse, the guest is transferred to a car for a short motorcade ride to the South lawn.

The motorcade moves slowly across South Executive Place and enters the White House grounds through the East gate. As it moves up the driveway to the mansion, it passes through a cordon of uniformed military troops from the Third Infantry Regiment, "The Old Guard". In their dress blues, they are standing at attention and carrying flags. The car stops just short of the mansion and the honored guest and spouse exit. From there, they are escorted to the President by the Chief of Protocol.

The U.S. Army Military Band is playing. The Army's "Herald Trumpets", resplendent in white uniform jackets, are spread across the imposing steps and on the first level of the Truman balcony, over the diplomatic entrance to the White House. They play a traditional heraldic horn greeting. Then, at the conclusion of their performance, the band launches into "Ruffles and Flourishes," the introduction to "Hail to the Chief."

Already lined up at attention on the south lawn are formations of each of the four military services and the Coast Guard. The visitor and the President inspect the troops, their military aides trailing behind. After the inspection is completed, the President and his guest take the podium and deliver short speeches exchang-

ing greetings from each other's countries. These remarks are delivered to the carefully-selected guests who are members of the visitor's embassy staff, the Department of State and the White House staff. Other attendees are drawn from White House guest lists and Congress, and they are all honored, if not thrilled, to be there.

Though the whole ceremony is within the secure 18-acre White House complex, the Secret Service and their uniformed division, the "White House Police", are vigilant. Each of the guests has been subjected to a computer background check and issued a special pass to the ceremony. There are sharpshooters poised on the White House roof. The Washington Monument is closed to visitors for the occasion, no small interruption to the hundreds of visitors who come to see it in a single day. In short, every precaution is taken to protect the life of the President, his visitor, and his visitor's entourage.

In spite of these measures, the Secret Service knows that there remains one area of vulnerability: The possibility that an individual is willing to sacrifice his own life in order to take the life of a President. And the Service also knows that such an action is unpredictable, and there is no protection from it.

There is just worry.

:0500

Reveille sounded through the barracks at Fort Myers. It was no longer a bugler. That custom had ended shortly after WWII. Then a phonograph record had been substituted. Now it was a tape cassette.

Corporal Joseph Sly, one of the "cannon cockers" of the ceremonial salute battery of the 3rd infantry, was facing a busy day. He dressed in his "blues" and went to mess. After mess, he would head for the motor pool.

:0615

Corporal Sly and the rest of the Battery crew logged out of the motor pool four M-1078s (Light Mobility Tactical Vehicle), the Army's latest version of the traditional "deuce-and-a-half."

These had been hitched to the salute cannons the night before. The M5, 155mm, anti-tank guns, were manufactured in 1943. To a modern soldier the guns, with their long tubes and splinter shields, looked strange. To Sly, they looked beautiful.

:0625

The Salute Battery departed Fort Myers for the 15-minute drive to the Ellipse.

:0628

Gloria Macapagal Arroyo, The president of the Republic of the Philippines, woke up with a start. At first she didn't remember where she was. She was not a good airplane traveler. She had trouble adjusting to a number of changes in time zones. Accordingly, on this trip to meet with the President of the United States, she had flown first from the Philippines to Hawaii. The next day she did Hawaii to Chicago. Yesterday they had done the Chicago to Washington leg. Suddenly, she remembered. She was in Blair House, the lovely official guest house for the President's visitors.

:0642

Deputy Chief of Protocol, Neill Hawthorne, was in the basement of his house, polishing his shoes. Upstairs, in the kitchen, his wife was ironing his trousers. He owned two expensive custom-made suits. Both of them were at the cleaners. Twenty minutes earlier his boss, the Chief of Protocol, had called to inform him that he was going to have to do the Arroyo arrival ceremony. The Chief had suddenly come down with a stomach virus.

The Chief of Protocol was, as is the case in most Administrations, a wealthy and prominent individual. Neill was a loyal campaign worker, an advance man. He cursed the relative poverty that limited his wardrobe. He bet his boss had a whole closet full of hand-tailored suits.

:0700

The column of five olive drab military buses carrying the honor guard from the 3rd Infantry and the 60-piece U.S. Army band left Fort Myers in Virginia for the 15 minute trip to the south lawn of the White House. There the troops would unload, form up, and march onto the south lawn to a cadence beat out by the drummers. Click, click......click click click. Click, click...... click click click.

Simultaneously, detachments from The Marine Barracks at 8th and I Streets, the Air Force at Bolling Air Force Base, The Coast Guard from the Alexandria Coast Guard Station and the U.S. Navy from the Washington Navy Yard, also boarded buses for the south lawn. These troops would be used in the "review of troops" ceremony. The standing schedule required that all troops be in place 90 minutes before the beginning of a ceremony.

:0710

A service truck from the District of Columbia Police Department unloaded a dozen rubber traffic cones at the intersection of 17th Street and Constitution Avenue and then proceeded to E Street where the process was repeated. These would be used to block all traffic on 17th Street during the arrival ceremony. This procedure was not normally done. The Secret Service had requested it for President Arroyo, for some unexplained security reason.

:0712

A large truck, a motorcycle and a van left Nanjemoy, Maryland and headed for Route 210 north and the District of Columbia. Because Route 210 became very busy during commuting times, George Wilkinson decided they should allow plenty of time for delays.

:0730

Twelve Secret Service agents from the Washington Field Office began dispersing themselves around the perimeter of the south lawn of the White House and the Ellipse. They were identifiable by the colored pin they wore in their suit jacket lapels. A practiced eye would also detect the presence of shoulder holsters. These agents enhanced the security forces provided by a dozen men from their uniformed division. The Washington Metropolitan Police Force already had 15 uniformed officers on 17th Street including four at each set of traffic cones. The National Park Police, with jurisdiction in the Federal Center, had another dozen men on the mall and the ellipse.

:0732

Deputy Chief of Protocol Hawthorne departed his home in Mitchellville, Maryland, for Blair House. He was satisfied he looked presentable.

:0745

President of the Philippines Gloria Macapagal Arroyo finished applying her makeup.

As she was not due to depart Blair House until:0857, she had plenty of time for breakfast in Blair House's very beautiful dining room.

:0800

The invited guests began arriving for the ceremony. Among these were members of the staff of the Philippine Embassy. (So that everyone could attend the ceremony, the embassy hired temporary telephone operators. Only the third Secretary was left behind in case of emergency. The Ambassador put him on the guest list for the State dinner as compensation). Other guests were members of the diplomatic corps, members of Congress, and guests of the White House. Members of the White House staff did not need an invitation. If they could spare the time, they had only to leave their offices and walk out on the south lawn from the gates by either the East or the West Wing.

:0830

Danielle Lamaze-Smith departed the Headquarters of the Central Intelligence Agency for the White House. She had hoped to leave earlier, but had gotten involved in a conference call. Now, with the morning commuter traffic to contend with, she feared she would miss the opening ceremony that was scheduled to begin at :0900. She told the driver to hurry.

:0845

In the abundance of caution that is characteristic of security people everywhere, the District of Columbia Police emplaced the traffic cones. This blocked off traffic on 17th street, E street and Pennsylvania Avenue.

:0857

President and Mr. Arroyo departed Blair House in a five-car motorcade controlled by the Secret Service. They would head in gate B3 of the White House and circle the drive to the Diplomatic Entrance.

:0859

The Arroyo motorcade arrived at the White House and deposited president and Mr. Arroyo at the Diplomatic Entrance.

:0900.51

An Army M35A3, a two and one half-ton truck with camouflage and black *MDW, 3rd Inf* markings stenciled on it's bumper and hood pulled up to the traffic cones on Constitution Avenue at 17th Street. The soldier driving explained that he had to get through as he was carrying the spare blank shells for the cannons. These had been forgotten when they loaded. "Sometimes there are misfires and then we have to have another shell" the soldier related. "It wouldn't do to have only a 19 or 20-gun salute instead of a 21-gun." The driver further explained, "that one of the cannon prime movers had experienced some engine fuel supply troubles on the way over from Fort Meyer. The motor pool had sent another deuce, instead of a humvee, in case the cannon needed a tow vehicle."

The police officer, not having served in the Army, did not recognize the difference between an *M35A3* and a *M1078*. They were both "deuce and a halves." The officer moved the traffic cones. The truck proceeded up 17th street.

:0901

The Army Herald Trumpets performed Honors, followed by Ruffles and Flourishes.

:0902

The Army Band played "Hail to the Chief."

:0902.18

Due to the police barricade, Danielle's driver could not get to 17th Street from E Street as he had planned. Danielle told her driver that she would walk the last several 100 feet. The driver returned to Langley.

:0903.23

Deputy Chief of Protocol Hawthorne, introduced the President and First Lady to president Arroyo and her husband;

:0903.46

The driver of the M35A3 stopped on 17th Street at the E Street entrance to the Ellipse. Again, this was for a police check. At that same instant Danielle also reached the corner of 17th and E Street. As the driver stuck his head out of the window to repeat his story about the blanks, Danielle caught sight of a handsome soldier with blond hair. He looked strangely familiar, but she couldn't quite place him. The second policeman, already conditioned by the fact that the truck had passed the first check, waved him through. Danielle started up 17th Street toward State Place, the entrance to the south lawn.

:0903.51

Clive Owens, the Secret Service duty officer in W16, the Secret Service command post directly under the Oval Office, in the West Wing of the White House, observed an army "deuce and a half" on his monitor. This image was from the video camera on the roof of the White House. As the truck was not supposed to be there during the ceremonies, he started the video recorder. He also radioed for agent Harry Duncan to go over to the truck and check out the driver.

:0904.38

Danielle suddenly remembered where she had seen the soldier before. It was five years earlier, in a mud hut in Afghanistan. She turned around and walked back to the E Street entrance to the Ellipse as rapidly as she could in her high heels.

:0904.42

The President introduced the Vice President and his wife, the Secretary of State and his wife and the Chairman of the Joint Chiefs of Staff and his wife to president Arroyo and her husband.

:0905.03

George Wilkinson pulled the truck into the middle of the Ellipse and slipped the gearshift to neutral. Then he reached for the silver toggle switch he had installed on the dash. He flipped the switch and heard a loud click from behind the dash. He pushed the switch back to its original position. Again he was rewarded with the loud click. Then he tried the other direction, the same result. Something was terribly wrong with the electrical system. The solenoids weren't working. *And he had carefully tested each of them when he installed them!* He would have to get in the back of the truck and drop the mortar shells by hand.

George Wilkinson jumped out of the truck, ran to the rear, and began to frantically undo the knots on the ropes holding the truck bed end tarp.

:0905.05

The President of the United States and the president of the Republic of the Philippines moved to the reviewing stand and began to climb the steps.

:0905.07

Danielle arrived at the E Street entrance to the Ellipse at the same time as Secret Service Agent, Harry Duncan. She spotted his pin, flashed her CIA identification card at him and asked, "Are you carrying?" When Duncan, with a surprised look on his face, nodded affirmatively, Danielle, in a calm low voice, to prevent all of the police officers around them from overhearing, said; "We've got to get to that truck. Its driver is a known terrorist. Let's go." She reached down, pulled off her heels, and started running. Duncan, still a little unsure of what was happening, ran alongside.

:0905.11

The two presidents stood at attention at the front of the reviewing stand. Suddenly, the 21-gun salute started. On the Ellipse, Danielle could hear the OIC (Officer in Charge) shouting "ready.....fire," timing his orders with a stopwatch to the three seconds spacing traditionally used in salutes.

:0906.11

As Danielle and Duncan got close to the truck, Wilkinson untied the last of the knots and climbed into the bed. When he pulled back the canvas flap, he exposed all of his welding handiwork. Duncan, who had been an infantryman in Desert Storm, the first gulf war, recognized mortars when he saw them. He pulled out his weapon. Danielle cried out. "Anwar, don't." Anwar stopped. He looked up in shock and amazement as he recognized Danielle.

Agent Duncan pulled the trigger just as the 20th cannon fired. The puny report of his pistol shot was totally drowned out by the boom of the 155mm blank round. As Duncan was on the ground and Belhadj was in the truck, the shot had an upward trajectory. It went in the top of Belhadj's chest and came out the back of his neck. He fell backward into the truck. The canvas tailgate flap that he had been holding open, dropped down.

:0906.15

The U.S. Army Band played the National Anthem of the Republic of the Philippines. This was immediately followed by the National Anthem of the United States of America.

:0911

The President escorted president Arroyo off the stand and led her on a formal review of the assembled troops.

:0915

The President led president Arroyo back to the reviewing platform where they watched a musical review of the troops. When this was finished, the Commander of the Troops concluded the Honors.

:0920

The President began his remarks of welcome.

:0925

President Arroyo responded to the President's remarks.

:0930

The Arrival Ceremony was concluded.

:0935

Peter Nichols drove up 17th Street on his motorcycle. He saw the truck, surrounded by four men and one woman. There was no sign of George.

As Peter drove back to link up with Carl on New York Avenue, he was thinking about the plan changes they would have to execute. Although they didn't know if George was alive, they had to react as though he was. George knew Dawit's private number in Detroit. They had to call Dawit and warn him that his phone number may be compromised. They could make that call later in the day, from someplace in Virginia. Instead of going to Detroit, they would drive south to Myrtle Beach and hide out for a week until they got their next instructions. He would write the letter, seeking new direction from their unknown handler in New York, once they got to the motel. With luck, maybe even that evening.

Anwar Belhadj died just a few yards from the spot on the mall where his parents had first met, more than twenty years earlier. He was buried four days later in an unmarked grave, facing East as Islam requires (even a terrorist deserves that little respect, the government had determined.) Danielle Lamaze-Smith was the only person in attendance. She lingered at the gravesite until after the backhoe had finished filling the hole and then walked slowly back to the waiting car with the seal of the Central Intelligence Agency on the door. She felt very weary, but very relieved.

Chapter 100
The White House: May 24, 2003

"Welcome to the Oval Office, Danielle."

With those words the President of the United States met her at the doorway. Partially with the pull of his hand and partially with the pull of some unseen magnetic force, Danielle found herself in the world's most famous office. She had just reached the center of the room when the telephone on the desk sounded a subdued buzz. The President dropped her hand and waved her to a chair in front of the elaborately carved marble fireplace. He strode to the desk in two steps and, still standing, picked up the receiver.

"Thank you for calling me back Senator."

Danielle made a motion that suggested that she would leave the room. The President vigorously shook his head in opposition. He put his hand over the mouthpiece, gave her an exaggerated wink, and whispered, "Stay, you'll enjoy this."

Danielle was treated to seven minutes of salesmanship of a sort of which she did not expect the President capable. He was trying to win the senator over to his position on a bill. The President pulled out all of the stops. Danielle heard only one side of the conversation, but it was clear to her that the President was being successful. This was a presidential skill that was not apparent from reading the Washington press reports. The reporters and commentators generally downplayed the President's linguistic attributes.

When the call was completed, the President replaced the phone and got up from his chair. "With this job, it is always something. It's a wonder we all fight so hard for it" And then he grinned, "of course Air Force One makes it all worthwhile. Now, let's get out of here before I get caught again."

The President opened the door to the rose garden and led her down the colonnaded walk to the entry to a wide, vaulted corridor running under the mansion. As they walked, he kept up a running commentary.

"Although I spent a lot of time here prior to being President, it isn't until you actually are *the President* that the full sense of history of this place overwhelms you. Even knowing that this isn't the White House of Lincoln and Adams and Jefferson, it gets to you. When I say that this isn't the White House of those three Presidents, I mean that they probably wouldn't recognize the place. Hell, the only thing original to the White House of 1800 is the Gilbert Stuart painting of George Washington hanging in the East Room. That's the one Dolly Madison saved from the British fire by cutting out it of the frame."

"The White House has been modified a number of times, it even got a third story in 1927. During the Truman Administration, the place was completely gutted. Only the exterior walls were left standing. Several additional basement levels were excavated, a steel supporting structure was fabricated and modern utilities were installed including air conditioning. Then the rooms were replaced in approximately their original locations. So the Red Room, the Green Room and Lincoln's bedroom are not actually the original rooms, they only occupy the same space. It still goes on. Nixon, in a controversial move, covered up FDR's swimming pool and turned it into a press room. Of course, many of the fireplaces are original, and the woodwork and plasterwork were replicated. Anyway, it looks better now than it ever did in the old days. The furnishings are all period antiques, gifts from wealthy donors. When Teddy Roosevelt was President he had his hunting trophies hanging in the State Dining Room. I don't imagine the anti-gun, anti-hunting crowd and PETA would let him get away with that today."

They reached a seated guard who leapt to his feet as they approached. "Good afternoon Mr. President."

"Good afternoon, Tom." the President responded. Danielle was impressed to see that he knew the guard's name; she had long concluded that the most successful people she had ever met were usually also the most thoughtful and courteous.

They passed the guard by a few steps and went to the left side of the corridor to a very small elevator. Continuing his gentlemanly behavior, the President motioned her in first, got in and pressed the "2" button. In the confined space, the sense of the President's masculinity was overpowering.

"When I first got here, I resolved not to take the elevator and to always walk upstairs in my own house. A President needs all the exercise he can get. But from where we were, on the ground floor, it is a little bit of 'you can't get there from here.' We would have had to walk all the way to the end of the hall, climb the stairs to the State floor, and walk back to the main staircase. Also, there are always people buzzing around on the State floor. I want to limit the number of people seeing us together today."

As Danielle pondered this last remark, the elevator opened and she found herself on the Family living quarters floor of the White House. They turned right and walked down a hallway running down the center of the whole building to the northwest corner. The President led her into an elegant room with a vaulted ceiling and a mahogany Sheraton dining table for eight, set with two places. There was no doubt about the seating arrangements. The President pulled out her chair, to the right of his at the head of the table.

"This is the Family Dining Room, Danielle. I don't usually bring guests here, but today I wanted to do something special." As he said that a waiter appeared. Using the customary salutation "Mr. President", he asked if he should serve the soup. The President said "yes." The waiter re-appeared with a silver tureen of crème of celery soup which, beginning with Danielle, he proceeded to carefully ladle out.

In front of each of them was a buff colored card four inches by five inches. Along the top of the long edge *The President's House* was printed in raised gold letters. Under that was the date, and under that the menu de jour.

The President's House
May 24, 2003

Crème of Celery Soup
Boeuf Bourguignon with Wild Rice
Mixed Salad with Raspberry Vinaigrette
Sacher Torte with Whipped Cream
Coffee

It was a wonderful menu. Danielle picked it up admiringly. She longed to slip into her purse, but dared not appear gauche. The President came to her rescue. "When I first ate here and saw this little extravaganza, menus for each meal, my first reaction was to put a stop to it. Then the chef told me that their sole purpose was for souvenir value. Since then I have been saving mine in a scrapbook as a tangible reminder of how good I had it when I was in office. Take yours with you too." He said this with a warm smile that fairly beamed. Danielle was becoming more and more impressed with this man who was so solicitous of his guests.

The President sipped a spoonful of soup and assumed a serious mien.

"Danielle, do you know what an *ampere* is?"

"Sir, I was a poor student of physics in high school. It was one of the few subjects I've had difficulty with. I guess it was one of those 'left brain, right brain' things. I remember an ampere is a unit of electrical measurement, but that is all. I can't tell you the difference between volts and amperes."

"To tell you the truth, I was the same. If you had asked me to define ampere last week, I wouldn't have known either. However, based upon a report I received several days ago, amperes suddenly took on a critical importance for me. For you too. For a lot of people."

"An ampere is a unit of electrical power. The 100-watt bulb

in a common desk lamp draws about one ampere of current. The chandelier over our heads has six 25-watt bulbs. It takes about 1.5 amperes to power it. A difference of just ten amperes would have resulted in a vastly different ending in the incident on the mall last Monday."

"After you and the Secret Service agent shot the would-be assassin, what's his name?"

Danielle interjected, "Anwar Belhadj."

"Yes, Anwar Belhadj, well, you wisely had the Secret Service commandeer the truck. That was very smart thinking on your part. If the Army had gotten into it every general in the world would have known about the assassination attempt by the end of the day. The military has the best back channel gossip communication system in existence. We would never have been able to keep the thing a secret."

"The Secret Service EOD team dismantled ninety-six 60mm mortar shells and put safety wires in them. Then they drove the truck to their training facility in Greenbelt. And guess what they found? The electric solenoids that controlled the firing of the mortars were wired to the light switch. When Belhadj threw the switch in the cab to drop all the shells, the headlights were still on. Army trucks always have their headlights lit when on the road. The current load was too great and blew the circuit breaker. Just like when you plug the electric iron and the toaster into the same outlet. If he had turned the headlights off, you and I wouldn't be here talking. The load was too much by just ten amperes. We guess that was the way they were taught to make car bombs. Take the power from the light switch rather than run an electric line directly to the battery. If someone lifts the hood, everything appears normal. A damned close call, too close for my comfort."

"The ninety-six mortar tubes were welded in a pattern to destroy everything from Pennsylvania Avenue to the Washington Monument. While there was not enough explosive power to reduce the White House to rubble, there was enough to do considerable damage. And of course, everyone in the area would have been killed. Perhaps more than were killed on 9/11."

"Because Agent Duncan fired his weapon at precisely the same moment as the next to the last cannon shot, no one heard the gunfire. And of course, Belhadj died in the truck, out of view. So far, we have been able to ascertain that only 16 people, including you and me, are familiar with what happened. Most of the rest are Secret Service agents. That is too large a number to keep a secret forever, but I have decided we should try. There is no sense in scaring the public or giving bin Laden the pleasure of knowing that he came close. There is also no reason to give the newsies or the Congress something to beat us up with. I have therefore made the decision that we will keep the entire incident under wraps. In a few years, if and when somebody leaks some of the story, the rest of us will deny it. And, of course, there will be no official government records, even at the CIA. I am sure you see the logic in this."

"Mr. President, I entirely agree with your decision. Personally, from the very beginning I thought this was the direction you should take. I have told no one, not my husband, not the DCI or my immediate superior. That is why I got several Secret Service agents to guard the truck and why I cautioned agent Duncan about keeping quiet. To me, it is one of those incidents that 'never occurred.'"

The President smiled. "I thought you would see it that way."

The President again grew serious. "The only problem I have is what to do with you."

"Danielle, you have been of enormous service to America. I have been furnished with your files from the NSC and the CIA. I found them fascinating reading. Your trip to Afghanistan, your hunch about the madrasses, your analysis of the nature of our enemies; were inspired. You have been on the cutting edge of this thing for seven years. You have constantly kept one step ahead of bin Laden, including last Monday. I owe you my life. The country owes you more. I can think of no event comparable in American history. Certainly there were men such as Washington and Lincoln who created or preserved our republic. You didn't do that. What you did was to persevere over a period of years and ultimately prevent a great catastrophe from occurring. That deserves some sort of special recognition."

"There is a basic counter-productive aspect to awards and honors. To be significant and respected, an honor must be known and recognized. To be recognized, an honor must be widely held. And therein lays the problem. How to make an honor respected without cheapening it through overuse. Our nation's highest tribute, The Medal of Honor, is awarded for exceptional valor on the field of battle. Yet even this medal at one time came dangerously close to being reduced in prestige. In the Civil war, it was once awarded to an entire Yankee company, every man. It wasn't until the past century that the War Department finally put in place a system and standards for its issuance. Now, when you see a soldier with an MOH, you know he is really something. I guess one could define this as a sort of Gresham's law of medals."

Danielle spoke up. "Sir, I really don't understand the reference to Gresham and his law."

The President smiled and explained. "Gresham was a 16th century economist who posited that 'cheap money drives out dear.' When there is an abundance of counterfeit money in circulation, people are unwilling to part with their real money. Its value is lowered by the counterfeit. When I related it to medals and honors, I was referring to the cheapening of their value by overuse."

"The Presidential Medal of Freedom, the highest honor I can bestow, was created by President Truman to recognize certain civilians who had contributed significantly to the victory in World War II. In 1962 President Kennedy expanded the eligibility to include members of the public at large, whose contributions to America enriched our way of life. These included movie stars, athletic coaches, philanthropists, etc. I am not saying this shouldn't have been done. I am saying that when a truly deserving person, such as yourself, comes along, there is no fitting tribute."

"I had my staff do some research on this subject. They found that President Nixon must have recognized this void. In particular, he wanted to recognize the contributions of foreign nationals to our country. He asked John Ehrlichman, his counsel, to come up with some suggestions. Mr. Ehrlichman, in turn, passed the assignment along to a creative young man on his staff. This fellow proposed the creation of an honorary society, *The Order of Friends of the United States*. It was patterned after your French Legion of Honor. Nixon bought into the idea. An Executive Order was drafted and sent to the Bureau of the Budget, now the Office of Management and Budget, for final formatting."

"Then the matter gets interesting. It went through a vetting process in the bureaucracy you wouldn't believe. This review procedure included an Assistant Attorney General named William Rehnquist, now the Chief Justice of the Supreme Court. Finally, months later, some faceless clerk at DOD drafted a memorandum for the signature of an unknown Colonel on the NSC staff of Dr. Kissenger. The Colonel signed the memo and sent it back to John Ehrlichman, the man who Nixon had originally told to come up with something new in the way of awards. Probably the Colonel also slipped a copy of his memo to Ehrlichman in Nixon's reading file. Anyway, the DOD's arguments about not needing a new award won the day. Nixon dropped the idea. Incidentally, the Colonel went on to become a Four-Star General and NATO Commander. Later he served with distinction as the Secretary of State in the Reagan Administration. If you haven't figured out whom it is I'm talking about, his name was Alexander Haig."

"In spite of the fact that the original executive order went through several drafts, a name change, and was approved by a number of departments and agencies, no executive order was ever issued. The DOD's objection was the death sentence. It is a case study of how difficult it is to get things accomplished in the government. Even for a President. It is also an example of the power of the Pentagon."

"Danielle, on the day after tomorrow at 3 o' clock in the afternoon, there will be a private ceremony in my office. The Vice-President, and the Secretary of State will be present, as will the DCI and the Director of the National Security Agency, the Secretary of Defense and your husband. I invited the Attorney General, but he is out of town. The Secretary of the Treasury, as you probably know, is recovering from surgery. These people will watch me invest you with the exclusive membership in *The Order of Friends of the United States.* I have asked all of these officials to be witnesses and to sign the commendation. I believe this award is probably the most important recognition I shall present during my Presidency."

"The order includes a neck medallion that is currently being cast in gold by the mint. Thomas Jefferson himself presented the original of this medallion to several French diplomats who were helpful to our revolution. I find this whole thing strangely eerie. Thomas Jefferson originally awarded this medal to several Frenchmen for their service to America. Now, 213 years later, I am awarding it to a French woman for the same thing."

"Yes, I know you are not an American citizen, but you now have lived here for some time, and you have done more for your adopted country than almost anyone I can think of. And because you are *not* a citizen of the United States, you actually meet the qualifications for the medal!"

"My only regret is that the ceremony must be private. However, we can't very well have the presentation public and the *raison d'etre* a secret, can we?" Danielle thought the President's French pronunciation was pretty good.

Danielle couldn't remember any of the rest of the meal or their conversation. It all floated by on an adjacent cloud.

Only the thought that at least two boys were still at large, dampened their spirits for a few minutes...

Then, when she was leaving the historic building, the President walked her to the car and gave her a large brown envelope. "For your interest, here is the whole file on *The Order of Friends of the United States*, just as it was drafted thirty six years ago, from inception to 'death by Haig'."

As she sunk into the rear seat cushion of the White House car returning her to the CIA headquarters, Danielle opened up the folder the President had given her. She saw that the author of the original memo creating the order was named Charles E. Stuart. As she read his work, she began thinking that he was the sort of person who would be interested in what happened to his little project of so long ago. She determined when she got to her office, she would track him down. She would tell him that she was now the sole and exclusive member of his *order*. She just couldn't tell him why.

Perhaps, if Stuart sounded interesting on the telephone, she might even invite him to lunch. There might even be the idea for a book in her story!

On the following pages are but three of the numerous documents that she found in the collection of papers given to her by the President on May 24, 2003, regarding the Friend of the United States *medal awarded to Dr. Danielle Lamaze-Smith by the President of the United States on that date.*

March 11, 1969

FOR: John D. Ehrlichman
FROM: Charles E Stuart
RE: Award: Foreign Nationals

As you requested, I have investigated the various means by which a foreign diplomat may be officially recognized for services rendered to the United States.

The State Department has little to offer. They utilize the Scroll of Appreciation (exhibit A) and in cases of greater criticality have on several occasions mounted a State Department seal on a walnut plaque and used it as an award.

The Johnson Administration must have found need for an appropriate award for in 1965 Harry McPherson prompted the State Department to develop prototypes of five medals. These are:

> Liberty Medal for Peace and Freedom
> Cross of Valor
> Department of State Distinguished Service Medal
> Department of State Meritorious Service Medal
> Scroll of Freedom

None of these medals was ever officially recognized or put into production. (artwork and descriptions – exhibit B)

It has occurred to me that this may be a propitious time for a more ambitious program than the establishment of another "distinguished service award." Suppose, for example, that we take the case that large numbers of foreigners, over the years, have made profound contributions to America. Further, that these contributions have never been uniformly recognized. Could we not now, capitalize on those overtures to brotherhood expressed in Europe last week, and officially recognize specific foreigners who have substantially contributed to the greatness of this country.

The French have done this successfully for several centuries with the Legion of Honor. Despite the fact that it is widely held, the ribbon is worn with pride by Legionnaires everywhere.

Page 1 Text: Charles E. Stuart Memorandum proposing "Order of Friends of the United States" medal. (see p. 401)

I propose a similar organization. Let us create "The Order of Friends of the United States".

Historically, Americans have shied away from the creation of official orders, societies, etc. This is a natural reaction from a people whose society, from the beginning, was intended to be classless. Nonetheless, we are sophisticated enough today to accept the concept of an honorary class of foreigners who have contributed to our country.

In order to give the decoration sufficient prestige, considerable promotion should be done and in fact the President should announce it on some auspicious occasion. Posthumous awards should be made to such men as Lafayette, Pulaski, von Steuben, etc. In order to accommodate such historic greats as these, as well as lesser beings, the medal will be awarded in degrees, i.e., with honors. Grand honors, etc.

Recipients, individuals or governments in the case of long-dead conferees will receive a scroll, ribbon, and gold medal.

Thomas Jefferson, in 1790, created the "Diplomatic Medal" and awarded it to two French diplomats. It has not been utilized since that time. (Description and artwork – exhibit C) The only thing mitigating against the use of this medal is the fact that, unfortunately, the U.S. mint has been reproducing these in bronze since 1876. It has never been a very good seller and in recent years has been averaging about 50 medals a year. If the medals to be awarded were produced only in gold and the mint were to cease the sale of the bronze items, I should think the comparatively small distribution of the bronze medals would cause no problems.

To establish this or any other award program or presentation medal, an Executive Order is required. I have drafted one which is complete but for the language describing the means for funding which I shall let the Bureau of the Budget insert. (Executive Order – Exhibit D)

You may find a program of this magnitude unreasonable. If so, a simple medal of recognition can easily be put into effect inasmuch as the State Department has already executed the design.

Page 2 Text: Charles E. Stuart Memorandum proposing "Order of Friends of the United States" medal. (see p. 401)

(Above) The author's original memo to John Erlichman, President Nixon's Counsel. The text is reproduced on pages 399-400.
(Courtesy Nixon Archives)

(Above) The Executive Order draft which served as the authority for Danielle's medal. The text is on page 402-403.
(Courtesy Nixon Archives)

Executive Order
Establishing the "Order of Friends of the United States"

By virtue of the authority vested in me as President of the United States, it is ordered as follows:

Section 1. Order established. The Order of Friends of the United States (hereinafter referred to as the order) is hereby established for the purpose of giving due recognition to those citizens of other countries who have performed exemplary deeds of service for the United States.

Section 2. Medal established. An award medal representing the Order is hereby established together with accompanying ribbons and appurtenances. The medal shall be in three degrees, the degree of "with honors" being intermediate, and quote "with grand honors" being the highest.

Section 3. Conferring the order.

(a) The Order may be bestowed by the President upon any foreign national who has made an especially meritorious contribution to the national interest of the United States.

(b) The president may select for the order any person nominated by the board provided for in Section 4 of this order, any person otherwise recommended to the president, or any person selected by the President upon his own initiative.

(c) The announcement of the granting of the order may take place at any time during the calendar year. The presentation ceremonies shall take place on the anniversary of the birth of the late Dwight David Eisenhower, 34th president of the United States, the 14th day of October.

(d) Subject to the provisions of this executive order, the award may be conferred posthumously.

Section 4. Order awards Board.

(a) There is hereby established the Order Awards Board (hereinafter referred to as "the Board").

(b) The Board shall be comprised of the following:

(1) The Secretary of State. (2) Such other members of the executive branch as the President may designate. (3) Five members who shall be appointed by the president from among persons outside the federal government. The terms of service of these members should be five years except that the first five appointees shall have terms expiring on the 31st of July, 1970, 1971, 1972,

1973, and 1974, respectively. Any person appointed to fill a vacancy occurring during a term shall serve for the remainder of the term. Any member whose term expires May, in the discretion of the President, be reappointed.

(c) The Board shall have a chairman who shall be designated by the President from among its members and shall serve in the capacity of chairman at the pleasure of the President.

Section 5. Functions of the Board.

(a) Any individual or group may recommend recipients for the order and the Board shall consider such recommendations.

(b) Giving full consideration to the criteria expressed in section 3 of this order, the Board shall screen such recommendations and, on the basis of such recommendations are upon its own motion, shall from time to time submit to the President nominations of individuals for recognition.

Section 6. Expenses.

(a) Necessary administrative expenses of the board incurred in connection with its responsibilities under this order including those under section 6 (b) hereof, during the fiscal year 1969 may be paid from the appropriation appearing under the heading "Special Projects" in the executive office appropriation act, 1969, public Law at 90-350, 82 Stat. 195, and, to the extent permitted by law, from any corresponding appropriations which may be made for subsequent years. Such payments shall be made without regard to the provisions of section 3681 of the revised statutes and section 9 of the Act of March 4, 1909, 35 Stat. 1027 (31 U.S.C. 672 and 673).

(b) The members of the Board appointed under section 4 b3 hereof shall serve without compensation but shall be entitled to receive travel and expenses, including per diem in lieu of subsistence, as authorized by law (5 U.S.C. 5701-5708) for persons in the Government service employed intermittently.

Section 7. Design of the medal. The Army Institute of Heraldry shall prepare for the approval of the President a design of the medal, citation, and ribbon.

The White House, 1969.

Above and opposite page: Draft of Executive Order which established Danielle's "Order of Friends of the United States".

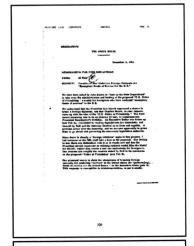

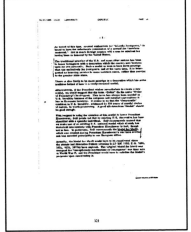

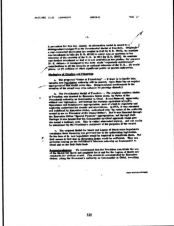

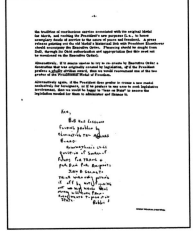

(Above) *The letter from Alexander Haig in the State Department which killed the idea from Charles E. Stuart which had been endorsed by President Richard Nixon, for the "Friend of the United States" medal.* In the memo, Haig says, "Our feeling is that there are difficulties with it as it stands now and that the President should reactivate an existing national medal (like the Medal of Merit) rather than create a new one exclusively for foreigners…"

(Courtesy Nixon Archives, College Park, Maryland)

Acknowledgements

There are a number of people who helped me with facts or the verification of information:

I thank Maggie Garner for her approval of my remembrances of high school biology genetics; Dr. Jay Iaconetti, my anesthesiologist friend, for educating me about the drug "Narcan"; Captain David Maxwell, USN (Ret), formerly the Commanding Officer of The Indian Head Naval Ordinance Station (as it was known during his tenure) for details about that interesting post which has been my neighbor for the past 35 years. Also, major general Craig Hagan, USA (Ret.), for providing technical information about the 60 mm mortar.

I pay special thanks to Ted Gropple, Director of the Ceremonies Office for the Military District of Washington, who was kind enough to meet with me to answer questions and to provide me with the actual schedule for President Arroyo's visit with President Bush.

For doing what they get paid to do, but doing it well and with extra effort, I thank Leslie Phillips of the Public Affairs office of the Department of State and Michelle Ness in Public Affairs at the CIA. (Did the KGB ever have a public affairs office?) John Roberts and his staff at the Nixon Archives in College Park, Maryland managed to find all of those old memos of so long ago, without which the book would have had a vastly different ending. I also owe thanks to Don Martin, formerly with the National Security Agency, who offered me insights into NSA.

My civil engineer friend, Ipreham Chehab, helped me with Arabic vocabulary and loaned me his Troxler so that I could take its measurements.

I recognize Major General Ted Atkeson, USA (Ret.), a long time friend who was for several years the number three in command at the Central Intelligence Agency. Ted was, quite consciously, the unnamed general from military intelligence in the second chapter. He was also kind enough to review an early draft and offer many useful suggestions.

Laura Kalpakian, herself a successful author, helped me with her skilled and insightful review of the manuscript and made many valuable suggestions for improvement.

My friend and physical therapist, Lucy Dettor, has been an enormous help to me as this book was readied for publication, reading me chapters as they were edited. Her patience and support have been invaluable as we refined the manuscript. She was a vital link between me and my editor, Joe Coons.

Finally, I am grateful to my wife Connie, for contributing the title and for believing in my work during the long period of production.

Charles E. Stuart

August, 2007

Editor's Note

I first met Charles E. "Chuck" Stuart in 1955 when we were freshmen at Union College in Schenectady, N.Y. We became fast friends and active in a wide range of endeavors both curricular and extra-curricular. After our 1959 graduation he served in the U.S. Army, and then in 1961 joined me in acquiring a small Ohio AM-FM radio station where he served as sales manager. I was 26, he was 23, and we worked together intensively and successfully building our small business. After three years he moved to New York City to work in advertising, then finance, and became an active volunteer fund raiser for the Republican Party. Eventually hired as an "Advance Man" for the Richard Nixon campaign, his great creativity and management skill was recognized and he was asked to be an assistant to the White House Chief Counsel, John Ehrlichman, even though Stuart was not an attorney. At the end of Nixon's first term Charles resigned (he had nothing to do with the "Watergate" scandal) and became a senior executive for a development company. He remained involved in quality property developments for the rest of his life.

When he was only 34 he found he had *menengioma,* a disease which causes frequent brain tumors to grow. After his first successful brain surgery he soon had more tumors and surgeries until he had been "under the knife" a total of thirteen times by the age of 69, a record he wryly said he "would gladly forego." In spite of the enormous impact his health problems had on his life, he remained vigorous, engaged, active, and a positive-thinker. Almost until his death he focused on what he *could* do and made the most of it.

This book was written during the last several years of life, some of it dictated using voice-recognition software on his computer because he had been so paralyzed by his ailment and resultant surgeries that he could not operate a computer keyboard.

This is his book! It was only because he couldn't type that I had anything to do with it. Here was the procedure: I got his original manuscript in WORD form. I checked for errors and suggested changes to him by phone (we lived in different states) and he would approve. I then would make the necessary edits, and at regular intervals send him and our friend, Lucy Dettor, a copy. Lucy would read him the new pages (by then he couldn't hold a book himself), and the process would repeat.

Just as the book was finished, Charles died. His body had endured all the pain it could, and he found relief from it at last. Sadly, he had not lived to see the book published, a personal goal that many of us thought was sustaining him through his difficult last weeks.

Even in his last days, he was able to have flashes of his great sense of humor, his amazing knowledge of history and the world, and a great capacity for clearly telling a compelling story. He was one of the most kind, ethical, intelligent, loyal, and powerful personalities I have ever known, and he was always a realist.

Charles developed a huge assemblage of devoted friends, and they were an important part of his life. I join them in trying to carry out his wishes. At his request, the proceeds from the sales of this book will *all* go into a trust to support charities that are in areas that were selected by him, including, particularly, scholarship funds and organizations related to brain surgery.

Chuck, we miss you. You were one of a kind.

Joseph D. Coons, September 2007

Made in the USA